18 March 2003

To Edwin Weihe,

With many thanks

and best wishes,

David Medalie

ENCOUNTERS

An Anthology of South African Short Stories

Selected and Introduced by

DAVID MEDALIE

Witwatersrand University Press

Witwatersrand University Press
1 Jan Smuts Avenue
2001 Johannesburg
South Africa

ISBN 1 86814 325 2

First published 1998

Typeset by Positive Proof, Johannesburg
Printed and bound by Kohler Carton and Print, Pinetown

CONTENTS

PUBLISHING HISTORY

'The Schoolmaster' was first published in *The Little Karoo* by Pauline Smith in 1925. Republished in *The Little Karoo* (Africasouth Paperbacks by David Philip Publisher (Pty) Ltd, 1990)

'The Barren Woman' (from *When Evening Falls*, unpublished manuscript written in the 1940s), published in *H I E Dhlomo: Collected Works* edited by Nick Visser and Tim Couzens (Ravan Press, 1985)

'The Kafir Drum' was first published in *On Parade* in 1949. Republished in *Unto Dust: Stories by Herman Charles Bosman*, edited by Lionel Abrahams (Human & Rousseau, 1963, 1964, 1969, 1971)

'The Home-coming' was first published in *On Parade* in 1949. Republished in *Unto Dust: Stories by Herman Charles Bosman*, edited by Lionel Abrahams (Human & Rousseau, 1963, 1964, 1969, 1971)

'Kwashiorkor' was written in the 1950s and published in *The Will To Die* by Can Themba, selected by Donald Stuart and Roy Holland (Heinemann Educational Books Ltd, 1972; Africasouth Paperbacks, David Philip Publisher (Pty) Ltd, 1982)

'Stop Thief!' was published in *A Long Way from London* by Dan Jacobson (Weidenfeld & Nicolson, 1958) and is reprinted by permission of the author and A M Heath & Company Ltd

'Enemies' was published in *Six Feet of the Country* by Nadine Gordimer (Victor Gollancz Ltd, 1956) and is reprinted by permission of A P Watt Ltd on behalf of Nadine Gordimer

'Blankets' was first published in *Black Orpheus* in 1964 and republished in *A Walk in the Night and other stories* by Alex La Guma (Heinemann Educational Books, 1968; Africasouth Paperbacks, David Philip Publisher (Pty) Ltd, 1991)

'The Hajji' was published in *The Hajji and Other Stories* by Ahmed Essop (Ravan Press, 1978)

'The Silva Cup is Broken' was first published in *My Cousin Comes To Jo'Burg and other stories* by Mbulelo Mzamane (Ravan Press (Pty) Ltd, 1980; Longman Drumbeat, 1981) and is reprinted by kind permission of the author and of Shelley Power Literary Agency Ltd

'Learning To Fly' was published in *Private Parts & Other Tales* by Christopher Hope (Bateleur Press, 1981) and is reprinted by kind permission of the author

'The Prophetess' was published in *Fools and other stories* by Njabulo S Ndebele (Ravan Press, 1983, 1987, 1989, 1990) and is reprinted by kind permission of the author and of Shelley Power Literary Agency Ltd

'A Trip to the Gifberge' was published in *You Can't Get Lost in Cape Town* by Zoë Wicomb (Virago Press, London, 1987)

'Devil At a Dead End' was first published in *Soweto Stories* (Pandora Press, 1989). The title of the collection was changed to *Footprints in the Quag: Stories and Dialogues from Soweto* by Miriam Tlali (David Philip, Publisher (Pty) Ltd, 1989). In 1979, Devil At a Dead End was banned in South Africa after the author had read it at a seminar of writers at the University of Iowa under the title 'Just the Two of Us'. It is published here by kind permission of the author and of Peake Associates

'Comrades' was published in *Jump and Other Stories* by Nadine Gordimer (Bloomsbury, 1991; Penguin Books, 1993) and is reprinted by permission of A P Watt Ltd on behalf of Nadine Gordimer

'Holding Back Midnight' was published in *Holding Back Midnight* by Maureen Isaacson (COSAW Publishing (Pty) Ltd, 1992)

'Butch Goes to Botswana' was published in *The Six Dead Ballerinas* by Brendan Cline (Justified Press, 1994)

'Relatives' was published in *Crossing Over: New writing for a new South Africa* compiled by Linda Rode with the assistance of Jakes Gerwel (Kwela Books, 1995) It won the Sanlam Award (published story category) in 1996

'The Awakening of Katie Fortuin' was published in *New Contrast* Vol 24, Number 4, December 1996 and is reprinted by kind permission of the author

'There Are Virgins in the Township' was published in *The Naked Song and other stories* by Mandla Langa (Africasouth New Writing by David Philip Publishers (Pty) Ltd, 1996)

'Recognition' by David Medalie is published here for the first time. It won the Sanlam Award (unpublished story category) in 1996

'Autopsy' was published in *Propaganda by Monuments & other stories* by Ivan Vladislavić (David Philip Publishers (Pty) Ltd, 1996)

INTRODUCTION

Every story in this anthology has an *explicit* South African focus. This means something more than that the setting or scenario presented in the story should be recognisably South African: it should also be *intrinsically a part of what the story is about*, and thus not merely a backdrop to events or concerns that could as easily be located elsewhere. Stories by South African writers in which the South African context is absent, muted or negligible have not been included.

Although the anthology was envisaged as one which would appeal to the general reader and to anyone interested in South African literature, its possible use as a teaching text at high schools or universities was a crucial consideration from the start. Stories were sought which, it is hoped, will be interesting and enjoyable to teach and study in themselves, but which may also be valuable to consider in relation to one another for the purposes of comparison and contrast.

Some stories are undoubtedly more challenging in certain ways – linguistic, conceptual or contextual – than others, and this is intentional: the presupposition was that teachers and lecturers would select for study those stories which are appropriate to the particular needs and levels of their students. At the same time, it should be noted that even the less obviously 'difficult' stories in the collection are not without complexity: where, for instance, the language is easier to follow, the concepts or implications raised by the story may require other kinds of knowledge or understanding. The stories have been chosen in the hope that they will encourage readers to *encounter* what may be removed from their own experiential or linguistic range, so that the effect of working through the collection may be more than merely the appeasement or confirmation of their own experiences and predilections. The anthology serves to introduce some of the different ways within the short story form in which language and narrative have been used to represent or reflect upon past or contemporary South African experiences. If what emerges is a sense that these are multi-faceted and that the modes of representation are correspondingly varied – reminding us, in Njabulo Ndebele's words, that 'the problems of the South African social formation are complex and all-embracing ... they cannot be reduced to a single, simple formulation'[1] – then the collection will have succeeded in one of its aims.

It is in the light of this that the broad theme of the encounter (which runs through the anthology) should be regarded. Every story presents an 'encounter' of one kind or another, and this has also been one of the considerations underlying the choice of stories. The idea of the encounter lends cohesion to the collection as a whole, suggesting another way in which the short stories may be considered in relation to one another. The notion of the encounter does not, however, constitute an attempt to force stories that are dissimilar into a conceptual net and thus to suppress or flatten difference; it acts rather as a loose framework in which they may be brought together and into juxtaposition with one another in order to allow the various emphases to emerge. It is intended to be a useful starting-point for the reader, an approach to the anthology; it is not a destination.

---

1. Njabulo Ndebele, *Rediscovery of the Ordinary: Essays on South African Literature and Culture*. Johannesburg: Cosaw, 1991, p55.

The encounters presented in these twenty-two stories are multiple and diverse: some are interpersonal, some socio-political, some ideological; in a number of the stories, the encounter which is described includes all of these elements and invites us, as so many works of South African literature have done, to consider the extent to which the personal or private experience is often inseparable from the wider political or social currents. Some of the encounters are antagonistic, some sympathetic; some are tragic, some comic. Many of them offer reversals or surprises whereby initial assumptions about the nature of the encounter need to be revised. The tenor of our South African encounters, these stories seem to suggest, is neither predictable nor simple; everything that is complex, unique or bizarre within the South African experience leaves its mark on the encounters between individuals.

The anthology does not neglect the political history of South Africa, nor does it present it in terms of a single trajectory or set of developments. Most of the stories in this collection record the impact of broad social contexts on the lives of individuals: they present history and politics in terms of lived experience and provide a sense of the *texture* of people's lives within a wide range of South African scenarios. Within the discrete experiences conveyed in the stories, many of them embrace broad issues pertaining to politics, race, class and gender.

For instance, the encounter between two vividly-rendered elderly white women in Gordimer's 'Enemies' carries strong overtones of class divisions. Essop's 'The Hajji' offers an investigation of issues relating to culture and gender within the explicit apartheid context of the Group Areas Act, the Mixed Marriages Act and the Immorality Act. In Smith's 'The Schoolmaster', the pain of a young girl's first experience of love and sexuality and the preoccupation with suffering, guilt and absolution are inseparable from the Calvinist context within which Smith frames these events.

One of the effects of considering these stories within the broad framework of the 'encounter' is an impression of the interlacing of people's lives across ostensibly entrenched political and social divisions. For all that separation has been the ideological ambition of many who wielded power in South Africa, these stories would seem to suggest that encounters across the categorical divisions nevertheless have constituted and continue to constitute the rough fabric of many South African experiences. At the same time, the stories do not give the impression of blithely dismissing difficulties: many of the encounters depicted in the anthology are abrasive ones which bear the marks of a scarred, suspicious or ignorant society. This may take the form of violence or the threat of violence, as in Hope's 'Learning to Fly', Jacobson's 'Stop Thief!', Tlali's 'Devil at a Dead End' and van Wyk's 'Relatives'. Alternatively, attempts to do good or to break down barriers of class or race may meet with frustration, as in Themba's 'Kwashiorkor' and Gordimer's 'Comrades'.

The encounter may also take the form of a confrontation with oneself or with different facets within the self: such an encounter may be as unsettling or threatening as any other. In Smith's 'The School-master', for instance, Jan Boetje's struggle is with the demons that lurk within himself. Wicomb's 'A Trip to the Gifberge', although describing an awkward and complex encounter between a mother and her daughter, deals also with the way in which the daughter is compelled to encounter her own ambivalent feelings and the power of the past she has sought to escape.

In Gordimer's 'Enemies', the adversarial relationship intimated by the title refers, in part, to opposing tendencies within one individual. Mrs Clara Hansen combats those impulses within herself which, if indulged, would lead to the loss of her rigid, even obsessive self-control and haughty dignity. These impulses bear the collective name of 'old fool':

> The train had dumped her out of the way; good thing, too, she thought, chastising herself impatiently: counting the luggage, fussing, when in ten years Alfred's never forgotten anything. Old fool, she told herself, old fool. Her ageing self often seemed to her an enemy of her real self, the self that had never changed. The enemy was a stupid one, fortunately; she merely had to keep an eye on it in order to keep it outwitted. Other selves that had arisen in her life had been much worse; how terrible had been the struggle with some of *them*. (p 55)

The old woman whom she meets on the train is the 'enemy' precisely because she represents that which Mrs Hansen dreads: the surrender of the body to appetite, obesity and age. A chance encounter on a train thus brings into focus a struggle within the battleground of the self. As a result, the words Clara Hansen sends by telegram to Alfred at the end of the story are far more than merely an attempt to avert a possible error or mistaken deduction: seen in the light of the contest between the enemies, the brief message is coloured with attestations of survival, defiance and even conquest. A story like 'Enemies' reminds us that certain encounters may be haphazard and banal on the surface, yet profoundly significant if, as in this case, the tensions and fears which lie hidden are exposed.

The anthology seeks neither to underplay the importance of apartheid in the experiences of South Africans and within twentieth century South African history, nor to present it deterministically as the only conceivable kind of political or social experience. A number of stories deal explicitly with apartheid – its laws, its injustices and its repercussions. These include Essop's 'The Hajji', Hope's 'Learning to Fly', Tlali's 'Devil at a Dead End', Gordimer's 'Comrades', Medalie's 'Recognition' and Dowling's 'The Awakening of Katie Fortuin'. Others assume the apartheid context in their investigation of issues such as racialism, privilege, poverty or exile – examples of these are Jacobson's 'Stop Thief!', Themba's 'Kwashiorkor', La Guma's 'Blankets' and Wicomb's 'A Trip to the Gifberge'. What emerges clearly in these stories is that apartheid has not been monolithic in its effects or in the ways in which it has been represented.

One of its effects has been the suppression in practice – and often in literature – of other important cultural and social concerns. Underlying the selection of the stories in this anthology was a determination that the representation of the lives and experiences of historically marginalised South African communities should *not* invariably be represented in relation to dominant groups or ideologies. Several stories concern themselves with a range of issues in which the apartheid context is relatively muted, but in which indigenous cultural practices, beliefs and taboos are explored – for instance, Dhlomo's 'The Barren Woman' and Ndebele's 'The Prophetess'. There are also stories which concentrate upon township life and provide a variety of encounters within that environment: these include La Guma's 'Blankets', Langa's 'There Are Virgins in the Township' and Mzamane's 'The Silva Cup Is Broken', as well as van Wyk's 'Relatives', which focuses specifically on problems of violence and gangsterism.

Not surprisingly, what one finds if one considers the collection as a whole, is that many of the encounters have to do with the exercise of power. Dhlomo's 'The Barren Woman', Bosman's 'The Kafir Drum', Themba's 'Kwashiorkor' and Ndebele's 'The Prophetess' deal, in their very different ways, with the power of belief and ritual in traditional societies. 'The Kafir Drum' works ironically to undermine the supremacy of Western technology and the various phenomena of modernity; in 'Kwashiorkor', on the other hand, modernity, education and enlightened attitudes are themselves a potential form of power, set against ignorance, superstition and the attenuation of traditional ways of life.

Many of Bosman's stories expose the colonial settlers as parvenus and inauthentic occupiers of the land: hence, in 'The Kafir Drum', the men who gather in the post office on Jurie Bekker's farm are the butt of a satirical undermining of their cultural chauvinism. Old Mosigo, 'the last of the drum-men at Gaberones' represents, in contrast, the dwindling power of the old Africa, since the drum-men are becoming redundant as a result of 'the competition of the white man's telegraph wires.' Even in the description of old Mosigo there is the suggestion that he has gathered within himself the vestiges of an untrammelled, pre-colonial Africa:

> The wrinkles on his face were countless. They made me
> think of the kafir footpaths that go twisting across the length
> and breadth of Africa, and that you can follow for mile after
> mile and day after day, and that never come to an end. (p 23)

The story, in its homage to Mosigo and what he represents, and its unflattering treatment of more modern modes of communication and those who use them, seeks to recognise the power of old Africa – seen in nostalgic and romantic terms – even as its passing is being marked. There are several kinds of power in this story: the power of modernity, which lies in the fact that it will inevitably prevail, but which the mocking irony of the story holds in abeyance; and the power of old Mosigo and what he stands for, which is waning in real terms, but is perpetuated and invigorated within the scope of the story by being endowed with attributions of 'authenticity' and in being spared any satirical lashing.

In 'Stop Thief!', the confluence of several different forms of power is described: the power of the male in a patriarchal society, the power of wealth and privilege, and the power of white supremacy in a racist society. There is no innocence where there is power, the story implies; no relationship that is exempt from it. Within the typical nuclear family – father, mother, son, daughter – violence is nurtured, taught, and, finally, handed down as a legacy, like the family's wealth. The games the father plays with his children are tinged with the threat of violence, while the mother's apparently easeful existence expresses, as the narrator of the story indicates, her own acceptance of her relative disempowerment – both as a woman in a patriarchal society, and as someone who does not originally come from a wealthy home and has recourse to wealth only through her husband:

> She seemed sunken under her husband, under his wealth,
> under his strength; they had come down upon her as the
> sun did where she lay at the side of the swimming bath, and
> she questioned them no more than she could have
> questioned the sun. She had submitted to them. (p 46)

The story suggests how different forms of power operate in relation to each other. The passivity and complicity of the mother are required in order for the power of the father to operate unchallenged. The power of wealth makes her indolence possible; yet her inactivity is also the mark of her submission to the power her husband wields.

When the young burglar is apprehended, the violence that is latent within the family is directed towards him in response to his intrusion into the home where their wealth guards itself aggressively. The end of the story shows how well the children have learned their lessons as the son assumes power over the father. The pattern of violence is shown to be self-perpetuating. What is more, where the father is concerned, the implication is that power, like wealth, must be eternally vigilant on its own behalf: there will always be those who will respond to the first sign of weakness.

'Butch Goes to Botswana' is also a story about power. Within the gay relationship depicted by Cline, the class status and wealth of the narrator give him power over the male prostitute, Butch; but Butch, in turn, has power too – the power of his sexual appeal, which holds the older man in thrall. The fact that power is to play a crucial role in their relationship and in the story as a whole is marked very clearly at the beginning of the story, when the first meeting of the two men is described:

> What pleasant power one feels at such a moment. He had
> his looks, I had my money, things seemed to be even. But I
> had also my experience, my personality, or force of
> character; which he could oppose only with weakness and
> fecklessness. The physical strength which he could turn
> against me – those broad shoulders and hands – would avail
> him nothing. That was what I was buying. (p 159)

The complacency expressed here is not sustained as the story continues, for the balance of power turns out neither to be neat nor fixed. The relationship itself is complex and contains a number of surprises and reversals within its ostensible predictability. In addition, another form of power intrudes abruptly and complicates matters further: the power of the apartheid state, expressed in this instance in the form of conscription for young white men. At odds with the more fluid or contested expressions of maleness and male sexuality presented in the story, there is also the militaristic definition of maleness and whiteness which makes victims of both men and almost supersedes their private struggle for power.

'Devil at a Dead End' is an interesting story to consider in this regard, for, like a number of other stories in the anthology, it subverts the expectations which at first it seems to construe. Tlali's story seems initially to be predictable in its conferring of power and powerlessness: the white bureaucrats and officials have an immense amount of power; the black woman, who is the protagonist of the story, has none (except, of course, for the powerful support of the narrator's sympathetic depiction of her situation). As in 'Butch Goes to Botswana', the expression of sexual desire is shown to be inseparable from other forms of power: the inevitable and logical conclusion of the story would seem to be the rape of the black woman by the white guard. But the ending of the story shows that the refusal of the expected pattern confers a kind of power upon the story-teller herself: that of inducing surprise and reconsideration in the reader. The woman on the train, it turns out, is not wholly without power after all; her responses to the threat represented by the guard are both more complex and more resourceful than her earlier helplessness suggests.

A number of the stories in the anthology suggest that those who have power, no matter how entrenched and secure their position seems to be, may be forced to contemplate its loss: in some of them, the reversal in the fortunes of these characters is located within the context of changes within the political system of the country itself. In Isaacson's 'Holding Back Midnight' and Medalie's 'Recognition', characters who have lost some of their erstwhile power as a result of these changes are left contemplating or denying the attrition of their former power and status.

It cannot be denied that the anthology consists for the most part of realistic stories. This is largely because most South African short fiction written in English is firmly realistic: it is undoubtedly the dominant orientation within the genre. A realistic story is one in which time, place and historical context are clearly identified. These do not function simply as a backdrop to the characters or events depicted, but are crucial to the reader's understanding of the story. Realism assumes an intimate and profound relationship between the individual and the socio-historical contexts which pertain in his or her life. In realistic texts, events, actions and choices tend to emerge from and to embody that crucial relationship: they do not occur in isolation.

For instance, in Dhlomo's 'The Barren Woman', the narrator of the story takes great pains to contextualise the story of Mamkazi Zondi by emphasising that social and cultural factors exacerbate the sense of loss that arises from her barrenness; her private pain is inseparable from the broader preoccupations of her community:

> The Bantu love of children is well known. This love is partly natural, just like that of other human beings. It is partly the result of a social system in which lobola, the demands and difficulties of labour, and a man's prestige and status in society all put a premium on the size of the family. (p 10)

This first paragraph alerts us to the fact that this is a story in which the actions and choices of individuals cannot be considered in isolation, for they are coloured to such an extent by their location within tribal society and its values that even something as ostensibly 'natural' or 'universal' as the love of children takes on a specific cultural resonance.

In Themba's 'Kwashiorkor', on the other hand, the particular instance and the general tendency are played off against one another to show how the consideration of the one has constantly to be adjusted in the light of the other. The narrator's journalistic bias is towards the uniqueness of the individual 'human-interest story'; his sister, Eileen, is a social worker who works in generalities and social trends:

> ... she probes into the derelict lives of the unfortunate poor in Johannesburg. She studies their living habits, their recreational habits, their sporting habits, their drinking habits, the incidence of crime, neglect, malnutrition, divorce, aberration, and she records all this in cyclostyled forms that ask the questions ready-made. She has got so good that she could tell without looking whether such-and-such a query falls under paragraph so-and-so. She has got so

clinical that no particular case rattles her, for she has met
its like before and knows how and where to classify it. (p 31)

What is telling is that the story does not go on to affirm or deny either
perspective unequivocally: the distinctive identities and carefully-
evoked suffering of the Mabiletsa family force us to consider them as
individuals – we cannot merely relegate them to a set of statistics, and,
in that sense, the clinical approach of Eileen (even if she were able to
sustain it and not become emotionally involved, as she does) would
dilute the acuteness and the particularity of their suffering. At the
same time, however, it is clear that, the distinctiveness of the family
aside, they nonetheless embody and exemplify widespread patterns of
behaviour, arising out of poverty, urbanisation and ignorance. The
story does not allow us to dismiss the approach of either the brother or
the sister, but invites us to recognise that, between them, they are
pointing us towards the knotty and complex relationship that exists
between the individual and his or her society – the recurrent preoccupation of realistic fiction.

Despite the preponderance of realism within the South African
short story written in English, there are stories which depart to a
greater or lesser extent from that realism and yet maintain an explicit
South African focus. Examples of these are Isaacson's 'Holding Back
Midnight', Dowling's 'The Awakening of Katie Fortuin' and Vladislavić's
'Autopsy'. These stories suggest that realism is not the only viable
mode; that alternative literary methods may be just as substantial and
vivid in their representation of South African realities.

The departure from realism in 'Holding Back Midnight' and 'The
Awakening of Katie Fortuin' lies in the use of *allegorical* elements. An
allegory is a story which has its own inner logic and narrative thread,
but which contains a set of meanings which lie beyond the surface or
frame of the story. There is an untold story, as it were; another layer of
implications to be uncovered.

'Holding Back Midnight' treats allegorically the recalcitrance of the
past and those who adhere to it in a reactionary manner, even when
confronted with newness and ostensibly inevitable change. The story

is set at the time of the birth of the new millennium. The narrator and her generation represent those who have embraced newness, while her parents and their generation are intensely threatened by it. The world of the parents is that of a decadent residual colonialism, saturated with nostalgia and the reminders of former wealth and power. Isaacson carefully marks the political and ideological inferences that lie within the description of the rather bizarre New Year's Eve party:

> Hopefully the moment we are waiting for will release
> (my father) from the grip of history. History is ever-present
> in my father, like the patterns that shimmer from the
> chandeliers over the cracked walls ... History hovers, with
> the ghosts of the illicit couplings that once heated the
> hotel's shadowy rooms. (p 154)

Such comments emphasise the allegorical stratum of the story and direct our interpretation of it. For the father, history is like a vice, holding him back even as he stands on the brink of newness. Everything seems to suggest that his former power – derived from his wealth, the apartheid system and his status as a patriarch – is gone, and that he is an anachronistic and impotent figure. Yet the end of the story holds a number of surprises or reversals, for it seems that the father may have retained some of his power after all: the ending may be read as a futile attempt to avert inevitable change, or as an expression of the capacity of the past, even when it seems to be enfeebled, to hold the future hostage.

'The Awakening of Katie Fortuin' is an elaboration on the Rip Van Winkle story. The reader is alerted to the allegorical dimension so that, the humour of the story notwithstanding, the political significance of Katie's long sleep is made apparent. This is also the interpretation which the community places upon it, so that, although she is not a political figure in herself, her sleep is read as a form of protest:

> ... word got round that Katie Fortuin had gone to sleep
> because of Group Areas, in resistance to it. Then, because

> people always talk and dream and imagine, it was circulated
> that Katie wasn't going to wake up till justice returned. Our
> cottage became something of a shrine to a woman who
> turned herself into a barometer of oppression, who refused
> to be moved. (p 184)

Yet when Katie finally wakes up to find herself in a post-apartheid
South Africa, her habitual suspiciousness and churlishness are
apparent. The narrator's last words are that he 'fear(s) the reawakening
of Katie Fortuin.' Is she to become a political 'barometer' once more,
one wonders, pointing this time to uncongenial realities within the
new South Africa? The ending – as in many short stories – is suggestive
rather than conclusive.

In 'Autopsy', the conventional realist concern with the specifics of
time and place, the importance accorded to detail and careful
observation, are confounded by the central event of the story, namely
the pursuit, by the narrator, of 'the King' in Hillbrow. The story has
been built around the popular myth that Elvis Presley is still alive and
has been sighted in various parts of the world. Proceeding from this
comical premise, Vladislavić shows the power of latter-day 'myths'
within popular culture, advertising and the media, and, in particular,
the centrality of the United States in this process of myth-generation.
Although the narrator finds himself in what he calls 'the new improved
South Africa', the Hillbrow that he moves through as he follows 'the
King' is a maelstrom of discrepant cultural signals, all of which he
consumes unquestioningly, just as, in his perfect disingenuousness, he
never doubts for a moment the identity of 'the King'.

'Learning to Fly' is, in some ways, the most provocative story of all
to consider in relation to the question of realism, for it may be regarded
both as a surreal story and as a hyper-realistic one. Hope's account of
Colonel 'Window-jumpin'' du Preez seems, from a certain perspective,
to be a comical story, veering constantly towards the absurd and the
preposterous; yet it is also a bitter and precise satire of the abuse of
power by the apartheid government, particularly in relation to the
brutal treatment meted out to political detainees. The apartheid

premise of essential or intrinsic racial difference takes on a particularly bizarre dimension in the 'celebrated thesis' of du Preez that 'all men, when brought to the brink, will contrive to find a way out if the least chance is afforded them and the choice of the means is always directly related to the racial characteristics of the individual in question.' Thus we are made aware as readers that it is the South African political situation which is truly bizarre: the uncertain status of realism in 'Learning to Fly' points us towards a recognition of the perversions that constituted normality in apartheid South Africa.

No single, all-encompassing definition will succeed in capturing the many faces and moods of the short story genre; what is more, although there are common characteristics that can be isolated, there will always be stories which do not conform even to these broad tendencies. Description will inevitably fall short of practice; indeed, it should be so. Short stories can be cunning, elusive and eccentric; they can be complex, simple (or ostensibly simple), direct or subtle; they can also, one should admit, be trite, predictable and boring.

It is *generally* true to say that effective short stories imbue their relative brevity with a measure of intensity. Although there are limited opportunities for extended description or extended characterisation, they manage to convey a great deal within the economy which the constraints of the form impose upon them.

La Guma's 'Blankets' is a good example of this type of story: although it is extremely short, it presents a series of swiftly-changing – almost kaleidoscopic – scenes which, taken together, tell us much about Choker and the life he has lead. Common to all these memories is the presence of a blanket. What emerges is that the blanket does not represent anything in itself; it assumes a certain significance or meaning within a particular context. In this way, while dispensing with extended descriptions of setting, or references of a sociological nature to modes of conduct within a particular society, as in 'The Barren Woman' or 'Kwashiorkor', La Guma manages, nonetheless, to suggest the power of factors such as poverty and deprivation in human life:

'It's cold, mos, man,' Choker said. But it wasn't the guard to
whom he was talking. He was six years old and his brother,
Willie, a year senior, twisted and turned in the narrow,
cramped, sagging bedstead which they shared, dragging the
thin cotton blanket from Choker's body. (p 65)

The woman was saying, half-asleep, 'No, man. No, man.'
Her body was wet and sweaty under the blanket, and the
bed smelled of a mixture of cheap perfume, spilled powder,
human bodies and infant urine. (p 65)

What these two scenes have in common – the blanket, the sharing of
the bed, the sense of intolerable closeness, the verbal echo ('man') –
points also to what is different: one refers to Choker's childhood, the
other to an adult sexual encounter. There is a sense of randomness, but
also of cohesion as the blankets draw the disparate events of Choker's
life together even as they draw the story itself together. Just as the
blanket does not have a meaning, only *meanings*, so the story itself
relies on meanings that accrue around the rapidly-changing scenarios
it presents.

Just as brevity and swiftness of pace are central to 'Blankets', so are
the relative length and slower pace of a story like Ndebele's 'The
Prophetess' crucial in that context. Here, too, there is a sense that
every detail contributes to the effect of the story as a whole. What
seems to be random or a diversion from the main story line turns out
to be an important ingredient in Ndebele's recreation of the community life of Charterston township, which is at the heart of the story.
The slow unfolding of the narration gives an impression of a world in
which slower rhythms still have a place, despite the pressures being
exerted upon them. The figure of the prophetess is central to Ndebele's
investigation of tradition in relation to the pull towards a sceptical
modernity. Her power (or lack thereof) raises the question of the
efficacy of traditional beliefs and value systems. This is not an issue
which the story resolves: instead, the conglomeration of different
personalities, perspectives and modes of interaction contributes to the
fascination and richness of the world which the young boy inhabits.

In a good short story, the language is not merely a vehicle by which plot and characterisation are conveyed, but a crucial part of the story's meanings and effects. In some of these stories, the 'encounter' is played out in the field of language and even takes the form of a clash between different *kinds* of language. In 'Kwashiorkor', for example, the clinical, theoretical language of Eileen, the emotive, descriptive language of her brother, and the colloquial, street-wise language of Maria suggest more vividly than anything their discrepant perspectives.

In 'The Prophetess', language is implicated in the enquiry into what has potency or value. The advice that the prophetess gives the young boy may profitably be considered also as a comment upon the importance of the judicious use of language within the process of story-telling itself:

> '... You see, you should learn to say what you mean. Words,
> little man, are a gift from the Almighty, the Eternal Wisdom.
> He gave us all a little pinch of His mind and called on us
> to think. That is why it is folly to misuse words or not to
> know how to use them well ...' (p 107)

The evocation of the township environment in Mzamane's 'The Silva Cup Is Broken' depends heavily on the different types of language which we find in the story. These range from the high-register speech of Fr Nqamakwe, which bears no trace of an African influence, to the very earthy and abrasive speech of Makhumalo, flavoured with the dialect of the township, and in which both English and Zulu words appear. Fluency, idiomatic richness and the gift of quick repartee are forms of power in this story. It is deeply significant, therefore, that the story ends with another kind of language, as seen in Jersey's letter to Mbuyiselo, which comes in the form of 'an ink-stained scrap of paper, torn from a disused exercise book'. Jersey has been given almost no voice in the story prior to this. Now the poignancy of her predicament and her sense of rejection are marked by the guileless simplicity; the spelling errors seem to betoken her lack of access to a language of power. Yet, at the same time, there *is* a kind of strength conveyed in her letter, despite her invidious position as a poorly-educated young black woman, subject to the whims and negligence of Mbuyiselo. Her letter is an assertion of her refusal to allow herself to be abused any longer:

> I have born you a child but you hold me like a dog. I will
> not forgiv or forget. You have showed me your truest
> khalas. Now I must tell you the paynful thing of that I no
> more love you. The silva cup is broken. (p 90)

Every story has a narrator: the kind of narrator that is used and his or her perspective in relation to the events or issues being presented are crucial, inseparable from other elements within the story. There is always a distinctive *voice* doing the telling and that influences the reader's response to what is being conveyed.

In Smith's 'The Schoolmaster', Themba's 'Kwashiorkor', van Wyk's 'Relatives', Wicomb's 'A Trip to the Gifberge' and Langa's 'There Are Virgins in the Township', a first-person narrator, who is also a participant in the story, is used. The extent to which the narrator is involved in what is happening may vary, but one of the characteristics of this form of narration is that the insight or understanding of the narrator is necessarily constrained by his or her *position* in relation to what is being described or experienced. Hence, in such stories, there is often a gap between what the narrator perceives and what the reader comes to recognise or understand. This tends to be acutely the case where the narrator is clearly a *persona* – a distinctive character whom we are not invited to identify in any way with the writer of the story. Bosman's 'Oom Schalk Lourens' is such a persona; so, too, are the narrators in Vladislavić's 'Autopsy', Isaacson's 'Holding Back Midnight', Dowling's 'The Awakening of Katie Fortuin', Cline's 'Butch Goes to Botswana' and Medalie's 'Recognition'.

In 'There Are Virgins in the Township', the first-person narrator is clearly commenting and reflecting upon earlier experiences: the story moves from his childhood to his adulthood, but the narration is coloured throughout by hindsight. As the title suggests, attitudes to women and female sexuality are central to the story, and, indeed, sexual rivalries and deceptions make up a great deal of the plot. The dual role of the narrator – as a participant in the unfolding events of the story and as someone retrospectively evaluating what has occurred – allows Langa to expose the sexual chauvinism of the young man, but also to include the altered perspective which comes later. This makes possible the presence of the following two passages, for instance, within the same story:

> In fact, Maisie had confided in my current girl-friend that *she* rather fancied Arthur. A bit of a laugh, really, since Maisie had a tendency to balloon out as if at will. That she carried a torch for Arthur was a subject that drove some of the more unsympathetic students to hysterics; it was tantamount to being fancied by a Goodyear blimp. (p 196)

> An earlier guilt returned; in not acknowledging what had happened between us, I had effectively put Zodwa at Arthur's mercy, where she was treated like a shop-soiled article, of no account. I felt the weight of what we men do to put women at a disadvantage, where we blaspheme those intimate moments of love and codify them as conquests – we, the eternal swordsmen – while they retreat, maimed, to lick their wounds in that most private, unreachable corner of their hearts. (p 205)

'There Are Virgins in the Township' moves from an apartheid context into a post-apartheid South Africa, and it makes a revised and more acute understanding of gender issues and the predicament of a number of characters – including Zodwa, Arthur and Jonathan – a part of that progressive trajectory.

The first-person narrator in 'A Trip to the Gifberge' has been living in exile in London, in flight from the political situation in South Africa. Her return home inspires a welter of ambivalent and contradictory sensations, provoked by the country itself, the community she had been a part of, and, in particular, her mother. Although the mother is a very important presence in the story, our responses to her are filtered entirely through the narrator's perspective: we are not given access to her thoughts and know her only in terms of her daughter's perceptions of her. There is no alternative perception to suggest objectivity or balance, nothing to demarcate the rights and wrongs in the fraught relationship; indeed, it is precisely upon the *absence* of these kinds of certainty that the story centres. Resentment, antagonism, nostalgia and tenderness vie with one another and the restriction of the narrative perspective to that of the daughter immerses us as readers in her struggle to resolve these contending impulses.

Njabulo Ndebele has diagnosed a certain kind of superficiality in much South African literature:

> This superficiality comes from the tendency to produce
> fiction that is built around the interaction of surface
> symbols of the South African reality. These symbols can
> easily be characterised as either good or evil, or, even more
> accurately, symbols of evil on the one hand, and symbols of
> the victims of evil on the other hand.[2]

The stories in this anthology tend, as a whole, to avoid this kind of superficiality. There is, for instance, no simplistic characterisation or glib attribution of moral superiority in 'A Trip to the Gifberge'. The mother, who is politically conservative and entirely unsympathetic to her daughter's attempts to become a writer, seems at first to be a character whom it will be easy to dismiss or reject. Yet it is she who is given the most important pronouncement on the vexed question of patriotism, one of the core concerns of the story. The narrator feels 'revulsion' when Aunt Cissie gives her proteas at the airport, for they are the 'national blooms'. In her rejection of them is encapsulated all the distaste for the country of her birth which has driven her abroad. Yet, as the story unfolds, it is clear that there is much that still has a

---

2. Njabulo Ndebele, *Rediscovery of the Ordinary: Essays on South African Literature and Culture*. p23.

hold on her, that stirs feelings of affection and identification despite herself. Hence, the mother's comments about proteas towards the end of the story are authoritative, precisely because they suggest what the entire story has been moving towards – the recognition that there are affiliations and sympathies that, in their largeness and complexity, survive a narrow and exclusionary kind of patriotism:

> '...You who're so clever ought to know that proteas belong to the veld. Only fools and cowards would hand them over to the Boers. Those who put their stamp on things may see in it their own histories and hopes. But a bush is a bush; it doesn't become what people think they inject into it.'
> (p 133)

The presence of a third-person narrator who is not a participant in the story, but who, instead, recounts what occurs and comments upon it from a position of greater or lesser involvement may be seen in Dhlomo's 'The Barren Woman', Jacobson's 'Stop Thief!', Gordimer's 'Enemies' and 'Comrades', Essop's 'The Hajji', Ndebele's 'The Prophetess' and Mzamane's 'The Silva Cup Is Broken'.

The most common kind of third-person narrator is the *omniscient* narrator who is particularly authoritative, unrestricted not only in his or her access to situations that unfold within the plot of the story, but also to the thoughts and inner lives of the characters. Omniscient narrators tend to be very powerful presences within the story (often intrusively so), directing the responses of the reader and, in many cases, marking the shortcomings in the behaviour or understanding of the characters. A story with a narrator of this sort does not need to embody all the different viewpoints or perspectives which it wishes to present in its *characters*, for it has recourse to the uniquely powerful voice of the story-teller.

The most extreme example of the use of this kind of narrator is perhaps Dhlomo's 'The Barren Woman', where the narrator offers various elucidations of a sociological nature, generalities to do with Time and Nature, and goes to great pains to ensure that the tragic tale of Mamkazi and her barrenness, followed by the death of her child, is understood within the context of these truisms. Yet, even in a story like 'The Hajji', where the omniscient narrator is not so overwhelming a presence, it is nonetheless clear that we are being guided throughout in our responses to Hajji Hassen and his refusal to forgive his dying brother. In contrast to 'The Prophetess', where the third-person narrator remains very close to the perceptions and consciousness of the young boy, here the narrator frequently marks his distance from Hajji Hassen, particularly when his cultural or sexual chauvinism is at its most pronounced:

> He sat beside (Catherine). The closeness of her
> presence, the perfume she exuded stirred currents of feeling
> within him ...There was something so businesslike in her
> attitude and bearing, so involved in reality (at the back
> of his mind there was Salima, flaccid, cowlike and
> inadequate) that he could hardly refrain from expressing
> his admiration. (p 70)

The pejorative description of Salima proceeds from Hajji Hassen, not from the narrator; in fact, the latter takes pains to establish her as a compassionate figure, offering solace to Catherine and visiting Karim, despite her husband's intractability. In marking the difference in perspective, the narrator is also pointing to a failure in generosity, a spiritual niggardliness, in Hajji Hassen, at odds with his status as one who has recently returned from the pilgrimage to Mecca. In his attraction to Catherine, there is also the suggestion of hypocrisy: he is not immune to that which he has condemned so bitterly in his brother. On other occasions in the story, there is sympathy for Hassen, especially when he encounters naked racism in Hillbrow; but, in each case, there is a standard of judgement and compassion against which he is implicitly being measured. The effect is to indicate that, his status as a Hajji notwithstanding, he is not the sole moral arbiter in the story: there is Salima, Mr Mia, other members of the community, and, in particular, the narrator.

Another common (although by no means inevitable) pattern to be discerned in short stories is that many of them record incidents of heightened or dramatic significance, often accompanied by revelations or new kinds of understanding which, even if not grasped by or available to the characters, are nonetheless communicated to the reader. Stories of this sort tend to suggest that, whatever the future holds, it will not be the same as the present: the irruption of the significant event or revelation means that something fundamental has been altered. Versions of this very common pattern are to be found in a number of the stories in this anthology, including Smith's 'The Schoolmaster', Jacobson's 'Stop Thief!', Essop's 'The Hajji', Gordimer's 'Comrades', Ndebele's 'The Prophetess', Medalie's 'Recognition' and van Wyk's 'Relatives'.

In 'The Schoolmaster', the revelations contained within the story are situated in the context of notions of teaching and learning, which operate at many levels. In his lessons, Jan Boetje introduces the children to forms of knowledge and experiences that are, to them, exotic and fascinating:

> Geography also he taught them, but it was such a
> geography as had never before been taught in the Platkops
> district. Yes, surely the world could never be so wonderful
> and strange as Jan Boetje made it to us (for I also went to
> his geography class) in my grandfather's waggon-house.
> (p 4)

Yet the narrator, Engela, also has areas of knowledge at her disposal. These are derived from her immediate context and are experientially acquired:

> And it was now that I taught Jan Boetje which berries he
> might eat and which would surely kill him, which leaves
> and bushes would cure a man of many sicknesses, and
> which roots and bulbs would quench his thirst. Many such
> simple things I taught him in the veld, and many, many
> times afterwards I thanked God that I had done so. (p 4)

The implication is that knowledge and understanding do not exist in absolute terms: they gain power and value in relation to the contexts that inform them. This is true also of love, as Engela's grandmother suggests towards the end of the story, her wisdom endowing her comment with the status both of a revelation and as the culminating lesson in a series of lessons:

> Grandmother! Grandmother! Is love then such sorrow?'
> And still I can hear the low clear voice that answered so
> strangely: 'A joy and a sorrow – a help and a hindrance –
> love comes at the last to be but what one makes it.' (p 8)

The insights that Engela gains empower her and revelation in this story is granted a practical and consequential value as she takes over Jan Boetje's position and becomes a schoolteacher herself.

Gordimer's 'Comrades' presents not only an encounter between individuals who subscribe to different political creeds within a broadly leftist orientation, but, perhaps more importantly, offers an investigation of the way in which the different circumstances of people's lives have created vastly different *sensibilities*. The title suggests joint or shared commitment, and the gathering attended by Mrs Telford at the beginning of the story seems to accommodate a broad spectrum of political persuasions:

> They were the people to be educated; she was one of the
> committee of white and black activists (convenient generic
> for revolutionaries, leftists secular and Christian, fellow-
> travellers and liberals) up on the platform. (p 148)

Yet the story goes on to show the unravelling of assumptions of common purpose and shared ideals. The nature of Hattie·Telford's political involvement is vastly different from that of the young activists whom she brings to her home for a meal. She is a liberal and, consequently, the sanctity of the individual is both an ideological cornerstone and a refuge to her. She feels somewhat estranged from the large crowd at the gathering and their collectivist political rhetoric:

> At the end of a day like this she wanted a drink, she
> wanted the depraved luxury of solitude and quiet in which
> she would be restored (enriched, oh yes! by the day) to the
> familiar limits of her own being. (p 149)

Hers is a world of space, carefully-chosen African art and material comforts; the young men, however, have been schooled in 'the literacy of political rhetoric, the education of revolt against having to live the life their parents live.' The revelation which forms the conclusion to the story – the final paragraph even contains the word 'revelation' – has to do with the fact that, in feeding them, she is giving them precisely that: food. She can give them nothing of her home, her space, her finely-honed aesthetic sense: to them these are 'phenomena undifferentiated, undecipherable.'

Within the promise of comradeship, the story ends with the revelation of the breakdown of all commonality in a situation of radically disjunctive experiences, pointing to a chasm that exists between ostensible common purpose and the reality of mutually exclusive experiences.

The unfolding of a revelation may also be seen in 'Relatives'. Here, too, a 'chance encounter' on a train turns out to be of momentous, even ominous significance. The idea (suggested in many of the stories) that those who meet in random circumstances may turn out, unexpectedly, to be bound to one another in profound ways, is pivotal to this story. The narrator wishes to be a writer and is inclined to believe in the virtue of writers' manuals and formulaic constructions in the telling of stories:

> Then I began a story which I had already tested on my
> uncle in Carnarvon. There, among seasoned storytellers, it
> had passed my 'litmus' test – Listenable, Interesting,
> Telling, Meaningful, Unusual, Strange. (pp 173, 174)

The revelation which forms the conclusion to the story not only has to do with the narrator's relationship with the two young men with whom he shares a compartment in the train, but also with the inadequacy of such formulae when confronted with a situation of such extraordinary unpredictability that it eclipses earlier notions of what may be considered 'meaningful', 'unusual' or 'strange'.

'Relatives' is, therefore, in part a story about story-telling and story-writing: it is a good example of how short stories may self-consciously reflect upon and draw attention to their own construction. In doing so, they explicitly invite the reader to consider the implications of alternative modes of narration. Such stories point to the intimate relationship that may exist between the *form* of the story and its *content* – the 'how' and the 'what', so to speak. In van Wyk's story, as in Ndebele's, what seems at first to be a random sequence of events or reflections turns out to be carefully arranged and highly pertinent once one sees the *overall design*; in the same way, the revelations at the end enable the reader (and, in some cases, the narrator) to discern, retrospectively, what could not be grasped earlier.

This can also be seen in Bosman's sly and cunning stories, usually narrated by his sly and cunning narrator, Oom Schalk Lourens. Bosman manipulates the reader's expectations by establishing what seems to be a conventional or normative pattern and then subverting it, often to reveal a lurking darkness or malignity. This sense of reversal frequently takes the form of a surprise ending, but the surprise is carefully prepared in advance: as in many well-crafted short stories, the effect of the conclusion is that, rather than releasing us from the story, it returns us to it again, as it were, to ponder its implications anew.

In 'The Home-coming', Bosman takes up one of his favourite themes – betrayal. The story plays with two familiar narrative patterns, the first of which is the passion and devotion of young lovers:

> They were just of an age, the young Moolman couple, and
> they were both good to look at. And when they arrived
> back from Zeerust after the wedding, Hendrik made a
> stirring show of the way he lifted Malie from the mule-cart,
> to carry her across the threshold of the little farm-house in
> which their future life was to be cast. (p 28)

The second pattern is the well-known scenario of the husband's
infidelity. Hendrik is at the diamond diggings in the arms of the
'Woman of Zeerust', while Malie accepts his abandonment of her with
seeming resignation and does her best to tend to the farm, her earlier
devotion to Hendrik apparently unaltered. The ending of the story,
however, presents a shift that does not meet with the expectations
arising out of either of these patterns. The arrival in the mule-cart,
being lifted from it, Malie's laugh – these details all recur, but in a
wholly different configuration so that all prior expectations and
associations have to be reappraised. Yet, at the same time, the ending
validates Oom Schalk's observation at the beginning of the story in
relation to laughter and its many moods, contexts and incarnations:

> I suppose you could describe the way in which Frans Els
> carried on that day while he still thought that it was the
> ouderling's tent, as one kind of laughter. The fact is that
> there are more kinds of laughter than just that one sort,
> and it seems to me that this is the cause of a lot of
> regrettable awkwardness in the world. (p 27)

Malie laughs, as she did before, but her laughter has changed from one
kind to another, in fulfilment of Oom Schalk's warning. The throw-
away comment and the apparent digression have assumed momentous
significance, in compliance with Bosman's view that, in 'the first class
short story ... every word must count, every detail must be perfect.'[3]

Nadine Gordimer has described relations between blacks and whites in
South Africa in the following terms:

> ... there are things we know about each other that are
> never spoken, but are there to be written – and received
> with the amazement and consternation, on both sides, of

---

3. Herman Charles Bosman, 'The South African Short Story Writer'. In *Herman Charles Bosman*,
   edited by Stephen Gray. Johannesburg: McGraw-Hill, 1986, p 97.

having been found out ... What's certain is that there is no representation of our social reality without that strange area of our lives in which we have knowledge of one another.[4]

One could broaden the comment to include all the different segments and divisions within South African society. The short stories in this collection capture, in the encounters that they present, something of the curious commingling, the strange kinds of knowledge and the 'consternation' that Gordimer describes.

***

I am grateful to my colleagues and friends in the department of English at the University of the Witwatersrand for their commitment to this project, which they expressed in the form of encouragement, advice and constructive suggestions. In particular, I would like to thank Michelle Adler, Hazel Cohen, Victor Houliston, Karen Lazar, Marcia Leveson, Denise Newfield, Pamela Nichols, Hilary Semple, Ann Smith, Jennifer Stacey, Timothy Trengove-Jones, Shaun Viljoen and Merle Williams.

I have also benefited greatly from the advice of Maureen Isaacson, who made her vast knowledge of South African literature available to me.

Finally, I would like to thank Franscois McHardy and Pat Tucker of Wits University Press for their interest in this anthology from the start, their thoughtful and astute comments, and their patience.

David Medalie
Department of English
University of the Witwatersrand
December 1997

---

4. Nadine Gordimer, 'Living in the Interregnum'. In *The Essential Gesture: Writing, Politics and Places*, edited by Stephen Clingman. London: Penguin, 1988, p 279.

THE SCHOOLMASTER

Pauline Smith

Because of a weakness of the chest which my grandmother thought that she alone could cure, I went often, as a young girl, to my grandparents' farm of Nooitgedacht in the Ghamka valley. At Nooitgedacht, where my grandparents lived together for more than forty years, my grandmother had always young people about her – young boys and girls, and little children who clung to her skirts or were tossed up into the air and caught again by my grandfather. There was not one of their children or their grandchildren that did not love grandfather and grandmother Delport, and when aunt Betje died it seemed but right to us all that her orphans, little Neeltje and Frikkie and Hans, Koos and Martinus and Piet, should come to Nooitgedacht to live. My grandmother was then about sixty years old. She was a big stout woman, but as is sometimes the way with women who are stout, she moved very easily and lightly upon her feet. I had seen once a ship come sailing into Zandtbaai harbour, and grandmother walking, in her full wide skirts with Aunt Betje's children bobbing like little boats around her, would make me often think of it. This big, wise, and gentle woman, with love in her heart for all the world, saw in everything that befell us the will of the Lord. And when, three weeks after Aunt Betje's children had come to us, there came one night, from God knows where, a stranger asking for shelter out of the storm, my grandmother knew that the Lord had sent him.

The stranger, who, when my grandmother brought him into the living-room, gave the name of Jan Boetje, was a small dark man with a little pointed beard that looked as if it did not yet belong to him. His cheeks were thin and white, and so also were his hands. He seldom raised his eyes except when he spoke, and when he did so it was as if I saw before me the Widow of Nain's son, risen from the dead, out of my grandmother's Bible. Yes, as if from the dead did Jan Boetje come to us that night, and yet it was food that I thought of at once. And quickly I ran and made coffee and put it before him.

When Jan Boetje had eaten and drunk my grandparents knew all that they were ever to know about him. He was a Hollander, and had but lately come to South Africa. He had neither relative nor friend in the colony. And he was on his way up-country on foot to the goldfields.

For a little while after Jan Boetje spoke of the goldfields my grandmother sat in silence. But presently she said:

'Mijnheer! I that am old have never yet seen a happy man that went digging for gold, or a man that was happy when he had found it. Surely it is sin and sorrow that drives men to it, and sin and sorrow that comes to them from it. Look now! Stay with us here on the farm, teaching school to my grandchildren, the orphans of my daughter Lijsbeth, and it may be that so you will find peace.'

Jan Boetje answered her: 'If Mevrouw is right, and sin and sorrow have driven me to her country for gold, am I a man to be trusted with her grandchildren?'

My grandmother cried, in her soft clear voice that was so full of love and pity: 'Is there a sin that cannot be forgiven? And a sorrow that cannot be shared?'

Jan Boetje answered: 'My sorrow I cannot share. And my sin I myself can never forgive.'

And again my grandmother said: 'Mijnheer! What lies in a man's heart is known only to God and himself. Do now as seems right to you, but surely if you will stay with us I will trust my grandchildren to you and know that the Lord has sent you.'

For a long, long time, as it seemed to me, Jan Boetje sat before us and said no word. I could not breathe, and yet it was as if all the world must hear my breathing. Aunt Betje's children were long ago in bed, and only my grandparents and I sat there beside him. Long, long we waited. And when at last Jan Boetje said: 'I will stay,' it was as if he had heard how I cried to the Lord to help him.

So it was that Jan Boetje stayed with us on the farm and taught school to Aunt Betje's children. His schoolroom was the old waggon-house (grandfather had long ago built a new one), and here my grandmother and I put a table and stools for Jan Boetje and his scholars. The waggon-house had no window, and to get light Jan Boetje and the children sat close to the open half-door. From the door one looked out to the orange grove, where all my grandmother's children and many of her grandchildren also had been christened. Beyond and above the orange trees rose the peaks of the great Zwartkops mountains, so black in summer, and so white when snow lay upon them in winter. Through the mountains, far to the head of the valley, ran the Ghamka pass by which men travelled up country when they went looking for gold. The Ghamka river came down through this pass and watered all the farms in the valley. Coming down from the mountains to Nooitgedacht men crossed it by the Rooikranz drift.

Inside the waggon-house my grandfather stored his great brandy casks and his tobacco, his pumpkins and his mealies, his ploughs and his spades, his whips and his harness, and all such things as are needed at times about a farm. From the beams of the loft also there hung the great hides that he used for his harness and his veldschoen. Jan Boetje's schoolroom smelt always of tobacco and brandy and hides, and when the mud floor, close by the door, was freshly smeared with mist it smelt of bullock's blood and cow-dung as well.

We had, when Jan Boetje came to us, no books on the farm but our Bibles and such old lesson books as my aunts and uncles had thought

not good enough to take away with them when they married. Aunt
Betje's children had the Bible for their reading book, and one of my
grandfather's hides for a blackboard. On this hide, with blue clay from
the river bed, Jan Boetje taught the little ones their letters and the
bigger ones their sums. Geography also he taught them, but it was such
a geography as had never before been taught in the Platkops district.
Yes, surely the world could never be so wonderful and strange as Jan
Boetje made it to us (for I also went to his geography class) in my
grandfather's waggon-house. And always when he spoke of the cities
and the wonders that he had seen I would think how bitter must be the
sorrow, and how great the sin, that had driven him from them to us.
And when, as it sometimes happened, he would ask me afterwards:
'What shall we take for our reading lesson, Engela?' I would choose the
fourteenth chapter of Chronicles or the eighth chapter of Kings.

Jan Boetje asked me one day: 'What makes you choose the Prayer in
the Temple, Engela?'

And I, that did not know how close to love had come my pity,
answered him: 'Because, Mijnheer, King Solomon who cries, "Hear
thou in heaven thy dwelling-place, and when thou hearest forgive",
prays also for the stranger from a far country.'

From that day Jan Boetje, who was kind and gentle with his
scholars, was kind and gentle also with me. Many times now I found
his eyes resting upon me, and when sometimes he came and sat quietly
by my side as I sewed there would come a wild beating at my heart that
was joy and pain together. Except to his scholars he had spoken to no
one on the farm unless he first were spoken to. But now he spoke also
to me, and when I went out in the veld with little Neeltje and her
brothers, looking for all such things as are so wonderful to a child, Jan
Boetje would come with us. And it was now that I taught Jan Boetje
which berries he might eat and which would surely kill him, which
leaves and bushes would cure a man of many sicknesses, and which
roots and bulbs would quench his thirst. Many such simple things I
taught him in the veld, and many, many times afterwards I thanked
God that I had done so. Yes, all that my love was ever to do for Jan
Boetje was but to guide him so in the wilderness.

When Jan Boetje had been with us six months and more, it came to be little Neeltje's birthday. My grandmother had made it a holiday for the children, and Jan Boetje and I were to go with them, in a stump-cart drawn by two mules, up into a little ravine that lay beyond the Rooikranz drift. It was such a clear still day as often happens in our Ghamka valley in June month, and as we drove, Neeltje and her brothers sang together in high sweet voices that made me think of the angels of God. Because of the weakness of my chest I myself could never sing, and yet that day, with Jan Boetje sitting quietly by my side, it was as if my heart were so full of song that he must surely hear it. Yes, I that am now so old, so old, was never again to feel such joy as swept through my soul and body then.

When we had driven about fifteen minutes from the farm we came to the Rooikranz drift. There had been but little rain and snow in the mountains that winter, and in the wide bed of the river there was then but one small stream. The banks of the river here are steep, and on the far side are the great red rocks that give the drift its name. Here the wild bees make their honey, and the white wild geese have their home. And that day how beautiful in the still clear air were the great red rocks against the blue sky, and how beautiful against the rocks were the white wings of the wild geese!

When we had crossed the little stream Jan Boetje stopped the cart and Neeltje and her brothers climbed out of it and ran across the river bed shouting and clapping their hands to send the wild geese flying out from the rocks above them. Only I was left with Jan Boetje, and now when he whipped up the mules they would not move. Jan Boetje stood up in the cart and slashed at them, and they backed towards the stream. Jan Boetje jumped from the cart, and with the stick end of his whip struck the mules over the eyes, and his face, that had grown so dear to me, was suddenly strange and terrible to see. I cried to him: 'Jan Boetje! Jan Boetje!' but the weakness of my chest was upon me and I could make no sound. I rose in the cart to climb out of it, and as I rose Jan Boetje had a knife in his hand and dug it into the eyes of the mules to blind them. Sharp above the laughter of the children and the cries of the wild geese there came a terrible scream, and I fell from the cart on to the soft grey sand of the river bed. When I rose again the mules were far down the stream, with the cart bumping and splintering behind them, and Jan Boetje after them. And so quickly had his madness come upon him that still the children laughed and clapped their hands, and still the wild geese flew among the great red rocks above us.

God knows how it was that I gathered the children together and, sending the bigger boys in haste back to the farm, came on myself with Neeltje and the little ones. My grandfather rode out to meet us. I told him what I could, but it was little that I could say, and he rode on down the river. When we came to the farm the children ran up to the house to my grandmother, but I myself went alone to the waggon-house. I opened the door and closed it after me again, and crept in the dark to Jan Boetje's chair. Long, long I sat there, with my head on my arms on his table, and it was as if in all the world there was nothing but a sorrow that must break my heart, and a darkness that smelt of tobacco and brandy and hides. Long, long I sat, and when at last my grandmother found me, 'My little Engela,' she said. 'The light of my heart! My treasure!'

The mules that Jan Boetje had blinded were found and shot by my grandfather, and for long the splinters of the cart lay scattered down the bed of the river. Jan Boetje himself my grandfather could not find, though he sent men through all the valley looking for him. And after many days it was thought that Jan Boetje had gone up country through the pass at night. I was now for a time so ill that my father came down from his farm in Beaufort district to see me. He would have taken me back with him but in my weakness I cried to grandmother to keep me. And my father, to whom everything that my grandmother did was right, once again left me to her.

My father had not been many days gone when old Franz Langermann came to my grandparents with news of Jan Boetje. Franz Langermann lived at the toll-house at the entrance to the pass through the mountains, and here Jan Boetje had come to him asking if he would sell him an old hand-cart that stood by the toll-gate. The hand-cart was a heavy clumsy one that the road-men repairing the road through the pass had left behind them. Franz Langermann had asked Jan Boetje what he would do with such a cart? And Jan Boetje had answered: 'I that have killed mules must now work like a mule if I would live.' And he had said to Franz Langermann: 'Go to the farm of Nooitgedacht and say to Mevrouw Delport that all that is in the little tin box in my room is now hers in payment of the mules. But there is enough also to pay for the hand-cart if Mevrouw will but give you what is just.'

My grandmother asked Franz Langermann: 'But what is it then that Jan Boetje can do with a hand-cart?'

And Franz Langermann answered: 'Look now, Mevrouw! Through the country dragging the hand-cart like a mule he will go, gathering such things as he can find and afterwards selling them again that he may live. Look! Already out of a strap that I gave him Jan Boetje has made for himself his harness.'

My grandmother went to Jan Boetje's room and found the box as Franz Langermann had said. There was money in it enough to pay for the mules and the hand-cart, but there was nothing else. My grandfather took the box out to Franz Langermann and said:

'Take now the box as it is, and let Mijnheer give you himself what is just, but surely I will not take payment for the mules. Is it not seven months now that Jan Boetje has taught school to my grandchildren? God help Jan Boetje, and may he go in peace.'

But Franz Langermann would not take the box. 'Look now, Mevrouw,' he said, 'I swore to Jan Boetje that only for the hand-cart would I take the money, and all the rest would I leave.'

My grandmother put the box back in Jan Boetje's room, and gave to Franz Langermann instead such things as a man takes on a journey – biltong, and rusks and meal, and a little kid-skin full of dried fruits. As much as Franz Langermann could carry she gave him. But I, that would have given Jan Boetje all the world, in all the world had nothing that I might give. Only when Franz Langermann had left the house and crossed the yard did I run after him with my little Bible and cry:

'Franz Langermann! Franz Langermann! Say to Jan Boetje to come again to Nooitgedacht! Say to him that so long as I live I will wait!'

Yes, I said that. God knows what meaning my message had for me, or what meaning it ever had for Jan Boetje, but it was as if I must die if I could not send it.

That night my grandmother came, late in the night, to the room where I lay awake. She drew me into her arms and held me there, and out of the darkness I cried:

'Grandmother! Grandmother! Is love then such sorrow?'

And still I can hear the low clear voice that answered so strangely: 'A joy and a sorrow – a help and a hindrance – love comes at the last to be but what one makes it.'

It was the next day that my grandmother asked me to teach school for her in Jan Boetje's place. At first, because always the weakness of my chest had kept me timid, I did not think she could mean it. But she did mean it. And suddenly I knew that for Jan Boetje's sake I had strength to do it. And I called the children together and went down to the waggon-house and taught them.

All through the spring and summer months that year, getting books from the pastor in Platkops dorp to help me, I taught school for my grandmother. And because it was easy for me to love little children and to be patient with them, and because it was for Jan Boetje's sake that I did it, I came at last to forget the weakness of my chest and to make a good teacher. And day after day as I sat in his chair in the waggon-house I would think of Jan Boetje dragging his hand-cart across the veld. And day after day I would thank God that I had taught him which berries he might eat, and which bulbs would quench his thirst. Yes, in such poor and simple things as this had my love to find its comfort.

That year winter came early in the Ghamka valley, and there came a day in May month when the first fall of snow brought the river down in flood from the mountains. My grandfather took the children down to the drift to see it. I did not go, but sat working alone with my books in the waggon-house. And always on that day when I looked up through the open half-door, and saw, far above the orange grove, the peaks of the Zwartkops mountains so pure and white against the blue sky, there came a strange sad happiness about my heart, and it was as if I knew that Jan Boetje had at last found peace and were on his way to tell me so. Long, long I thought of him that day in the waggon-house, and when there came a heavy tramping of feet and a murmur of voices across the yard I paid no heed. And presently the voices died down, and my grandmother stood alone before me, with her eyes full of tears and in her hand a little damp and swollen book that I knew for the Bible I had sent to Jan Boetje ... Down in the drift they had found his body – his harness still across his chest, the pole of his cart still in his hand.

That night I went alone to the room where Jan Boetje lay and drew back the sheet that covered him.

Across his chest, where the strap of his harness had rubbed it, the skin was hard and rough as leather. I knelt down by his side, and pressed my head against his breast. And through my heart there ran in farewell such foolish, tender words as my grandmother used to me – 'My joy and my sorrow ... The light of my heart, and my treasure.'

THE BARREN WOMAN

H I E Dhlomo

The Bantu love of children is well known. This love is partly natural, just like that of other human beings. It is partly the result of a social system in which lobola, the demands and difficulties of labour, and a man's prestige and status in society all put a premium on the size of the family. Because of lobola girls are considered as valuable as boys. Perhaps more. Whatever may be said about the evils of the system today, in tribal society lobola enhanced the status of a woman and gave her protection and a high niche in a society where men held autocratic powers, and great value was placed on boys as potential military power.

Barrenness in women was a stigma and disgrace. Even today most Bantu people spend large sums of money and endure many hardships to fight it.

In the past African women were also reputed for their remarkable powers of surviving ante-natal, actual labour and post-natal troubles. Just as warriors regarded death as a matter of course, women took giving birth in their daily stride, as it were – not as an exceptional event requiring special preparation and associated with anxiety.

Of the two modern social evils reported from time to time, child stealing (although unknown in Bantu communities) is more in line with the tribal tradition of love for children, and the abandonment of unwanted babies foreign to it. But neither child stealing nor adoption as we know it was practised in tribal society. That is why barrenness was such a tragedy.

The story of Mamkazi Zondi is interesting because it involves most of the elements above. It is simple, has no dramatic climax, and no element of surprise. She lived in the remote but thriving and, therefore, well-populated village of Manzini. As in many other rural areas part of the population was tribal and 'heathen', and part 'Christian' – meaning anyone who wore European clothes, sent their children to school, lived in square houses no matter how humble and dilapidated, or did not conform to tribal patterns one way or another.

Mamkazi belonged to the 'Christian' group, had been married for three years, and would have been happy and her story not worth telling but for one curse.

She was barren.

She and her husband had gone to great trouble and wasted a fortune trying to get a baby. European doctors and African herbalists and witch-doctors had been consulted without success.

The couple were unhappy. Temba Zondi, her husband, loved her and was kind and devoted to her. Except on three or four occasions when they had had exceptionally violent quarrels, he never blamed her for her defect. However, the curse hung over their house and life. She was reminded about it frequently and in many ways. When her husband silently stared at her or took more than usual interest in a neighbour's or visitor's child, it hurt her deeply for she felt he was chiding and blaming her bitterly, if silently. Garrulous or unfeeling and spiteful neighbours gossiped about it. Innocent visitors and old, distant acquaintances who meant no harm hurt her when they asked if she had no child yet.

Of all her friends and neighbours, the best and most intimate was Ntombi Mate. But Mamkazi did not know whether to regard Ntombi as a blessing or a curse, a solace to her soul or a thorn in her flesh.

Unlike most 'Christian' women of her age in the village, who could only read and write (the younger generation were more progressive), Ntombi was considered 'educated'. She had passed Standard Six, had travelled to several big towns, and had worked for some time in a large mission hospital where she acquired a rudimentary knowledge of midwifery. Although she had not been out of Manzini village for years, was married and had a big family, she still retained her reputation and status. She was the unofficial, unqualified, but useful district midwife of the place. Whether she thought and believed it was professionally necessary or she was too lazy (and had grown fat) and too snobbish (was she not above others?), she insisted that those who needed her help must come to her 'clinic', which was a large hut with four beds. She never answered calls to homes, no matter what happened. Homes were far away and had no comforts, the way was rough, and calls came at inconvenient hours of the day and night. Well known and never without work, she was yet never inundated with cases because most women were strong and healthy enough to give birth successfully in their homes, and the others did not care about clinics and hospitals except in cases where there were complications.

The snag in the deep and warm friendship of Mamkazi and Ntombi was that whenever the latter referred to her work, Mamkazi was reminded of her plight. Otherwise each woman could do almost anything for the other. And Ntombi had done all to help her friend.

During the fourth year of her marriage, Mamkazi conceived. The fact lifted her to the seventh heaven of ecstasy, pride and expectation. But there were times when she was slain by doubts, fears and worse. Doubts and fears about miscarriage, stillbirth, and other accidents. Worse? Possibly. There was the sad case of the Kozas where the coming of a child after five years of barren marriage completely wrecked their home because of the allegation – supported by some and denied by others, and not open to proof or disproof in that backward society – that Koza's wife had been unfaithful and the child was illegitimate.

Mamkazi's fears were unfounded. Zondi was intoxicated with joy, and treated her with poignant tenderness and devotion. Doctors and hospitals were very far away. But, urged by their own gratitude and caution and Ntombi's strong advice, Mamkazi paid four visits to the nearest town to consult a doctor. When the time came she, of course, placed herself under the care of her friend who was determined to display to the utmost her knowledge and experience on this occasion.

The baby came without trouble. It was a girl. Mamkazi was so fit that she could have returned home the next day and gone about her business. Two other women were in the clinic at that time. The same night they, too, had children, one a girl, and the other twins – a boy and a girl. The twins were not identical – but at the time this struck no one, not even Ntombi, as being significant.

The following night Mamkazi's heaven changed into hell. Zondi had almost been overpowered with joy and pride, and had found it difficult to leave the clinic even for a few moments or to return home in the night. Ntombi and Mamkazi had congratulated one another a dozen times. Many friends had come and stood amazed at the 'miracle'. Ntombi had openly given special attention to her friend. Expensive and lovely things had been bought for the baby. Everything was in striking contrast to the two other poor women, one of whom was a 'Christian' and the other – the mother of the twins – a tribal person.

Ntombi insisted on cleanliness and on what other 'modern' professional rules and methods she knew. One of these was not to cover heavily with blankets the new arrivals (and other sick persons), as fond mothers and relatives were inclined to do.

In the still hours of the second night, Mamkazi, who could hardly sleep for joy, woke up to find that her precious child had been smothered to death! It was impossible! A thousand-to-one chance accident! And of all people, this to happen to her! No. God would not let it happen!

'O God, Almighty Father! It cannot be! Give life to my child! Restore it back to me! How can God be so cruel, mock with such evil! After years in hell, to lift me into heaven for a moment, only to plunge me back into deeper hell! Hear, Holiest Father, hear. I kiss and beg at Thy feet!'

Thus she prayed silently and insanely. But the ways of God are unfathomable. The child was dead. Demented, she had no power to cry out aloud or rave. After trying gently but excitedly to stir and suckle the baby into life, some demoniacal spirit descended upon her, making her cool and determined, and propelling her to some devilish scheme. There is no God! Why stand in the way of the Devil, then! In a flash, the evil plan was born and executed. Mechanically, rapidly, and with mad courage and precision, she undressed her dead baby, exchanged it with the scantily attired twin girl whom she dressed as her child, wrapped up the twin boy and the dead child heavily in a blanket as she had found them and retired to her bed in a state of nervous and insane anxiety.

'I have done it! Who will find out! Who dares accuse me! Three of us have girls – and how can they tell? I have the right to the living baby! It is mine! She does not need it. She has many other children. Come close to me, my dear one. Live and thrive! There is life in you, and your life is my life, hope and light. Let us sleep in peace.'

A raving maniac, she could not sleep, but managed to lie still.

As if by some evil spell, she had carried out her plan without disturbance. Hardly an hour later, a piercing cry rent the clinic. Soon there was bedlam. The mother of the twins had awakened and made the tragic discovery. Her lamentations were broadcast far and wide. The clinic was soon filled by the agitated Ntombi, members of her family and people who lived close by. The rare 'accident' left everyone dumbfounded and mentally paralysed. The mother of the twins could not be consoled.

The next day the whole village knew about the strange happenings. The husbands of the three women had rushed to the clinic early to stand by and comfort their wives. So did others. The tragedy was discussed excitedly, if in whispers.

After some time, the excitement and sense of grief subsided, and life in the village and in the families directly concerned took its normal course. No one had the least suspicion about foul play. The women of the village were amazed and impressed that Ntombi's constant and seemingly unnecessary and irritating warning about wrapping children in heavy blankets – advice she gave purely on 'hygienic' and snobbish grounds – had been justified so tragically. The old tribal superstition that giving birth to twins is bad luck was revived for a time. It helped seal the matter as 'natural' and in accordance with hoary tradition and sacrosanct custom.

The three women's agitation, sallowness and wild behaviour were considered natural and excusable under the circumstances. This was especially true of Mamkazi who received special and universal sympathy as her rare blessing coincided with such a misfortune. Of the three women, she was the most pitied and 'understood' for whatever strange behaviour and attitude she adopted. Her husband and friends repeatedly congratulated and consoled her with the words, 'Thank God, it did not happen to you!'

The excitement subsided and life in the village and in the families concerned took a normal course. No one had the least suspicion about foul play. Not so! Nature is 'scientific', omniscient and deeply jealous and revengeful when her course and ends are disturbed.

One person was keenly suspicious about the whole episode. It was Ntombi. Instinctively and intuitively the truth was revealed to her through a glass darkly. However, as a rational human being and a realist, she held her peace. But there was conflict, not peace, within her. She had carefully taken notice of Mamkazi's unnatural behaviour and agitation on the fateful day and after. More experienced, observant and trained than others, including the three mothers, she could tell the difference between newborn babes – in weight, behaviour, and even in physical features that would be imperceptible to others. Besides, she was the only person who had seen and handled all three girls. She was sure that there was something wrong. But was it possible? How could mediocre-minded and nervous Mamkazi have conceived and executed without help and discovery such a foul act?

What was she to do! The knowledge that, in bigger and more accessible centres, the thing would have led to an embarrassing, and even incriminating investigation, added to her uneasiness and inner conflict. It might be a sin in the eyes of God, also.

Thus, while the rest of the village had forgotten about the occurrence, two women – Mamkazi and Ntombi – remained restless, unhappy and guarded.

Time heals, makes us forget and helps solve problems. Pleasant but deceitful philosophy! Time festers old wounds, opens patched-up scars, complicates and increases problems, and makes us remember and grow afraid at every turn. Time plagues, derides, incapacitates.

Far from achieving happiness and triumph, Mamkazi found that she had set herself a problem that became more complicated as time went on. If someone spoke of Jabu Buthelezi, the mother of the twins, her child or her family, she became apprehensive. If she herself met one of the family, it was worse.

The passage of years had wrought many changes in Manzini village. The population had increased rapidly. With the opening up of new roads and the introduction of a bus service, there was more progress. A European District Surgeon now visited the village on certain days of the week. He had a trained nurse assisting him. Ntombi's 'clinic' was a thing of the past. There was a fine large new school, and the local store had been expanded and the goods improved in quantity and quality. There was no need for children and adults to trudge many weary miles to the distant school or the better store. Some tribal families – among them the Buthelezis – had become 'Christians'.

Mamkazi was reminded of her act at every turn.

'Ma! I met Zidumo Buthelezi and his mother at the store,' her daughter Simangele would report innocently and excitedly. 'His mother said "I love you as much as my boy. You look like one another." She kissed me and gave me sweets.'

Returning from a beer-drinking party her husband would blabber, '... And there was Buthelezi who said that he would be disappointed if our little Simangele did not marry into his family when she grew up. He is crazy about the child, just like the others. Ha! Ha!'

On such occasions she would weep, burst out into a violent temper or behave in some inexplicable manner. And remarks and incidents of this kind came every day.

She had quarrelled with her husband when she tried arbitrarily to restrict the movements of the little girl; when she said the child must be sent to the distant not the local school; when she suggested that they should go and live in another district. Zondi could not understand all this, and they became increasingly unhappy.

Mamkazi and Ntombi were hardly on speaking terms now for the latter had tried to discover the truth by subtle and friendly hints at first, but, at last, had bluntly demanded to know the truth.

'We are the best of friends. You can rely on me. We are growing old and must not die with certain secrets. Let me know the truth if only to ease my conscience. You can trust me not to tell. It would serve no purpose,' Ntombi had implored.

'Inquisitive spy! Blackmailing informer! Nagging cheat! It would wreck you as completely as myself! Of course you dare not tell! It was your clinic. You are more educated! You should have known, and it was your responsibility. I can also blackmail you! The police and the people would believe it was done with your connivance. In fact, that it was your evil idea and scheme. For how else could a convalescent, ignorant, grieved woman like me have succeeded to carry out the thing without your help and knowledge! Know then that your suspicions are true. I "switched" the two girls! I did! Simangele is her twin child! But she is forever mine! Mine, you hear! Go and tell! I hate you! Get out of my sight!'

Mamkazi aged rapidly. She cut herself off from society almost completely. Old villagers talked about it, but, unsuspecting, gave the wrong reason for the change. Newcomers and the young did not care. Her husband drank heavily and more frequently. From being one of the most loving and happy couples, they became one of the most unhappy in the village. She had done all this for her husband's and her own triumph and happiness. Instead, she had wrecked both. Retreat was impossible. She clung to her tragic secret and followed her deadly course as if for life.

It is summer. The grass is green. Birds sing. Wild flowers gently sway everywhere. Near a humming stream rest two shy young lovers, Simangele Zondi and Zidumo Buthelezi. They are nineteen years of age, good-looking and in the full bloom of health. It is college vacation time. Although they grew up together, they have had little time to see one another in the past three years for they have been attending different and distant colleges.

'In youth when we were always together, we did not care whether we were together or not. Now that we crave always to be together we cannot always be together,' said Zidumo.

'Always speaking as if you were a full-grown man. I like to stay young,' laughed Simangele.

'I am a man. You will always be young.'

'But you were right. And mother would be raving mad to know that I have been seen with you, let alone that I am in love with you!'

'I cannot understand it. It has always been so, I am told, since we were tots. But I never noticed it. Did you?'

'I knew it. Perhaps some silly old family feud.'

'Possibly. But I doubt it, for my people love you and have nothing against your people. They seem just as puzzled. There is one solution. As soon as I complete my degree studies next year, I will elope with and marry you!'

At this, they laughed and kissed.

Tormented and vigilant Mamkazi had heard of their meeting and of their being in love. The climax followed rapidly.

Zondi's largest room was soon crowded with distressed, puzzled and expectant people. The audience had been carefully selected. They had been hurriedly and secretly summoned at the persistent and intolerable ravings of Mamkazi who appeared to be near death and wanted to say something. There was Ntombi and her husband; Buthelezi, his wife and Zidumo; the Priest and his assistant; the Zondis.

Aware of impending tragedy, the Priest had prayed for peace and guidance. But Mamkazi could not wait or be controlled. She groaned and raved in her bed. Supported, she sat up and spoke. There was mingled supreme triumph and utter despair, joy and bitterness, sanity and madness in her words and visage. She wept and laughed, defied and implored.

'Silence! Who dares! Ha! Ha! Listen to me. They shall not, cannot, marry. Yes, you two! The Buthelezis shall not have my daughter. Foiled? Indeed, you are! Ha! She is mine and I will have my way. Mind, I tell you, forever mine! O God, O Evil, the daughter you gave me!

What? Yes, I stole her from you – your girl twin. Your child lives forever mine! How can brother and sister be married? Can't you leave her – me – alone! Ask her – ask my nagging, evil friend, there – the midwife. She knows! She will ...'

Mamkazi collapsed. Jabu Buthelezi wept aloud and sank on the floor. There was amazement, incredulity and confusion.

But the Priest was equal to the situation. He called for and restored some measure of order, sent his assistant to call for the doctor at once, asked for God's help in a sentence, and finally commanded Ntombi to speak and explain. Trembling and old, she wept and stammered.

'It is true. It happened long ago in my clinic ...' she began.

© H I E Dhlomo

THE KAFIR DRUM

Herman Charles Bosman

Old Mosigo was the last of the drum-men left at Gaberones when they brought the telegraph wires on long poles to this part of the country (Oom Schalk Lourens said). You can hear some kafir drums going now, down there in the vlakte – there they are again ... tom-tom-tom-*tom*-tom. There must be a big beer drink on at those huts in the vlakte. Of course, that's all the kafirs use their drums for these days – to summon the neighbours to a party. On a quiet night you can hear those drums from a long distance away. From as far as the Bechuanaland border sometimes.

But there was a time when the voice of the kafir drum travelled right across Africa. I can still remember how, many years ago, the kafirs received messages from thousands of miles away with their drums. The tom-tom men in every village understood the messages sent out by the drums of the neighbouring villages. Then in their turn they spread the message further, with the result that, if the news was important, the whole of Africa knew it within a few days. The peculiar thing about this was that even when such a message originated from a tribe with a completely strange language, the drum-man of the tribe receiving the message could still interpret it. In the old days there were two drum-men in each village. They were instructed in the code of the drum from boyhood, and then in their turn they taught the art of sending and receiving messages by drum to those who came after them.

No white man has ever been able to learn the language of the kafir's drums. The only white man who ever had any idea at all of what the drums said – and even his knowledge about it was of the slightest – was Gerhardus van Tonder who regularly travelled deep into Africa with his brother, Rooi Willem.

Gerhardus van Tonder told me that he had asked the drum-men of several tribes to teach him the meaning of the sounds they beat out on their tom-toms.

'But you know yourself how ignorant a kafir is,' Gerhardus van Tonder said to me. 'I could never understand what the drum-men tried over and over again to explain to me. Even when a drum-man told me the same thing up to ten times I still couldn't grasp it. So thick-skulled are they.'

Nevertheless, Gerhardus said that, because he heard the same message so often, he was able, later on, to make it out whenever the drums broadcast the message that his brother, Rooi Willem, had shot an elephant dead. But one day an elephant trampled Rooi Willem to death. Gerhardus listened to the message that the drums sent out after that. It was exactly the same as all those earlier messages, Gerhardus said. Only, it was the other way around.

Even in those days the prestige of the drum-man had fallen considerably, because a mission station had been started at Gaberones, and the missionaries had brought with them their own message which came into conflict with the heathen news from Central Africa. But when the telegraph wires were brought up here from Cape Town, taken past the Groot Marico and into the Protectorate – then everyone knew that, so to speak, the days of the kafir drum-man were numbered.

Yet on one occasion when I spoke to old Mosigo about the telegraph, what he had to say was: 'The drum is better than the copper wire that you white men bring on poles across the veld. I don't need copper wire for my drum's messages. Or long poles with rows of little white medicine bottles on them either.'

But whatever Mosigo thought, the authorities had the copper wires brought as far as Nietverdiend. A little post office had then been built on Jurie Bekker's farm, and a young telegraph operator from Pretoria appointed to serve as postmaster. This young man had arranged for a colleague in Pretoria to telegraph to him, from time to time, items from the newspapers. By means of these telegrams, which were pinned up on a notice board in the post office, we who live in this part of the bushveld kept in touch with the outside world.

The telegrams were all very short. In one of them we read of President Kruger's visit to Johannesburg and what he said, at a public meeting, about the Uitlanders.

'If that is all that the President could say about the Uitlanders,' said Hans Grobler, 'namely, "that they are a pest stop and that they should be more heavily taxed stop and that a miners' procession threw bottles stop," then I think that at the next elections I will simply vote for General Joubert. And why do these telegrams always repeat the word "stop" so monotonously?'

Those of us who were in the post office at the time agreed with Hans Grobler. Moreover we said that not only did we need a better president, but a better telegraph operator as well. We also agreed that extending the telegraph service to Nietverdiend was a waste of hundreds of miles of copper wire, not to speak, even, of all those long poles.

When we mentioned this to the telegraph operator, he looked from one to the other of us, thoughtfully, for a few moments, and then he said, 'Yes. Yes, I think it has been a waste.'

Thereupon At Buitendag made a remark that we all felt was very sensible. 'I can't read or write,' he declared, 'and I don't know what it is, exactly , that you are talking about. But I know that the best sort of news that I and my family used to get in the old days was the messages the kafirs used to thump out on their drums. I am not ashamed to say that I and my wife brought up seven sons and three daughters on nothing but that kind of news. I still remember the day old Mosigo –

even in those days he was old already – received the message about the three tax collectors who got eaten by crocodiles when their boat was upset on the Zambesi ...'

'And that sort of news was worth getting,' Hans Grobler interrupted him. 'I don't mean that we would be *pleased* if three tax collectors got eaten by crocodiles' – and we all said 'Oh, no,' and guffawed – 'They are also human. The tax collectors, I mean. But my point is that that sort of news was *news*. That is something that we understand. But look at this telegram. About "the fanatic who fired at the King of Spain stop and missed him by less than two feet stop". What use is a message like that to us bushveld Boers? And what sort of a thing is a fanatic, anyway?'

As a result of the conversations at the post office I decided to look up Mosigo, the last of the drum-men at Gaberones.

I found him sitting in front of his hut. The wrinkles on his face were countless. They made me think of the kafir footpaths that go twisting across the length and breadth of Africa, and that you can follow for mile after mile and day after day, and that never come to an end. And I thought how the messages that Mosigo received through his drum came from somewhere along the farthest paths that the kafirs followed across Africa, getting footsore on the way.

He was busy thumping his old drum. Tom-tom tom-tom, it went. It sounded almost like a voice to me. Now and again it seemed as if there floated on the wind a sound from very far away, which was either an answer to Mosigo's message, or the echo of his drum. But it wasn't like in the old days, when you could hear clearly how the message of one drum was taken up and spread over koppies and vlaktes by other drums. Anyone could see that there were not so many drum-men left in the bushveld, these days. And the reducing of their numbers wasn't because the chiefs had had them thrown to the vultures for bringing bad news.

It could only be due to the competition of the white man's telegraph wires.

I carried on a long conversation with old Mosigo, and in the course of it I told him about the King of Spain. And Mosigo said to me that he did not think much of that kind of news, and if that was the best the white man could do with his telegraph wires, then the white man still had a lot to learn. The telegraph people could come right down to his hut and learn. Even though he did not have a yellow rod – like they had shown him on the roof of the post office – to keep the lightning away, but only a piece of python skin, he said.

And looking at Mosigo's wrinkles I considered that he must have more understanding of things than that young upstart of a telegraph operator who had only been out of school for three or four years at the most. And who always put the word 'stop' in the middle of a message – a clear sign of his general uncertainty.

Even so, although I did not myself have a high opinion of the telegraph, I was not altogether pleased that an old kafir like Mosigo should speak lightly of an invention that came out of the white man's brain. And so I said that the telegraph was still quite a new thing and that it would no doubt improve in time. Perhaps how it would improve quite a lot would be if they sacked that young telegraph operator at Nietverdiend for a start, I said.

That young telegraph operator was too impertinent, I said.

Mosigo agreed that it would help. It was a very important thing, he said, that for such work you should have the right sort of person. It was no good, he explained, having news told to you by a man who was not suited to that kind of work.

'Another thing that is important is having the right person to tell the news to,' Mosigo went on. 'And you must also consider well concerning whom the news is about. Take that King, now, of whom you have told me, that you heard of at Nietverdiend through the telegraph. He is a great chief, that King, is he not?'

I said to Mosigo that I should imagine he must be a great chief, the King of Spain. I couldn't know for sure, of course, you can't really, with foreigners.

'Has he many herds of cattle and many wives hoeing in the bean-fields?' Mosigo asked. 'Do you know him well, this great chief?'

I told Mosigo that I did not know the King of Spain to speak to, since I had never met him. But if I did meet him – I was going on to explain, when Mosigo said that was exactly what he meant. 'What is the good of hearing about a man,' he asked, 'unless you know who that man *is*? When the telegraph operator told you about that big chief, he told it to the wrong man.'

And he fell to beating his drum again.

From then on I went regularly to visit Mosigo in order to find out what was happening in the world. We still read on the notice board in the post office about what had happened in, for instance, Russia – where a fanatic had opened fire on the Emperor 'and missed him by one foot stop'. We began to infer from the telegrams that a fanatic was someone who couldn't aim very well. But to get news that really meant something I had always, afterwards, to go and visit Mosigo.

Thus it happened that one afternoon, when I visited Mosigo on my way back from the post office, and found him again sitting in front of his hut before his drum, he told me that there would be no more news coming over his drum, because of a message about the death of a drum-man that he had just received.

It was a message that had come from a great distance, he said.

Still the following week I again rode over to Gaberones. It was after I had read a telegram on the notice board in the post office that said that a fanatic had missed the French President 'by more than twenty feet.'

And when I again rode away from Gaberones, where, this time, I had not seen Mosigo but had seen instead his drum, on which the skin stretched across the wooden frame had been cut, in accordance with the ritual carried out at the death of a drum-man – I wondered to myself on my way home, from how far, really, had it come – farther than France or Spain – that last message that Mosigo received.

THE HOME-COMING

Herman Charles Bosman

Laughter (Oom Schalk Lourens said). Well, there's a queer thing for you, now, and something not so easy to understand. And the older you get, the more things you seem to find to laugh at. Take old Frans Els, for instance. I can still remember the way he laughed, that time at Zeerust, when we were coming around the church building and we saw one of the tents from the Nagmaal camping-ground being carried away by a sudden gust of wind.

'It must be the ouderling's tent,' Frans Els called out. 'Well he never was any good at fixing the ground-pegs. Look, kêrels, there it goes right across the road.' And he laughed so much that his beard, which was turning white in places, flapped about almost like that tent in the wind.

Shortly afterwards, what was left of the tent got caught round the wooden poles of somebody's verandah, and several adults and a lot of children came running out of the house, shouting. By that time Frans Els was standing bent almost double over a fence. The tears were streaming down his cheeks and he had difficulty in getting his breath. I don't think I ever saw a man laugh so much in my life.

I don't think I ever saw a man stop laughing so quickly, either, as Frans Els did when some people from the camping-ground came up and spoke to him. They had to say it over twice before he could get the full purport of the message, which was to the effect that it was not the ouderling's tent at all, that had got blown away, but his.

I suppose you could describe the way in which Frans Els carried on that day while he still thought that it was the ouderling's tent, as one kind of laughter. The fact is that there are more kinds of laughter than just that one sort, and it seems to me that this is the cause of a lot of regrettable awkwardness in the world.

Another thing I have noticed is that when a woman laughs it usually means a good deal of trouble for a man. Not at that very moment, maybe, but afterwards. And more especially when it is a musical sort of laugh.

There is still another kind of laughter that you have also come across in your time, I am sure. That is the way we laugh when there are a number of us together in the Indian store at Ramoutsa, and Hendrik Moolman tells a funny story that he has read in the *Goede Hoop*. What is so entertaining about his way of telling these stories is that Hendrik Moolman always forgets what the point is. Then when we ask, 'But what's so funny about it?' he tries to make up another story as he goes along. And because he's so weak at that, it makes us laugh more than ever.

So when we talk about Hendrik Moolman's funny stories, it is not the stories themselves that we find amusing, but his lack of skill in telling them. But I suppose it's all the same to Hendrik Moolman. He joins heartily in our laughter and waves his crutch about. Sometimes he even gets so excited that you almost expect him to rise up out of his chair without help.

It all happened very long ago, the first part of this story of Hendrik Moolman and his wife Malie. And in those days, when they had just married, you would not, if the idea of laughter had come into your mind, have thought first of Hendrik Moolman telling jokes in the Indian store.

They were just of an age, the young Moolman couple, and they were both good to look at. And when they arrived back from Zeerust after the wedding, Hendrik made a stirring show of the way he lifted Malie from the mule cart, to carry her across the threshold of the little farmhouse in which their future life was to be cast. Needless to say, that was many years before Hendrik Moolman was to acquire the nickname of Crippled Hendrik, as the result of a fall into a diamond claim when he was drunk. Some said that his fall was an accident. Others saw in the occurrence the hand of the Lord.

What I remember most vividly about Malie, as she was in those early days of her marriage, are her eyes, and her laughter that was in strange contrast to her eyes. Her laughter was free and clear and ringing. Each time you heard it, it was like a sudden bright light. Her laughter was like a summer's morning. But her eyes were dark and did not seem to belong with any part of the day at all.

It was the women who by-and-by started to say about the marriage of Hendrik and Malie this thing, that Malie's love for Hendrik was greater than his love for her. You could see it all, they said, by that look that came on her face when Hendrik entered the voorkamer, called in from the lands because there were visitors. You could tell it too, they declared, by that unnatural stillness that would possess her when she was left alone on the farm for a few days, as would happen each time her husband went with cattle or mealies to the market town.

With the years, also, that gay laugh of Malie Moolman's was heard more seldom, until in the end she seemed to have forgotten how to laugh at all. But there was never any suggestion of Malie having been unhappy. That was the queerest part of it – that part of the marriage of Malie and Hendrik that confuted all the busybodies. For it proved that Malie's devotion to Hendrik had not been just one-sided.

They had been married a good many years before that day when it became known to Malie – as a good while before that it had become known to the rest of the white people living on this side of the

Dwarsberge – that Hendrik's return from the market town of Zeerust would be indefinitely delayed.

Those were prosperous times, and it was said that Hendrik had taken a considerable sum with him in gold coins for his journey to the Elandsputte diamond diggings, whither he had gone in the company of the Woman of Zeerust. Malie went on staying on the farm, and saw to it that the day-to-day activities in the kraal and on the lands and in the homestead went on just as though Hendrik were still there. Instead of in the arms of the Woman of Zeerust.

This went on for a good while, with Hendrik Moolman throwing away, on the diggings, real gold after visionary diamonds.

There were many curious features about this thing that had happened with Hendrik Moolman. For instance, it was known that he had written to his wife quite a number of times. Jurie Bekker, who kept the post office at Drogedal, had taken the trouble on one occasion to deliver into Malie's hands personally a letter addressed to her in her husband's handwriting. He had taken over the letter himself, instead of waiting for Malie to send for it. And Jurie Bekker said that Malie had thanked him very warmly for the letter, and had torn open the envelope in a state of agitation, and had wept over the contents of the letter, and had then informed Jurie Bekker that it was from her sister in Kuruman, who wrote about the drought there.

'It seemed to be a pretty long drought,' Jurie Bekker said to us afterwards in the post office, 'judging from the number of pages'.

It was known, however, that when a woman visitor had made open reference to the state of affairs on the Elandsputte diggings, Malie had said that her husband was suffering from a temporary infatuation for the Woman of Zeerust, of whom she spoke without bitterness. Malie said she was certain that Hendrik would grow tired of that woman, and return to her.

Meanwhile, many rumours of what was happening with Hendrik Moolman on the Elandsputte diggings were conveyed to this part of the Marico by one means and another – mainly by donkey-cart. Later on it became known that Hendrik had sold the wagon and the oxen with which he had trekked from his farm to the diggings. Still later it became known why Malie was sending so many head of cattle to market. Finally, when a man with a waxed moustache and a notebook appeared in the neighbourhood, the farmers hereabouts, betokening no surprise, were able to direct him to the Moolman farm, where he went to take an inventory of the stock.

By that time the Woman of Zeerust must have discovered that Hendrik Moolman was about at the end of his resources. But nobody knew for sure when she deserted him – whether it was before or after that thing had happened to him which paralysed the left side of his body.

And that was how it came about that in the end Hendrik Moolman did return to his wife, Malie, just as she had during all that time maintained that he would. In reply to a message from Elandsputte diggings she had sent a kafir in the mule-cart to fetch Baas Hendrik Moolman back to his farm.

Hendrik Moolman was seated in a half-reclining posture against the kafir who held the reins, that evening when the mule-cart drew up in front of the home into which, many years before, on the day of their wedding, he had carried his wife, Malie. There was something not unfitting about his own home-coming in the evening, in the thought that Malie would be helping to lift him off the mule cart, now.

Some such thought must have been uppermost in Malie's mind also. At all events, she came forward to greet her errant husband. Apparently she now comprehended for the first time the true extent of his incapacitation. Malie had not laughed for many years. Now the sound of her laughter, gay and silvery, sent its infectious echoes ringing through the farmyard.

KWASHIORKOR

Can Themba

'Here's another interesting case ...'

My sister flicked over the pages of the file of one of her case studies, and I wondered what other shipwrecked human being had there been recorded, catalogued, statisticised and analysed. My sister is a social worker with the Social Welfare Department of the Non-European Section of the Municipality of Johannesburg. In other words, she probes into the derelict lives of the unfortunate poor in Johannesburg. She studies their living habits, their recreational habits, their sporting habits, their drinking habits, the incidence of crime, neglect, malnutrition, divorce, aberration, and she records all this in cyclostyled forms that ask the questions ready-made. She has got so good that she could tell without looking whether such-and-such a query falls under paragraph so-and-so. She has got so clinical that no particular case rattles her, for she has met its like before and knows how and where to classify it.

Her only trouble was ferocious Alexandra Township, that hell-hole in Johannesburg where it was never safe for a woman to walk the streets unchaperoned or to go from house to house asking testing questions. This is where I come in. Often I have to escort her on her rounds just so that no township rough-neck molests her. We arranged it lovely so that she only went to Alexandra on Saturday afternoons when I was half-day-off and could tag along.

'Dave,' she said, 'here's another interesting case. I'm sure you would love to hear about it. It's Alex again. I'm interested in the psychological motivations and the statistical significance, but I think you'll get you a human-interest story. I know you can't be objective, but do, I beg you, do take it all quietly and don't mess me up with your sentimental reactions. We'll meet at two o'clock on Saturday, okay?'

That is how we went to that battered house in 3rd Avenue, Alexandra. It was just a lot of wood and tin knocked together gawkily to make four rooms. The house stood precariously a few yards from the sour, cider-tasting gutter, and in the back there was a row of out-rooms constructed like a train and let to smaller families or bachelor men and women. This was the main source of income for the Mabiletsa family – mother, daughter and daughter's daughter.

But let me refer to my sister Eileen's records to get my facts straight.

Mother: Mrs Sarah Mabiletsa, age 62, widow, husband Abner Mabiletsa died 1953 in motor-car accident. Sarah does not work. Medical Report says chronic arthritis. Her sole sources of support are rent from out-rooms and working daughter, Maria. Sarah is dually illiterate.

Daughter: Maria Mabiletsa, age 17, Reference Book No. F/V 118/32N1682. Domestic servant. Educational standard: 5. Reads and writes English, Afrikaans, Sepedi. Convictions: 30 days for shoplifting. One illegitimate child unmaintained and of disputed paternity.

Child: Sekgametse Daphne Lorraine Mabiletsa, Maria's child, age 3 years. Father undetermined. Free clinic attendance. Medical Report: Advanced Kwashiorkor.

Other relatives: Sarah's brother, Edgar Mokgomane, serving jail sentence, 15 years, murder and robbery.

Remarks (Eileen's verdict): This family is desperate. Mother: ineffectual care for child. Child: showing malnutrition effects. Overall quantitative and qualitative nutritional deficiency. Maria: good-time girl, seldom at home, spends earnings mostly on self and parties. Recommend urgent welfare aid and/or intervention.

Although Eileen talks about these things clinically, *objectively*, she told me the story and I somehow got the feel of it.

Abner Mabiletsa was one of those people who was not content with life in the reserves in Pietersburg district where he was born and grew up. He did not see where the tribal set-up of chief and *kgotla* – the tribal council – and customs, taboos, superstitions, witchcraft and the lackadaisical dreariness of rotating with the sun from morn till eve, would take the people and would take him. Moreover, the urge to rise and go out to do things, to conquer and become someone, the impatience of the blood, seized him. So he upped and went to Johannesburg, where else? Everybody went there.

First, there were the ordinary problems of adjustment; the tribal boy had to fit himself into the vast, fast-moving, frenetic life in the big city. So many habits, beliefs, customs had to be fractured overnight. So many reactions that were sincere and instinctive were laughed at in the city. A man was continually changing himself, leaping like a flea from contingency to contingency. But Abner made it, though most of the time he did not know who he was, whither he was going. He only knew that this feverish life had to be lived, and identity became so large that a man sounded ridiculous for boasting he was a Mopedi or a Mosuto or a Xhosa or a Zulu – nobody seemed to care. You were just an African *here*, and somewhere *there* was a white man: two different types of humans that impinged, now and then – indeed often – but painfully.

Abner made it. He was helped by his home-boys, those who had come before. They showed him the ropes. They found him a job. They accommodated him those first few months until he found a room of his own in Alexandra. They took him to parties, to girls, to dice schools. Ultimately, they showed him where he could learn to drive a car. Soon, soon, he could negotiate all the byways and back-alleys of Johannesburg by himself. He had escapades, fun, riotous living ... Until one day one of his escapades became pregnant and bore him a daughter. He paid the *lobola* – that hard-dying custom of paying the bride-price – getting some of his friends and home-boys to stand for him *in loco parentis*; he did not even apprise his folk back home in Pietersburg of his marriage; he did it all himself.

But life in Johannesburg was such that he did not find much time to look after his family. He was not exactly the delinquent father, but there was just not the time or the room for a man to become truly family-bound. Then suddenly, crash! He died in a motor car accident, and his unprovided-for wife had to make do.

His daughter, Maria, grew up in the streets of Alexandra. The spectre of poverty was always looming over her life; and at the age of fourteen she left school to work in the white man's kitchens. It helped, at first, to alleviate the grim want, the ever-empty larder, at home. But soon she got caught up in the froth of Johannesburg's titillating nether life. She had a boyfriend who came pretty regularly to sleep in her room at the back of her place of employment; she had other boyfriends in the city, in the townships, with whom she often slept. And of the billions of human seed so recklessly strewn, one was bound some time to strike target.

When her condition became obvious, Maria nominated the boy she liked best, the swankiest, handsomest, most romantic and most moneyed swain in her repertoire. But he was a dangerous *tsotsi*, and when she told him of what he had wrought, he threatened to beat the living spit out of her. She fondly, foolishly persisted; and he assaulted her savagely. The real boyfriend – the one who slept in her room – felt bitter that she had indicated another. Had he not already boasted to his friends that he had 'bumped' her? Now the whole world judged that he had been cuckolded.

Poor Maria tried the somersault and turned to him, but by then he would have none of it. He effectively told the Native Commissioner, 'I am this girl's second opinion. She does not know who is responsible for her condition. There she stands, now too scared to nominate the man she first fancied, so she looks for a scapegoat, me.'

The commissioner had some biting things to say to Maria, and concluded that he could not, in all conscience, find this man guilty of her seduction. As they say, he threw out the case.

So, Sekgametse Daphne Lorraine was born without a father; an event in Alexandra, in Johannesburg, in all the urban areas of our times, that excites no surprise whatsoever.

First, Maria shed all her love – that is, the anguish and pain she suffered, the bitterness, the humiliation, the sense of desolation and collapse of her tinsel world – upon this infant. But people either perish or recover from wounds; even the worst afflictions do not gnaw at you forever. Maria recovered. She went back to her domestic work, leaving the baby with her mother. She would come home every Thursday – Sheila's Day – or the day-off for all the domestics in Johannesburg. She came to her baby, bringing clothing, blankets, pampering little goodies and smothering treacly love.

But she was young still, and the blood burst inside her once she recovered. Johannesburg was outside there calling, calling, first wooingly, alluringly, then more and more stridently, irresistibly. She came home less often, but remorsefully, and would crush the child to her in those brief moments. Even as she hugged the rose, the thorns tore at her. Then suddenly she came home no more.

'It is quite a typical case of recidivism,' Eileen explained scholastically to me on our way to Alexandra. 'You see, there's a moment's panic as a result of the trauma. The reaction varies according to the victim. One way is that for most of our girls there's a stubborn residue of moral upbringing from home or church, sometimes really only from mamma's personality and mamma probably comes from an older, steadier, more inhibited and tribe-controlled environment ...' Eileen shrugged helplessly, '... and detribalisation, modernisation, adaptation, acculturation, call it what you like, has to tear its way into their psychological pattern, brute-like. At first, before the shock, these girls really float loosely about in the new freedoms, not really willing evil, not consciously flouting the order, but they're nevertheless playing with fire, and there's no-one knows how to tell them no. Their parents themselves are baffled by what the world's come to and there's no invisible reality like tribe, or comprehensible code like custom or taboo, to keep some kind of balance. Meanwhile, the new dispensation – the superior culture, they call it; the diabolical shadow-life, I call it –

pounds at them relentlessly. Suddenly, some traumatic event, a jail-sentence, a sudden encounter with brute, bloody death, or a first pregnancy pulverises them into what we credulous monitors consider repentance. It's really the startled whimper of a frightened child vaguely remembering that in some remote distance mamma or tribe or school or church has whispered, "Thou shalt not," and the horror that it's too late.'

'But,' Eileen almost cursed out the words, 'the superior culture keeps pounding at them, and it's a matter of time before your repentant maiden sings again, "Jo'burg, here I come".'

I was shaken, 'Eileen, you know that much and yet you continue tinkering with statistics!'

She pulled herself together with an effort. But though she spoke confidently, it sounded unconvincing: 'Lad, I'm a social scientist, not a conjuress.'

So we went to that house in 3rd Avenue, off Selbourne Road. A deep gully ran in front of the house but the uneven street did not allow it to function effectively as a drain, and puddles of murky, noisome water and collected waste-matter stood pooled in it, still, thick, appalling, like foul soup that makes you nauseous – as if some malevolent devil bade you gulp it down. On the other side the rotting carcass of a long-dead dog was sending malodorous miasmata from its surface to befoul the air. And on either side the street, moated by these stinking gullies, lived people.

Eileen jumped smartly over the trench and I followed. We walked into the fenceless yard, round to the back of the house, and she knocked. After a moment a wrinkled old lady opened the door. The ploughshares of the years had wobbled across her face; but then again, you thought it could not have been the years alone that had ravaged her so; something else …

'Oh, come in, nurse.' They called everybody 'nurse' who came to their hovels to promise assuagement of their misery.

Although it was bright day outside, you had to get used to the dark inside, and then when your eyes, by slow degrees, adjusted themselves, things seemed to come at you. A big sideboard tilted into view first.

Then a huge stove whose one grey arm reached into the ceiling hole obscenely, and near it a double-bed, perched on four large polish tins filled with sand. The bed was sunken in the middle like a crude canoe, and the blankets on it were yellow with age and threadbare with wear. In the middle of the top blanket was a great hole from some past misadventure, and through the hole glowered a crimson eye, the red disc of a piece-patched quilt-like thing.

I stumbled into a wooden table in the centre, and in my retreat hit a kitchen-dresser. Dark-brown cockroaches scrambled for cover.

'Don't be so clumsy,' Eileen hissed, and in the same syntax, as it were, to the old lady, 'Mother Mabiletsa, it's so dark in here. You really must open that window.'

I had not known there was a window there, but Eileen swept a piece of blanket aside and in flushed the light of day.

'How are you, Mother Mabiletsa? How are the legs today? Sit down please and tell me how is the baby.'

Mother Mabiletsa groaned into a chair, and I took a bench by the side of the table. Eileen stood a moment holding the old woman in scrutiny. When the old woman did not reply, Eileen lifted her bag and put it on the table.

'Look, I've brought little Sekgametse some skimmed milk. It's very good for babies, you know.'

I turned to look at the old lady and it seemed to me she was past caring about either Grace or Damnation. She was just enveloped in a dreadful murk of weariness.

She pressed down on arthritic knees, rose painfully and limped into another room. I could hear her moving about, heaving with effort though she sounded alone. Then she came in with a bundle in her arms which she put down on the great bed beside Eileen.

'Come and look,' Eileen whispered to me as she unfurled the bundle.

There sat a little monkey on the bed. It was a two to three years' old child. The child did not cry or fidget, but bore an unutterably miserable expression on its face, in its whole bearing. It was as if she was the grandmother writ small; pathetically, wretchedly she looked out upon the world.

'Is it in pain?' I asked in an anxious whisper.

'No, just wasting away.'

'But she looks quite fat.'

To be sure, she did. But it was a ghastly kind of fatness, the fatness of the 'hidden hunger' I was to know. The belly was distended and sagged towards the bed. The legs looked bent convexly and there were light-brown patches on them, and on the chest and back. The complexion of the skin was unnaturally light here and there so that the creature looked piebald. The normally curly hair had a rusty tint and had lost much of its whorl. Much of it had fallen out, leaving islets of skull surfacing.

The child looked aside towards me, and the silent reproach, the quiet, listless, abject despair flowed from the large eyes wave upon wave. Not a peep, not a murmur. The child made no sound of complaint except the struggling breathing.

But those haunted eyes of despair. Despair? I brooded. To despair, you should have had knowledge before. You should have gone through the tart sensations of experience, have felt the first flush of knowledge, the first stabs of hope, have encountered reality and toyed with the shifting, tantalising promises that shadow-play across life's tapestries, have stretched out, first tentative arms, then wildly grasping hands, and have discovered the disappointment of the evanescence of all things that come from the voids to tickle men's fancies, sharpen men's appetites and rouse their futile aspirations, only to vanish back into the voids. Ultimately you should have looked into the face of death and known the paralysing power of fear.

What of all this, could this little monkey know? And, yet, there it all was in those tragic eyes.

Then I thought, 'So this is kwashiorkor!' Hitherto, to me, the name had just been another scare-word that had climbed from the dark caves of medical nomenclature to rear its head among decent folk; it had just been another disgusting digit, a clipped statistic that health officials hurled at us reporters, and which we laced our copy with to impress sensation-seeking editors who would fulminate under headlines like KWASHIORKOR AT YOUR DOOR. It had seemed right, then, almost sufficient that we should link it with the other horrors like 'Infant Mortality', 'Living Below the Bread-Line', 'The Apathy of the People' and 'The Cynical Indifference of the Affluent Society to the Problem'.

But here in this groanless, gloomy room, it seemed indecent to shriek banner headlines when the child, itself, was quiet. It spoke no protest, it offered no resistance.

But while I was romanticising, my sister was explaining to the old lady how to care for and feed the child, how to prepare and use the skim milk, how often to give it Cod Liver Oil, how often to. take it out into the air and the sunlight, how often to take it to the clinic.

Her mistressy voice, now urgent and straining, now clucking and scolding, now anxiously explaining, thinking in English, translating to itself first into Sepedi, begging, stressing, arguing, repeating, repeating, repeating – that restless voice tinkled into my consciousness, bringing me back.

The old lady muttered, 'I hear you, child, but how can I buy all these things with the R1.50 that's left over each month, and how can I carry this child to the clinic with my creaking bones?'

I was subdued.

'Well,' said Eileen later to me as we returned to the bus-stop. 'Think you've seen bottomless tragedy? I could give you figures for kwashiorkor in Alexandra alone ...'

'Please, Eileen, please.'

My life, a reporter's life, is rather full and hectic, and I am so vortically cast about in the whirlpools of Johannesburg that no single thought, no single experience, however profound, can stay with me for long. A week, two weeks, or less, and the picture of the kwashiorkor baby was jarred out of me, or perhaps lost into the limbo where the psyche hides unpleasant dreams.

Every day during that spell, I had to traffic with the ungodly, the wicked, the unfortunate, the adventurous, the desperate, the outcast and the screwy.

One day, I was in E Court waiting for a rather spectacular theft case to come. I had to sit through the normal run of petty cases. I was bored and fishing inside myself for a worthwhile reverie when suddenly I heard: 'Maria Mabiletsa! Maria Mabiletsa!' My presence of mind hurried back.

The prosecutor said, 'This one is charged with receiving stolen goods, Your Worship.'

A white man rose and told the court, 'Your Worship, I appear for the accused. I M Karotsky, of Mendelsohn and Jacobs, Sansouci House, 235 Bree Street.'

The prosecutor asked for an adjournment as 'other members of the gang are still at large'.

There was a wrangle about bail, but it was refused and the case was adjourned to August 25th.

It jolted me. After my case, I went down to the cells, and there, after sundry buffetings despite the flashing of my Press Card, I managed to see her.

She was sweet; I mean, looked sweet. Of course, now she was a mixture of fear and defiance, but I could see beyond these façades the real simplicity of her.

I do not know how long she had been in the cells, but she was clean and looked groomed. Her hair was stretched back and neatly tied in the ring behind the crown. She had an oval face, eyes intelligent and alive. Her nose stood out with tender nostrils. Her mouth was delicate but now twisted into a bitter scowl, and a slender neck held her head like the stem of a flower. Her skin-colour was chestnut, but like ... like ... like the inside of my hand. She had a slight figure with pouts for breasts, slight hips, but buttocks rounded enough to insist she was African.

She wore atop a white blouse with frills, and amidships one of those skirts cut like a kilt, hugging her figure intimately and suddenly relenting to flare out.

But now she was importunate. For her all time was little, and lots had to be said quickly. Before I could talk to her she said, 'Au-boetie, please, my brother, please, go and tell Lefty I'm arrested. Marshall Square maybe No 4. Tell him to bail me out. I'm Maria Mabiletsa, but Lefty calls me Marix. Please, Au-boetie, please.'

'Easy Maria,' I soothed, 'I know about you. I'm Dave from The Courier.'

'Ho-man, Boeta Dave, man. You we know, man. I read The Courier. But, please, Boeta Dave, tell Lefty my troubles, my mother's child.'

A cop was hurrying them away. 'Come'n, phansi! – down! Phansi! – down!'

'Please, Au-boetie Dave, don't forget to tell Lefty!'

'Maria,' I shouted as she was being rushed off, 'I've seen Sekgametse, she's well looked after.'

'Oh! –'

'Phansi– down!' Bang! The iron gates fell with a clangour.

That night I told Eileen. She stared at me with knitted brows for a long time. Then she said, 'The main thing is not to panic the old lady. Saturday, you and I will have to go there, but don't do or say anything to make her panic. Leave me to do all the talking.' But I could see Eileen was near panic herself.

Then I went to see Lefty. He was suave, unperturbed, taking all this philosophically.

'You reporter-boys take everything to head. Relax. You must have rhythm and timing. I've already got Karotsky to look after her and tomorrow Marix will be out. Relax, and have a drink.'

She was not out that tomorrow nor the day after. She had to wait for August 25. Meantime, Saturday came and Eileen and I went to the house in 3rd Avenue, Alexandra. When we got there we found – as they say – 'House To Let'. The old lady had heard about what had happened to Maria; she was faced with debts and the threat of starvation, so she packed her things, took the child, and returned to the reserve in Pietersburg.

The neighbours shrugged their shoulders and said, 'What could the old lady do?'

Eileen was livid.

'Dave, do you know what this means?' she erupted. 'It means that child is doomed. In the country, they love children, they look after them, they bring them up according to a code and according to what they know, but what they know about the nutrition of children is homicidal and, s'true's God, they live under such conditions of poverty that they may turn cannibals any moment. That's where goes the child

I tried to rehabilitate. And when adversity strikes them, when drought comes and the land yields less and less, and the cows' udders dry up, who are the first to go without? The children, those who need the milk most, those who need the proteins, the fats, the oils, the vegetables, the fruit; of the little there is, those who need it most will be the first to go without. There, indeed, they live on mielie-pap and despair. A doctor once told me, Dave, "Kwashiorkor hits hardest between the ages of one and five when protein is needed most and when it's least available to African children." Least available! Why, Dave, why? Because the ignorant African does not realise that when milk is short, give the children first; when meat is little, give the children first. It's not as if ...' she wailed '... it's not as if my over-detribalised self wants to give grown-ups' food to children, but my Sekgametse's sick. I've been trying to coax her back from unnecessary and stupid child-death. Now this.'

Tactlessly, I said, 'Come now, Eileen, you've done your bit. Go and make your report, you're not a nurse, and in any case you can't solve the whole world's troubles one-out.'

'The whole world's troubles!' She spat at me as if I was a child-stealer. 'I only wanted to save that one child, damn you!'

Of course, she made her social worker's report, and other human problems seized her, and I often wondered later whether she had forgotten he kwashiorkor baby. Once, when I asked her if she had heard anything about the baby, she gave a barbed-wire reply, 'Outside our jurisdiction.' It sounded too official to be like Eileen, but I sensed that she felt too raw about it to be anything else than professional, and I held my war within me.

Then I met Maria. It was at a party in Dube, one of those class affairs where thugs and tarts appear in formal dress, and though none of the chicken flew, the liquor flowed.

'Remember me?' I asked her in the provocative style in vogue. She screwed her face and wrinkled her nose and said, 'Don't tell me, don't tell me, I know I know you.' But strain as hard as she tried, she could not identify me. So in mercy I told her I was the news reporter she once sent to Lefty when she was arrested. It half registered. I told her my sister was the 'nurse' who looked after her Sekgametse. A cloud crossed her brow.

'He, man, Au-boetie, man, Africans are cruel,' she moaned. 'You know, I sent my child to the reserve in Pietersburg, and every month I used to send her nice things until she was the smartest kid in the countryside. Then they bewitched her. *Kaffir-poison!*' she said darkly. 'The child's stomach swelled and swelled with the beast they'd planted in it, until the child died. The Lord God will see those people , *mmcwi!*'

Viciously, I asked: 'And did you ever send the child Soya beans?'

© Can Themba

STOP THIEF!

Dan Jacobson

A black-browed angry-looking man he was, and the games he played
with his children were always angry games; he was chasing them, he
was growling at them, he was snapping his teeth at them, while they
shrieked with delight and fear, going pale and tense with fear, but
coming back for more, and hanging on to his hands when he declared
that he had had enough. There was a boy and a girl, both dark-haired
and thin, the boy a little older than his sister and protective towards
her with servants and strangers, with everyone but his father: he did
not dare to protect her when his father sprang at her from behind a
bush, and carried her shrieking, upside down, to his lair that was, he
told them, littered with the bones of other children that he had already
eaten.

The mother sat aside from these games – she sat at the tea table at
the head of the small sweep of lawn towards the swimming bath,
beyond which were the trees where her husband and children played,
or she lay in the sun on the side of the swimming bath, with a towel

about her head, and it was only rarely that she called to them or warned them of their father's stealthy, mock approaches. She sun-bathed or she read in the sun; they were all sun-tanned in that family, from spending so much time at their swimming bath, and from their annual six-weeks' holiday at the Cape, where they lived the life simple in a seaside cottage with only one servant. The big house in Johannesburg seemed to have innumerable servants, all black men in gleaming white jackets and aprons and little white caps like those of an Indian political movement, but in fact only another sign of their servitude, and these black men kept the house like a house on show: the house shone, unmarked by the pressures, the stains and splashes, the disorder of living. Not that the children were the least bit tidy – they dropped things about them as they went, and left the toys and the sticks and the items of clothing lying where they had been dropped, but the servants followed picking up things and putting them in drawers, as though that was all that they had been born for, this dance of attendance on the two nervous, dark-haired children. And the mother, who had been poorly brought up, loved it in the children that they had, so without question or wonder, the insolence of wealth. Once when he had hardly been more than a baby she had asked the boy: 'Would you like to be a little black boy?'

The child had been puzzled that his mother should have asked this. 'No,' he said, frowning, bringing his dark eyebrows together, and looking up in puzzled distaste.

'Why not?'

The puzzlement had left the boy's face, and there had been only distaste as he replied, 'They have nasty clothes.' And for this he had been given a kiss, which he accepted demurely. The children accepted their mother's affection as a matter of course; it was for their father's mock-anger that they lived. The mother knew this and did not resent it: she believed that the insolence she loved in them had come from their father, and for her husband's violence was profoundly confused with his wealth.

But sometimes, watching the children at their perilous play with their father, even the mother would be afraid. She would lift her eyes from her book, or unwrap the towel which had been muffling the sun's rays to a yellow blur on her eyes, and her heart would sink with fear to see them run and stand breathing behind some tree while their father prowled on tiptoe towards them. So frail they seemed, with their bony elbows poking out from their short-sleeved blouses, and their knees large and round below the dress or khaki shorts that each wore. And he seemed so determined, so muscular in the casual clothing he wore in the evenings, after he had come from work, so large above the children. But she accepted his violence and his strength, and she never protested against the games. She would sometimes watch them play, but her eyes would go back to the book, or she would again carefully wrap the towel about her eyes and her ears, and sink back into her drowse. She seemed sunken under her husband, under his wealth, under his strength; they had come down upon her as the sun did where she lay at the side of the swimming bath, and she questioned them no more than she could have questioned the sun. She had submitted to them.

The father laughed, showing his white teeth, when the children ran yelling from him. In the shadows of the trees they waited for him to come again. He moved slowly towards them, and a lift of his arm made them scamper. He was king of his castle – and castle enough the house was too, in its several acres of ground, and its trees that cut it off from sight of the road.

Then one night the burglar came to their house. It was not for nothing that their house, like every other house in Johannesburg, had every window barred with steel burglar-proofing, that every door had a double lock, that two large dogs were let loose in the grounds at night. It was not for nothing that the father had a revolver in his wardrobe, always loaded and on a high shelf out of reach of the children. For the burglars in Johannesburg can be an ugly lot – gangsters, marauders, hard black men who seem to have nothing to lose, who carry with them knives and knuckledusters and guns.

But this one was not one of these. This one was a boy, a fool, a beginner, come by himself to the wrong house, barked at by the dogs where he stood in the darkness of a corner of the garage between the large painted mudguard of a car and a workbench behind him. He did not even reach for one of the chisels on the bench behind him, but stood squeezing the fingers of one hand in the grasp of the other, as though by that alone he might be able to stop the shivering which shook his shoulders in quick, awful spasms.

But the house did not know what he was and what he might do. The whole house was wild with lights and shouts and the banging of doors. Men, women, they had tumbled out pell-mell from the rooms in which they slept: one of the servants had been roused by the barking of dogs and had seen the burglar slipping into the garage. The house had all been in darkness, and still, so still that not even the trees had moved under the brilliance of the stars in the early morning sky, when the shouts of the servant had first come calamitously upon it. Wild, hoarse, archaic, the shouts had sounded, like the shouts a dreamer might dream he is making, in his deep terror of the darkness around him. Then there had been the other shouts, the house in uproar.

And the father in his pyjamas and dressing gown, with the revolver thrust unsteadily before him, was advancing across the back-yard. The servants fell in behind him, even the one who had been guarding the window of the garage. 'Get to the window, you fool!' the father shouted. 'Guard the window!' Unwillingly, one or two went to the window, while the father came closer to the garage door.

He did not know what might be behind the door; he found that he could not push the garage door open, for fear the burglar might spring at him. He was a stranger to himself, roused out of bed by hoarse shouts, hurried downstairs by danger, chilled by the early morning air: to him it seemed that he had never before seen the place he was in; never before felt the lock under his hand; and when he looked back, the house, with the light falling on the paved yard from the open kitchen door, was the house of a stranger, not his at all. The servants were simply people, a throng, some carrying improvised clubs in their hands, all half-dressed, none of them known.

He could not push the door open. The dread of opening himself to whatever might be there was too great. The servants pushed a little closer; and he felt his fear growing tighter and closer within him. They pressed so closely upon him his fear had no room to move, and when he did at last lift up the revolver it was in desperation to drive away the people, who were constricting his fear and pressing it upon him. He lifted the revolver and shouted, 'Leave me!' He tilted it towards the stars and fired. The clamour of the shot was more loud and gross in his ears than he could have imagined, and with it there sprang from the muzzle a gout of flame, vivid in the darkness. When the servants shrank back he felt a momentary sense of release and relaxation, as though he had done the thing for which he had been dragged out of bed, and could be left now to go in peace. Then he felt the door behind him budge.

He leaped away from the door so violently that he stumbled and fell, and he was on his knees with the revolver scratching uselessly against the paving when the burglar came out of the garage. The servants too had staggered back when their master had leaped towards them, so the burglar stood alone in the doorway, with his hands still squeezed together, but lifted now to his chest, like someone beseeching mercy. From where he sprawled on the ground the master could only gasp: 'Catch him. Get round him!' And one or two of the men-servants came forward. They hesitated, and then they saw the spasms shaking the burglar, so they came to him and took him roughly, pinioning him. Their master was struggling to his feet.

'Bring him into the kitchen,' he said. There was a sigh from the group of servants, and a babble, then eagerly they began jostling the burglar towards the kitchen, and he went unresistingly.

To the father the kitchen too looked harsh and strange, a place of urgency, and there seemed to be too many people in it: all the servants, and his wife, and the two children, and the burglar, and the servant' friends, those who had been sleeping illegally but without harmful intent in the rooms in the back yard. These shrank back now, as if only now realising that the events of the night might have consequences for themselves too, and not only for the burglar they had helped to catch.

'You've phoned the police?' the father asked.

'Yes,' the mother said. 'The flying squad's coming.'

The father sat down at the kitchen table, blowing his cheeks out with exhaustion, feeling the tension beginning to ebb from the pit of his stomach. He could not look at the burglar. The mother too, for different reasons, avoided looking at the burglar, but the two children, in their neat white pyjama suits, had eyes for nothing else. They knew all about burglars: they had grown up in Johannesburg, and they knew why the steel bars lay across their bedroom windows, and why they were not allowed outside the house after nightfall, and why the dogs roamed loose at night. But this was the first burglar they had seen. Even the revolver loose in their father's hand could not draw their eyes from the burglar.

He stood in the middle of the kitchen, and his dark eyes were dazed, unseeing. He was a young African – he looked no more than seventeen – an undersized, town-bred seventeen years of age. He was wearing a soiled grey sports coat and a pair of ragged trousers that reached only about half-way down his shins, and when the spasms came he shook from his shoes upwards, even his strained brown ankles shaking, his knees, his loins, his shoulders, his head, all shaking. Then the fit would pass and he would simply stand, supported on each side by the household servants.

He seemed to see nothing, to look at nothing, to hear nothing: there seemed to be within him a secret war between his will and the spasms of shaking that came upon him, like a fit. The colour of his face was terrible: he was grey, an ash-grey, a grey like that of the first thinning of the darkness after a rain-sodden night. Sometimes when every other part of his body was free of the spasm, his mouth would still be shaking; his lips were closed, but they shook, as if there were a turbulence in his mouth that he had to void. Then that too would pass.

The little boy at last looked away from the burglar to his father, and saw him sitting weakly in the chair, exhausted. The hand that held the revolver lay laxly on the kitchen table, and from it there rose a faint acrid scent, but the gun looked in his hand like a toy. The father could not move and he could not speak, he sat collapsed, until even the servants looked curiously at him, as the little boy had done, from the burglar to him, and then back to the burglar again. They murmured a little, uncertainly; the two who were holding the burglar loosened their grip on him and shuffled their feet. They waited for direction from their master, but no direction came. The little boy waited for action from his father, but no action came. The son was the first to see that his father could make no action, could give no word.

So he gave the word himself. In a voice that was barely recognisable as his own, his face with its little point of a nose contorted, he screamed in rage and disappointment: 'Hit the burglar! Hit the burglar!' He danced on his bare feet, waving his small fists in the air. 'Why don't you hit the burglar? You must hit the burglar.' He danced like a little demon in his light pyjamas. 'Hit!' he screamed. 'Hit!' His little sister joined in because she heard her brother shouting, and she added her high yell to his: 'Hit the burglar!'

'Get the children out of here!' the father shouted. The children had raised their voices for a moment only, but it had seemed endless, their little voices shrilling for blood. 'What are they doing here?' the father shouted in a fury at the mother, pulling himself up at last. 'Get them out of here!' But he made no move to help the mother, though he saw that she could not manage both dancing, capering children. And when the little boy saw that his father did not move towards him, again he screamed, 'Hit the burglar!'

'Jerry,' the mother gasped to one of the servants, 'help me. Don't stand there!' She was grappling at arm's length with the flailing hands of the little girl.

The dark body of the servant bent over the boy. Then he sprang back, waving his hand. The boy had bitten him. So he too being near-distraught with excitement and this last unexpected little assault, reached out and hit the little boy across the back of the head. The boy staggered; he fell down and lay on the sparkling kitchen floor. But it was only for a moment. He came up growling, with hands lifted, curled inwards, and fell upon the burglar. It took two servants to prise him off, and when he was finally carried away over the black powerful shoulder of the one, he had left two deep scratches on the face of the burglar, both from the forehead down, broken by the shelf of bone over the eyes, and continued down the cheeks. The burglar had made no effort to defend himself, knowing what would happen to him if he did anything to hurt the child.

Then the police came and took the burglar away. By that time the children were safe and quiet in the nursery; and later the mother too fell asleep after taking a sedative.

But the servant who had hit the boy was dismissed the very next day, by the mother, who could not bear it that a servant should have struck a child of hers. Least of all the son to whom she now submitted, the son who after the night the burglar had come to the house was not afraid to protect his sister, when her father fell upon her in their games in the garden, and who fought, when he himself was picked up and carried away, as an adult might fight, with his fists and his feet and his knees, to hurt. His will was stronger than his father's, and soon they were facing each other like two men, and the wild games and the shrieking among the trees grew rarer. For the father was afraid of the games he sometimes still had to play with his son, and there was none among them who did not know it, neither the son, nor the daughter, nor the mother, nor the father from whose hands in one night the violence in the family had passed.

ENEMIES

Nadine Gordimer

When Mrs Clara Hansen travels, she keeps herself to herself. This is usually easy, for she has money, has been a baroness and a beauty, and has survived dramatic suffering. The crushing presence of these states in her face and bearing is nearly always enough to stop the loose mouths of people who find themselves in her company. It is only the very stupid, the senile, or the self-obsessed who blunder up to assail that face, withdrawn as a castle, across the common ground of a public dining-room.

Last month, when Mrs Hansen left Cape Town for Johannesburg by train, an old lady occupying the adjoining compartment tried to make of her apologies, as she pressed past in the corridor loaded with string bags and paper parcels, an excuse to open one of those pointless conversations between strangers which arise in the nervous moments of departure. Mrs Hansen was giving last calm instructions to Alfred, her Malay chauffeur and manservant, whom she was leaving behind, and she did not look up. Alfred had stowed her old calf cases from Europe firmly and within reach in her compartment, which, of course, influence with the reservation office had ensured she would have to herself all the way. He had watched her put away in a special pocket in her handbag, her train ticket, a ticket for her de-luxe bed, a book of tickets for her meals. He had made sure that she had her two yellow sleeping pills and the red pills for that feeling of pressure in her head, lying in cottonwool in her silver pillbox. He himself had seen that her two pairs of spectacles, one for distance, one for reading, were in her overnight bag, and had noted that her lorgnette hung below the diamond bow on the bosom of her dress. He had taken down the folding table from its niche above the wash-basin in the compartment, and placed on it the three magazines she had sent him to buy at the bookstall, along with the paper from Switzerland that, this week, had been kept aside, unread, for the journey. For a full fifteen minutes before the train left, he and his employer were free to ignore the to-and-fro of voices and luggage, the heat and confusion. Mrs Hansen murmured down to him; Alfred, chauffeur's cap in hand, dusty sunlight the colour of beer dimming the oil-shine of his black hair, looked up from the platform and made low assent. They used the half sentences, the hesitations, and the slight changes of tone or expression of people who speak the language of their association in the country of their own range of situation. It was hardly speech; now and then it sank away altogether, into the minds of each, but the sounds of the station did not well in its place. Alfred dangled the key of the car on his little finger; the old face beneath the toque noted it, the lips, the infinitely weary corners of the eyes drooped in the indication of a smile. Would he really put the car away into the garage for six weeks after he'd seen that it was oiled and greased?

Unmindful of the finger, he said, his face empty of the satisfaction of a month's wages in advance in his pocket, two friends waiting to be picked up in a house in the Malay quarter of the town, 'I must make a note that I mustn't send madam's letters on after the 26th.'

'No. Not later than the 26th.'

Did she know; with that face that looked as if it knew everything, could she know, too, about the two friends in the house in the Malay quarter?

She said, and neither of them listened, 'In case of need, you've always got Mr Van Dam.' Van Dam was her lawyer. This remark, like a stone thrown idly into a pool to pass the time, had fallen between them into the widening hiatus of parting time and again. They had never questioned or troubled to define its meaning. In ten years, what need had there ever been that Alfred couldn't deal with himself, from a burst pipe in the flat, to a jammed fastener on Mrs Hansen's dress?

Alfred backed away from the ice-cream carton a vendor thrust under his nose; the last untidy lump of canvas luggage belonging to the woman next door thumped down like a dusty animal at Mrs Hansen's side; the final bell rang.

As the train ground past out of the station, Alfred stood quite still with his cap between his hands, watching Mrs Hansen. He always stood like that when he saw her off. And she remained at the window, as usual, smiling slightly, inclining her head slightly, as if in dismissal. Neither waved. Neither moved until the other was borne out of sight.

When the station was gone and Mrs Hansen did turn slowly to enter her compartment to the quickened rhythm of the train, she met the gasping face of the old woman next door. Fat overflowed not only from her jowl to her neck, but from her ankles over her shoes. She looked like a pudding that had risen too high and run down the sides of the dish. She was sprinkling cologne on to a handkerchief and hitting with it at her face as if she were trying to kill an insect. 'Rush like that, it's no good to you' she said, 'Something went wrong with my son-in-law's car, and what a job to get a taxi! *They* don't care, get you here today or tomorrow. I thought I'd never get up those steps ...'

Mrs. Hansen looked at her very slowly. 'When one is no longer young, one must always give oneself exactly twice as much time as one needs. I have learnt that. I beg your pardon ___' And she passed before the woman into her compartment.

'I wonder if they're serving tea yet? Shall we go along to the dining-car?' The woman stopped her in the doorway.

'I always have my tea brought to me in my compartment,' said Mrs Hansen, in the low, dead voice that had been considered a pity, in her day, but that now made young people who could have been her grandchildren ask if she had been an actress. And she glided the door to.

Alone, she stood a moment in the secretive privacy, where everything swayed and veered in obedience to the gait of the train. She began to look anxiously over the stacked luggage, her lips moving, but she had grown too set to adjust her balance from moment to moment, and, suddenly, she found herself sitting down. The train had dumped her out of the way; good thing, too, she thought, chastising herself impatiently: counting the luggage, fussing, when in ten years Alfred's never forgotten anything. Old fool, she told herself, old fool. Her ageing self often seemed to her an enemy of her real self, the self that had never changed. The enemy was a stupid one, fortunately; she merely had to keep an eye on it in order to keep it outwitted. Other selves that had arisen in her life had been much worse; how terrible had been the struggle with some of *them*.

She sat down with her back to the engine, beside the window, and put on her reading glasses and took up the newspaper from Switzerland. But for some minutes she did not read. She heard again inside herself the words *alone, alone*, just the way she had heard them fifty-nine years ago when she was twelve years old and crossing France by herself for the first time. As she had sat there, bolt upright in the corner of a carriage, her green velvet fur-trimmed cloak around her, her hamper beside her, and the locket with the picture of her grandfather hidden in her hand, she had felt a swelling terror of exhilaration, the dark, drowning swirl of cutting loose; had tasted the strength to be brewed out of self-pity and the calm to be lashed together out of panic, that belonged to other times and other journeys approaching her from the distance of her future. *Alone, alone.* This that her real self had known years before it happened to her – before she had lived the journey that took her from a lover, or those others that took her from the alienated faces of madness and death – that same self remembered years after those journeys had dropped behind into the past. Now she was alone, lonely, lone – whatever you liked to call it – all the time; there is nothing of the drama of an occasion about it, for me, she reminded herself, drily. Still, there was no denying it, *alone* was not the same as lonely; even old fool could not blur the distinction of that. The blue silk coat quivered where Alfred had hung it, the bundle of magazines edged along the table, somewhere above her head a loose strap tapped; she felt again aloneness as the carapace that did not shut her off but shielded her strong sense of survival – against it, and all else.

She opened the paper from Switzerland, and, with her left foot (the heat had made it a little swollen) up on the seat opposite, began to read. She felt lulled and comfortable and was not even irritated by the thuds and dragging noises coming from the partition behind her head: it was clear that that was the woman next door – *she* must be fussing with her luggage. Presently a steward brought the tea-tray which Alfred had ordered before the train left. Mrs. Hansen drew in her mouth with pleasure at the taste of the strong tea as connoisseurs do when they drink old brandy, and read the afternoon away.

She took her dinner in the dining-car because she had established in a long experience that it was not a meal that could be expected to travel train corridors and remain hot, and also because there was something shabby, something *petit bourgeois* about taking meals in the stuffy cubicle in which you were also to sleep. She tidied her hair round the sides of her toque – it was a beautiful hat, one of four, always the same shape, that she had made every second year, in Vienna – took off her rings and washed her hands, and powdered her nose, pulling a critical, amused face at herself in the compact mirror. Then she put on her silk coat, picked up her handbag, and went with upright dignity, despite the twitchings and lurchings of the train, along the corridors to the dining-car. She seated herself at an empty table for two, beside a window, and, of course, although it was early and there were many other seats vacant, the old woman from the compartment next door, entering five minutes later, came straight over and sat down opposite her.

Now it was impossible not to speak to the woman, and Mrs Hansen listened to her with the distant patience of an adult giving half an ear to a child, and answered her when necessary, with a dry simplicity calculated to be far above her head. Of course, old fool was tempted to unbend, to lapse into the small boastings and rivalries usual between two old ladies. But Mrs Hansen would not allow it; and certainly not with this woman, this acquaintance thrust upon her in a train. It was bad enough that only the week before, old fool had led her into one of these pathetic pieces of senile nonsense; cleverly disguised – old fool could be wily enough – but, just the same, unmistakably the kind of thing that people found boring. It was about her teeth. At seventy-one, they were still her own, which was a self-evident miracle. Yet she had allowed herself, at a dinner party given by some young friends who were obviously impressed by her, to tell a funny story (not quite true, either) about how when she was a weekend guest in a house with an over-solicitous hostess, the jovial host had hoaxed his wife by impressing upon her the importance of providing a suitable receptacle for their guest's teeth when she took them out overnight. There was a glass beside the jug of water on the bedside table; the hostess appeared, embarrassedly, with another. 'But my dear, what is the other glass for?' The denouement, laughter etc. Disgusting. Good teeth as well as bad aches and pains must be kept to oneself; when one is young, one takes the first for granted, and does not know the existence of the others.

So it was that when the menu was held before the two women, Mrs Hansen ignored the consternation into which it seemed to plunge her companion, forestalled the temptation to enter, by contributing her doctor's views, into age's passionate preoccupation with diet, and ordered fish.

'D'you think the fish'll be all right? I always wonder, on a train, you know ...' said the woman from the next compartment.

Mrs Hansen merely confirmed her order to the waiter by lowering her eyes and settling her chin slightly. The woman decided to begin at the beginning, with soup. 'Can't go far wrong with soup, can you?'

'Don't wait, please,' said Mrs Hansen, when the soup came.

It was watery, the woman said. Mrs Hansen smiled her tragic smile, indulgently. The woman decided that she'd keep Mrs Hansen company, and risk the fish, too. The fish lay beneath a pasty blanket of white sauce, and while Mrs Hansen calmly pushed aside the sauce and ate, the woman said 'There's nothing like the good, clean food cooked in your own kitchen.'

Mrs Hansen put a forkful of fish to her mouth and spoke at last when she had finished it. 'I'm afraid it's many years since I had my own kitchen for more than a month or two a year.'

'Well, of course, if you go about a lot, you get used to strange food, I suppose. I find I can't eat half the stuff they put in front of you in hotels. Last time I was away, there were some days I didn't know what to have at all, for lunch. I was in one of the best hotels in Durban, and all there was was this endless curry, curry this, curry that, and a lot of dried-up cold meats.'

Mrs Hansen shrugged. 'I always find enough for my needs. It does not matter much.'

'What can you do? I suppose this sauce is the wrong thing for me, but you've got to take what you get when you're travelling,' said the woman. She broke off a piece of bread and passed it swiftly round her plate to scoop up what was left of the sauce. 'Starchy,' she added.

Mrs Hansen ordered a cutlet, and, after a solemn study of the menu, the other woman asked for the item listed immediately below the fish – ox-tail stew. While they were waiting she ate bread and butter, and, shifting her mouthful comfortably from one side of her mouth to the other, accomplished a shift of her attention, too, as if her jaw and her brain had some simple mechanical connection. 'You're not from here, I suppose?' she asked, looking at Mrs. Hansen with the appraisal reserved for foreigners and the licence granted by the tacit acceptance of old age on both sides.

'I have lived in the Cape, on and off, for some years,' said Mrs Hansen. 'My second husband was Danish, but settled here.'

'I could have married again. I'm not boasting, I mean, but I did have the chance, if I'd've wanted to,' said the woman. 'Somehow, I couldn't face it, after losing my first – fifty-two, that's all, and you'd have taken a lease on his life. Ah, those doctors. No wonder I feel I can't trust them a minute.'

Mrs Hansen parted the jaws of her large, elegant black bag to take out a handkerchief; the stack of letters that she always had with her, new ones arriving to take the place of old with every air mail, lay exposed. Thin letters, fat letters, big envelopes, small ones; the torn edges of foreign stamps, the large, sloping, and small, crabbed hands of foreigners writing foreign tongues. The other woman looked down upon them like a tourist, curious, impersonally insolent, envious. 'Of course, if I'd been the sort to run about a lot, I suppose it might have been different. I might have met someone really *congenial*. But there's my daughters. A mother's responsibility is never over, that's what I say. When they're little, it's little troubles; when they're grown up, it's big ones. They're all nicely married, thank God, but you know, it's always something – one of them sick, or one of the grandchildren, bless them ... I don't suppose you've got any children? Not even from your first, I mean?'

'No,' said Mrs Hansen. 'No.' And the lie, as always, came to her as a triumph against that arrogant boy (old fool persisted in thinking of him as a gentle-browed youth bent over a dachshund puppy, though he was a man of forty-five by now) whom, truly, she had made, as she had warned she would, no son of hers. When the lie was said, it had the effect of leaving her breathless, as if she had just crowned a steep rise. Firmly and calmly, she leaned forward and poured herself a glass of water, as one who has deserved it.

'My, it does look fatty,' the other woman was saying, over the ox-tail that had just been placed before her. 'My doctor'd have a fit if he knew I was eating this.' But eat it she did, and cutlet and roast turkey to follow. Mrs Hansen never knew whether or not her companion rounded off the meal with rhubarb pie (the woman had remarked, as she saw it carried past, that it looked soggy), because she herself had gone straight from cutlet to coffee, and, her meal finished, excused herself before the other was through the turkey course. Back in her compartment, she took off her toque at last, and tied a grey chiffon scarf round her head. Then she took her red-and-gold Florentine leather cigarette-case from her bag and settled down to smoke her nightly cigarette, while she waited for the man to come and convert her seat into the de-luxe bed Alfred had paid for in advance.

It seemed to Mrs Hansen that she did not sleep very well during the early part of the night, though she did not quite know what it was that made her restless. She was woken, time and again, apparently by some noise that had ceased by the time she was conscious enough to identify it. The third or fourth time this happened, she woke to silence and a sense of absolute cessation, as if the world had stopped turning. But it was only the train that had stopped. Mrs Hansen lay and listened; they must be at some deserted siding, in the small hours: there were no lights shining in through the shuttered window, no footsteps, no talk. The voice of a cricket, like a fingernail screeching over glass, sounded, providing, beyond the old woman's closed eyes, beyond the dark compartment and the shutters, a landscape of grass, dark, and telephone poles.

Suddenly, the train gave a terrific reverberating jerk, as if it had been given a violent push. All was still again. And in the stillness, Mrs Hansen became aware of groans coming from the other side of the partition against which she lay. The groans came bumbling and nasal through the wood and leather; it sounded like a dog with its head buried in a cushion, worrying at the feathers. Mrs Hansen breathed out, once, hard, in annoyance, and turned over: the greedy old pig, now she was suffering agonies of indigestion from that ox-tail, of course. The groans continued at intervals. Once there was a muffled tinkling sound, as if a spoon had been dropped. Mrs Hansen lay tense with irritation, waiting for the train to move on and drown the woman's noise. At last, with a shake that quickly settled into a fast clip, they were off again, lickety-lack, lickety-lack, past (Mrs Hansen could imagine) the endless telephone poles, the dark grass, the black-coated cricket. Under the dialogue of the train, she was an unwilling eavesdropper to the vulgar intimacies next door; then, either the groans stopped or she fell asleep in spite of them, for she heard nothing till the steward woke her with the arrival of early morning coffee.

She sponged herself, dressed, and had a quiet breakfast, undisturbed by anyone, in the dining-car. The man sitting opposite her did not even ask her so much as to pass the salt. She was back in her compartment, reading, when the ticket examiner came in to take her ticket away (they would be in Johannesburg soon) and, of course, she knew just where to lay her hand on it, in her bag. He leaned against the doorway while she got it out. 'Hear what happened?' he said. 'What happened,' she said uncertainly, screwing up her face because he spoke indistinctly, like most young South Africans. 'Next door,' he said, 'The lady next door, elderly lady. She died last night.'

'She died? That woman died?' She stood up and questioned him closely, as if he were an irresponsible person.

'Yes,' he said, checking the ticket on his list. 'The bed boy found her this morning, dead in her bed. She never answered when the steward came round with coffee, you see.'

'My God,' said Mrs Hansen, 'My God. So she died, eh?'

'Yes, lady,' he held out his hand for her ticket; he had the tale to tell all up and down the train.

With a gesture of futility, she gave it to him.

After he had gone, she sank down on the seat, beside the window, and watched the veld go by, the grasses streaming past in the sun like the long black tails of the widow-birds blowing where they swung upon the fences. She had finished the papers and magazines. There was no sound but the sound of the hurrying train.

When they reached Johannesburg she had all her luggage trimly closed and ready for the porter from the hotel at which she was going to stay. She left the station with him within five minutes of the train's arrival, and was gone before the doctors, officials and, she supposed, newspaper reporters, came to see the woman taken away from the compartment next door. What could I have said to them? she thought, pleased with her sensible escape. Could I tell them she died of greed? Better not to be mixed up in it.

And then she thought of something. Newspaper reporters. No doubt there would be a piece in the Cape papers tomorrow. *Elderly woman found dead in Cape-Johannesburg train.* As soon as she had signed the register at the hotel she asked for a telegram form. She paused a moment, leaning on the marble-topped reception desk, looking out over the heads of the clerks. Her eyes, that were still handsome, crinkled at the corners, her nostrils lifted, her mouth, that was still so shapely because of her teeth, turned its sad corners lower in her reluctant, calculating smile. She printed Alfred's name and the address of the flat in Cape Town, and then wrote quickly, in the fine hand she had mastered more than sixty years ago: IT WAS NOT ME. CLARA HANSEN.

BLANKETS

Alex La Guma

Choker lay on the floor of the lean-to in the back yard where they had carried him. It was cooler under the sagging roof, with the pile of assorted junk in one corner; an ancient motor tyre, sundry split and warped boxes, an old enamel display sign with patches like maps of continents on another planet where the enamelling had cracked away, and the dusty footboard of a bed. There was also the smell of dust and chicken droppings and urine in the lean-to.

From outside, beyond a chrome-yellow rhomboid of sun, came a clatter of voices. In the yard they were discussing him. Choker opened his eyes and, peering down the length of his body, past the bare, grimy toes, he saw several pairs of legs, male and female, in tattered trousers and laddered stockings.

Somebody, a man, was saying: '... that was coward ... from behind, mos.'

'Ja. But look what he done to others ...'

Choker thought, to hell with those baskets. To hell with them all.

Somebody had thrown an old blanket over him. It smelled of sweat and having-been-slept-in-unwashed, and it was torn and threadbare and stained. He touched the exhausted blanket with thick, grubby fingers. The texture was rough in parts and shiny thin where it had worn away. He was used to blankets like this.

Choker had been stabbed three times, each time from behind. Once in the head, then between the shoulder blades and again in the right side, out in the street, by an old enemy who had once sworn to get him.

The bleeding had stopped and there was not much pain. He had been knifed before, admittedly not as bad as this, but, he thought through the pain, the basket couldn't even do a decent job. He lay there and waited for the ambulance. There was blood drying slowly on the side of his hammered-copper face, and he also had a bad headache.

The voices, now and then raised in laughter, crackled outside. Feet moved on the rough floor of the yard and a face not unlike that of a brown dog wearing an expiring cloth cap, looked in.

'You still awright, Choker? Am'ulance is coming just now, hey.'

'___ off,' Choker said. His voice croaked.

The face withdrew, laughing: 'Ou Choker. Ou Choker.'

He was feeling tired now. The grubby fingers, like corroded iron clamps, strayed over the parched field of the blanket ... He was being taken down a wet, tarred yard with tough wire netting over the windows which looked into it. The place smelled of carbolic disinfectant, and the bunch of heavy keys clink-clinked as it swung from the hooked finger of the guard.

They reached a room fitted with shelving that was stacked here and there with piled blankets. 'Take two, jong,' the guard said, and Choker began to rummage through the piles, searching for the thickest and warmest blankets. But the guard, who somehow had a doggish face and wore a disintegrating cloth cap, laughed and jerked him aside and, seizing the nearest blankets, found two and flung them at Choker. They were filthy and smelly and within their folds vermin waited like irregular troops in ambush.

'Come on. Come on. You think I got time to waste?'

'It's cold, mos, man,' Choker said. But it wasn't the guard to whom he was talking. He was six years old and his brother, Willie, a year senior, twisted and turned in the narrow, cramped, sagging bedstead which they shared, dragging the thin cotton blanket from Choker's body. Outside the rain slapped against the cardboard-patched window, and the wind wheezed through cracks and corners like an asthmatic old man.

'No, man, Willie, man. You got all the blanket, jong.'

'Well, I can't mos help it, man. It's cold.'

'What about me?' Choker whined. 'What about me. I'm also cold mos.'

Huddled together under the blanket, fitted against each other like two pieces of a jigsaw puzzle. The woman's wiry hair got into his mouth and smelled of stale brilliantine. There were dark stains made by heads on the crumpled, grey-white pillow, and a rubbed smear of lipstick, like a half-healed wound.

The woman was saying, half-asleep, 'No man. No, man.' Her body was wet and sweaty under the blanket, and the bed smelled of a mixture of cheap perfume, spilled powder, human bodies and infant urine. The faded curtain over a window beckoned to him in the hot breeze. In the early slum-coloured light a torn under-garment hanging from a brass knob was a spectre in the room.

The woman turned from him under the blankets, protesting, and Choker sat up. The agonised sounds of the bedspring woke the baby in the bathtub on the floor, and it began to cry, its toothless voice rising in a high-pitched wail that grew louder and louder ...

Choker opened his eyes as the wail grew to a crescendo and then quickly faded as the siren was switched off. Voices still splattered the sunlight in the yard, now excited. Choker saw the skirts of white coats and then the ambulance men were in the lean-to. His head was aching badly, and his wounds were throbbing. His face perspired like a squeezed-out washrag. Hands searched him. One of the ambulance attendants asked: 'Do you feel any pain?'

Choker looked at the pink-white face above his, scowling. 'No, sir.'

The layer of old newspapers on which he was lying was soaked with his blood. 'Knife wounds,' one of the attendants said. 'He isn't bleeding much,' the other said. 'Put on a couple of pressure pads.'

He was in mid-air, carried on a stretcher and flanked by a procession of onlookers. Rubber sheeting was cool against his back. The stretcher rumbled into the ambulance and the doors slammed shut, sealing off the spectators. Then the siren whined and rose, clearing a path through the crowd.

Choker felt the vibration of the ambulance through his body as it sped on its way. His murderous fingers touched the folded edge of the bedding. The sheet around him was white as cocaine, and the blanket was thick and new and warm. He lay still, listening to the siren.

THE HAJJI

Ahmed Essop

When the telephone rang several times one evening and his wife did not attend to it as she usually did, Hajji Hassen, seated on a settee in the lounge, cross-legged and sipping tea, shouted: 'Salima, are you deaf?' And when he received no response from his wife and the jarring bell went on ringing, he shouted again: 'Salima, what's happened to you?'

The telephone stopped ringing. Hajji Hassen frowned in a contemplative manner, wondering where his wife was now. Since his return from Mecca after the pilgrimage, he had discovered novel inadequacies in her, or perhaps saw the old ones in a more revealing light. One of her salient inadequacies was never to be around when he wanted her. She was either across the road confabulating with her sister, or gossiping with the neighbours, or away on a shopping spree. And now, when the telephone had gone on assaulting his ears, she was not in the house. He took another sip of the strongly spiced tea to stifle the irritation within him.

When he heard the kitchen door open he knew that Salima had entered. The telephone burst out again in a metallic shrill and the Hajji shouted for his wife. She hurried to the phone.

'Hullo ... Yes ... Hassen ... Speak to him?... Who speaking? ... Caterine?... Who Caterine? Au-right ... I call him.'

She put the receiver down gingerly and informed her husband in Gujarati that a woman named 'Caterine' wanted to speak to him. The name evoked no immediate association in his memory. He descended from the settee and, squeezing his feet into a pair of crimson sandals, went to the telephone.

'Hullo ... Who?... Catherine?... No, I don't know you ... Yes ... yes ... Yes ... Oh ... now I remember ...Yes ...'

He listened intently to the voice, urgent, supplicating. Then he gave his answer:

'I am afraid I can't help him. Let the Christians bury him. His last wish means nothing to me ... Madam, it's impossible ... No ... Let him die ... Brother? Pig! Pig! Bastard!' He banged the receiver onto the telephone in explosive annoyance.

'O Allah!' Salima exclaimed. 'What words! What is this all about?'

He did not answer, but returned to the settee, and she quietly went to the bedroom.

Salima went to bed and it was almost midnight when her husband came into the room. His earlier vexation had now given place to gloom. He told her of his brother Karim who lay dying in Hillbrow. Karim had cut himself off from his family and friends ten years ago; he had crossed the colour line (his fair complexion and grey eyes serving as passports) and gone to cohabit with a white woman. And now that he was on the verge of death he wished to return to the world he had forsaken and to be buried under Moslem funeral rites and in a Moslem cemetery.

Hajji Hassen had, of course, rejected the plea, and for good reason. When his brother had crossed the colour line, he had severed his family ties. The Hajji at that time had felt excoriating humiliation. By going over to the white Herrenvolk, his brother had trampled on something that was vitally part of him, his dignity and self-respect. But the rejection of his brother's plea involved a straining of the heartstrings

and the Hajji did not feel happy. He had recently sought God's pardon
for his sins in Mecca, and now this business of his brother's final earthly
wish and his own intransigence was in some way staining his spirit.

The next day Hassen rose at five to go to the mosque. When he
stepped out of his house in Newtown the street lights were beginning
to pale and clusters of houses to assume definition. The atmosphere
was fresh and heady, and he took a few deep breaths. The first trams
were beginning to pass through Bree Street and were clanging along
like decrepit yet burning spectres towards the Johannesburg City Hall.
Here and there a figure moved along hurriedly. The Hindu fruit and
vegetable hawkers were starting up their old trucks in the yards,
preparing to go out for the day to sell to suburban housewives.

When he reached the mosque the Somali muezzin in the ivory-
domed minaret began to intone the call for prayers. After prayers, he
remained behind to read the Koran in the company of two other men.
When he had done the sun was shining brilliantly in the courtyard
onto the flowers and the fountain with its goldfish.

Outside the house he saw a car. Salima opened the door and whispered,
'Caterine'. For a moment he felt irritated, but realising that he might as
well face her he stepped boldly into the lounge.

Catherine was a small woman with firm, fleshy legs. She was seated
cross-legged on the settee, smoking a cigarette. Her face was almost
boyish, a look that partly originated in her auburn hair which was cut
very short, and partly in the smallness of her head. Her eye-brows,
firmly pencilled, accentuated the grey-green glitter of her eyes. She
was dressed in a dark grey costume.

He nodded his head at her to signify that he knew who she was. Over
the telephone he had spoken with aggressive authority. Now, in the
presence of the woman herself, he felt a weakening of his masculine
fibre.

'You must, Mr Hassen, come to see your brother.'

'I am afraid I am unable to help,' he said in a tentative tone. He felt
uncomfortable; there was something so positive and intrepid about her
appearance.

'He wants to see you. It's his final wish.'

'I have not seen him for ten years.'

'Time can't wipe out the fact that he's your brother.'

'He is a white. We live in different worlds.'

'But you must see him.'

There was a moment of strained silence.

'Please understand that he's not to blame for having broken with you. I am to blame. I got him to break with you. Really you must blame me, not Karim.'

Hassen found himself unable to say anything. The thought that she could in some way have been responsible for his brother's rejection of him had never occurred to him. He looked at his feet in awkward silence. He could only state in a lazily recalcitrant tone: 'It is not easy for me to see him.'

'Please come Mr Hassen, for my sake, please. I'll never be able to bear it if Karim dies unhappily. Can't you find it in your heart to forgive him, and to forgive me?'

He could not look at her. A sob escaped from her, and he heard her opening her handbag for a handkerchief.

'He's dying. He wants to see you for the last time.'

Hassen softened. He was overcome by the argument that she had been responsible for taking Karim away. He could hardly look on her responsibility as being in any way culpable. She was a woman.

'If you remember the days of your youth, the time you spent together with Karim before I came to separate him from you, it will be easier for you to pardon him.'

Hassen was silent.

'Please understand that I am not a racialist. You know the conditions in this country.'

He thought for a moment and then said: 'I will go with you.'

He excused himself and went to his room to change. After a while they set off for Hillbrow in her car.

He sat beside her. The closeness of her presence, the perfume she exuded, stirred currents of feeling within him. He glanced at her several times, watched the deft movements of her hands and legs as she controlled the car. Her powdered profile, the outline taut with a resolute quality, aroused his imagination. There was something so businesslike in her attitude and bearing, so involved in reality (at the back of his mind there was Salima, flaccid, cowlike and inadequate) that he could hardly refrain from expressing his admiration.

'You must understand that I'm only going to see my brother because you have come to me. For no one else would I have changed my mind.'

'Yes, I understand. I'm very grateful.'

'My friends and relatives are going to accuse me of softness, of weakness.'

'Don't think of them now. You have decided to be kind to me.'

The realism and the commonsense of the woman's words! He was overwhelmed by her.

The car stopped at the entrance of a building in Hillbrow. They took the lift. On the second floor three white youths entered and were surprised at seeing Hassen. There was a separate lift for non-whites. They squeezed themselves into a corner, one actually turning his head away with a grunt of disgust. The lift reached the fifth floor too soon for Hassen to give a thought to the attitude of the three white boys. Catherine led him to apartment 65.

He stepped into the lounge. Everything seemed to be carefully arranged. There was her personal touch about the furniture, the ornaments, the paintings. She went to the bedroom, then returned and asked him in.

Karim lay in bed, pale, emaciated, his eyes closed. For a moment Hassen failed to recognise him: ten years divided them. Catherine placed a chair next to the bed for him. He looked at his brother and again saw, through ravages of illness, the familiar features. She sat on the bed and rubbed Karims's hands to wake him. After a while he began to show signs of consciousness. She called him tenderly by his name. When he opened his eyes he did not recognise the man beside him, but by degrees, after she had repeated Hassen's name several times, he seemed to understand. He stretched out a hand and Hassen took it, moist and repellent. Nausea swept over him, but he could not withdraw his hand as his brother clutched it firmly.

'Brother Hassen, please take me away from here.'

Hassen's agreement brought a smile to his lips.

Catherine suggested that she drive Hassen back to Newtown where he could make preparations to transfer Karim to his home.

'No, you stay here. I will take a taxi.' And he left the apartment.

In the corridor he pressed the button for the lift. He watched the indicator numbers succeeding each other rapidly, then stop at five. The doors opened – and there they were again, the three white youths. He hesitated. The boys looked at him tauntingly. Then suddenly they burst into deliberately brutish laughter.

'Come into the parlour,' one of them said.

'Come into the Indian parlour,' another said in a cloyingly mocking voice.

Hassen looked at them, annoyed, hurt. Then something snapped within him and he stood there, transfixed. They laughed at him in a raucous chorus as the lift doors shut.

He remained immobile, his dignity clawed. Was there anything so vile in him that the youths found it necessary to maul that recess of self-respect within him? 'They are whites,' he said to himself in bitter justification of their attitude.

He would take the stairs and walk down the five floors. As he descended he thought of Karim. Because of him he had come there and because of him he had been insulted. The enormity of the insult bridged the gap of ten years when Karim had spurned him, and diminished his being. Now he was diminished again.

He was hardly aware that he had gone down five floors when he reached ground level. He stood still, expecting to see the three youths again. But the foyer was empty and he could see the reassuring activity of street life through the glass panels. He quickly walked out as though he would regain in the hubbub of the street something of his assaulted dignity.

He walked on, structures of concrete and glass on either side of him, and it did not even occur to him to take a taxi. It was in Hillbrow that Karim had lived with the white woman and forgotten the existence of his brother; and now that he was dying he had sent for him. For ten years Karim had lived without him. O Karim! The thought of the youth he had loved so much during the days they had been together at the Islamic Institute, a religious seminary though it was governed like a penitentiary, brought the tears to his eyes and he stopped against a shop window and wept. A few pedestrians looked at him. When the shopkeeper came outside to see the weeping man, Hassen, ashamed of himself, wiped his eyes and walked on.

He regretted his pliability in the presence of the white woman. She had come unexpectedly and had disarmed him with her presence and subtle talk. A painful lump rose in his throat as he set his heart against forgiving Karim. If his brother had had no personal dignity in sheltering behind his white skin, trying to be what he was not, he was not going to allow his own moral worth to be depreciated in any way.

When he reached central Johannesburg he went to the station and took the train. In the coach with the blacks he felt at ease and regained his self-possession. He was among familiar faces, among people who respected him. He felt as though he had been spirited away by a perfumed well-made wax doll, but had managed with a prodigious effort to shake her off.

When he reached home Salima asked him what had been decided and he answered curtly, 'Nothing.' But, feeling elated after his escape from Hillbrow, he added condescendingly, 'Karim left of his own accord. We should have nothing to do with him.'

Salima was puzzled, but she went on preparing supper.

Catherine received no word from Hassen and she phoned him. She was stunned when he said: 'I'm sorry but I am unable to offer any help.'

'But ...'

'I regret it. I made a mistake. Please make some other arrangements. Goodbye.'

With an effort of will he banished Karim from his mind. Finding his composure again he enjoyed his evening meal, read the paper and then retired to bed. Next morning he went to mosque as usual, but when he returned home he found Catherine there again. Angry that she should have come, he blurted out: 'Listen to me, Catherine. I can't forgive him. For ten years he didn't care about me, whether I was alive or dead. Karim means nothing to me now.'

'Why have you changed your mind? Do you find it so difficult to forgive him?'

'Don't talk to me of forgiveness. What forgiveness, when he threw me aside and chose to go with you? Let his white friends see to him, let Hillbrow see to him.'

'Please, please, Mr Hassen, I beg you...'

'No, don't come here with your begging. Please go away.'

He opened the door and went out. Catherine burst into tears. Salima comforted her as best she could.

'Don't cry Caterine. All men hard. Dey don't understand.'

'What shall I do now?' Catherine said in a defeated tone. She was an alien in the world of the non-whites. 'Is there no one who can help me?'

'Yes, Mr Mia help you,' replied Salima.

In her eagerness to find some help, she hastily moved to the door. Salima followed her and from the porch of her home directed her to Mr Mia's. He lived in a flat on the first floor of an old building. She knocked and waited in trepidation.

Mr Mia opened the door, smiled affably and asked her in.

'Come inside, lady; sit down ... Fatima,' he called to his daughter, 'bring some tea.'

Mr Mia was a man in his fifties, his bronze complexion partly covered by a neatly trimmed beard. He was a well-known figure in the Indian community. Catherine told him of Karim and her abortive appeal to his brother. Mr Mia asked one or two questions, pondered for a while and then said: 'Don't worry, my good woman. I'll speak to Hassen. I'll never allow a Muslim brother to be abandoned.'

Catherine began to weep.

'Here, drink some tea and you'll feel better.' He poured tea. Before Catherine left he promised that he would phone her that evening and told her to get in touch with him immediately should Karim's condition deteriorate.

Mr Mia, in the company of the priest of the Newtown mosque, went to Hassen's house that evening. They found several relatives of Hassen's seated in the lounge (Salima had spread the word of Karim's illness). But Hassen refused to listen to their pleas that Karim should be brought to Newtown.

'Listen to me Hajji,' Mr Mia said. 'Your brother can't be allowed to die among the Christians.'

'For ten years he has been among them.'

'That means nothing. He's still a Muslim.'

The priest now gave his opinion. Although Karim had left the community, he was still a Muslim. He had never rejected the religion and espoused Christianity, and in the absence of any evidence to the contrary it had to be accepted that he was a Muslim brother.

'But for ten years he has lived in sin in Hillbrow.'

'If he has lived in sin that is not for us to judge.'

'Hajji, what sort of a man are you? Have you no feeling for your brother?' Mr Mia asked.

'Don't talk to me about feeling. What feeling had he for me when he went to live among the whites, when he turned his back on me?'

'Hajji, can't you forgive him? You were recently in Mecca.'

This hurt Hassen and he winced. Salima came to his rescue with refreshments for the guests.

The ritual of tea-drinking established a mood of conviviality and Karim was forgotten for a while. After tea they again tried to press Hassen into forgiving his brother, but he remained adamant. He could not now face Catherine without looking ridiculous. Besides he felt integrated now; he would resist anything that negated him.

Mr Mia and the priest departed. They decided to raise the matter with the congregation in the mosque. But they failed to move Hassen. Actually his resistance grew in inverse ratio as more people came to learn of the dying Karim and Hassen's refusal to forgive him. By giving in he would be displaying mental dithering of the worst kind, as though he were a man without an inner fibre, decision and firmness of will.

Mr Mia next summoned a meeting of various religious dignitaries and received their mandate to transfer Karim to Newtown without his brother's consent. Karim's relatives would be asked to care for him, but if they refused Mr Mia would take charge.

The relatives, not wanting to offend Hassen and also feeling that Karim was not their responsibility, refused.

Mr Mia phoned Catherine and informed her of what had been decided. She agreed that it was best for Karim to be amongst his people during his last days. So Karim was brought to Newtown in an ambulance hired from a private nursing home and housed in a little room in a quiet yard behind the mosque.

The arrival of Karim placed Hassen in a difficult situation and he bitterly regretted his decision not to accept him into his own home. He first heard of his brother's arrival during the morning prayers when the priest offered a special prayer for the recovery of the sick man. Hassen found himself in the curious position of being forced to pray for his brother. After prayers several people went to see the sick man, others went up to Mr Mia to offer help. Hassen felt out of place and as soon as the opportunity presented itself he slipped out of the mosque.

In a mood of intense bitterness, scorn for himself, hatred of those who had decided to become his brother's keepers, infinite hatred for Karim, Hassen went home. Salima sensed her husband's mood and did not say a word to him.

In his room he debated with himself. In what way should he conduct himself so that his dignity remained intact? How was he to face the congregation, the people in the streets, his neighbours? Everyone would soon know of Karim and smile at him half sadly, half ironically, for having placed himself in such a ridiculous position. Should he now forgive the dying man and transfer him to his home? People would laugh at him, snigger at his cowardice, and Mr Mia perhaps even deny him the privilege: Karim was now *his* responsibility. And what would Catherine think of him? Should he go away somewhere (on the pretext of a holiday) to Cape Town, to Durban? But no, there was the stigma of being called a renegade. And besides, Karim might take months to die, he might not die at all.

'O Karim, why did you have to do this to me?' he said, moving towards the window and drumming at the pane nervously. It galled him that a weak, dying man could bring such pain to him. An adversary could be faced, one could either vanquish him or be vanquished, with one's dignity unravished, but with Karim what could he do?

He paced his room. He looked at his watch; the time for afternoon prayers was approaching. Should he expose himself to the congregation? 'O Karim! Karim!' he cried, holding on to the burglar-proof bar of his bedroom window. Was it for this that he had made the pilgrimage – to cleanse his soul in order to return into the penumbra of sin? If only Karim would die he would be relieved of his agony. But what if he lingered on? What if he recovered? Were not prayers being said for him? He went to the door and shouted in a raucous voice: 'Salima!'

But Salima was not in the house. He shouted again and again, and his voice echoed hollowly in the rooms. He rushed into the lounge, into the kitchen, he flung the door open and looked into the yard.

He drew the curtains and lay on his bed in the dark. Then he heard the patter of feet in the house. He jumped up and shouted for his wife. She came hurriedly.

'Salima, Salima, go to Karim, he is in a room in the mosque yard. See how he is, see if he is getting better. Quickly!'

Salima went out. But instead of going to the mosque, she entered her neighbour's house. She had already spent several hours sitting beside Karim. Mr Mia had been there as well as Catherine – who had wept.

After a while she returned from her neighbour. When she opened the door her husband ran to her. 'How is he? Is he very ill? Tell me quickly!'

'He is very ill. Why don't you go and see him?'

Suddenly, involuntarily, Hassen struck his wife in the face.

'Tell me, is he dead? Is he dead?' he screamed.

Salima cowered in fear. She had never seen her husband in this raging temper. What had taken possession of the man? She retired quickly to the kitchen. Hassen locked himself in the bedroom.

During the evening he heard voices. Salima came to tell him that several people, led by Mr Mia, wanted to speak to him urgently. His first impulse was to tell them to leave immediately; he was not prepared to meet them. But he had been wrestling with himself for so many hours that he welcomed a moment when he could be in the company of others. He stepped boldly into the lounge.

'Hajji Hassen,' Mr Mia began, 'please listen to us. Your brother has not long to live. The doctor has seen him. He may not outlive the night.'

'I can do nothing about that,' Hassen replied, in an audacious, matter-of-fact tone that surprised him and shocked the group of people.

'That is in Allah's hand,' said the merchant Gardee. 'In our hands lie forgiveness and love. Come with us now and see him for the last time.'

'I cannot see him.'

'And what will it cost you?' asked the priest, who wore a long black cloak that fell about his sandalled feet.

'It will cost me my dignity and my manhood.'

'My dear Hajji, what dignity and what manhood? What can you lose by speaking a few kind words to him on his death-bed? He was only a young man when he left.'

'I will do anything, but going to Karim is impossible.'

'But Allah is pleased by forgiveness,' said the merchant.

'I am sorry, but in my case the circumstances are different. I am indifferent to him and therefore there is no necessity for me to forgive him.'

'Hajji,' said Mr Mia, 'you are only indulging in glib talk and you know it. Karim is your responsibility, whatever his crime.'

'Gentlemen, please leave me alone.'

And they left. Hassen locked himself in his bedroom and began to pace the narrow space between bed, cupboard and wall. Suddenly, uncontrollably, a surge of grief for his dying brother welled up within him.

'Brother! Brother!' he cried, kneeling on the carpet beside his bed and smothering his face in the quilt. His memory unfolded a time when Karim had been ill at the Islamic Institute and he had cared for him and nursed him back to health. How much he had loved the handsome youth!

At about four in the morning he heard an urgent rapping. He left his room to open the front door.

'Brother Karim dead,' said Mustapha, the Somali muezzin of the mosque, and he cupped his hands and said a prayer in Arabic. He wore a black cloak and a white skull-cap. When he had done he turned and walked away.

Hassen closed the door and went out into the street. For a moment his release into the street gave him a feeling of sinister jubilation, and he laughed hysterically as he turned the corner and stood next to Jamal's fruitshop. Then he walked on. He wanted to get away as far as he could from Mr Mia and the priest who would be calling upon him to prepare for the funeral. That was no business of his. They had brought Karim to Newtown and they should see to him.

He went up Lovers' Walk and at the entrance of Orient House he saw the night-watchman sitting beside a brazier. He hastened up to him, warmed his hands by the fire, but he did this more as a gesture of fraternisation as it was not cold, and he said a few words facetiously. Then he walked on.

His morbid joy was ephemeral, for the problem of facing the congregation at the mosque began to trouble him. What opinion would they have of him when he returned? Would they not say: he hated his brother so much that he forsook his prayers, but now that his brother is no longer alive he returns. What a man! What a Muslim!

When he reached Vinod's Photographic Studio he pressed his forehead against the neon-lit glass showcase and began to weep.

A car passed by, filling the air with nauseous gas. He wiped his eyes, and looked for a moment at the photographs in the showcase; the relaxed, happy, anonymous faces stared at him, faces whose momentary expressions were trapped in film. Then he walked on. He passed a few shops and then reached Broadway Cinema where he stopped to look at the lurid posters. There were heroes, lusty, intrepid, blasting it out with guns; women in various stages of undress; horrid monsters from another planet plundering a city; Dracula.

Then he was among the quiet houses and an avenue of trees rustled softly. He stopped under a tree and leaned against the trunk. He envied the slumbering people in the houses around him, their freedom from the emotions that jarred him. He would not return home until the funeral of his brother was over.

When he reached the Main Reef Road the east was brightening up. The lights along the road seemed to be part of the general haze. The buildings on either side of him were beginning to thin and on his left he saw the ghostly mountains of mine sand. Dawn broke over the city and when he looked back he saw the silhouettes of tall buildings bruising the sky. Cars and trucks were now rushing past him.

He walked for several miles and then branched off onto a gravel road and continued for a mile. When he reached a clump of blue-gum trees he sat down on a rock in the shade of the trees. From where he sat he could see a constant stream of traffic flowing along the highway. He had a stick in his hand which he had picked up along the road, and with it he prodded a crevice in the rock. The action, subtly, touched a chord in his memory and he was sitting on a rock with Karim beside him. The rock was near a river that flowed a mile away from the Islamic Institute. It was a Sunday. He had a stick in his hand and he prodded at a crevice and the weather-worn rock flaked off and Karim was gathering the flakes.

'Karim! Karim!' he cried, prostrating himself on the rock, pushing his fingers into the hard roughness, unable to bear the death of that beautiful youth.

He jumped off the rock and began to run. He would return to Karim. A fervent longing to embrace his brother came over him, to touch that dear form before the soil claimed him. He ran until he was tired, then walked at a rapid pace. His whole existence precipitated itself into one motive, one desire, to embrace his brother in a final act of love.

His heart beating wildly, his hair dishevelled, he reached the highway and walked on as fast as he could. He longed to ask for a lift from a passing motorist but could not find the courage to look back and signal. Cars flashed past him, trucks roared in pain.

When he reached the outskirts of Johannesburg it was nearing ten o'clock. He hurried along, now and then breaking into a run. Once he tripped over a cable and fell. He tore his trousers in the fall and found his hands were bleeding. But he was hardly conscious of himself, wrapped up in his one purpose.

He reached Lovers' Walk, where cars growled around him angrily; he passed Broadway Cinema, rushed towards Orient House, turned the corner at Jamal's fruitshop. And stopped.

The green hearse with the crescent moon and stars emblem passed by; then several cars with mourners followed, bearded men, men with white skull-caps on their heads, looking rigidly ahead, like a procession of puppets, indifferent to his fate. No one saw him.

THE SILVER CUP IS BROKEN

(For Zani)

Mbulelo Mzamane

The service was to start at nine and not, as it usually did, at seven. The announcement had been made the previous Sunday. Makhumalo – who had been feeling too weak to come to church – was not informed, so she had come at the usual time. She had been standing outside the church for more than half an hour, joined from time to time by others who, like her, had missed the previous Sunday's announcement. After waiting till eight, they decided to go their various ways.

Makhumalo always arrived too early for church services. Every Thursday she came at two, although meetings of the Mothers' Union started at three on that day. Her reason was that she always wanted to have a good rest before the service. She was well past her sixties and found the mile-and-a-half walk to church strenuous. On this Sunday, rather than walk all the way back home as the others had done, she decided to go to the rectory which was only a few yards from the church. There was something on her mind which she wanted to discuss with the priest.

At the rectory Makhumalo found Majevrou, the priest's wife, preparing her children for Sunday school. Fr Nqamakwe had not yet returned from his out-stations. As Makhumalo was dressed in the black skirt and white blouse of the Mothers' Union, Majevrou guessed that she had come too early for the service. 'Good morning, Khumsie,' she said, addressing the old lady by her pet name. She drew out a chair for her. 'Please sit down. I can see you had no idea the service would start at nine today. What about a cup of tea?'

'I'd appreciate that very much, Majevrou,' Makhumalo said, panting. She perched herself on the seat and, not without a touch of envy, watched the priest's energetic wife moving briskly about the house. 'I have been waiting outside the church for the last hour or so.' She paused to recapture her breath. 'My sickness caught up with me last week. I couldn't come to church and so I missed the announcements.'

'Oh! I'm sorry to hear that. Let me see if I can't get you something for your rheumatism.' Majevrou, who was also a nurse at the local hospital, often brought tablets for Makhumalo. She slipped into one of the bedrooms and came back with an envelope full of tablets. 'The usual dosage, two every night before you go to bed.'

'Thank you, Majevrou. The last ones you gave me made me stronger than I've been since I was your age, years before that fathead, Mbuyiselo, was born. I'm sure I'd be well on the way to my recovery if it wasn't for him.'

'What has he done this time? By the way, has he been able to find work yet?'

'Ho! Ho! Ho!' When Makhumalo laughed she displayed the depths of her toothless mouth. 'He still goes on jabbering about how he is not prepared to work for any white man. "What do you feed on in the meantime?" I ask, and as usual he is out of the house before answering. In fact, I've come to talk to Father about him. He must marry, instead of filling the location with children.'

Mbuyiselo lived with Makhumalo who was his maternal grandmother. His mother was a widow and worked for a white family in town. She was not allowed to bring anybody to stay with her in the little room which had been apportioned to her. Occasionally she sent Makhumalo some money, but the bulk of the money on which Makhumalo and Mbuyiselo lived came from Makhumalo's old age pension. Mbuyiselo, athletically built, was, at the age of eighteen, a brilliant footballer who saw his future solely in terms of soccer. He refused to work, although other professional footballers played over weekends and augmented their meagre earnings by taking on regular jobs on weekdays.

Makhumalo also told Majevrou that Mbuyiselo had had two children. The burden of paying 'damages' for the two girls had been laid squarely on Makhumalo's shoulders. She was afraid that if appropriate steps were not taken in time, there'd soon be a third child by a third girl. She'd asked him once which of the two women he preferred and he'd chosen Jersey, the mother of his second child. Makhumalo was now keen that he should marry Jersey. She could come in handy with the housework too, which Makhumalo was finding increasingly exacting. Perhaps if Fr Nqamakwe intervened in person, Mbuyiselo would see sense and marry.

Majevrou assured her that Fr Nqamakwe would come and talk to Mbuyiselo. The old lady's burden felt considerably lighter. An hour later she took her leave to wait the remaining period before the service outside the church.

A few days later Fr Nqamakwe visited Makhumalo. Fortunately Mbuyiselo had just returned from football practice, so they discussed his marriage plans. Representations had already been made to Jersey's family by Mbuyiselo's uncles. These were actually willing neighbours hastily gathered for the purpose. The sum of fifty rand had already been deposited with Jersey's family. The bulk of that deposit had come from Makhumalo, with the rest coming from Mbuyiselo's mother. There was still an outstanding amount of seventy rand, but it was not unheard of these days for young couples to settle the balance themselves, after the wedding.

'Now, my son,' Fr Nqamakwe said, 'you and your intended should start attending confirmation classes as from Monday. Your child cannot be baptised until you have both become full members of the

church, nor can you receive the sacrament of holy matrimony until
then. The church's canons are explicit on that. Can I depend on you
to bring watchumacall ... eh ...'

'Jersey, Father,' Makhumalo said.

'Yes, Jersey. Can I depend on you to bring her with you to the church
on Monday evening at five?'

'Yes, Father.' Mbuyiselo scratched his tilted head.

'Oho!' Makhumalo said. 'I know this one. He'll just say "Yes"
although he intends doing nothing of the sort.'

Fr Nqamakwe smiled patronisingly. 'I think we shall prove you
wrong this time, Khumsie.' He gave Mbuyiselo a look of alliance.
'Mbuyiselo will come and bring watchumacall ... eh ...'

'Jersey, Father.'

'Yes, he'll bring her with him. Not so, my son?'

Mbuyiselo nodded and continued to scratch his tilted head. Fr
Nqamakwe rose, patted him reassuringly on the shoulder and bade
them both farewell.

Promptly at five on the appointed Monday, Mbuyiselo and Jersey
were at the church. When Fr Nqamakwe saw them, an involuntary
smile lit up his face and a sigh of satisfaction escaped him as he
thought of his success with the young, which had earned him his
reputation in the parish. At the end of the catechism lesson Fr
Nqamakwe exhorted the couple not to deviate from the path which
the Lord had mapped out for them.

Mbuyiselo never set foot in church again. Fr Nqamakwe drove to
Makhumalo's. Mbuyiselo was seated near the municipality-supplied
stove, in his track suit, and having his supper of pap, meat and *morogo*.
When he saw Fr Nqamakwe he felt as uncomfortable as a booked
player before the disciplinary committee of the league. Fr Nqamakwe
greeted him and followed Makhumalo into the sitting room.

Mbuyiselo, sniffing the sweet scent of freedom, was already dashing
for the kitchen exit when Makhumalo reappeared. She shouted as
jubilantly as a prize-winner at bingo, 'Hey, *uyaphi*? Where on earth do
you think you are going to? Come back, Father wants to talk to you.'

Makhumalo remained in the kitchen and made tea. With the uneasy, clumsy gait of a closely marked forward, Mbuyiselo shuffled his way to the sitting room.

'Sit down, my son, please sit down.'

Mbuyiselo grunted as if he had been fouled, and remained standing.

'It has come ... ahem ... there's a disturbing rumour that reached my ears this afternoon. Your fiancée tells me that you've not been to see her for a considerable period. Is that true, my son?'

'Yes, Father,' Mbuyiselo said softly and scratched his tilted head.

'Is there any reason for your unkind behaviour towards your intended, my son?'

'I am working.' Mbuyiselo had 'struck' a job as a delivery boy with a furniture shop in town.

'That is very nice, my son, that is indeed very nice. Where do you work and for how long have you been working?'

Makhumalo brought in two cups of tea, one for Fr Nqamakwe and the other for herself. She overheard some of the priest's words. 'He's been working for just over a week now. He actually received his first pay two day ago. When I asked him to give me some money, he told me that I'd never smell a single penny from his pocket. Yet when you came in, Father, he was eating money from this pocket.' She pointed at the pocket of her apron with the flourish of an eight-year-old displaying a newly-purchased dress.

'Henceforth,' she continued, 'I'm going to request his whites to hand his pay-packet to me, every week.'

Fr Nqamakwe had prepared a systematic, fatherly approach but Makhumalo's random outburst looked like putting him off.

'You haven't been attending ... ahem ... I mean, I haven't been seeing you at confirmation classes recently ...'

'Because he hasn't been coming, Father.'

Makhumalo's wagging tongue had the obstructive effect of heavy traffic upon a learner-driver.

'Can you explain this ... ahem ... is it possible for you to ... ahem ... explain this watchumacall ... this apparent laxity on your part, my son?'

'I am working,' Mbuyiselo said.

'Liar! *Unamanga.*' Makhumalo's militancy had been reinforced by the priest's protective presence. 'You've only been working for a week. What about all these other weeks? I've been urging you every Monday to attend classes; instead, you take your football boots and rudely walk out.' She had about her the recklessness of a tigress long encaged and only recently released. '*Nalemalinyana yalebhola asiyiboni. Iphi? Jà,* that's right, show us the money you earn from your soccer!'

Fr Nqamakwe coughed to indicate that things had taken a turn for the worse. He began to see his duty as being to establish peace within this household, even before attempting to reconcile Jersey with Mbuyiselo. 'It's not as if he's no longer working now.' He cleared his throat. 'Surely some good must come out of that?'

'Where's it?'

'Ahem ... I mean, Khumsie,' Fr Nqamakwe continued, 'he now needs to slightly adjust his priorities in keeping with his new status in life. He could give his pay to his granny, some of it, instead of keeping it all to himself; he could attend confirmation classes only on Monday, instead of going for football practices which are important, no doubt, if he must retain his place in the team. I've been a footballer, too, though you wouldn't guess that today. But wasn't it our Lord Himself who said, "Render unto Caesar those things that belong to Caesar and unto God those things that belong to Him?" Don't you think you could bring yourself to do at least that much, my son?'

'Oho!' Makhumalo refused to entertain any grand illusions about her grandson. '*Ngiyamazi lo. Uyazihlupha nje.* He's my grandson and I know just what rot's in that head.'

Fr Nqamakwe had now finished his cup of tea, most of which he drank cold. There was nothing left but to commend whatever a man could not resolve to God's infinite wisdom. After offering a prayer for the unity of the church, the world and its families, especially Khumsie's family, he bade them both farewell and left. Makhumalo saw him to his car. She felt like a starved beast which had recently smelt fresh, warm blood.

When she returned to the house she pounced upon Mbuyiselo once more. 'Did you hear? I hope you are going to pay heed to Father's advice. Do you hear me? I hope those flapping ears are not just mere decorations – because if they are, they are very poor decorations.'

'I'll do none of the things which either you or any watchumacall tells me to do.' Mbuyiselo threw his arms recklessly, menacingly into the air. 'And I shall repeat it again,' he pursued. 'You'll never smell a single penny from me.'

'We'll see where your next meal is going to come from,' Makhumalo said. 'We shall see.'

Mbuyiselo banged the door on his way out.

When he returned, an hour later, Makhumalo was already in bed. She woke up to the sound of a woman's screams, just beneath her window. Mbuyiselo had brought Jersey with him and was taking her to task for washing their dirty linen, as it were, in Fr Nqamakwe's presence.

'I'll teach you to go on blurting out things to every watchumacall.'

'What are you doing, Mbuyiselo? What are you doing ...? Okay, kill me then, kill me.'

Makhumalo got out of bed. She suddenly remembered that, in her anger, she had forgotten to lock the back door. She crept towards the kitchen. As she entered, Jersey catapulted in, followed by Mbuyiselo. He was wielding a butcher's knife menacingly. She stood still.

'Mbuyiselo, what are you doing to that child, whoever she is?'

Only a weak streak of light filtered into the kitchen from her bedroom.

'When I have done with her, may that be a warning to your ancient, wagging tongue too.' Mbuyiselo sounded as composed as a song.

'Yeyeni bo!' Makhumalo exclaimed. 'Must you kill her in my presence, in my own house. Must you bring damnation ...'

Mbuyiselo pricked at Jersey's ribs with the knife. She screamed and looked at her ribs.

Makhumalo was horrified. She charged in blindly. 'Not in my house, you don't.'

Mbuyiselo retreated. Makhumalo dived for the poker, next to the stove. Mbuyiselo was now as close to the door as could be. Makhumalo charged with the fury of an irritated bull whereupon Mbuyiselo withdrew to the comparative safety of the dark night.

Makhumalo shouted from the door, 'You won't sleep in my house tonight, you won't.'

'I don't care,' Mbuyiselo said from the dark night, but his voice had lost much of its former sting. 'You will never see me in your house again.' He stalked out of the yard.

Makhumalo locked the kitchen door and went to ascertain that the front door as well as the windows were locked. She came back to her guest whom she had almost forgotten. 'What are you called, my child?'

'Jersey, granny.'

She took a closer look at the girl. 'Oh! It's you, my girl, is it? To think it's you he wants to murder instead of marry. You'll not go to your home tonight. I'll take you there myself, tomorrow. You'll sleep here tonight. If he thinks he is going to waylay you, he is very much mistaken.'

Makhumalo prepared a sleeping place for Jersey on the floor, beside her bed. Mbuyiselo did not turn up again that night.

Returning from work the following evening, he decided to touch Jersey's place. He stood at the corner under a lamppost, and sent a child to go and call her. He watched a number of little children at play outside Jersey's house and thought he recognised one. It could have been his child.

Jersey sent back a message to say she'd be coming.

It was getting dark. He leaned against the lamppost and pulled nonchalantly at his Lexington.

Two boys walked past, recognised him and hailed him by his football name. 'Heit, Danger!'

He threw them a glance and responded, 'Heit!'

Jersey came out, picked up a small boy, and disappeared back into the house.

Another group of boys passed by, saw him and greeted.

In the middle of his third Lexington, a child came up to him with a note written on an ink-stained scrap of paper torn from a disused exercise book. He leaned against the lamppost and began to read the almost illegible scrawl:

Dear Mbuyiselo,

You have broken my hut very much. I have born you a child but you hold me like a dog. I will not forgiv or forget. You have showed me you truest khalas. Now I must tell you the paynful thing of that I no more love you. The silva cup is broken.

Your X,

Jersey.

LEARNING TO FLY

Christopher Hope

An African Fairy Tale

Long ago, in the final days of the old regime, there was a colonel who held an important job in the State Security Police and his name was Rocco du Preez. Colonel du Preez was in charge of the interrogation of political suspects and because of his effect on the prisoners of the old regime he became widely known in the country as 'Window-jumpin'' du Preez. After mentioning his name it was customary to add 'thank God', because he was a strong man and in the dying days of the old regime everyone agreed that we needed a strong man. Now Colonel du Preez acquired his rather strange nickname not because he did any window jumping himself but rather because he had been the first to draw attention to this phenomenon which affected so many of the prisoners who were brought before him.

The offices of State Security were situated on the thirteenth floor of a handsome and tall modern block in the centre of town. Their high windows looked down on to a little dead end street far below. Once this street had been choked with traffic and bustling with thriving shops. Then one day the first jumper landed on the roof of a car parked in the street, and after that it was shut to traffic and turned into a pedestrian shopping mall. The street was filled in and covered with crazy paving and one or two benches set up for weary shoppers. However, the jumpings increased and became a spate: sometimes one or two a week and several accidents on the ground began to frighten off the shoppers.

Whenever a jump had taken place the whole area was cordoned off to allow in the emergency services; the police, the undertaker's men, the municipal workers brought in to hose down the area of impact which was often surprisingly large. The jumpings were bad for business and the shopkeepers grew desperate. The authorities were sympathetic and erected covered walkways running the length of the street leaving only the central area of crazy pavings and the benches, on which no one had never been known to sit, exposed to the heavens; the walkways, protected by their overhead concrete parapets, were guaranteed safe against any and all flying objects. But still trade dwindled and one by one the shops closed and the street slowly died and came to be known by the locals, who gave it a wide berth, as the 'landing field'.

As everyone knows, window jumpings increased apace over the years and being well placed to study them probably led Colonel Rocco du Preez to his celebrated thesis, afterwards included in the manual of psychology used by recruits at the Police College and known as Du Preez's Law. It states that all men, when brought to the brink, will contrive to find a way out if the least chance is afforded them and the choice of the means is always directly related to the racial characteristics of the individual in question. Some of Du Preez's remarks on the subject have come down to us, though these are almost certainly apocryphal, as are so many of the tales of the final days of the old regime. 'Considering your average white man,' Du Preez is supposed to have said, 'my experience is that he prefers hanging – whether by pyjama cord, belt, strips of blanket; providing he finds the handy protuberance, the cell bars, say, or up-ended bedstead he needs, you'll barely have turned your back and he'll be up there swinging from the light cord or other chosen noose. Your white man in his last throes has a wonderful sense of rhythm – believe me, whatever you may have heard to the contrary – I've seen several whites about to cough it and all of them have been wonderful dancers. Your Indian, now, he's something else, a slippery customer who prefers smooth surfaces. I've known Asians to slip and crack their skulls in a shower cubicle so narrow you'd have sworn a man couldn't turn in it. This innate slitheriness is probably what makes them good businessmen. Now, your coloured, per contra, is more clumsy a character altogether. His hidden talent lies in his amazing lack of co-ordination. Even the most sober rogue can appear hopelessly drunk to the untrained eye. On the surface of things it might seem that you can do nothing with him; he has no taste for the knotted strip of blanket or the convenient boot-lace; a soapy bathroom floor leaves him unmoved – yet show him a short, steep flight of steps and he instinctively knows what to do. When it comes to Africans I have found that they, perverse as always, choose another way out. They are given to window jumping. This phenomenon has been very widespread in the past few years. Personally, I suspect its roots go back a long way, back to their superstitions – i.e. to their regard for black magic and witchcraft. Everyone knows that in extreme instances your average Blackie will believe anything: that his witchdoctors will turn the white man's bullets to water; or, if he jumps out of a window thirteen stories above terra firma he will miraculously find himself able to fly. Nothing will stop him once his mind's made up. I've seen up to six Bantu jump from a high window on one day. Though the first landed on his head and the others saw the result they were not deterred. It's as if despite the evidence of their senses they believed that if only they could practise enough they would one day manage to take off.'

'Window-jumpin'' du Preez worked in an office sparsely furnished with an old desk, a chair, a strip of green, government-issue carpet, a very large steel cabinet marked 'Secret' and a bare, fluorescent light in the ceiling. Poor though the furnishings were, the room was made light and cheerful by the large windows behind his desk and nobody remembers being aware of the meanness of the furnishings when Colonel du Preez was present in the room. When he sat down in his leather swivel chair behind his desk, witnesses reported that he seemed to fill up the room, to make it habitable, even genial. His reddish hair and green eyes were somehow enough to colour the room and make it complete. The eyes had a peculiarly steady glint to them. This was his one peculiarity. When thinking hard about something he had the nervous habit of twirling a lock of the reddish hair, a copper colour with gingery lights, in the words of a witness, around a finger. It was his only nervous habit. Since these were often the last words ever spoken by very brave men, we have to wonder at their ability to register details so sharply under terrible conditions; for it is these details that provide us with a glimpse of the man Du Preez, as no photographs have come down to us.

It was to this office that three plainclothes men one day brought a new prisoner. The charge-sheet was singularly bare: it read simply, Mpahlele ... Jake. 'Possession of explosives.' Obviously they had got very little out of him. The men left, closing the door softly, almost reverently, behind them.

The prisoner wore an old black coat, ragged grey flannels and a black beret tilted at an angle which gave him an odd, jaunty, rather continental look, made all the more incongruous by the fact that his hands were manacled behind him. Du Preez reached up with his desk ruler and knocked off the beret revealing a bald head gleaming in the overhead fluorescent light. It would have been shaved and polished, Du Preez guessed, by one of the wandering barbers who traditionally gathered on Sundays down by the municipal lake, setting up three-legged stools and basins of water and hanging towels and leather strops for their cutthroat razors from the lower branches of a convenient tree and draping their customers in large red and white check cloths, giving them little hand mirrors so that they could look on while the barbers scraped, snipped, polished and gossiped away the sunny afternoon by the water's edge beneath the tall bluegums. Clearly Mpahlele belonged to the old school, of whom there were fewer each year as the fashion for Afro-wigs and strange woollen bangs took increasing hold among younger blacks. Du Preez couldn't help warming to this just a little. After all, he was one of the old school himself in the new age of trimmers and ameliorists. Mpahlele was tall, as tall as Du Preez and, he reckoned, about the same age – though it was always difficult to tell with Africans. A knife scar ran from his right eye down to his collar, the flesh fused in a livid welt as if a tiny mole had burrowed under the black skin pushing up a furrow behind it. His nose had been broken, too, probably as the result of the same township fracas, and had mended badly, turning to the left and then sharply to the right as if unable to make up its mind. The man was obviously a brawler. Mpahlele's dark brown eyes were remarkably calm – almost to the point of arrogance. Du Preez thought for an instant, before dismissing the absurd notion with a tiny smile. It shocked him to see an answering smile on the prisoner's lips. However he was too old a hand to let this show.

'Where are the explosives?'

'I have no explosives,' Mpahlele answered. 'Also, I will tell you nothing.'

He spoke quietly, but Du Preez thought he detected a most unjustifiable calm amounting to confidence, or worse, to insolence, and he noted how he talked with special care. It was another insight. On his pad he wrote the letters M.K. The prisoner's diction and accent betrayed him: Mission Kaffir. Raised at one of the stations by a foolish clergy as though he was one day going to be a white man. Of course, the word 'kaffir' was not a word in official use any longer. Like other names at that time growing less acceptable as descriptions of Africans: 'native', 'coon' and even 'bantu', the word had given way to softer names in an attempt to respond to the disaffection springing up among people. But Du Preez, as he told himself, was too old a dog to learn new tricks. Besides, he was not interested in learning to be more 'responsive'. He did not belong to the ameliorists. His job was to control disaffection and where necessary to put it down with proper force. And anyway, his notes were strictly for his own reference, private reminders of his first impressions of a prisoner, useful when, and if, a second interview took place. The number of people he saw was growing daily and he could not expect to keep track of them all in his head.

Du Preez left his desk and slowly circled the prisoner. 'Your comrade who placed the bomb in the shopping centre was a bungler. There was great damage. Many people were killed. Women and children among them. But he wasn't quick enough, your friend. The blast caught him too. Before he died he gave us your name. The paraffin tests show you handled explosives recently. I want the location of the cache. I want the make-up of your cell with names and addresses as well as anything else you might want to tell me.'

'If the bomb did its business then the man was no bungler,' Mpahlele said.

'The murder of women and children – no bungle?'

Mpahlele shrugged. 'Casualties of war.'

Du Preez circled him and stopped beside his right ear. 'I don't call the death of children war. I call it barbarism.'

'Our children have been dying for years but we have never called it barbarism. Now we are learning. You and I know what we mean. I'm your prisoner of war. You will do whatever you can to get me to tell you things you want to know. Then you will get rid of me. But I will tell you nothing. So why don't you finish with me now? Save time.' His brown eyes rested briefly and calmly on Du Preez's empty chair, and then swept the room as if the man had said all he had to say and was now more interested in getting to know that terrible office.

A muscle in Du Preez's cheek rippled and it took him a moment longer than he would have liked to bring his face back to a decent composure. Then he crossed to the big steel cabinet and opened it. Inside was the terrible, tangled paraphernalia of persuasion – the electric generator, the leads and electrodes, the salt water for sharpening contact, and the thick leather straps necessary for restraining the shocked and writhing victim. At the sight of this he scored a point; he thought he detected a momentary pause, a faltering in the steady brown eyes taking stock of his office, and he pressed home the advantage. 'It's very seldom that people fail to talk to me after this treatment.' He held up the electrodes. 'The pain is intense.'

In fact, as we know now, the apparatus in the cabinet was not that actually used on prisoners – indeed, one can see the same equipment on permanent exhibition in the National Museum of the Revolution. But Du Preez, in fact, kept it for effect. The real thing was administered by a special team in a soundproof room on one of the lower floors. But the mere sight of the equipment, whose reputation was huge among the townships and shanty towns, was often enough to have the effect of loosening stubborn tongues. However, Mpahlele looked at the tangle of wires and straps as if he wanted to include them in his inventory of the room and his expression suggested not fear but rather – and this Du Preez found positively alarming – a hint of approval. There was nothing more to be said. He went back to his desk, pressed the buzzer and the plainclothes men came in and took Mpahlele downstairs.

Over the next twenty-four hours 'Window-jumpin'' du Preez puzzled over his new prisoner. It was a long time before he put his finger on some of the qualities distinguishing this man from others he'd worked with under similar circumstances. Clearly, Mpahlele was not frightened. But then other men had been brave too – for a while. It was not only bravery, one had to add to it the strange fact that this man quite clearly did not hate him. That was quite alarming: Mpahlele had treated him as if they were truly equals. There was an effrontery about this he found maddening and the more he thought about it, the more he raged inside. He walked over to the windows behind his desk and looked down to the dead little square with its empty benches and its crazy paving which, with its haphazard joins where the stones were cemented one to the next into nonsensical, snaking patterns, looked from the height of the thirteenth story as if a giant had brought his foot down hard and the earth had shivered into a thousand pieces. He was getting angry. Worse, he was letting his anger cloud his judgement. Worse still, he didn't care.

Mpahlele was in a bad way when they brought him back to Du Preez. His face was so bruised that the old knife scar was barely visible, his lower lip was bleeding copiously and he swayed when the policemen let him go and might have fallen had he not grabbed the edge of the desk and hung there swaying. In answer to Du Preez's silent question the interrogators shook their heads. 'Nothing. He never said *nothing*.'

Mpahlele had travelled far in the regions of pain and it had changed him greatly. It might have been another man who clung to Du Preez's desk with his breath coming in rusty pants; his throat was choked with phlegm or blood he did not have the strength to cough away. He was bent and old and clearly on his last legs. One eye was puffed up in a great swelling shot with green and purple bruises, but the other, he noticed with a renewed spurt of anger, though it had trouble focusing, showed the same old haughty gleam when he spoke to the man.

'Have you any more to tell me about your war?'

Mpahlele gathered himself with a great effort, his one good eye flickering wildly with the strain. He licked the blood off his lips and wiped it from his chin. 'We will win,' he said, 'soon.'

Du Preez dismissed the interrogators with a sharp nod and they left his presence by backing away to the door, full of awe at his control. When the door closed behind them he stood up and regarded the swaying figure with its flickering eye. 'You are like children,' he said bitterly, 'and there is nothing we can do for you.'

'Yes,' said Mpahlele, 'we are children. We owe you everything.'

Du Preez stared at him. But there was not a trace of irony to be detected. The madman was quite plainly sincere in what he said and Du Preez found that insufferable. He moved to the windows and opened them. It was now that, so the stories go, he made his fateful remark. 'Well, if you won't talk, then I suppose you had better learn to fly.'

What happened next is not clear except in broad outline even today, the records of the old regime which were to have been made public have unaccountably been reclassified as secret, but we can make an informed guess. Legend then says that Du Preez recounted for his prisoner his 'theory of desperate solutions' and that, exhausted though he was, Mpahlele showed quickening interest in the way out chosen by white men – that is to say, dancing. We know this is true because Du Preez told the policemen waiting outside the door when he joined them in order to allow Mpahlele to do what he had to do. After waiting a full minute, Du Preez entered his office again closing the door behind him, alone, as had become customary in such cases, his colleagues respecting his need for a few moments of privacy before moving on to the next case. Seconds later these colleagues heard a most terrible cry. When they rushed into the room they found it was empty.

Now we are out on a limb. We have no more facts to go on. All is buried in obscurity or say, rather, it is buried with Du Preez, who plunged from his window down to the landing field at the most terrible speed, landing on his head. Jake Mpahlele has never spoken of his escape from Colonel 'Window-jumpin'' du Preez. All we have are the stories. Some firmly believe to this day that it was done by a special magic and Mpahlele had actually learnt to fly and that the Colonel, on looking out of his window, was so jealous at seeing a black man swooping in the heavens that he had plunged after him on the supposition, regarded as axiomatic in the days of the old regime, that anything a black man could do, a white man could do ten times better. Others, more sceptical, said that the prisoner had hidden himself in the steel cabinet with the torture equipment and emerged to push Du Preez to hell and then escaped in the confusion you will get in a hive if you kill the queen bee. All that is known for sure is that Du Preez lay on the landing field like wet clothes fallen from a washing line, terribly twisted and leaking everywhere. And that in the early days of the new regime Jake Mpahlele was appointed chief investigating officer in charge of the interrogation of suspects and that his work with political prisoners, especially white prisoners, was soon so widely respected that he won rapid promotion to the rank of Colonel and became known throughout the country as Colonel Jake 'Dancin'' Mpahlele, and after his name it was customary to add 'thank God', because he was a strong man and in the early days of the new regime everyone agreed we needed a strong man.

THE PROPHETESS

Njabulo S Ndebele

The boy knocked timidly on the door, while a big fluffy dog sniffed at his ankles. That dog made him uneasy; he was afraid of strange dogs and this fear made him anxious to go into the house as soon as possible. But there was no answer to his knock. Should he simply turn the doorknob and get in? What would the prophetess say? Would she curse him? He was not sure now which he feared more: the prophetess or the dog. If he stood longer there at the door, the dog might soon decide that he was up to some mischief after all. If he left, the dog might decide he was running away. And the prophetess! What would she say when she eventually opened the door to find no one there? She might decide someone had been fooling, and would surely send lightning after the boy. But then, leaving would also bring the boy another problem: he would have to leave without the holy water for which his sick mother had sent him to the prophetess.

There was something strangely intriguing about the prophetess and holy water. All that one was to do, the boy had so many times heard

in the streets of the township, was fill a bottle with water and take it
to the prophetess. She would then lay her hands on the bottle and
pray. And the water would be holy. And the water would have curing
powers. That's what his mother had said too.

The boy knocked again, this time with more urgency. But he had to
be careful not to annoy the prophetess. It was getting darker and the
dog continued to sniff at his ankles. The boy tightened his grip round
the neck of the bottle he had just filled with water from the street tap
on the other side of the street, just opposite the prophetess's house. He
would hit the dog with this bottle. What's more, if the bottle broke he
would stab the dog with the sharp glass. But what would the prophetess
say? She would probably curse him. The boy knocked again, but this
time he heard the faint voice of a woman.

'*Kena!*' the voice said.

The boy quickly turned the knob and pushed. The door did not yield.
And the dog growled. The boy turned the knob again and pushed. This
time the dog gave a sharp bark, and the boy knocked frantically. Then
he heard the bolt shoot back, and saw the door open to reveal darkness.
Half the door seemed to have disappeared into the dark. The boy felt
fur brush past his leg as the dog scurried into the house.

'*Voetsek!*' the woman cursed suddenly.

The boy wondered whether the woman was the prophetess. But as
he was wondering, the dog brushed past him again, slowly this time. In
spite of himself, the boy felt a pleasant, tickling sensation and a slight
warmth where the fur of the dog had touched him. The warmth did
not last, but the tickling sensation lingered, going up to the back of his
neck and seeming to caress it. Then he shivered and the sensation
disappeared, shaken off in the brief involuntary tremor.

'Dogs stay out!' shouted the woman, adding, 'This is not at the white
man's.'

The boy heard a slow shuffle of soft leather shoes receding into the
dark room. The woman must be moving away from the door, the boy
thought. He followed into the house.

'Close the door,' ordered the woman who was still moving somewhere
in the dark. But the boy had already done so.

Although it was getting dark outside, the room was much darker and the fading day threw some of its waning light into the room through the windows. The curtains had not yet been drawn. Was it an effort to save candles, the boy wondered. His mother had scolded him many times for lighting up before it was completely dark.

The boy looked instinctively towards the dull light coming in through the window. He was anxious, though, about where the woman was now, in the dark. Would she think he was afraid when she caught him looking out to the light? But the thick, dark green leaves of vine outside, lapping lazily against the window, attracted and held him like a spell. There was no comfort in that light; it merely reminded the boy of his fear, only a few minutes ago, when he walked under that dark tunnel of vine which arched over the path from the gate to the door. He had dared not touch that vine and its countless velvety, black, and juicy grapes that hung temptingly within reach, or rested lusciously on forked branches. Silhouetted against the darkening summer sky, the bunches of grapes had each looked like a cluster of small cones narrowing down to a point.

'Don't touch that vine!' was the warning almost everyone in Charterston township knew. It was said that the vine was all coated with thick, invisible glue. And that was how the prophetess caught all those who stole out in the night to steal her grapes. They would be glued there to the vine, and would be moaning for forgiveness throughout the cold night, until the morning, when the prophetess would come out of the house with the first rays of the sun, raise her arms into the sky, and say: 'Away, away, sinful man; go and sin no more!' Suddenly, the thief would be free, and would walk away feeling a great release that turned him into a new man. That vine; it was on the lips of everyone in the township every summer.

One day when the boy had played truant with three of his friends, and they were coming back from town by bus, some grown-ups in the bus were arguing about the prophetess's vine. The bus was so full that it was hard for anyone to move. The three truant friends, having given their seats to grown-ups, pressed against each other in a line in the middle of the bus and could see most of the passengers.

'Not even a cow can tear away from that glue,' said a tall, dark man who had high cheek-bones. His balaclava was a careless heap on his head. His moustache, which had been finely rolled into two semi-circular horns, made him look fierce. And when he gesticulated with his tin lunch box, he looked fiercer still.

'My question is only one,' said a big woman whose big arms rested thickly on a bundle of washing on her lap. 'Have you ever seen a person caught there? Just answer that one question.' She spoke with finality, and threw her defiant scepticism outside at the receding scene of men cycling home from work in single file. The bus moved so close to them that the boy had feared the men might get hit.

'I have heard of one silly chap that got caught!' declared a young man. He was sitting with others on the long seat at the rear of the bus. They had all along been laughing and exchanging ribald jokes. The young man had thick lips and red eyes. As he spoke he applied the final touches of saliva with his tongue to brown paper rolled up with tobacco.

'When?' asked the big woman. 'Exactly when, I say? Who was that person?'

'These things really happen!' said a general chorus of women.

'That's what I know,' endorsed the man with the balaclava, and then added, 'You see, the problem with some women is that they will not listen; they have to oppose a man. They just have to.'

'What is that man saying now?' asked another woman. 'This matter started off very well, but this road you are now taking will get us lost.'

'That's what I'm saying too,' said the big woman, adjusting her bundle of washing somewhat unnecessarily. She continued: 'A person shouldn't look this way or that, or take a corner here or there. Just face me straight: I asked a question.'

'These things really happen,' said the chorus again.

'That's it, good ladies, make your point; push very strongly,' shouted the young man at the back. 'Love is having women like you,' he added, much to the enjoyment of his friends. He was now smoking, and his rolled up cigarette looked small between his thick fingers.

'Although you have no respect,' said the big woman, 'I will let you know that this matter is no joke.'

'Of course this is not a joke!' shouted a new contributor. He spoke firmly and in English. His eyes seemed to burn with anger. He was young and immaculately dressed, his white shirt collar resting neatly on the collar of his jacket. A young nurse in a white uniform sat next to him. 'The mother there,' he continued, 'asks you very clearly whether you have ever seen a person caught by the supposed prophetess's supposed trap. Have you?'

'She didn't say that, man,' said the young man at the back, passing the roll to one of his friends. 'She only asked when this person was caught and who it was.' The boys at the back laughed. There was a lot of smoke now at the back of the bus.

'My question was,' said the big woman turning her head to glare at the young man, 'have you ever seen a person caught there? That's all.' Then she looked outside. She seemed angry now.

'Don't be angry, mother,' said the young man at the back. There was more laughter. 'I was only trying to understand,' he added.

'And that's our problem,' said the immaculately dressed man, addressing the bus. His voice was sure and strong. 'We laugh at everything; just stopping short of seriousness. Is it any wonder that the white man is still sitting on us? The mother there asked a very straightforward question, but she is answered vaguely about things happening. Then there is disrespectful laughter at the back there. The truth is you have no proof. None of you. Have you ever seen anybody caught by this prophetess? Never. It's all superstition. And so much about this prophetess also. Some of us are tired of her stories.'

There was a stunned silence in the bus. Only the heavy drone of an engine struggling with an overloaded bus could be heard. It was the man with the balaclava who broke the silence.

'Young man,' he said, 'by the look of things you must be a clever, educated person, but you just note one thing. The prophetess might just be hearing all this, so don't be surprised when a bolt of lightning strikes you on a hot sunny day. And we shall be there at your funeral, young man, to say how you brought misfortune upon your head.'

Thus had the discussion ended. But the boy had remembered how, every summer, bottles of all sizes filled with liquids of all kinds of colours would dangle from vines and peach and apricot trees in many yards in the township. No one dared steal fruit from those trees. Who wanted to be glued in shame to a fruit tree. Strangely, though, only the prophetess's trees had no bottles hanging from their branches.

The boy turned his eyes away from the window and focused into the dark room. His eyes had adjusted slowly to the darkness, and he saw the dark form of the woman shuffling away from him. She probably wore those slippers that had a fluff on top. Old women seem to love them. Then a white receding object came into focus. The woman wore a white *doek* on her head. The boy's eyes followed the *doek*. It took a right-angled turn – probably round the table. And then the dark form of the table came into focus. The *doek* stopped, and the boy heard the screech of a chair being pulled; and the *doek* descended somewhat and was still. There was silence in the room. The boy wondered what to do. Should he grope for a chair? Or should he squat on the floor respect-fully? Should he greet or wait to be greeted? One never knew with the prophetess. Why did his mother have to send him to this place? The fascinating stories about the prophetess, to which the boy would add graphic details as if he had also met her, were one thing; but being in her actual presence was another. The boy then became conscious of the smell of camphor. His mother always used camphor whenever she complained of pains in her joints. Was the prophetess ill then? Did she pray for her own water? Suddenly, the boy felt at ease, as if the discovery that a prophetess could also fee pain somehow made her explainable.

'Lumela 'me,' he greeted. Then he cleared his throat.

'Eea ngoanaka,' she responded. After a little while she asked: 'Is there something you want, little man?' It was a very thin voice. It would have been completely detached had it not been for a hint of tiredness in it. She breathed somewhat heavily. Then she coughed, cleared her throat, and coughed again. A mixture of rough discordant sounds filled the dark room as if everything was coming out of her insides, for she seemed to breathe out her cough from deep within her. And the boy wondered: if she coughed too long, what would happen? Would something come out? A lung? The boy saw the form of the woman clearly now: she had bent forward somewhat. Did anything come out of her on to the floor? The cough subsided. The woman sat up and her hands fumbled with something around her breasts. A white cloth emerged. She leaned forward again, cupped her hands and spat into the cloth. Then she stood up and shuffled away into further darkness away from the boy. A door creaked, and the white *doek* disappeared. The boy wondered what to do because the prophetess had disappeared before he could say what he had come for. He waited.

More objects came into focus. Three white spots on the table emerged. They were placed diagonally across the table. Table mats. There was a small round black patch on the middle one. Because the prophetess was not in the room, the boy was bold enough to move near the table and touch the mats. They were crocheted mats. The boy remembered the huge lacing that his mother had crocheted for the church altar. ALL SAINTS CHURCH was crocheted all over the lacing. There were a number of designs of chalices that carried the Blood of Our Lord.

Then the boy heard the sound of a match being struck. There were many attempts before the match finally caught fire. Soon, the dull, orange light of a candle came into the living room where the boy was, through a half closed door. More light flushed the living room as the woman came in carrying a candle. She looked round as if she was wondering where to put the candle. Then she saw the ashtray on the middle mat, pulled it towards her, sat down and turned the candle over into the ashtray. Hot wax dropped on to the ashtray. Then the prophetess turned the candle upright and pressed its bottom on to the wax. The candle held.

The prophetess now peered through the light of the candle at the boy. Her thick lips protruded, pulling the wrinkled skin and caving in the cheeks to form a kind of lip circle. She seemed always ready to kiss. There was a line tattooed from the forehead to the ridge of a nose that separated small eyes that were half closed by large, drooping eyelids. The white *doek* on her head was so huge that it made her face look small. She wore a green dress and a starched green cape that had many white crosses embroidered on it. Behind her, leaning against the wall, was a long bamboo cross.

The prophetess stood up again, and shuffled towards the window which was behind the boy. She closed the curtains and walked back to her chair. The boy saw another big cross embroidered on the back of her cape. Before she sat down she picked up the bamboo cross and held it in front of her.

'What did you say you wanted, little man?' she asked slowly.

'My mother sent me to ask for water,' said the boy, putting the bottle of water on the table.

'To ask for water?' she asked with mild exclamation, looking up at the bamboo cross. 'That is very strange. You came all the way from home to ask for water?'

'I mean,' said the boy, 'holy water'.

'Ahh!' exclaimed the prophetess, 'you did not say what you meant, little man.' She coughed, just once. 'Sit down, little man,' she said, and continued, 'You see, you should learn to say what you mean. Words, little man, are a gift from the Almighty, the Eternal Wisdom. He gave us all a little pinch of his mind and called on us to think. That is why it is folly to misuse words or not to know how to use them well. Now, who is your mother?'

'My mother?' asked the boy, confused by the sudden transition. 'My mother is staff nurse Masemola.'

'Ao!' exclaimed the prophetess, 'you are the son of the nurse? Does she have such a big man now?' She smiled a little and the lip circle opened. She smiled like a pretty woman who did not want to expose her cavities.

The boy relaxed somewhat, vaguely feeling safe because the prophetess knew his mother. This made him look away from the prophetess for a while, and he saw that there was a huge mask on the wall just opposite her. It was shining and black. It grinned all the time showing two canine teeth pointing upwards. About ten feet away at the other side of the wall was a picture of Jesus in which His chest was open, revealing His heart which had many shafts of light radiating from it.

'Your mother has a heart of gold, my son,' continued the prophetess. 'You are very fortunate indeed to have such a parent. Remember, when she says, "My boy, take this message to that house," go. When she says, "My boy, let me send you to the shop," go. And when she says, "My boy, pick up a book and read," pick up a book and read. In all this she is actually saying to you, learn and serve. Those two things, little man, are the greatest inheritance.'

Then the prophetess looked up at the bamboo cross as if she saw something in it that the boy could not see. She seemed to lose her breath for a while. She coughed deeply again, after which she went silent, her cheeks moving as if she was chewing.

'Bring the bottle nearer,' she said finally. She put one hand on the bottle while with the other she held the bamboo cross. Her eyes closed, she turned her face towards the ceiling. The boy saw that her face seemed to have contracted into an intense concentration in such a way that the wrinkles seemed to have become deep gorges. Then she began to speak.

'You will not know this hymn, boy, so listen. Always listen to new things. Then try to create too. Just as I have learnt never to page through the dead leaves of hymn books.' And she began to sing.

If the fish in a river
boiled by the midday sun
can wait for the coming of evening,
we too can wait
in this wind-frosted land,
the spring will come,
the spring will come.
If the reeds in winter
can dry up and seem dead
and then rise
in the spring,
we too will survive the fire that is coming
the fire that is coming,
we too will survive the fire that is coming.

It was a long, slow song. Slowly, the prophetess began to pray.

'God, the All Powerful! When called upon, You always listen. We direct our hearts and thoughts to You. How else could it be? There is so much evil in the world; so much emptiness in our hearts; so much debasement of the mind. But You, God of all power, are the wind that sweeps away evil and fills our hearts and minds with renewed strength and hope. Remember Samson? Of course You do, O Lord. You created him, You, maker of all things. You brought him out of a barren woman's womb, and since then, we have known that out of the desert things will grow, and that what grows out of the barren wastes has a strength that can never be destroyed.'

Suddenly, the candle flame went down. The light seemed to have gone into retreat as the darkness loomed out, seemingly out of the very light itself, and bore down upon it, until there was a tiny blue flame on the table looking so vulnerable and so strong at the same time. The boy shuddered and felt the coldness of the floor going up his bare feet.

Then out of the dark, came the prophetess's laugh. It began as a giggle, the kind the girls would make when the boy and his friends chased them down the street for a little kiss. The giggle broke into the kind of laughter that produced tears when one was very happy. There was a kind of strange pleasurable rhythm to it that gave the boy a momentary enjoyment of the dark, but the laugh gave way to a long shriek. The boy wanted to rush out of the house. But something strong, yet intangible, held him fast to where he was. It was probably the shriek itself that had filled the dark room and now seemed to come out of the mask on the wall. The boy felt like throwing himself on the floor to wriggle and roll like a snake until he became tired and fell into a long sleep at the end of which would be the kind of bliss the boy would feel when he was happy and his mother was happy and she embraced him, so closely.

But the giggle, the laugh, the shriek, all ended as abruptly as they had started as the darkness swiftly receded from the candle like the way ripples run away from where a stone has been thrown in the water. And there was light. On the wall, the mask smiled silently, and the heart of Jesus sent out yellow light.

'Lord, Lord, Lord,' said the prophetess slowly in a quiet, surprisingly full voice which carried the same kind of contentment that had been in the voice of the boy's mother when one day he had come home from playing in the street, and she was seated on the chair close to the kitchen door, just opposite the warm stove. And as soon as she saw him come in, she embraced him all the while saying: 'I've been so ill for so long, but I've got you. You're my son. You're my son. You're my son.'

And the boy had smelled the faint smell of camphor on her, and he too embraced her, holding her firmly although his arms could not go beyond his mother's armpits. He remembered how warm his hands had become in her armpits.

'Lord, Lord, Lord,' continued the prophetess, 'have mercy on the desert in our hearts and in our thoughts. Have mercy. Bless this water; fill it with your power; and may it bring rebirth. Let her and all others who will drink of it feel the flower of newness spring alive in them; let those who drink it break the chains of despair, and may they realise that the desert wastes are really not barren, but that the vast sands that stretch into the horizon are the measure of the seed in us.'

As the prophetess stopped speaking, she slowly lowered the bamboo cross until it rested on the floor. The boy wondered if it was all over now. Should he stand up and get the blessed water and leave? But the prophetess soon gave him direction.

'Come here, my son,' she said, 'and kneel before me here.' The boy stood up and walked slowly towards the prophetess. He knelt on the floor, his hands hanging at his sides. The prophetess placed her hands on his head. They were warm, and the warmth seemed to go through his hair, penetrating deep through his scalp into the very centre of his head. Perhaps, he thought, that was the soul of the prophetess going into him. Wasn't it said that when the prophetess placed her hands on a person's head, she was seeing with her soul deep into that person; that, as a result, the prophetess could never be deceived? And the boy wondered how his lungs looked to her. Did she see the water that he had drunk from the tap just across the street? Where was the water now? In the stomach? In the kidneys?

Then the hands of the prophetess moved all over the boy's head, seeming to feel for something. They went down the neck. They seemed cooler now, and the coolness seemed to tickle the boy for his neck was colder than those hands. Now they covered his face, and he saw, just before he closed his eyes, the skin folds on the hands so close to his eyes that they looked like many mountains. Those hands smelled of blue soap and candle wax. But there was no smell of snuff. The boy wondered. Perhaps the prophetess did not use snuff after all. But the boy's grandmother did, and her hands always smelled of snuff. Then the prophetess spoke.

'My son,' she said, 'we are made of all that is in the world. Go. Go and heal your mother.' When she removed her hands from the boy's face, he felt his face grow cold, and there was a slight sensation of his skin shrinking. He rose from the floor, lifted the bottle with its snout, and backed away from the prophetess. He then turned and walked towards the door. As he closed it, he saw the prophetess shuffling away to the bedroom carrying the candle with her. He wondered when she would return the ashtray to the table. When he finally closed the door, the living room was dark, and there was light in the bedroom.

It was night outside. The boy stood on the veranda for a while, wanting his eyes to adjust to the darkness. He wondered also about the dog. But it did not seem to be around. And there was that vine archway with its forbidden fruit and the multicoloured worms that always crawled all over the vine. As the boy walked under the tunnel of vine, he tensed his neck, lowering his head as people do when walking in the rain. He was anticipating the reflex action of shaking off a falling worm. Those worms were disgustingly huge, he thought. And there was also something terrifying about their bright colours.

In the middle of the tunnel, the boy broke into a run and was out of the gate: free. He thought of his mother waiting for the holy water; and he broke into a sprint, running west up Thipe Street towards home. As he got to the end of the street, he heard the hum of the noise that came from the ever-crowded barber shops and the huge beer hall just behind those shops. After the brief retreat in the house of the prophetess, the noise, the people, the shops, the street lights, the buses and the taxis all seemed new. Yet, somehow, he wanted to avoid any contact with all this activity. If he turned left at the corner, he would have to go past the shops into the lit Moshoeshoe Street and its Friday night crowds. If he went right, he would have to go past the now dark, ghostly Bantu-Batho post office, and then down through the huge gum tress behind the Charterston Clinic, and then past the quiet golf course. The latter way would be faster, but too dark and dangerous for a mere boy, even with the spirit of the prophetess in him. And were not dead bodies found there sometimes? The boy turned left.

At the shops, the boy slowed down to manoeuvre through the crowds. He lifted the bottle to his chest and supported it from below with the other hand. He must hold on to that bottle. He was going to heal his mother. He tightened the bottle cap. Not a drop was to be lost. The boy passed the shops.

Under a street lamp just a few feet from the gate into the beer hall was a gang of boys standing in a tight circle. The boy slowed down to an anxious stroll. Who were they, he wondered. He would have to run past them quickly. No, there would be no need. He recognised Timi and Bubu. They were with the rest of the gang from the boy's neighbour-hood. Those were the bigger boys who were either in Standard Six or were already in secondary school or were now working in town.

Timi recognised the boy.

'Ja, sonny boy,' greeted Timi. 'What's a piccaninny like you doing alone in the streets at night?'

'Heit, bra Timi,' said the boy, returning the greeting. 'Just from the shops, bra Timi,' he lied, not wanting to reveal his real mission. Somehow that would not have been appropriate.

'Come on, you!' yelled another member of the gang, glaring at Timi. It was Biza. Most of the times when the boy had seen Biza, the latter was stopping a girl and talking to her. Sometimes the girl would laugh. Sometimes Biza would twist her arm until she 'agreed'. In broad daylight!

'You don't believe me,' continued Biza to Timi, 'and when I try to show you some proof you turn away to greet an ant.'

'Okay then,' said another, 'what proof do you have? Everybody knows that Sonto is a hard girl to get.'

'Come closer then,' said Biza, 'and I'll show you.' The boy was closed out of the circle as the gang closed in towards Biza, who was at the centre. The boy became curious and got closer. The wall was impenetrable. But he could clearly hear Biza.

'You see? You can all see. I've just come from that girl. Look! See? The liquid? See? When I touch it with my finger and then leave it, it follows like a spider's web.'

'Well, my man,' said someone, 'you can't deceive anybody with that. It's the usual trick. A fellow just blows his nose and then applies the mucus there, and then emerges out of the dark saying he has just had a girl.'

'Let's look again closely,' said another, 'before we decide one way or the other.' And the gang pressed close again.

'You see? You see?' Biza kept saying.

'I think Biza has had that girl,' said someone.

'It's mucus man, and nothing else,' said another.

'But you know Biza's record in these matters, gents.'

'Another thing, how do we know it's Sonto and not some other girl. Where is it written on Biza's cigar that he has just had Sonto? Show me where it's written "Sonto" there.'

'You're jealous, you guys, that's your problem,' said Biza. The circle went loose and there was just enough time for the boy to see Biza's penis disappear into his trousers. A thick little thing, thought the boy. It looked sad. It had first been squeezed in retreat against the fly like a concertina, before it finally disappeared. Then Biza, with a twitch of alarm across his face, saw the boy.

'What did you see, you?' screamed Biza. 'Fuck off!'

The boy took to his heels wondering what Biza could have been doing with his penis under the street lamp. It was funny, whatever it was. It was silly too. Sinful. The boy was glad that he had got the holy water away from those boys and that none of them had touched the bottle.

And the teachers were right, thought the boy. Silliness was all those boys knew. And then they would go to school and fail test after test. Silliness and school did not go together.

The boy felt strangely superior. He had the power of the prophetess in him. And he was going to pass that power to his mother, and heal her.

Those boys were not healing their mothers. They just left their mothers alone at home. The boy increased his speed. He had to get home quickly. He turned right at the charge office and sped towards the clinic. He crossed the road that went to town and entered Mayaba Street.

Mayaba Street was dark and the boy could not see. But he did not lower his speed. Home was near now, instinct would take him there. His eyes would adjust to the darkness as he raced along. He lowered the bottle from his chest and let it hang at his side, like a pendulum that was not moving. He looked up at the sky as if light would come from the stars high up to lead him home. But when he lowered his face, he saw something suddenly loom before him, and, almost simultaneously, felt a dull yet painful impact against his thigh. Then there was a grating of metal seeming to scoop up sand from the street. The boy did not remember how he fell but, on the ground, he lay clutching at his painful thigh. A few feet away, a man groaned and cursed.

'Blasted child!' he shouted. 'Shouldn't I kick you? Just running in the street as if you owned it. Shit of a child, you don't even pay tax. Fuck off home before I do more damage to you!' The man lifted his bicycle and the boy saw him straightening the handles. And the man rode away.

The boy raised himself from the ground and began to limp home, conscious of nothing but the pain in his thigh. But it was not long before he felt a jab of pain at the centre of his chest and his heart beating faster. He was thinking of the broken bottle and the spilt holy water and his mother waiting for him and the water that would help to cure her. What would his mother say? If only he had not stopped to see those silly boys he might not have been run over by a bicycle. Should he go back to the prophetess? No. There was the dog, there was the vine, there were the worms. There was the prophetess herself. She would not let anyone who wasted her prayers get away without punishment. Would it be lightning? Would it be the fire of hell? What would it be? The boy limped home to face his mother. He would walk in to his doom. He would walk into his mother's bedroom, carrying no cure, and face the pain in her sad eyes.

But as the boy entered the yard of his home, he heard the sound of bottles coming from where his dog had its kennel. Rex had jumped over the bottles, knocking some stones against them in his rush to meet the boy. And the boy remembered the pile of bottles next to the kennel. He felt grateful as he embraced the dog. He selected a bottle from the heap. Calmly, as if he had known all the time what he would do in such a situation, the boy walked out of the yard again, towards the street tap on Mayaba Street. And there, almost mechanically, he cleaned the bottle, shaking it many times with clean water. Finally, he filled it with water and wiped its outside clean against his trousers. He tightened the cap, and limped home.

As soon as he opened the door, he heard his mother's voice in the bedroom. It seemed some visitors had come while he was away.

'I'm telling you, *Sisi*,' his mother was saying, 'and take it from me, a trained nurse. Pills, medicines, and all those injections, are not enough. I take herbs too, and then think of the wonders of the universe as our people have always done. Son, is that you?'

'Yes, Ma,' said the boy, who had just closed the door with a deliberate bang.

'And did you bring the water?'

'Yes, Ma.'

'Good. I knew you would. Bring the water and three cups. MaShange and MaMokoena are here.'

The boy's eyes misted with tears. His mother's trust in him: would he repay it with such dishonesty? He would have to be calm. He wiped his eyes with the back of his hand, and then put the bottle and three cups on a tray. He would have to walk straight. He would have to hide the pain in his thigh. He would have to smile at his mother. He would have to smile at the visitors. He picked up the tray; but just before he entered the passage leading to the bedroom, he stopped, trying to muster courage. The voices of the women in the bedroom reached him clearly.

'I hear you very well, Nurse,' said one of the women. 'It is that kind of sense I was trying to spread before the minds of these people. You see, the two children are first cousins. The same blood runs through them.'

'That close!' exclaimed the boy's mother.

'Yes, that close. MaMokoena here can bear me out; I told them in her presence. Tell the nurse, you were there.'

'I have never seen such people in all my life,' affirmed MaMokoena.

'So I say to them, my voice reaching up to the ceiling, "Hey, you people, I have seen many years. If these two children really want to marry each other, then a beast *has* to be slaughtered to cancel the ties of blood ..."'

'And do you want to hear what they said?' interrupted MaMokoena.

'I'm listening with both ears,' said the boy's mother.

'Tell her, child of Shange,' said MaMokoena.

'They said that was old, crusted foolishness. So I said to myself, "Daughter of Shange, shut your mouth, sit back, open your eyes, and watch." And that's what I did.'

'Two weeks before the marriage, the ancestors struck. Just as I had thought. The girl had to be rushed to hospital, her legs swollen like trousers full of air on the washing line. Then I got my chance, and opened my mouth, pointing my finger at them, and said, "Did you ask the ancestors' permission for this unacceptable marriage?" You should have seen their necks becoming as flexible as a goose's. They looked this way, and looked that way, but never at me. But my words had sunk. And before the sun went down, we were eating the insides of a goat. A week later, the children walked up to the altar. And the priest said to them, "You are such beautiful children!"'

'Isn't it terrible that some people just let misfortune fall upon them?' remarked the boy's mother.

'Only those who ignore the words of the world speaking to them,' said MaShange.

'Where is this boy now?' said the boy's mother. 'Son! Is the water coming?'

Instinctively the boy looked down at his legs. Would the pain in his thigh lead to the swelling of his legs? Or would it be because of his deception? A tremor of fear went through him; but he had to control it, and be steady, or the bottle of water would topple over. He stepped forward into the passage. There was his mother! Her bed faced the passage, and he had seen her as soon as he turned into the passage. She had propped herself up with many pillows. Their eyes met, and she smiled, showing the gap in her upper front teeth that she liked to poke her tongue into. She wore a fawn chiffon *doek* which had slanted into a careless heap on one side of her head. This exposed her undone hair on the other side of her head.

As the boy entered the bedroom, he smelled camphor. He greeted the two visitors and noticed that, although it was warm in the bedroom, MaShange, whom he knew, wore her huge, heavy, black, and shining overcoat. MaMokoena had a blanket over her shoulders. Their *doeks* were more orderly than the boy's mother's. The boy placed the tray on the dressing chest close to his mother's bed. He stepped back and watched his mother, not sure whether he should go back to the kitchen, or wait to meet his doom.

'I don't know what I would do without this boy,' said the mother as she leaned on an elbow, lifted the bottle with the other hand, and turned the cap rather labouriously with the hand on whose elbow she was resting. The boy wanted to help, but he felt he couldn't move. The mother poured water into one cup, drank from it briefly, turned her face towards the ceiling, and closed her eyes. 'Such cool water!' she sighed deeply, and added, 'Now I can pour for you,' as she poured water into the other two cups.

There was such a glow of warmth in the boy as he watched his mother, so much gladness in him that he forgave himself. What had the prophetess seen in him? Did she still feel him in her hands? Did she know what he had just done? Did holy water taste any differently from ordinary water? His mother didn't seem to find any difference. Would she be healed?

'As we drink the prophetess's water,' said MaShange, 'we want to say how grateful we are that we came to see for ourselves how you are.'

'I think I feel better already. This water, and you ... I can feel a soothing coolness deep down.'

As the boy slowly went out of the bedroom, he felt the pain in his leg, and felt grateful. He had healed his mother. He would heal her tomorrow, and always with all the water in the world. He had healed her.

A TRIP TO
THE GIFBERGE

Zoë Wicomb

You've always loved your father better.

That will be her opening line.

The chair she sits in is a curious affair, crude, like a crate with arm-rests. A crate for a large tough-skinned vegetable like hubbard squash which is of course not soft as its name suggests.

I move towards her to adjust the goatskin karos around her shoulders. It has slipped in her attempt to rise out of the chair. I brace myself against the roar of distaste but no, perhaps her chest is too tight to give the words their necessary weight. No, she would rather remove herself from my viperous presence. But the chair is too low and the gnarled hands spread out on the armrests cannot provide enough leverage for the body to rise with dignity. ('She doesn't want to see you,' Aunt Cissie said, biting her lip.)

Her own words are a synchronic feat of syllables and exhalations to produce a halting hiss. 'Take it away. I'll suffocate with heat. You've tried to kill me enough times.' I drop the goatskin on to the ground before realising that it goes on the back of the chair.

I have never thought it unreasonable that she should not want to see me. It is my insistence which is unreasonable. But why, if she is hot, does she sit here in the last of the sun? Her chair stands a good twenty yards from the house, beyond the semi-circle of the grass broom's vigorous expressionistic strokes. From where I stand, having made the predicted entrance through the back gate, she is a painterly arrangement alone on the plain. Her house is on the very edge of the location. Behind her the Matsikamma Range is interrupted by two swollen peaks so that her head rests in the cleavage.

Her chair is uncomfortable without the karos. The wood must cut into the small of her back and she is forced to lean forward, to wriggle. Our eyes meet for a second, accidentally, but she shuts hers instantly so that I hold in my vision the eyes of decades ago. Then they flashed coal-black, the surrounding skin taut across the high cheekbones. Narrow, narrow slits which she forced wide open and, like a startled rabbit, stared entranced into a mirror as she pushed a wave into the oiled black hair.

'If only,' she lamented, 'if only my eyes were wider I would be quite nice, really nice,' and with a snigger, 'a princess.'

Then she turned on me. 'Poor child. What can a girl do without good looks? Who'll marry you? We'll have to put a peg on your nose.'

And the pearled half moon of her brown fingertip flashed as she stroked appreciatively the curious high bridge of her own nose. Those were the days of the monthly hairwash in the old house. The kitchen humming with pots of water nudging each other on the stove, and afterwards the terrible torments of the comb as she hacked with explorer's determination the path through the tangled undergrowth, set on the discovery of silken tresses. Her own sleek black waves dried admirably, falling into place. Mother.

Now it is thin, scraped back into a limp plait pinned into a bun. Her shirt is the fashionable cut of this season's muttonleg sleeve and I remember that her favourite garments are saved in a mothballed box. Now and then she would bring something to light, just as fashion tiptoeing out of a dusty cupboard would crack her whip after bowing humbly to the original. How long has she been sitting here in her shirt and ill-matched skirt and the nimbus of anger?

She coughs. With her eyes still closed she says, 'There's Jantjie Bêrend in an enamel jug on the stove. Bring me a cup.'

Not a please and certainly no thank you to follow. The daughter must be reminded of her duty. This is her victory: speaking first, issuing a command.

I hold down the matted Jantjie Bêrend with a fork and pour out the yellowish brew. I do not anticipate the hand thrust out to take the drink so that I come too close and the liquid lurches into the saucer. The red dry earth laps up the offering of spilled infusion which turns into a patch of fresh blood.

'Clumsy, like your father. He of course never learned to drink from a cup. Always poured it into a saucer, that's why the Shentons all have lower lips like spouts. From slurping their drinks from saucers. Boerjongens, all of them. My Oupa swore that the English potteries cast their cups with saucers attached so they didn't have to listen to Boers slurping their coffee. Oh, he knew a thing or two, my Oupa. Then your Oupa Shenton had the cheek to call me a Griqua meid.'

Her mouth purses as she hauls up the old grievances for which I have no new palliatives. Instead I pick up the bunch of proteas that I had dropped with my rucksack against the wall. I hand the flowers to her and wonder how I hid my revulsion when Aunt Cissie presented them to me at the airport.

'Welcome home to South Africa.' And in my arms the national blooms rested fondly while she turned to the others, the semi-circle of relatives moving closer. 'From all of us. You see everybody's here to meet the naughty girl.'

'And Eddie,' I exclaimed awkwardly as I recognised the youngest uncle now pot-bellied and grey.

'Ag no man, you didn't play marbles together. Don't come here with disrespectful foreign ways. It's your Uncle Eddie,' Aunt Cissie reprimanded. 'And Eddie,' she added, 'you must find all the children. They'll be running all over the place like chickens.'

'Can the new auntie ride in our car?' asked a little girl tugging at Aunt Cissie's skirt.

'No man, don't be so stupid, she's riding with me and then we all come to my house for something nice to eat. Did your mammie bring some roeties?'

I rubbed the little girl's head but a tough protea had pierced the cellophane and scratched her cheek which she rubbed self-pityingly.

'Come get your baggage now,' and as we waited Aunt Cissie explained. 'Your mother's a funny old girl, you know. She just wouldn't come to the airport and I explained to her the whole family must be there. Doesn't want to have anything to do with us now, don't ask me why, jus turned against us jus like that. Doesn't talk, not that she ever said much, but she said, right there at your father's funeral – pity you couldn't get here in time – well, she said, "Now you can all leave me alone," and when Boeta Danie said, "Ag man sister you musn't talk so, we've all had grief and the Good Lord knows who to take and who to leave," well you wouldn't guess what she said...' and Aunt Cissie's eyes roved incredulously about my person as if a good look would offer an explanation ' ... she said plainly, jus like that, "Danie," jus dropped the Boeta there and then in front of everybody, she said ... and I don't know how to say it because I've always had a tender place in my heart for your mother, such a lovely shy girl she was...'

'Really?' I interrupted. I could not imagine her being described as shy.

'Oh yes, quite shy, a real lady. I remember when your father wrote home to ask for permission to marry, we were so worried. A Griqua girl, you know, and it was such a surprise when he brought your mother, such nice English she spoke and good features and a nice figure also.'

Again her eyes took in my figure so that she was moved to add in parenthesis, 'I'll get you a nice step-in. We get good ones here with the long leg, you know, gives you a nice firm hip-line. You must look after yourself man; you won't get a husband if you let yourself go like this.'

Distracted from her story she leaned over to examine the large ornate label of a bag bobbing by on the moving belt.

'That's not mine,' I said.

'I know. I can mos see it says Mev H J Groenewald,' she retorted. Then, appreciatively as she allowed the bag to carry drunkenly along, 'But that's now something else hey. Very nice. There's nothing wrong in admiring something nice man. I'm not shy and there's no Apartheid at the airport. You spend all that time overseas and you still afraid of Boers.' She shook her head reproachfully.

'I must go to the lavatory,' I announced.

'OK. I'll go with hey.'

And from the next closet her words rose above the sound·of abundant pee gushing against the enamel of the bowl, drowning my own failure to produce even a trickle.

'I made a nice pot of beans and samp, not grand of course but something to remind you you're home. Stamp-en-stoot we used to call it on the farm,' and her clear nostalgic laughter vibrated against the bowl.

'Yes,' I shouted, 'funny, but I could actually smell beans and samp hovering just above the petrol fumes in the streets of London.'

I thought of how you walk along worrying about being late, or early, or wondering where to have lunch, when your nose twitches with a teasing smell and you're transported to a place so specific and the power of the smell summons the light of that day when the folds of a dress draped the brick wall and your hands twisted anxiously, 'Is she my friend, truly my friend?'

While Aunt Cissie chattered about how vile London was, a terrible place where people slept under the arches in newspapers and brushed the pigeonshit off their brows in the mornings. Funny how Europeans could sink so low. And the coloured people from the West Indies just fighting on the streets, killing each other and still wearing their doekies from back home. Really, as if there weren't hairdressers in London. She had seen it all on TV. Through the door I watched the patent-leather shoes shift under the heaving and struggling of flesh packed into corsets.

'Do they show the riots here in South Africa on TV?'

'Ag, don't you start with politics now,' she laughed, 'but I got a new TV you know.'

We opened our doors simultaneously, and with the aid of flushing water she drew me back, 'Yes, your father's funeral was a business.'

'What did Mamma say?'

'Man, you musn't take notice of what she says. I always say that half the time people don't know what they talking about and blood is thicker than water so you jus do your duty hey.'

'Of course Auntie. Doing my duty is precisely why I'm here.' It is not often that I can afford the luxury of telling my family the truth.

'But what did she say?' I persisted.

'She said she didn't want to see you. That you've caused her enough trouble and you shouldn't bother to go up to Namaqualand to see her. And I said, "Yes Hannah it's no way for a daughter to behave but her place is with you now."' Biting her lip she added, 'You mustn't take any notice. I wasn't going to say any of this to you, but seeing that you asked ... Don't worry man, I'm going with you. We'll drive up tomorrow.'

'I meant what did she say to Uncle Danie?'

'Oh, she said to him, "Danie," jus like that, dropped the Boeta right there in the graveyard in front of everyone, she said, "He's dead now and I'm not your sister so I hope you Shentons will leave me alone." Man, a person don't know what to do.'

Aunt Cissie frowned.

'She was always so nice with us you know, such a sweet person, I jus don't understand, unless ...' and she tapped her temple, 'unless your father's death jus went to her head. Yes,' she sighed, as I lifted my rucksack from the luggage belt, 'it never rains but pours; still, every cloud has a silver lining,' and so she dipped liberally into her sack of homilies and sowed them across the arc of attentive relatives.

'It's in the ears of the young,' she concluded, 'that these thoughts must sprout.'

She has never seemed more in control than at this moment when she stares deep into the fluffy centres of the proteas on her lap. Then she takes the flowers still in their cellophane wrapping and leans them, heads down, like a broom against the chair. She allows her hand to fly to the small of her back where the wood cuts.

'Shall I get you a comfortable chair? There's a wicker one by the stove which won't cut into your back like this.'

Her eyes rest on the eaves of the house where a swallow circles anxiously.

'It won't of course look as good here in the red sand amongst the thornbushes,' I persist.

A curt 'No'. But then the loose skin around her eyes creases into lines of suppressed laughter and she levers herself expertly out of the chair.

'No, it won't, but it's getting cool and we should go inside. The chair goes on the stoep,' and her overseer's finger points to the place next to a tub of geraniums. The chair is heavy. It is impossible to carry it without bruising the shins. I struggle along to the unpolished square of red stoep that clearly indicates the permanence of its place, and marvel at the extravagance of her gesture.

She moves busily about the kitchen, bringing from the pantry and out of the oven pots in advanced stages of preparation. Only the peas remain to be shelled but I am not allowed to help.

'So they were all at the airport hey?'

'Not all, I suppose; really I don't know who some of them are. Neighbours for all I know,' I reply guardedly.

'No you wouldn't after all these years. I don't suppose you know the young ones at all; but then they probably weren't there. Have better things to do than hang about airports. Your Aunt Cissie wouldn't have said anything about them ... Hetty and Cheryl and Willie's Clint. They'll be at the political meetings, all UDF people. Playing with fire, that's what they're doing. Don't care a damn about the expensive education their parents have sacrificed for.'

Her words are the ghostly echo of years ago when I stuffed my plaits into my ears and the sour guilt rose dyspeptically in my throat. I swallow, and pressing my back against the cupboard for support I sneer, 'Such a poor investment children are. No returns, no compound interest, not a cent's worth of gratitude. You'd think gratitude was inversely proportionate to the sacrifice of parents. I can't imagine why people have children.'

She turns from the stove, her hands gripping the handles of a pot, and says slowly, at one with the steam pumping out the truth, 'My mother said it was a mistake when I brought you up to speak English.

Said people spoke English just to be disrespectful to their elders, to You and Your them about. And that is precisely what you do. Now you use the very language against me that I've stubbed my tongue on trying to teach you it. No respect! Use your English as a catapult!'

I fear for her wrists but she places the pot back on the stove and keeps her back turned. I will not be drawn into further battle. For years we have shunted between understanding and failure and I, the Caliban, will always be at fault. While she stirs ponderously, I say, 'My stories are going to be published next month. As a book I mean.'

She sinks into the wicker chair, her face red with steam and rage.

'Stories,' she shouts, 'you call them stories? I wouldn't spend a second gossiping about things like that. Dreary little things in which nothing happens, except ... except ...' and it is the unspeakable which makes her shut her eyes for a moment. Then more calmly, 'Cheryl sent me the magazine from Joburg, two, three of them. A disgrace. I'm only grateful that it's not a Cape Town book. Not that one could trust Cheryl to keep anything to herself.'

'But they're only stories. Made up. Everyone knows it's not real, not the truth.'

'But you've used the real. If I can recognise places and people, so can others, and if you want to play around like that why don't you have the courage to tell the whole truth? Ask me for stories with neat endings and you won't have to invent my death. What do you know about things, about people, this place where you were born? About your ancestors who roamed these hills? You left. Remember?' She drops her head and her voice is barely audible.

'To write from under your mother's skirts, to shout at the world that it's all right to kill God's unborn child! You've killed me over and over so it was quite unnecessary to invent my death. Do people ever do anything decent with their education?'

Slumped in her chair she ignores the smell of burning food so that I rescue the potatoes and baste the meat.

'We must eat,' she sighs. 'Tomorrow will be exhausting. What did you have at Cissie's last night?'

'Bobotie and sweet potato and stamp-en-stoot. They were trying to watch the television at the same time so I had the watermelon virtually to myself.'

She jumps up to take the wooden spoon from me. We eat in silence the mutton and sousboontjies until she says that she managed to save some prickly pears. I cannot tell whether her voice is tinged with bitterness or pride at her resourcefulness. She has slowed down the ripening by shading the fruit with castor-oil leaves, floppy hats on the warts of great bristling blades. The flesh is nevertheless the colour of burnt earth, a searing sweetness that melts immediately so that the pips are left swirling like gravel in my mouth. I have forgotten how to peel the fruit without perforating my fingers with invisible thorns.

Mamma watches me eat, her own knife and fork long since resting sedately on the plate of opaque white glass. Her finger taps the posy of pink roses on the clean rim and I am reminded of the modesty of her portion.

'Tomorrow,' she announces, 'we'll go on a trip to the Gifberge.'

I swallow the mouthful of pips and she says anxiously, 'You can drive, can't you?' Her eyes are fixed on me, ready to counter the lie that will attempt to thwart her and I think wearily of the long flight, the terrible drive from Cape Town in the heat.

'Can't we go on Thursday? I'd like to spend a whole day in the house with the blinds drawn against the sun, reading the *Cape Times*.'

'Plenty of time for that. No, we must go tomorrow. Your father promised, for years he promised, but I suppose he was scared of the pass. Men can't admit that sort of thing, scared of driving in the mountains, but he wouldn't teach me to drive. Always said my chest wasn't good enough. As if you need good lungs to drive.'

'And in this heat?'

'Don't be silly, child, it's autumn and in the mountains it'll be cool. Come,' she says, taking my arm, and from the stoep traces with her finger the line along the Matsikamma Range until the first deep fold. 'Just there you see, where the mountains step back a bit, just there in that kloof the road goes up.'

Maskam's friendly slope stops halfway, then the flat top rises perpendicularly into a violet sky. I cannot imagine little men hanging pegged and roped to its sheer sides.

'They say there are proteas on the mountain.'

'No,' I counter, 'it's too dry. You only find proteas in the Cape Peninsula.'

'Nonsense,' she says scornfully, 'you don't know everything about this place.'

'Ag, I don't care about this country; I hate it.'

Sent to bed, I draw the curtains against huge stars burning into the night.

'Don't turn your light on, there'll be mosquitoes tonight,' she advises.

My dreams are of a wintry English garden where a sprinkling of snow lies like insecticide over the stubbles of dead shrub. I watch a flashing of red through the wooden fence as my neighbour moves along her washing line pegging out the nappies. I want to call to her that it's snowing, that she's wasting her time, but the slats of wood fit closely together and I cannot catch at the red of her skirt. I comfort myself with the thought that it might not be snowing in her garden.

Curtains rattle and part and I am lost, hopelessly tossed in a sharp first light that washes me across the bed to where the smell of coffee anchors me to the spectre of Mamma in a pale dressing gown from the past. Cream, once primrose seersucker, and I put out my hand to clutch at the fabric but fold it over a saucer-sized biscuit instead. Her voice prises open the sleep seal of my eyes.

'We'll go soon and have a late breakfast on the mountain. Have another biscuit,' she insists.

At Van Rhynsdorp we stop at the store and she exclaims appreciatively at the improved window dressing. The wooden shelves in the window have freshly been covered with various bits of patterned fablon on which oil lamps, toys and crockery are carefully arranged. On the floor of blue linoleum a huge doll with blonde curls and purple eyes grimaces through the faded yellow cellophane of her box. We are the only customers.

Old Mr Friedland appears not to know who she is. He leans back from the counter, his left thumb hooked in the broad braces while the right hand pats with inexplicable pride the large protruding stomach.

His eyes land stealthily, repeatedly, on the wobbly topmost button of his trousers as if to catch the moment when the belly will burst into liberty.

She has filled her basket with muddy tomatoes and takes a cheese from the counter.

'Mr Friedland,' she says in someone else's voice, 'I've got the sheepskins for Mr Friedland in the bakkie. Do ... er ... does Mr Friedland want them?'

'Sheepskins?'

His right hand shoots up to fondle his glossy black plumage and at that moment, as anyone could have predicted, at that very moment of neglect, the trouser button twists off and shoots into a tower of tomato cans.

'Shenton's sheepskins.' She identifies herself under cover of the rattling button.

The corvine beak peck-pecks before the words tumble out hastily, 'Yes, yes, they say old Shenton's dead hey? Hardworking chap that!' And he shouts into a doorway, 'Tell the boy to get the skins from the blue bakkie outside.'

I beat the man in the white polystyrene hat to it and stumble in with the stiff salted skins which I dump at his fussy directions. The skin mingles with the blue mottled soap to produce an evil smell. Mr Friedland tots up the goods in exchange and I ask for a pencil to make up the outstanding six cents.

'Ugh,' I grunt, as she shuffles excitedly on the already hot plastic seat, her body straining forward to the lure of the mountain, 'How can you bear it?'

'What, what?' She resents being dragged away from her outing. 'Old Friedland you mean? There are some things you just have to do whether you like it or not. But those people have nothing to do with us. Nothing at all. It will be nice and cool in the mountains.'

As we leave the tarred road we roll up the windows against the dust. The road winds perilously as we ascend and I think sympathetically of Father's alleged fear. In an elbow of the road we look down on to a dwarfed homestead on the plain with a small painted blue pond and a willow lurid against the grey of the veld. Here against the black rock the bushes grow tall, verdant, and we stop in the shadow of a cliff. She bends over the bright feathery foliage to check, yes it is ysterbos, an infallible remedy for kidney disorders, and for something else, but she can't remember other than that the old people treasured their bunches of dried ysterbos.

'So close to home,' she sighs, 'and it is quite another world, a darker, greener world. Look, water!' And we look up into the shaded slope. A fine thread of water trickles down its ancient worn path, down the layered rock. Towards the bottom it spreads and seeps and feeds woman-high reeds where strange red birds dart and rustle.

The road levels off for a mile or so but there are outcroppings of rock all around us.

'Here we must be closer to heaven,' she says. 'Father would've loved it here. What a pity he didn't make it.'

I fail to summon his face flushed with pleasure; it is the stern Sunday face of the deacon that passes before me. She laughs.

'Of course he would only think of the sheep, of how many he could keep on an acre of this green veld.'

We spread out our food on a ledge and rinse the tomatoes in a stone basin. The flask of coffee has been sweetened with condensed milk and the Van Rhynsdorp bread is crumbly with whole grains of wheat. Mamma apologises for no longer baking her own. I notice for the first time a slight limp as she walks, the hips working unevenly against a face of youthful eagerness as we wander off.

'And here,' I concede, 'are the proteas.'

Busy bushes, almost trees, that plump out from the base. We look at the familiar tall chalice of leathery pink and as we move around the bush, deciding, for we must decide now whether the chalice is more attractive than the clenched fist of the imbricated bud, a large whirring insect performs its aerobatics in the branches, distracting, so that we linger and don't know. Then the helicopter leads us further, to the next bush where another type beckons. These are white protea torches glowing out of their silver-leafed branches. The flowers are open, the petals separated to the mould of a cupped hand so that the feathery parts quiver to the light.

'I wonder why the Boers chose the protea as national flower,' I muse, and find myself humming mockingly:

Suikerbossie'k wil jou hê,
Wat sal jou Mamma daarvan sê...

She harmonises in a quavering voice.

'Do you remember,' she says, 'how we sang? All the hymns and carols and songs on winter evenings. You never could harmonise.' Then generously she adds, 'Of course there was no one else to sing soprano.'

'I do, I do.'

We laugh at how we held concerts, the three of us practising for weeks as if there would be an audience. The mere idea of public performance turns the tugging condition of loneliness into an exquisite terror. One night at the power of her command the empty room would become a packed auditorium of rustles and whispers. And around the pan of glowing embers the terror thawed as I opened my mouth to sing. With a bow she would offer around the bowl of raisins and walnuts to an audience still sizzling with admiration.

'And now,' she says, 'I suppose you actually go to concerts and theatres?'

'Yes. Sometimes.'

'I can't imagine you in lace and feathers eating walnuts and raisins in the interval. And your hair? What do you do with that bush?'

'Some perfectly sensible people,' I reply, 'pay pounds to turn their sleek hair into precisely such a bushy tangle.'

'But you won't exchange your boskop for all the daisies in Namaqualand! Is that sensible too? And you say you're happy with your hair? Always? Are you really?'

'I think we ought to go. The sun's getting too hot for me.'

'Down there the earth is baking at ninety degrees. You won't find anywhere cooler than here in the mountains.'

We drive in silence along the last of the incline until we reach what must be the top of the Gifberge. The road is flanked by cultivated fields and a column of smoke betrays a hidden farmhouse.

'So they grow things on the mountain?'

'Hmm,' she says pensively, 'someone once told me it was fertile up here, but I had no idea of the farm!'

The bleached mealie stalks have been stripped of their cobs and in spite of the rows lean arthritically in the various directions that pickers have elbowed them. On the other side a crop of pumpkins lies scattered like stones, the foliage long since shrivelled to dust. But the fields stop abruptly where the veld resumes. Here the bushes are shorter and less green than in the pass. The road carries on for two miles until we reach a fence. The gate before us is extravagantly barred; I count thirteen padlocks.

'What a pity,' she says in a restrained voice, 'that we can't get to the edge. We should be able to look down on to the plain, at the strip of irrigated vines along the canal, and the white dorp and even our houses on the hill.'

I do not mind. It is mid-afternoon and the sun is fierce and I am not allowed to complain about the heat. But her face crumples. For her the trip is spoiled. Here, yards from the very edge, the place of her imagination has still not materialised. Nothing will do but the complete reversal of the image of herself in the wicker chair staring into the unattainable blue of the mountain. And now, for one brief moment, to look down from these very heights at the cars crawling along the dust roads, at the diminished people, at where her chair sits empty on the arid plain of Klein Namaqualand.

Oh, she ought to have known, at her age ought not to expect the unattainable ever to be anything other than itself. Her disappointment is unnerving. Like a tigress she paces along the cleared length of fence. She cannot believe its power when the bushes disregard it with such ease. Oblivious roots trespass with impunity and push up their stems on the other side. Branches weave decoratively through the diamond mesh of the wire.

'Why are you so impatient?' she complains. 'Let's have an apple then you won't feel you're wasting your time. You're on holiday, remember.'

I am ashamed of my irritation. In England I have learnt to cringe at the thought of wandering about, hanging about idly. Loitering even on

this side of the fence makes me feel like a trespasser. If someone were
to question my right to be here ... I shudder.

She examines the padlocks in turn, as if there were a possibility of
picking the locks.

'You could climb over, easy,' she says.

'But I've no desire to.'

'Really? You don't?' She is genuinely surprised that our wishes do not
coincide.

'I think I saw an old hut on our way up,' she says as we drive back
through the valley. We go slow until she points, there, there, and we
stop. It is further from the road than it seems and her steps are so slow
that I take her arm. Her fluttering breath alarms me.

It is probably an abandoned shepherd's hut. The reed roof, now
reclaimed by birds, has parted in place to let in shafts of light. On the
outside the raw brick has been nibbled at by wind and rain so that the
pattern of rectangles is no longer discernible. But the building does
provide shelter from the sun. Inside, a bush flourishes in the earth floor.

'Is it ghanna?' I ask.

'No, but it's related, I think. Look, the branches are a paler grey,
almost feathery. It's Hotnos-kooigoed.'

'You mean Khoi-Khoi-kooigoed.'

'Really, is that the educated name for them? It sounds right doesn't
it?' And she repeats Khoi-Khoi-kooigoed, relishing the alliteration.

'No, it's just what they called themselves.'

'Let's try it,' she says, and stumbles out to where the bushes grow in
abundance. They lift easily out of the ground and she packs the
uprooted bushes with the one indoors to form a cushion. She lies down
carefully and mutters about the heat, the fence, the long long day, and
I watch her slipping off to sleep. On the shaded side of the hut I pack
a few of the bushes together and sink my head into the softness. The
heat has drawn out the thymish balm that settles soothingly about my
head. I drift into a drugged sleep.

Later I am woken by the sun creeping round on to my legs. Mamma
starts out of her sleep when I enter the hut with the remaining coffee.

'I must take up a little white protea bush for my garden,' she says as we walk back to the bakkie.

'If you must,' I retort. 'And then you can hoist the South African flag and sing "Die Stem".'

'Don't be silly; it's not the same thing at all. You who're so clever ought to know that proteas belong to the veld. Only fools and cowards would hand them over to the Boers. Those who put their stamp on things may see in it their own histories and hopes. But a bush is a bush; it doesn't become what people think they inject into it. We know who lived in these mountains when the Europeans were still shivering in their own country. What they think of the veld and its flowers is of no interest to me.'

As we drive back we watch an orange sun plummet behind the hills. Mamma's limp is pronounced as she gets out of the bakkie and hobbles in to put on the kettle. We are hungry. We had not expected to be out all day. The journey has tired her more than she will admit.

I watch the stars in an ink-blue sky. The Milky Way is a smudged white on the dark canvas; the Three Kings flicker, but the Southern Cross drills her four points into the night. I find the long axis and extend it two and a half times, then drop a perpendicular, down on to the tip of the Gifberge, down on to the lights of the Soeterus Winery. Due South.

When I take Mamma a cup of cocoa, I say, 'I wouldn't be surprised if I came back to live in Cape Town again.'

'Is it?' Her eyes nevertheless glow with interest.

'Oh, you won't approve of me here either. Wasted education, playing with dynamite and all that.'

'Ag man, I'm too old to worry about you. But with something to do here at home perhaps you won't need to make up those terrible stories hey?'

DEVIL AT A DEAD END

Miriam Tlali

She arrived at Ficksburg Station at 2.30pm. It would be a good half hour before the Durban train to Bethlehem arrived. The thought made her smile. She was early. Her mother would have congratulated her for the achievement. She remembered, with the smile still on her face, how she would always say to them, 'My children, learn to be in time always. The passenger should wait for the train, and not expect the train to wait for her.'

She descended the stairs facing the open window of the booking office. Through the round opening at eye level she could hear that the booking clerk was engaged in conversation with someone, a female.

She carefully place a R10 banknote on the small, concave, coin-eroded wooden base, letting it protrude into the other side through the semi-circular opening over the plank. She waited, wondering about the contact and remembering what the taxi driver had said: 'You don't know this Boer clerk here. He can be very furious when you ask for a second-class ticket without having made a booking beforehand. Anyway, try. Speak to him in 'Se-Buru' and not English. They are more tolerant when you address them in their own language.'

'Ja?' the clerk said, banging impatiently on the base and startling her.

'Can I ... Kan ek 'n tweede-klas kaartjie kry na Johannesburg-toe, asseblief?'

'Het jy bespreking gemaak?'

'Nee, ek ...'

'Wel, nee. Natuurlik kan jy nie!' he snapped.

And without much ado, he grabbed the money and deposited (or shall I say he flung) a ticket and change in banknotes with some silver and bronze coins on the base. The girl tried to plead, saying she was from very far away, in the outlying areas of Leribe district in Lesotho. The clerk gazed at her, his fierce-looking, cat-like, bespectacled grey eyes looking like an abyss, with the pupils dilating and contracting. She flinched and dropped her eyes. In that instant, the furious clerk grunted and, with a hard bang, drew the wooden shutter over the window-pane. The girl bent down slowly. A black railway policeman who was standing a few metres away scurried nearer, and together they picked up some of the coins which had landed on the concrete floor. He asked, 'Did you want a second-class ticket, my sister?'

'Yes.'

'They usually insist that you make a booking two weeks before the intended date of departure.'

'How does one make a booking when you come from so far away? I would have to spend two days along the way. You know where Nqechane is.'

'I know,' said the policeman, nodding. 'And when you make a booking by phone, they ignore you. Some even try sending telegrams; but these are never noted. Anyway, don't worry. When you get to Bethlehem, ask the ticket examiner to convert your ticket to second class. The new Line trains via Balfour are usually not fully booked. Then at least you won't have to stand the whole night right up to Johannesburg.'

The siren of the oncoming steam locomotive became audible and minutes later the train pulled into the platform. The kind policeman helped the girl into the packed third-class coach and one of the passengers on the train extended his arms to receive the girl's bags. She thanked both men for their courtesy.

There seemed to be no sitting space available, and there was no point in attempting to move any further than where she was. She leaned against a window and arranged her three bags on the floor along the side of the passage wall. One bag she clamped between her feet and the other two she nestled against her jutting slim ankles. She could at least *feel* her bags all the time, she thought gratefully, as she clung to her handbag.

The train moved on slowly, stopping at the many sidings and stations and winding its way laboriously over the steep slopes. She closed her eyes and listened, wishing that she were at least lying down. That distance she had walked on foot! She thought of the booking clerk at Ficksburg and his eyes.

'It will be raining by the time we get to Bethlehem, can you see that, my sister?'

Only then was she aware of the presence of the kind man who had received her on to the train. She opened her eyes and noticed that the clouds were gathering fast and she nodded in response to the question. She could not make out whether the young man was coloured or Indian or African; she finally decided to dismiss the matter and not let her mind dwell on it. She looked through the open window into the peaceful receding landscape outside. Her searching eyes quickly spotted the mountain peak of Nqechane and she thought of the tranquillity of the past three weeks she had spent at the beautiful village bearing the name of the peak. Everything was just as she remembered it when she was still a child.

She closed her eyes and her thoughts drifted on, rocked by the swaying rhythmic movements of the train... She thought of the horrible eyes of the booking clerk at Ficksburg.

She recollected that she had not been in contact with a single white person for the duration of her holiday. She had had perfect peace. No; she corrected herself – with the exception of 'Mè Sistèrè', the Mother Superior at the nearby Nqechane Anglican Mission, and 'Ntate Fatèrè', the Priest-in-Charge. But those were different, she argued with herself.

They even extended a friendly arm to greet you. That is why she had forgotten about them. But of course there was her first contact with those white people at the border post of Ficksburg – how on earth could she forget that? She could not remember that contact because she had the Open-Sesame – the *brown* Travel Document of the Republic and not the *green* Lesotho Local Passport. It was precisely because of those first *contacts* that she had at last decided to change from green to brown. The nauseating numerous questions they used to ask when you wanted to come to any part of this Republic, especially Johannesburg. As if crossing a mere river meant the same thing as going from heaven to hell or vice versa. What did it matter what you crossed to get where anyway? They would ask you:

Why do you want to go to Johannesburg?
To what address?
How long are you going to be there?
How much money have you got in your purse – will you be able to pay for a return ticket?

And more often than not, you would be refused permission. Your *green* document would be flung at you and you would have to turn right back with your carefully prepared chicken provision and dumplings in your tin trunk and all. They wouldn't even consider the sacrifices you made to get to that post at all. Like how many days and nights you travelled on foot; or whether there are any buses where you come from; or, if there are buses, whether you were able to pay the fare or not. Whether your reasons for visiting the Republic were valid or not depended mainly on whether the 'nonnie' had prepared a good breakfast for the particular 'baas' at the post at the time or not. Of late, even when you claimed that there was a death of a close relation of yours at that address in the Republic, they would turn you back. *Death*, not illness, Death – what is worse than Death? And even if you actually produced a telegram to prove your claim they were not ashamed to ask you whether you were going to *eat* that corpse. 'What are you going to do with the dead person?' they ask you. She remembered how, when she got tired of all those stinking questions, she had taken the advice of her friend: leave the green thing in the bag and cross the river – walk or swim over it or across it, that's all.

But that too presented problems: the inevitable arrangements with the 'professional' river escorts, the ones who knew, or professed to know, when, where, and how to cross the Caledon in order to avoid contact with the whites at the border post with your green book. Armed sentries are known to carry on continuous patrols along the banks of the river. And these do not hesitate to open fire. These are some of the reasons which make those escorts indispensable.. In addition, the escorts would have to come to some agreement with the inspectors at the customs barriers. These would have to pass your luggage without asking too many questions. There would have to be some prior negotiations with people near the river on the other side to accommodate you where you could sit and dry your clothes while you waited to be reunited with your luggage. Some accidents were known to happen and this could incur heavy losses of valuables especially if the escorts were not adequately compensated. The whole process became more and more expensive.

She thought of the last straw, when she decided to bury her green book for ever and vowed to go to any lengths to acquire a brown one. She recalled bitterly that it was all because of that abominable barbed wire fence. Who ever thought that those white officials on this side would ever think of going to the extent of actually erecting a barbed wire fence right along the meandering Caledon River? Honestly! Just to bring about that contact. She had first to be carried across the full river, and then over a nearly seven-foot-high barbed wire fence by yelling, giggling, curious youths who obviously found it amusing and gratifying – the experience of coddling ordinarily inaccessible parts of the anatomy of a partially clad woman! She had her *brown* travel documents in her handbag now, and all that ordeal was over, thank God.

She thought of those eyes of the white booking clerk.

Just after 6pm, the train steamed steadily into Platform One at Bethlehem. A strong wind blew from the Drakensberg Mountains in the east and swept the raindrops into the faces of the alighting passengers, now rushing towards the smelly non-white waiting-rooms just outside the station, about twenty metres from the railway line.

'I will take these, my sister,' said the voice of the kind young man, relieving her of two of her bags.

'Thanks,' she said.

They joined the seemingly endless moving stream of passengers to the waiting-rooms.

At exactly 7pm the black announcer came round swinging a large loudspeaker and shouting into its mouthpiece, 'Ba eang Gauteng ba ee ho Platform Three! Ba eang Gauteng ba ee ho Platform Three! ...'

Still accompanied by the willing strange young man, the girl followed the long procession over the narrow bridge.

On Platform Three, there were two guards standing and chatting near the wooden benches. The girl said to the young man, 'I want to ask the guard to convert my ticket from third- to second-class, but I'm reluctant. I travelled on foot and by bus the whole day and I'm tired. I wouldn't be able to stand the whole night right to Johannesburg.'

'Where are you from, my sister?'

'Nqechane, in the Leribe District.'

'Oh. I don't even know where that is; I'm from Bloemfontein. Do go. I'll accompany you into the compartment and return to the third-class coaches.'

'And where are you going to?'

'Also Johannesburg.'

Reluctantly, and with a feeling of apprehension, the girl moved towards the two guards, who looked at her questioningly as she approached. She suddenly became conscious of her high platform shoes. She moved slowly. She would have to avoid the risk of tripping, she thought. She was thankful that her wide-bottomed balooba denim pair of slacks concealed her knees which were by now impulsively knocking against each other. Her step, which was normally graceful and confident, was faltering ... She thought of the white booking clerk at Ficksburg. Not knowing who of the two white men to refer her request to, she held her ticket before them and asked, 'Kan ek hierdie kaartjie verander tot tweede-klas asseblief?'

And without appearing to pay much attention, the man on her right-hand side said, signalling to the nearby coach with the 'Non-Whites – Reserved' sign on it, 'Gaan in die "C" Kompartement.'

With great relief and a smile on her face, she obeyed. She had been fortunate ... She thought of the furious eyes of the clerk at the booking office in Ficksburg. On her way, she passed the 'B' compartment and noticed that there was only one black lady in it. She smiled and nodded expectantly when the girl greeted her. The girl hesitated. She stopped and asked her, 'Are you with other passengers in here, Mother?'

'No, my child, I'm alone in here. Haven't seen any others arriving.'

He *did* say 'C', she thought, puzzled.

She passed on to the next compartment. It was also unoccupied. She put her bags on the cushioned green bunk. She looked around. It was clean and comfortable – a welcome change from the third-class coaches she had been standing in from Ficksburg. Only the stale familiar odour of the inevitable Dettol that, she had come to know, one would have to learn to live with. It was permanent, and it seemed to have been built into the very heavily wood-panelled walls of the compartments. Like the inlaid, meaningless landscape photographs of the sunny South Africa which seemed to strive to create beauty in surroundings where most of the time only ugliness and cruelty prevailed.

She decided to speak to the elderly lady next-door. After exchanging the usual formalities, she remarked, 'I wonder why the guard said I must go into "C" when you are alone here. The usual procedure is to let females share the same compartment, and the male passengers also their own, isn't it?'

'I wondered why you passed into "C", but then I thought you had more ladies accompanying you, my child.'

'No. I'm alone.'

They both smiled. She folded her arms over her bosom and sighed, still smiling, and remarked, twisting the ends of her lips and raising her eyebrows, 'Perhaps he wants to pay you a visit.'

'A visit?' the girl asked, surprised ... She thought of the booking clerk at Ficksburg, and realised that she would have the image of those grey cruel eyes on her for a long time. She said, 'I don't thing he'd do that.'

'Why, my child?'

The girl shrugged her shoulders vigorously, and answered, 'I don't know. But somehow they don't seem to know that we are human beings like *them*.'

'You're still very young, aren't you?' and she peeped through the window, pointing. 'You see that train in that platform on the other side? It's full of soldiers. All those white soldiers there, can you see them?'

'Yes. All carrying guns and filing into the train with kitbags. What about them?'

'Yes. They're soldiers. I don't know who they are fighting or why. One teacher told me that they are fighting black people somewhere in the north. They have a big camp just outside Bethlehem. That's where they learn how to shoot and all about fighting. When you pass there, you'll always see them drilling, playing all sorts of games. No black woman moves in that area without men to protect her. They chase them into the dongas and grab them by force. Would they do that if they didn't think we're humans?'

The girls shook her head. 'I'd like to go into the cloakroom or toilet there and do some washing up before I sit and eat something. Shall I leave my bags in your compartment? Surely he can't expect me to sit alone there. What happens if I should want to visit the small house, take everything with me? The same thing applies with *you* too. People want to sit together and speak. It can be very lonely. I'd rather be in here with you.'

The train left Bethlehem. The ticket examiner came and issued the new second-class ticket without appearing to notice anything amiss or out of order. He did not seem to mind the two women being together. They both ordered bedding. He was very formal and to the point; he then left.

'I'll wait until you come back, then it will be my turn and you can stay with the luggage.'

The girl left, taking her handbag and adding into it a few of the items she would need. She returned about twelve minutes later, feeling refreshed and no longer so tired. 'It's *your* turn now, Mother,' she said to the smiling lady.

'Hm ...You smell sweet, and look like a fresh peach!'

'Thanks.' The girl blushed.

She was just reaching up to ease her sling bag into the baggage rack above, when the guard stood at the door. He looked at the girl, noticing the bare portion of her ebony torso and the pronounced umbilical groove, reducing her slim waistline even more. Trying to look at him and noticing his fixed stare, she withdrew her arm almost instinctively and readjusted the hem of her short blouse. She pulled it down to cover her bare waist and felt uncomfortable when he shifted his eyes from her body to meet hers.

'Where's your companion?' he asked, smiling and frowning.

'Who?'

'Your escort or husband. The man who was with you when you entered the coach.'

'Oh. He ...'

The man did not wait to hear what the girl said because just then the elderly woman appeared at the end of the narrow passage and he moved away, tapping at the next door, smiling and giving her way to pass. She went into the compartment and shut the door behind her, whispering and smiling. 'What did I tell you? Didn't I tell you that he'd pay you a visit?'

'He asked me where the man who was carrying my bags had gone to. He said something about "husband" and when I tried to explain, he saw *you* coming and just left.'

'Oh, jealous!'

They both laughed.

'He knows I'm getting off at Villiers; but don't worry, it will be dawn already. I suppose he'll get tired of waiting.'

Not long after they had shared their provisions and had exhausted their long 'introductions' in the usual African way, the coloured attendant came to prepare their beds from the 'non-white' bedding kits. They went to bed and switched off the lights. The swaying train and the steady drizzle outside lulled them into a peaceful sleep as it traversed the unending, beautiful maize fields.

During the early hours of the morning, the guard knocked at the door to warn the elderly lady that the train was nearing Villiers, and disappeared. She felt reluctant to wake up the girl to bid her goodbye; thinking that she might find it difficult to sleep again after her departure. She decided to wake her up, anyway, as she felt that it would be cruel for her to just walk out. She bade the girl farewell and assured her that there was the coloured attendant in the nearby compartment and that she thought she had heard other passengers move into the other compartments. She explained, 'I know most third-class people usually come to the coach where the guard is only to get their tickets and then go back to third. But perhaps some of them were second-class passengers.' She bent down and whispered into the girl's ear, 'I don't think he'll ignore their presence. Besides – the law! Just make sure you lock the door from inside, my child.'

The train glided out of the platform. It was a smooth, quiet motion and she remembered that the coaches were now being drawn by an electric engine. She lay quietly, listening ... She thought of the ticket examiner's strange behaviour, and she remembered those eyes of the booking clerk at Ficksburg station.

From afar, came the low rumble of thunder. She moved out of her bed and walked to the other window, rolled up the blind and opened it. She looked out. The wide expanse of farmlands lay completely deserted, enveloped in pitch-black darkness. The lights piercing through the train windows struck the falling raindrops and formed rays of oblique streaks of glittering lines, descending heavily against the side of the coaches. The rain was pouring in torrents. There was no sign of life in the coach in which she was. Where was the coloured attendant anyway – fast asleep, she wondered? Was Johannesburg still far to go? She could not sleep.

The train stopped. It was a big station – 'Balfour North', the sign read. When the train was about to leave, the guard emerged from a room on the platform and stood next to the train, facing expectantly towards the fore end. He noticed the girl withdraw her head into the compartment and draw the blinds.

He blew his whistle and shouted, 'Balfour North!' and the train pulled out of the platform.

The door yielded easily when the guard prised the lever with his key. She turned, startled, and aware that she was scantily dressed in her flimsy nightie. She tried to move towards her bed and he intercepted her saying, 'It's dark. You needn't be afraid. I've just come to chat with you, that's all, please. I'm lonely in my cubicle, please. Please,' he begged, speaking calmly.

She asked, 'Chat about what?'

He smiled, asking, 'Where did you say your husband went to?'

'He's not my husband. He was a stranger. He helped me carry my luggage over the steps in Bethlehem.'

'What is he of yours?'

'What do you mean?'

'Can I turn on the very dim light, please? I like to see your beautiful face; can I?' the man said, reaching for the switch. The dim light came on. He smiled into the girl's face, and she drew away.

'I mean: is he your 'nyatsi' or what?' he said, twisting his eyebrows and smiling mischievously.

She sat on the cushioned bunk and watched him remove his cap and put it on the steel peg above the door. It struck her that the man's manner and tone of speech, which had been formal and austere in the presence of the middle-aged lady, had now changed to familiarity. His behaviour had altered like a reversible cloak; like a garment you either decided to keep on or strip off, just like that. She was not sure she liked the metamorphosis, but she became more curious ... She thought of the Ficksburg station booking clerk's eyes.

She remembered that she once heard a person saying that most whites first learnt swear words in the vocabulary of the African languages. She asked, 'What did you say he was of mine?'

'Your "nyatsi",' he repeated, emphasising the word.

'We travelled together from Ficksburg. He helped me with my baggage; and I was late. The train nearly left me. I was lucky to meet a sympathetic person.'

' Why were you late? Flirting, I suppose.'

'No. I was pleading with the booking clerk to sell me a second-class ticket and he was refusing.'

'And so your companion came to *console* you?' and he mentioned the word 'troos' (console), already moving towards her. He asked, 'How about letting *me* do that, then? I'd like to comfort you. I'd enjoy it very much,' he said, coming near her as the girl receded, petrified. 'Don't be afraid, please. Come; just stand up. Come, man; don't be so lazy. Just stand up and let's have some fun. Just a little love making,' the guard implored, touching her slim shoulders tenderly and stroking them. 'Come. It won't hurt, please. Come on, hold me tight, tight!' he demanded, taking the girl's hands and crossing them behind him. The girl slackened her grip, but he stopped her. 'Don't do that, please. All right, just clasp me tightly against you and I'll be satisfied.'

He held her face in both his hands and pressed it against his warm, impetuous body, raising her chin. The girl closed her eyes. 'Don't close your eyes, please. They're *so* beautiful. Look at me. Look into my eyes, please.'

The girl kept her eyes closed. She was thinking of the haunting, furious eyes of the booking clerk at Ficksburg. He switched off the light. 'Come now. Stand up. We shall soon be in Johannesburg. Please. You're hard, man – unyielding. Why?' he asked. He looked at his wrist watch in the dark. The green arms and the circle of dots were vivid and luminous. 'Just wait for me; I'm coming. There's a station nearby.'

The girl sat trembling and feeling guilty. She reprimanded herself, I should be screaming for help or something. She sat waiting. She was surprised at herself. She had been like a bewildered beholder, powerless. She had abandoned herself into the arms of a strange white man who did not even know her name. An expert who obviously knew what he was doing. She was taken aback at what seemed to be a response by a part of herself over which she had no control. She felt like a being apart, looking on. She waited, dismayed.

She listened. It was quiet outside. The storm had subsided. There was no downpour here. The torrent seemed to have been cut with a knife.

She heard the now-familiar voice of the ticket examiner. He yelled, 'Union!'

The train glided slowly out of the platform.

The next moment, the guard darted stealthily up the two steps in a single stride. He sneaked quietly into the dimly lit compartment. Without uttering a word, and with one powerful wrench, he gathered the tender body of the woman in his arms and her face came to rest against his. He breathed the words tenderly into her ear, 'Come on now, please!'

She slowly wrapped her shaky, reluctant arms around the warm neck of the guard. They stood there and kissed. She could feel his strong muscles move as he gently stroked her back. He moved his exploring hands down her midriff and below. His knees seemed to sag and he knelt on the edge of the cushioned bunk. As his left hand caressed the girl's firm nipple, his right hand felt for the switch and lowered it. The darkness surrounded them completely, isolating them from the rest of the world. She thought of the fiery, bottomless eyes of the booking clerk at Ficksburg station.

Almost in a whisper, his warm breath pouring like steam over her naked body, he pleaded. 'Kom,' he said, 'kom nou, toe, kom. Dis net die twee van ons; toemaar. Dis net ons twee; kom.'

In the darkness, and with his eyes closed tightly, his warm, quavering, salivating tongue groped towards the girl's navel, and spotting it, sank into its hollow warmness.

'Oh God help me. Let *something* happen ...' The girl's conscience, her soul, stood aloof, untouched, admonishing. Her heart was pounding fast, but only with a feeling of guilt. 'What if my parents, my husband ... What if ...? Oh no, no, no!'

Still kneeling and salivating like Pavlov's dog, the man continued to plead anxiously, 'Kom nou, kom ... ag tog ... asseblief, kom ...'

She drew a deep breath, lifting her face and looking up into the darkness; waiting for something, some miracle.

In times of threat, some invisible omnipotent power seems always to be waiting to come to the aid of the helpless, the weak, the defenceless. It was not through a cannon that David vanquished Goliath.

The girl remembered ... Somewhere in the Christian scriptures, they say, a maiden had hidden a potion in her bosom, and she did not want to be searched. The words entered her mind and she uttered them mechanically: '*Ntate se nkame hobane ke silafetse* ...' Her lips mumbled the entreaty, softly and uncertainly ... 'Father, do not touch me because I am unclean ...'

Then repeating loudly, drawing back and pushing the kneeling man, she gasped, 'Se nkame hobane ke silafetse ... ke metse *mokoala!*' (Do not touch me because I am afflicted with a venereal sickness.)

'Mokoala!'... One of those detestable, ominous words. The impact of that word was quick, merciless, shocking and immediately disarming. Like when in a dark alley you suddenly grope into a dead end. She stood still, listening to the sound of receding breath. She reached below the bunk above and lowered the dim switch. She watched the recoiling devilish figure and drew a sigh of relief.

COMRADES

Nadine Gordimer

As Mrs Hattie Telford pressed the electronic gadget that deactivates the alarm device in her car a group of youngsters came up behind her. Black. But no need to be afraid; this was not a city street. This was a non-racial enclave of learning, a place where tended flowerbeds and trees bearing botanical identification plates civilised the wild reminder of campus guards and dogs. The youngsters, like her, were part of the crowd loosening into dispersion after a university conference on People's Education. They were the people to be educated; she was one of the committee of white and black activists (convenient generic for revolutionaries, leftists secular and Christian, fellow-travellers and liberals) up on the platform.

– Comrade ... – She was settling in the driver's seat when one so slight and slim he seemed a figure in profile came up to her window. He drew courage from the friendly lift of the woman's eyebrows above blue eyes, the tilt of her freckled white face: – Comrade, are you going to town? –

No, she was going in the opposite direction, home ... but quickly, in the spirit of the hall where these young people had been somewhere, somehow present with her (ah no, she with them) stamping and singing Freedom songs, she would take them to the bus station their spokesman named.

– Climb aboard! –

The others got in the back, the spokesman beside her. She saw the nervous white of his eyes as he glanced at and away from her. She searched for talk to set them at ease. Questions, of course. Older people always start with questioning young ones. Did they come from Soweto?

They came from Harrismith, Phoneng Location.

She made the calculation: about two hundred kilometres distant. How did they get here? Who told them about the conference?

– We are Youth Congress in Phoneng. –

A delegation. They had come by bus; one of the groups and stragglers who kept arriving long after the conference had started. They had missed, then, the free lunch?

At the back, no one seemed even to be breathing. The spokesman must have had some silent communication with them, some obligation to speak for them created by the journey or by other shared experience in the mysterious bonds of the young – these young. – We are hungry. – And from the back seats was drawn an assent like the suction of air in a compressing silence.

She was silent in response, for the beat of a breath or two. These large gatherings both excited and left her over-exposed, open and vulnerable to the rub and twitch of the mass shuffling across rows of seats and loping up the aisles, babies' fudge-brown soft legs waving as their napkins are changed on mothers' laps, little girls with plaited loops on their heads listening like old crones, heavy women swaying to chants, men with fierce, unreadably black faces breaking into harmony tender and deep as they sing to God for his protection of Umkhonto weSizwe, as people on both sides have always, everywhere, claimed divine protection for their soldiers, their wars. At the end of a day like this she wanted a drink, she wanted the depraved luxury of solitude and quiet in which she would be restored (enriched, oh yes! by the day) to the familiar limits of her own being.

Hungry. Not for iced whisky and feet up. It seemed she had scarcely hesitated: – Look, I live nearby, come back to my house and have something to eat. Then I'll run you into town. –

– That will be very nice. We can be glad for that. – And at the back the tight vacuum relaxed.

They followed her through the gate, shrinking away from the dog – she assured them he was harmless but he was large, with a fancy collar by which she held him. She trooped them in through the kitchen because that was the way she always entered her house, something she would not have done if they had been adult, her black friends whose sophistication might lead them to believe the choice of entrance was an unthinking historical slight. As she was going to feed them, she took them not into her living-room with its sofas and flowers but into her dining-room, so that they could sit at table right away. It was a room in confident taste that could afford to be spare: bare floorboards, matching golden wooden ceiling, antique brass chandelier, reed blinds instead of stuffy curtains. An African wooden sculpture represented a lion marvellously released from its matrix in the grain of a Mukwa tree-trunk. She pulled up the chairs and left the four young men while she went back to the kitchen to make coffee and see what there was in the refrigerator for sandwiches. They had greeted the maid, in the language she and they shared, on their way through the kitchen, but when the maid and the lady of the house had finished preparing cold meat and bread, and the coffee was ready, she suddenly did not want them to see that the maid waited on her. She herself carried the heavy tray into the dining-room.

They are sitting round the table, silent, and there is no impression that they stopped an undertone exchange when they heard her approaching. She doles out plates, cups. They stare at the food but their eyes seem focused on something she can't see; something that overwhelms. She urges them: – Just cold meat, I'm afraid, but there's chutney if you like it ... milk everybody?... is the coffee too strong, I have a heavy hand, I know. Would anyone like to add some hot water? –

They eat. When she tries to talk to one of the others, he says *Ekskuus*? And she realises he doesn't understand English, of the white man's languages knows perhaps only a little of that of the Afrikaners in the rural town he comes from. Another gives his name, as if in some delicate acknowledgement of the food. – I'm Shadrack Nsutsha. – She repeats the surname to get it right. But he does not speak again. There is an urgent exchange of eye-language, and the spokesman holds out the emptied sugar-bowl to her. – Please. – She hurries to the kitchen and brings it back refilled. They need carbohydrate, they are hungry, they are young, they need it, they burn it up. She is distressed at the inadequacy of the meal and then notices the fruit bowl, the big copper fruit bowl, filled with apples and bananas, and perhaps there is a peach or two under the grape leaves with which she likes to complete an edible still life. – Have some fruit. Help yourselves. –

They are stacking their plates and cups, not knowing what they are expected to do with them in this room which is a room where apparently people only eat, do not cook, do not sleep. While they finish the bananas and apples (Shadrack Nsutsha had seen the single peach and quickly got there first) she talks to the spokesman, whose name she has asked for: Dumile. – Are you still at school, Dumile? – Of course he is not at school – *they* are not at school; youngsters their age have not been at school for several years, they are the children growing into young men and women for whom school is a battleground, a place of boycotts and demonstrations, the literacy of political rhetoric, the education of revolt against having to live the life their parents live. They have pompous titles of responsibility beyond childhood: he is chairman of his branch of the Youth Congress, he was expelled two years ago – for leading a boycott? Throwing stones at the police? Maybe burning the school down? He calls it all – quietly, abstractly, doesn't know many ordinary, concrete words but knows these euphemisms – – political activity – . No school for two years? No. – So what have you been able to do with yourself, all that time? –

She isn't giving him a chance to eat his apple. He swallows a large bite, shaking his head on its thin, little-boy neck. – I was inside. Detained from this June for six months. –

She looks round the others. – And you? –

Shadrack seems to nod slightly. The other two look at her. She should know, she should have known, it's a common enough answer from youths like them, their colour. They're not going to be saying they've been selected for the 1st Eleven at cricket or that they're off on a student tour to Europe in the school holidays.

The spokesman, Dumile, tells her he wants to study by correspondence, 'get his matric' that he was preparing for two years ago; two years ago when he was still a child, when he didn't have the hair that is now appearing on his face, making him a man, taking away the childhood. In the hesitations, the silences of the table, where there is nervously spilt coffee among plates of banana skins, there grows the certainty that he will never get the papers filled in for the correspondence college, he will never get the two years back. She looks at them all and cannot believe what she knows: that they, suddenly here in her house, will carry the AK-47s they only sing about, now, miming death as they sing. They will have a career of wiring explosives to the undersides of vehicles, they will go away and come back through the bush to dig holes not to plant trees to shade home, but to plant landmines. She can see they have been terribly harmed but cannot believe they could harm. They are wiping their fruit-sticky hands furtively palm against palm.

She breaks the silence; says something, anything.

– How d'you like my lion? Isn't he beautiful? He's made by a Zimbabwean artist, I think the name's Dube. –

But the foolish interruption becomes revelation. Dumile, in his gaze – distant, lingering, speechless this time – reveals what has overwhelmed them. In this room, the space, the expensive antique chandelier, the consciously simple choice of reed blinds, the carved lion: all are on the same level of impact, phenomena undifferentiated, undecipherable. Only the food that fed their hunger was real.

HOLDING BACK MIDNIGHT

Maureen Isaacson

The night is shooting past. It is bright jet and hot. The air is as smooth as the whiskey we sip on the verandah of the old hotel that has become my parents' home. We are safe from the faded neon and slow-moving traffic lights outside. The bubbles of fifty chilled bottles of champagne are waiting to spill as we touch down on the new century. In our own way, we each believe that from that moment on nothing will ever be the same.

Anything could happen at midnight. President Manzwe has said that he has a surprise for us. What can it be?

'Cheers!' shouts my mother. Old opals shine dully against her sagging lobes, her webbed neck. She is flushed, like a dead person who has been painted to receive her final respects.

'Cheers!' echoes her friend Ethel.

Smoke and disillusion have ravaged their voices. Their tongues are too slack to roll an olive pip. They walk slowly among the guests, in silver dresses that were fashionable once. They teeter on sling-back stilettos. They offer salmon and bits of fish afloat on shells of lettuce leaves.

Don't the people at this party ever think about AIDS? Out there in the real world, they give you cling paper gloves in restaurants lest you should bleed from an unnoticed cut. Waiters wear them. Doctors. Environmentalists, like my husband Leon and me. The lack of sterility makes me queasy tonight.

'What is the time, Dad?' I ask.

'Be patient,' he says.

Hopefully the moment we are waiting for will release him from the grip of history. History is ever-present in my father, like the patterns that shimmer from the chandeliers over the cracked walls. It is trapped in the broken paving outside this hotel where angels of delight once fluttered eyelashes as if they were wings at white men. History hovers, with the ghosts of the illicit couplings that once heated the hotel's shadowy rooms. It is funnelled through my memory.

Here comes my Uncle Otto, ex-Minister of Home Affairs, glass in hand. Looking at his ginger moustache, I am seven years old again. I am sitting on his lap at the bar. Don't tell your mother, he is saying. His hand is on my knee. I feel the closeness of flesh. Angels are rubbing themselves against the men. Men against angels.

'Why angels?' I want to know.

'Because they take the white men to heaven,' says Uncle Otto.

Like the street names that have been removed for their Euro-centricity, my parents and their friends are displaced. They do not understand the new signs. Their silhouettes glide across the garden, outlining their nostalgia. Through the shrill chirp of the crickets, I catch the desolation in the voices. The talk of lifts that no longer work, of the rubbish that piles up. There goes our old dentist Louis Dutoit and his wife Joyce, speaking of 'Old Johannesburg'. For all the world we are still there. Except for Leon and me of course. We could not have married in the old days, him being coloured and all. Doctor Dutoit would not even have filled Leon's teeth.

How graciously they tolerate us now. We have breezed in from our communal plot in the outer limits of the mega-city these people are too afraid to visit.

'Not without an AK-4777 rifle,' my father has said.

Instead they ruminate in this, the last of the shrunken ghettos that began to decline when cheap labour went out. Not for them the spread of shebeens and malls that splash jazz from what used to be poverty-stricken townships to the City Hall. The place we now call Soweto City. Connected by skyway and flyway, over and underground, as steady as the steel and the foreign funding on which it runs. Talk about one door closing. The Old Order was not yet cold in its grave and the place was gyrating, like a woman in love.

And the people out there? There are millions of us – living the good life advertised by laser-honed graphics that dazzle the streets. We are fast-living. Street-wise. Natural. We till the land. Our food is organic. See this party dress? It's made of paper. Tomorrow I'll shred it. Recycle later.

I thank heavens for Leon. I envy him his equilibrium. Forgive and forget. That's what he said before we came here tonight. His kind of thinking has helped me cope with the effect my parents have on me.

'Thank the Lord Leon's surname is also Laubscher. Some people will never know,' is all they said when I told them about our marriage.

Dad is the perfect host. But earlier this evening his sentimentality got the better of him when Uncle Otto reminded him of the New Year's Eve parties, five times the size of this one, held at our old house. Foreign diplomats, caviar, black truffles in Italian rice. Now he embraces Ethel. One-two. One-two. He dances a little jig with her on the verandah, cooled by the breeze that fans the palm tree. I squirm, reminded of the way he used to cavort when the hotel was in its prime.

'I'm a miner at heart,' he used to say, insisting that the place was a private sideline of no consequence.

Was anyone fooled into believing it was anything but a thriving business? We had more maids than rooms that needed polishing in our double-storey house. My parents had owned three game farms and four cars. A relic of the Old Regime, my father will never forgive the New Order for destroying his life-style. I am sure that in his dreams he still sells the kisses of angels to those who would cross the forbidden colour line by night, endorse it by day.

'Would you like to dance?' asks Paul Schoeman, once the minister of Law and Order. 'Mona Lisa ...,' sings Nat King Cole. I shuffle. Our feet collide. He holds me close, looks into my eyes and says, 'How can you live in the native township?'

I am unable to persuade old Schoeman that the change has brought with it a downswing in crime. I say all the things my father will not hear. But like Dad he does not grasp a word about redistribution. About progress. How can they when they insist without blinking that English and Afrikaans are still the official languages?

'You talk too much,' he says and pulls me towards him, gripping me so tightly that my left nipple sets off his security panic button, the kind my parents pay a fortune to wear round their necks. A siren wails. Up here on the verandah, men remove the fleshy fingers they have been rolling over their wives' naked, sagging backs. The whites of the wives' eyes show. Paul Schoeman grabs my breast. I scream. I put my hands to my ears. I want to block out the wailing. The barking of the Rottweilers. The gibbering of the guests. Four armed response security guards appear. Their sobriety creates a striking contrast.

They are not amused when my father says, 'False alarm. Who let the dogs out?' Leon is nowhere to be seen.

'Have a snack,' mother offers. It is anchovy, tart and salty.

'Is it nearly time for champagne?' I want to know.

'It won't be long now,' says Dad, as if he were meting out a punishment.

'What is the time?' shouts someone. One minute to midnight, says my watch. My father pours me another whiskey.

'Be patient', he commands. Any minute now, I tell myself.

'To the year two thousand!' I shout. 'To the future!'

'There is nothing to look forward to.' Dad's voice is weighed down. Now two of him are saying, 'This is the future.' The thick curl of his cigar smoke throws me back into a time when I believed that he had power over the planets. Now I am starting to believe that my father is actually capable of holding back midnight. I want to call the security guards with their military boots and pistols to return.

'Do you want to see the real danger we face here tonight?' I will ask.

Then I will see what they can do about the fear that washes this party like a backward-moving current.

I am standing alone when it happens. The blackness of the sky is split as fire crackers explode brightly into two million broken stars. An ethereal chorus resounds above the voice of Nat King Cole, above the marabi jazz that plays on Station Nnwe in the background. As the heavens shift, time dissolves and my rapture rises.

Down below, the profusion of papyrus plants, the beds of lobelia, chrysanthemum and wild hydrangea, the lawn that is overrun with weeds, are illuminated by an unearthly light. 'Happy New Year!' Leon embraces me from behind. 'Did you hear what Manzwe said?' he asks.

From a great distance, I hear my father saying that there is still one minute to go.

BUTCH GOES TO BOTSWANA

Brendan Cline

I had lost count of the Bloody Marys swilling around my disgruntled guts when my reward strutted into the bar. He pulled out a stool, fitted a booted foot into the rungs and stood there, flexing his thigh. All my organs went out to him. There is something so defenceless about these no-longer-young rent boys; their toughness is so bruised, hurt simply flows out of them. They are like slightly spoiled fruit which will continue to be squeezed until it has no choice but to turn rotten. This one was about thirty, still young enough but with the bloom quite gone. A man's face, shapely and independent but tell-tale sullen; a man's body. Looking at him now it was as if I caught him in the moment before age and drink swelled that firm face, sagged the fine chest. And despair would do its work, of course, and perhaps violence, for he was violent, one could see that.

I smiled. He pretended not to notice, lighting a cigarette with rough gestures. But his animal consciousness was directed at me: he'd picked up my scent, of money and loneliness, and unusual interest. I signed to

Jack the barman, who supplied him with a drink. I then descended from my barstool and made for one of the dark alcoves.

He swaggered across, the last word in jauntiness – bowed legs, heedless face, the swing off the balls of the feet. Only schoolboys and hustlers are quite so studiedly male. His hair was cropped on top and long at the back in an old-fashioned seventies style; dirty blond or perhaps plain dirty. His face was fine, almost classical, with aquiline nose and regular features except that his mouth was very large. Eyes appeared to be light blue or green. The tightness of his jeans must have contributed to his walk. He stood at the entrance to the alcove, resting his weight on one hip, his lashes lowered and his voluptuous mouth pulled in a little grin of passive enquiry. He thanked me, in a flat, uneducated voice, for the drink. Stupidity, slyness, and a good nature which proceeded from both, radiated like a halo from his head. I told him to sit.

What pleasant power one feels at such a moment. He had his looks, I had my money, things seemed to be even. But I had also my experience, my personality, or force of character; which he could oppose only with weakness and fecklessness. The physical strength which he could turn against me – those broad shoulders and hands – would avail him nothing. That was what I was buying.

He sat, opposite to me, his gnawed hands, of which I had caught a glimpse, now back in his pockets. He saw no point in pretending, he did not talk nonsense, simply smiled coyly but with a manful disdain for his own prettiness. In the background the bar was rapidly filling, the noise rose, high energy music thumped from the speaker. My young man had drained off his beer.

'Get yourself another,' I said, putting a note into the front of his jacket. 'And get me a double Bloody Mary *without salt.*'

We were at the next stage. I had issued a command, money had changed hands, I had been firm as to my tastes. Still, he was beautiful, and he got up very slowly. I watched him at the bar. So did several others. He gazed past them blankly, not needing them now. A crony of his passed, a weather-beaten man in imitation leather, with whom he exchanged a few words. I was pointed out and commented upon. My young man came back with the drinks. He said that his name was Butch.

'Surely not. You cannot have been christened Butch.'

'I was christened Henery.'

'Butch will do.'

Oh yes, old men of my age and inclination are very sharp. Our lives have been a matter of continuous attrition, we have been ground and worn and pared and chiselled, expected to subside into flimsy gravel: but we end up sharpened weapons. The question is what we will use ourselves for, what we will stab or cut. If we are successful in our work it is something, if we have someone to love us it is all right. I am much in demand as an actor.

We sat on our worn scarlet velveteen bench, rather pleased with the way things were turning out, though a touch pensive as well. Henery-Butch lounged back, hair spread upon the scarlet fabric, leather jacket open upon a singlet and his chest; sex apparent in the bleached blue jeans. I thought how in half an hour he would be out of these clothes, naked and in my arms, and a totally unreasonable joy shot through me.

'I suppose you have a girlfriend,' I said.

He said not.

'Someone who keeps you?'

No.

'I suppose you've been in jail?'

Yes, he had.

'Ready to leave?'

All amusement vanished from his face as we stood outside waiting for a taxi. I wondered if he felt humiliated at being seen with me, a pampered old creature with only one thing on his mind. But it seemed it was rather that he was simply waiting for the next thing to happen. This was his job. And in the taxi he was almost taciturn. This continued until I ushered him into my house. He stood in the entrance hall, staring along the stretches of marble tiles to the wing staircase, with its Persian rugs, statues upon pedestals, and other such frippery. Then he turned to me and smiled very confidentially.

'I s'poze you got a jacuzzi and all that,' he suggested.

'Yes, as a matter of fact –'

'Can I take a look around?'

It was on the tip of my tongue to say that I did not usually take male prostitutes on guided tours, but he looked so young and enthusiastic, and anyway it isn't often I have someone to show off to. I showed him the reception rooms, bedrooms, bathrooms, the pool, squash court, everything, until we came to the terrace above the rose garden. The garden furniture had been left out and a slight mild breeze brought the smell of roses over the still warm stonework. Butch stretched out on one of the recliners and said he felt like a drink. I decided to humour him. In fact, now that the moment had come I felt a little nervous and I needed a drink too. I reflected as I prepared them that I really should encourage him to take a bath. Perhaps the jacuzzi would do the trick. I fetched him from the terrace and we went down to the poolroom.

For me the most exciting moment is always watching the person take off his clothes. That mysterious and hitherto forbidden flesh, that longed-for, much-imagined holy vessel, would slowly, miraculously and blasphemously come to view, with utterly intimate gestures, and the forbidden, the forbidden, would emerge – all for me. For a man to take off his clothes for me, I do assure you words could never describe what this means to me.

Butch was more beautiful than I had expected. It was not just that he was formed like one of my marble statues; it was a particular luminescence of skin, through which the veins could dimly be seen. His body was good and strong, but it was also subtle, and thus vulnerable.

I waited to see if he would be sulky-passive, suffering me, desiring only to get dressed and snatch his money and go; or whether he would find some satisfaction; whether, as frequently happened, he would become abusive. I took off my clothes and faced him, concealing (of course) my trepidation. He stepped into the foaming water, shifting slightly to make room for me.

During the night Butch had nightmares. It was unusual for me to allow a young man to spend the night and I was not quite sure why I had done it this time. I suppose it was that air of vulnerability, which has made a fool of me before. I woke in the night, then, with Butch whimpering in his sleep. I nudged him very slightly, wanting to relieve the nightmares but not wanting him to wake. After a particularly bad one, in which he actually screamed, I found I could not get back to sleep. Dawn was beginning to fill the french windows, the blinds not having been drawn. I lay watching the gradual light, with the young man's face on the pillow next to me. His hair, chosen by the morning light for its first irradiation, spilled over his shoulder onto the pillow. Birds sang in the cypresses. A little later the footsteps of one of the servants on the terrace outside. I fell asleep for a moment, waking when the maid came into the room with coffee and the paper. She did not glance at my companion but returned a moment later with another cup. Butch woke. He asked where he was.

'In the house of an elderly actor who picked you up last night,' I said. 'Well, what are you going to do with yourself today? Hang around town until the evening, I suppose, spending the money I will pay you on beer and cigarettes, or worse.'

'Give us a chance ...'

'Here's your coffee.'

The same old pattern emerged, of course. The 'child' had nowhere to go, and made it clear by a hundred gauche little signs that he would like to stay here.

'You must forgive me,' I said. 'I do not wish to be offensive or cause pain – but you *are* a prostitute. Prostitutes are not the most delightful of house guests. They are inconsiderate and horrible, and nearly always violent when one comes finally to evict them.'

'You shouldn't call a person a prostitute,' he replied.

'Well, male escort, whatever you will.'

'You seem to know a lot about it.'

'Yes, I am afraid it becomes rather a habit.'

'Jees, I'm hungry, I never got a thing to graze last night.'

I rang the bell.

Butch was neither as ingratiating nor as self-centred as one might fear. His great drawback was that of every hustler I have ever met, that of the need for continuous speech. Now that he had spent the night in my house, now that he had impressed me with his manly reserve, all he wanted to do was talk. Words, pages, volumes had been waiting to tumble out, for who knows how long. I listened. Some of the stories were amusing, of course, especially when the register changed and one observed some anecdote based on relative fact become pure improvisation.

'Lies, lies, lies,' I said, 'but charming , of course. You are such a typical young psychopath, Butch.'

'Ja,' he agreed, 'they told me in the prison.'

'What were you in for?'

'Attempted murder.'

'Of course. Tell me how it was in prison.'

'I s'poze you want to hear about rapes and that stuff.'

'Indeed, yes.'

He told me. After a couple of days I took him out and bought clothes for him, and toiletries, and patent medicines. Already on the first day I had known this would happen, that Butch was here for quite a while, but I managed to put off this expression of it for as long as possible.

I knew everything, of course. On the first night I instructed myself firmly not to fall in love with him, and by the time the morning came – that hair splashed on the pillow and over his shoulder – I would have moved heaven and earth to keep him there. But I did not let him know this, and much of the time I managed to prevent myself knowing it, too.

I was at this time between stage productions. My house and my income were my own, inherited from long-dead family, and there was no need for me to work if I did not wish it. A couple of months a year was quite sufficient to keep my name on the books.

So Butch came into an ordered but tranquil, and I suppose rather holiday-like, existence where there was no want except for that of amusement; and this he felt it his role to provide. He seemed happy, particularly after I had added pinball and space invaders to the video machine and other distractions. Apart from which there was lying by the pool, taking saunas, telephoning, and when all else palled, shopping. My friends accepted him, a little ironically of course, but without demonstrations; and he liked them tremendously, human beings endowed with the sense of hearing. Butch fitted in perfectly to the routine of my life.

'Don't you have friends you miss?' I asked more than once. 'Aren't there people you might like to see? Surely your life can't have been utterly empty and devoid of contact?'

'No,' he replied thoughtfully, oiling himself by the pool.' Maybe later. Well, there's one mate of mine, Lofty, he's not a bad oke but he's trouble. I wouldn't ask Lofty to come here.'

'You could go and visit him,' I said. 'You mustn't feel tied down.'

'I'll think about it.'

Of course I was protesting too much. I did not want him to visit anyone, nor even to think of them. But I had to be careful, I must not have him feeling trapped. And when I went into my study, or took a book down onto the lawn, I had to take care that he did not see my restlessness, my listening, my rapt consciousness of every pore and follicle of his skin.

Nor was this concern of mine helped by the knowledge that it was really women Butch liked.

'I don't mind,' he said when I drilled him about it. 'Man, woman, makes no difference to me.'

'I don't believe you,' I said. 'It's not possible to be indifferent on the issue. What do you think about? When you have fantasies, what are they of? Cocks? Or cunts?'

'No, you don't understand me man,' he protested. 'I'm not like that.'

So his limited intelligence, or invincible stupidity, came to the rescue whenever he wanted not to understand. I knew, though. He accepted men and even enjoyed them – he enjoyed them, oh yes – but his heart wasn't in it.

And yet I often caught myself thinking that it was much too late for his heart to be in anything. He was ruined already, completely corrupted. It was too late for him to fall in love with some girl and settle down, he didn't have the equipment for it. He was weak, he was wounded, he would take whatever came along, providing it could look after him. He needed looking after.

The months passed. We went on holiday together, I bought him a car so that he could go shopping, a gymnasium was installed for his use. His appearance improved; the slight gauntness in his face became a hard roundness, the marmoreal tones of his skin turned golden brown. He offered to cut his hair, now sun-bleached and very much longer, but I managed to prevent that.

There were conflicts. More than once I found it impossible to conceal my irritation at an evening which had been ruined by his ceaseless babble and want of restraint. This was almost balanced out by my delight in the pain he caused my enemies – Butch's looks entranced them, but then they had to listen to him speak: hazardous, and frequently so boring that one became quite hysterical.

'Can't we go see a film?'

'What film, Butch?'

'Any film, I don't mind. Did I ever tell you about this one film they showed in the reformatory –'

'I'm afraid I need a reason to go and sit in a –'

'No, any film, you choose. This ou in the film was on the run from the FBI, or was it the CIA, ja, the CIA, and then he got to this other place, Boston I think it was, or Chicago, ja, Chicago – '

'You have told me, you must have. All right, I see here in the paper there's a French –'

'New Orleans! It was New Orleans, my friend. So this ou, he was like the main character, he bumps this oke from the CIA, or the FBI – '

'Shut up, Butch, shut up.'

'Okay. Can I have a swim before we go?'

'Are you sure you want to go? It's such good weather.'

'Can't I tell you about the film? You told me I must stop telling you but you'd find it interesting, I promise you –'

I hit him once. He hit back a lot harder, more than once, then wept.

'You had a terrible childhood, I suppose?'

'Never, it was grand.'

'Well then, why are you such a child now?'

'Don't be like that. Look, feel here, there's a lump here where you threw that lamp at me last night.'

'Yes ... does it hurt?'

We went out. At the supper table of a famous director, at a charity premier in full dress, at a garden party wedding, Butch talked. It might be a dream he had had, or a joke he seemed to remember, or the details of some favourite ailment. He was a great hypochondriac, with the scandalised relish for illness of the lower classes. The chief regret of his life was that he had never had an operation.

'I had a boil on my thumb once,' he would blurt, eyes glittering. Would the guests rebel this time?

'Butch, when my friends come this evening, don't get too enthusiastic. Let them talk. Don't agree with everything they say. Just sit and look beautiful.'

'Fine, fine, whatever you say, I like just sitting and looking.'

'Don't let them get too familiar.'

'Look who's getting jealous!'

'I have never been jealous in my life!'

In fact I was almost relieved when he received his call-up papers for a month-long army camp. I needed time to collect my wits.

'How do you feel about serving in the army?' a young friend of mine asked one evening.

'Ag, all right,' Butch replied.

'What if you get sent into the townships? You might have to fire on your fellow citizens.'

'Uh-uh, what would my fellow citizens be doing in the townships?'

My friend swallowed.

'You don't think it's wrong that the army enforces apartheid?' he persisted.

'No, no, the army only forces the troublemakers,' Butch explained. 'Apartheid's dead, my friend.'

'Then why are the townships sealed off, why are the whites living in isolated luxury and buying guns?'

'No, you see, the k- the blacks like the townships better 'cause all their friends are there.'

My friends gazed at Butch, then at me.

He was away for four weeks. I went out a lot, drank, tried to have sex with someone else. But I woke in the mornings with the sun on the bed and imagined his body stretched out next to mine, the purity, the serene thereness of him, with his chest raised as he lay with hands behind his head, smiling at me; the curve of his thighs as he pulled them into jeans; the fall of hair on his neck; and the private parts of him which he gave so freely. There were also the wrinkles at his eyes, the not quite tight stomach, the skin beginning to turn leathery in places. With tenderness, pain, and resignation, I thought of him.

I could afford to be resigned because he was coming back. At the end of the month I met him at the station. He seemed unchanged, if a little dreamier. That night we were out on the town until early morning, when we came home and lay outside on the terrace, gazing up at the sky.

'I slept under the stars,' he said. 'There was too much racket in the tents, snoring and okes talking in their sleep. Under the stars you can be alone, you can feel real.'

'This is all most unlike you,' I commented.

'Well, this was only after the other ous were sleeping, don't forget. I couldn't sleep in that tent. Then I thought if I lie outside like this and there's a Terry creeping round he'll fall over me and that'll be it.'

'Don't tell me there were terrorists up there?'

'What you think we were there for?'

'Did you see any?'

'Of course we saw them! We had contacts, my friend, I myself shot –'

'Don't tell me.'

'Under the stars I lay thinking. I thought about you, too. I thought about what I used to think about when I was inside. I used to have this dream. I never told anyone before. I used to dream I'd go to Botswana.'

'Why Botswana? If you're going to dream –'

'In Botswana everyone's happy, there's peace and plenty in Botswana. They don't argue up there. There's diamond mines all over the place, and there's adventure, canoe trails through the swamps with lions watching you. Randy tourists into kinky stuff. Every night you can see the Milky Way.'

'You really used to dream that?'

'I still dream it.'

'Ah – well, you can go, there's nothing stopping you.'

'You reckon? Wouldn't you mind?'

'Why should I mind?'

As he settled in again it became apparent that in at least one respect Butch had changed. He had become lazy and indifferent to what was going on outside the house. The idea of a night out, a day spent shopping, held no attraction. This suited me quite well, for I liked going out with my friends and I liked finding Butch at home when I came back.

'Ashamed to be seen with me, I suppose,' I said when wishing to be difficult.

'Who, me? I never feel ashamed.'

That was undeniable.

'What are you going to do with your life?' I asked. 'You're not getting any younger lying by the pool drinking rum.'

'This is my life,' he replied.

'I only ask for your own sake,' I said. ' I wish you had something to fall back on.'

'I've got you.'

'You may not always –'

'I'm not good at anything. Just leave me, let me take life as it comes.'

The thing is, when you love someone you end up wanting for them precisely that which they cannot take. I managed to keep my mouth shut. To have Butch in my house, with that large pouting mouth simply dying to be loquacious, was enough.

And for him? He was smoking a lot of grass. I found the practice rather alarming in that it was something I did not understand. Grass smokers seem to become either silly or unhappy. But this does not come well from one dependent on alcohol and pills to make him sleep, and sometimes to wake as well. Apart from one or two memorable occasions grass did not affect Butch adversely. His silliness when smoked-up was probably matched by mine after a few drinks: my mind certainly was clearer, but this I had resigned myself to anyway.

'This carpet looks like a river. See the reeds and rushes and all the water flowing, and those lilypads.' I looked down rather dubiously at my oriental rug.

'Or a bog,' he said, 'or a swamp. All that stuff flowing, and you come into the swamp and there's just green and water, you can't see a thing but the birds are calling all over the place, and you stand there and you just hear birds, then there's a rustle, and right by your foot there creeps a python, or else a crocodile. Then you walk a bit, or sort of sludge along, and the green water creeps up, and all of a sudden you got leeches on you. Yuk! Yuk! You get rid of the leeches. Hippos come up out of the water and check you out, every time they come up the canoe waai's from side to side, I forgot to say you're in the canoe. In the water there's fish, little fish and big fish of every colour, rainbow stripes and pink and red, yellow, green, blue, the lot. You catch some, just sort of grab them, scoop them out with your hands and later that's going to be your graze. First you got the sunset, though, when you have your first beer, that you been keeping in the water to keep cold, you been smoking it up the whole day, of course. Then the sunset, ja, red and yellow, and you just stare and stare. Animals come to the edge of the water to drink, lions and buck, zebra, elephants, everything. The crocs check them out and they check the crocs out and they all check you out. Then ...'

Sometimes I listened, sometimes not. Sometimes I spoke (I should say somewhere that I myself am a great talker, not having met my match till Butch) – over the months we spent in my house he must have found out a great deal about me. Occasionally I related anecdotes from the theatre, which made him guffaw without any understanding. But more often I spoke of what he would understand, what my childhood had been and what I'd been like as a very young man.

'Repressed!' I cried. 'Repressed! You have no idea, Butch. If someone like you had been lying next to me like you're doing now, I'd have died of fright. Only afterwards would I have realised how exciting it was.'

'Ja, some people have problems that way,' he sighed.

'Even now, I sometimes wonder whether, had I been more liberated as a youth, I'd still have my taste for hust –' I stopped, but it was too late.

'Hustlers,' he supplied, without rancour. 'Ja, I wonder as well. If you went off hustlers you'd prob'ly go off me too.'

'I didn't mean it like that.'

'No problem, I can handle it.'

What was it he could handle? Much of the time now he was smoked-up. He'd start in the mornings. Was he more withdrawn? How did he really feel about things (meaning, of course, me)? And how much can we know about another human being? I started drinking more, there was a feeling of things running their course.

The knock at the door came early one morning. A man in some kind of uniform asked for Butch. My instincts told me to say that he was not in. The man said that he would call again. I said I did not know when Butch would be back. As it turned out this was almost true as Butch had climbed through a window and was hiding in the servants' quarters. It was a while before I found him.

'What sort of trouble are you in?'

'That was a MP.'

'Member of Parliament?'

'Military Police. If they catch me they'll put me inside.'

'What for? Did you do something against the law, when you were up there?'

Butch laughed. 'I might as well tell you 'cause I'm going to have to leave anyway. I never went to the camp.'

'Oh. Where did you go then, or shouldn't I ask?'

'I was around. I was with my mates.'

'But the stories you told – you described the nights up there –'

'I've got a mind too, haven't I?'

He was brazen in order to soften the blow. It did not help. I was not shocked at being lied to. The shock was that he would, indeed, have to leave.

'Oh, why couldn't you have just done the camp!'

'Didn't feel like it. Can you lend me some money, please, I have to get a move on.'

'Where will you go?'

He thought a moment; then his face cleared: 'Botswana!'

I stood in the hall of my house staring at Butch and it was extraordinary how my resentment and rage dispersed at that word. I began to laugh. The pain would come later; let it come when I was alone.

'Yes,' I cackled. 'You go to Botswana. Someone will remember you with love.'

Whose fault was it, after all, that I was strong and he was not?

RELATIVES

Chris van Wyk

When I was twenty-one I went down to the Cape to write a book. I had got it into my head that my first novel should be a family saga and that my own roots could be found in the arid dust of the Karoo, that famous semi-desert in the Cape, in a little dorp called Carnarvon.

I had first gone down to Cape Town for a week. How could one travel all the way to the Cape without a trip to the most beautiful city in the world, Table Mountain, the train ride from Simon's Town to the city meandering along the beach, the beautiful coloured girls with their lilting, singsong voices?

Then back to Hutchinson Station in the heart of the Karoo to be picked up by my grandfather's younger brother, Henkie. A bigger version of my oupa, Uncle Henkie's other difference was that he had mischief in his eyes where my oupa had brooding shadows.

Then followed an hour's drive to Carnarvon by way of long, hot, dusty, potholed roads past waving, poor people on foot or pushing bicycles, and carrying bundles of wood or things wrapped in newspaper.

Carnarvon was a place in the middle of nowhere where nothing happened. Simple breakfasts, lunches and suppers were linked together by chains of cigarettes and conversations consisting of long, trailing life histories that made the old men in their elbow patches stammer and squint into the past from behind their thick spectacles, as they dredged up anecdotes from the dry riverbeds of history.

Oh, how wonderful it was listening to those minutely detailed sagas. But after two weeks I was bored out of my wits. The novel could wait, I decided as I packed up and was driven back to Hutchinson Station. The train from Cape Town – the very same one that had brought me there two weeks before – slid into the station. I bade Uncle Henkie goodbye with a promise that I would feature him prominently and truthfully in my novel.

When the train slithered out, I turned to the passengers in the compartment with whom I was going to spend the next sixteen hours or so on the way to Johannesburg.

There were three young men, two bearded, two chubby. (If you think I can't count, remember the riddle of the two fathers and two sons who each shot a duck. Only three ducks were shot. Why? Because one was a grandfather, the other a father, and the last a son. The man in the middle was both a father and a son, got it?) All youthful and exuberant, they were drinking beer, straight from the can, and their conversation was full of the hammers and nails of their profession and punctuated with laughter and inane arguments. None of them swore and they all flashed smiles at me, accepting me into their midst with an easy friendliness.

'You been to Cape Town?' one of them enquired.

'Ja,' I said, shoving my bag into the space above the door among their own bags and stuff.

'Then you must've got your quota of ten girls,' he said with a wink.

Of course I knew exactly what he was talking about: in the Mother City there were at least ten girls to every boy. I gave them a supercilious nod, hoping to convey the impression that I had certainly got my fair share. The truth of it was very different. All I could truly claim was a brief encounter with Marina, a nurse from Tygerberg hospital. She had allowed me to kiss her in the back seat of her cousin's car, but my beer breath had proved too much for her and after administering a violet-flavoured Beechie, she bade me goodnight and told me to come and see her in the morning.

There were two other passengers in the compartment. They were not quite as friendly as the trio from the Cape. They sat huddled in a corner, muttering in undertones and casting sidelong glances down the green SAR leather seat at me and my new buddies. They were brothers. This was obvious from their identical features: sandy hair that had been cut so short that the hairs grew in sharp italic spikes. They both had dark, brooding eyes and thick pouting lips. They wore khaki shirts and pants.

Try to describe people you meet on a bus or train it said in the writer's manual. I slipped a blank sheet into my mental typewriter and went to town:

They sit huddled in the corner of the compartment, bent so low in their conniving that they almost stick to the green SAR leather like two unsightly stains. They are identical but for the fact that there is a two or three year difference between them. Juveniles in khaki, they look like fugitives from a boy scout patrol, runaways not prepared to abide by the rules of the Lord Baden Powell. Stripped of their badges, their epaulettes, their scarves, banished to ride forever, second class on the Trans-Karoo.

As I've said, I was only twenty-one at the time.

I turned away from them and back to the three big men who were asking me questions as if I was an old buddy. I was surprised and pleased by this unexpected attention and friendliness. One of them glanced at his watch from time to time and stared out of the window at the scrub that made up the dry, lonely landscape of the Karoo. They asked me how my journey down to the Cape had been. They all seemed genuinely interested. One of them slid a can of beer across the little panelite table. They all sat forward to listen to what I had to say. I lit a cigarette, passing the pack around to my three friends. Then I began a story which I had already tested on my uncle in Carnarvon. There, among seasoned storytellers, it had passed my 'litmus' test – Listenable, Interesting, Telling, Meaningful, Unusual, Strange. I knew I had a winner:

On my way down from Johannesburg my travelling companion – no one else had been booked into our compartment – had been a Capetonian man. He travelled in a flamboyant striped yellow and white suit, every time he spoke he injected an air of drama into the compartment, and when he was quiet he seemed all the time to be sizing me up. I remember his name, Georgie Abrahams, from Elsies River.

As the train started its long journey out of Johannesburg Station, Georgie began to tell me how he had once killed a man. Where? In a compartment exactly like the one he and I were sitting in, facing each other. Why? Because, Georgie was very eager to explain, this *skelm* tried to steal some of Georgie's possessions: food, money, and expensive watch? I can't remember what it was but Georgie caught him, beat him up, sliced him from his greasy fat neck down to his 'klein gatjie' – Georgie's words. He threw the remains of the dead man out of the window in the dead of night, and wiped the blood carefully from the windowpane, the green leather seat, the floor. When the conductor questioned the whereabouts of the missing man, Georgie merely shrugged and uttered a melodious 'How should I know? Nobody asked me to take care of him.'

But even as Georgie was relating this tale of theft and murder in all its horrific detail, I knew it was a lie, simply a more elaborate version of my mother's dire warnings to yours truly at seven, 'If you eat in bed you'll grow horns', or the more convincing 'Go to bed with wet hair and you'll suffer from a smelly nose for the rest of your life'. Georgie was in fact warning me to stay clear of his luggage! And the story had quite an amusing ending. When we reached Cape Town Station, a toothless woman in a lopsided jersey, stretched to twice its original size (which used to be XL) welcomed the murderer home with an unceremonious slap across his face, while I looked on together with a brood of his startled children who didn't know if they should laugh with delight at their papa's homecoming, or cry for the humiliating onslaught he was being subjected to.

'Ses maande en djy skryf niks, phone niks, not a blerry word van djou!'

My companions chuckled. They couldn't decide what was better, my story or my Cape accent.

I looked at the two sulking boys in the corner. They had followed the entire story, but they refused to laugh. So what! It hadn't been for their amusement anyway.

But then my journey took an unexpected turn. An hour or two from Hutchinson my three companions got up, stamped the pins and needles out of their feet, swept the crumbs from their pants and began to gather up their luggage. They shook my hand, slapped my back and said goodbye. And at the next station they were gone. It all happened so quickly that I was a little stunned. Now it was just me and the kids in khaki. And then a strange thing happened. I suddenly knew why they were dressed in khaki. In all probability they were from a Cape Town reformatory on their way home to Johannesburg! Why had I not realised this simple fact before? The answer was elementary. I had been far too preoccupied with my new friends to pay too much attention to these two boys and there were no guardians in sight. But now that I was alone I focused my attention full square on these two, and in an instant I realised where they were from.

The two juvenile delinquents also seemed to undergo some transformation. They no longer muttered but spoke loudly, spicing their conversation with vulgarities. And, in an act of territorial imperative, they claimed more than their fair share of the confined space, stretching their stocky legs along the seats, putting their luggage everywhere, littering the floor with clothes and greasy food packets.

Then they began a conversation which froze my blood. Their brother, the leader of a gang, had been killed by a rival gang in a Johannesburg township called Coronationville. They had been given a weekend off to attend the funeral. They would bury their brother like the hero that he was, but they vowed to avenge his death before the soil on his grave hardened. They even had an argument about how this murder would be carried out, a slow cutting of the throat was the younger's plan. No, the elder brother disagreed, stab him about a hundred times, but from the ankles to the neck.

As these plans were being discussed they kept looking me straight in the eye as if challenging me to say anything in protest or disagreement. Each time I looked away, not daring to utter a word.

Meanwhile the train seemed to be riding into the sunset. A cool breeze replaced the warmth and the grim brothers felt the cold and pulled up the windows.

I began to worry. How could I spend an entire night in a pitch black compartment with two juvenile delinquents! Maybe I could go out in search of the conductor and ask to be moved to another compartment. But if I did that my two little gangsters would know instinctively what I was up to. This also meant leaving my luggage unattended. As these thoughts went through my head, I looked down from the top bunk and saw the elder brother staring at me. He knows what I'm thinking, I thought.

Darkness came and we turned on the lights. A caterer opened our door and read out the menu for supper. The two boys ordered steak, buttered bread, and potato salad. I had no appetite. The caterer left and I heard him whistling down the corridor and opening the compartment next door. My companions glared at me again. They seemed to know why I had not ordered a meal.

On my way down to the Cape, Georgie Abrahams had joked about committing murder. This time there was no such threat – towards me anyway. But for every dark kilometre to Jo'burg I felt that my home city was moving further and further away.

'You!' I looked down from the bunk. It was the elder brother who was demanding my attention.

'Ja,' I answered as casually as my voice would allow.

'Are you not Aunty Ria's child – grandchild?'

'Yes!' I could not believe my ears. Aunty Ria, as they called her, was indeed my grandmother and the mother of my own mother.

'I knew it was you when I saw you,' he said, not smiling, but with some friendliness in his voice. His brother stared up at me with some interest.

'You're that clever boy who used to read books and write stuff, hey?'

'Yes, but who are you?'

'Me'n him we Aunty Visa's grandchildren.'

Aunty Visa was my granny's sister.

'Then we're cousins!' I said. This wasn't quite true but I was desperate to be as closely related to them as possible.

When their food arrived they insisted that I join them. And I did, for suddenly my appetite had returned.

I had forgotten all about my chance encounter with my two delinquent relatives until the other day, three years later.

I opened the newspaper and read a report about rampant gang crime in the streets of Western Township and adjacent Coronationville. The article spoke of streets running with the blood of gangsters, the death of innocents caught in the crossfire, the revenge killings, the tragic futility of it all. The writer paid particular attention to the two brothers who had been stabbed to death and who now lay dead in the same graveyard as their brother, killed three years ago.

They had never reached twenty-one.

THE AWAKENING OF KATIE FORTUIN

Finuala Dowling

Today my auntie, Katie Fortuin, woke up. She fell asleep in 1969. Quite long to be asleep nearly twenty-five years.

We sort of knew Katie was going to wake up so we were all standing around her bed. Me, my wife Sandra, my Ma, Uncle Richard (Ma's second husband), my brother Stan, my sisters Rosie and Maria, their husbands Shane and Achmat, my half-brothers Vincent, Clive and Johnny, my half-sister Agnes, and all their offspring. The first thing Katie asked for was a cup of tea. I'm glad she didn't express an urgent need to look at herself in a mirror. Shock might have killed her.

Not that she'd aged badly. Her skin was quite smooth for a 54-year-old, probably because she hadn't been yelling or smoking and had gotten plenty of beauty sleep. But Ma had let Katie's hair grow into this great big wiry bush, kind of Afro-style, and it was streaked with grey. Lying with her bushy head against Ma's best Edgars pillowslip, Auntie looked much paler than us. Because of not being in the sun, she looked almost white.

Anyway, Katie didn't want a mirror, she wanted tea. I was sure she recognised in me the little boy who used to do errands for her, running down Hanover Street with no money but my Auntie's fervent promises.

'And if there's still no sugar, run down to the Babie shop and get some. You can tell that *ou Slaamse* to put it on credit and don't mind if his face looks like *asyn*. And by the by, it's very cheeky for a coloured boy to grow a moustache, you know.' I remembered then that my aunt had always been a prejudiced woman.

'Katie,' said Ma, 'we've had just on a quarter of a century to replace the sugar so you can rest assured your tea will be sugared just the way you like it.'

Katie looked suspiciously at Ma.

'And who might you be?' she asked.

'Don't you remember me, Katie? I'm your sister, Desirée. You've been asleep so long, you don't recognise me.'

'I must've been asleep long enough for you to guzzle a hundred pounds worth of *vetkoek*,' replied Katie, looking pointedly at Ma's matronly girth.

'Is that the thanks I get for looking after you and keeping you clean and sanitary for twenty-five years? You know you peed on my sheets and in nappies till they put that bag on you? I swear you put out about a gallon a day.'

'Well I'll go to the toilet from now on by myself, thank you, and then I won't have to have my liquid output measured by the likes of you.'

'Don't thank me, thank Gawd you know me.'

I couldn't believe it. As a kid I always remember Ma and Auntie Katie *skelling* each other out. Now it was like they just picked up where they'd left off somewhere in November of 1969, when my auntie, who'd been feeling inexplicably tireder and tireder, finally fell into a sleep. That's how it happened. Not a car accident or a stroke. Not a blow on the head we don't think, unless she and Ma were quietly boxing each other on the side.

I was nine years old at the time and we were all living together in a little cottage in District Six, and I can tell you there wasn't much room for doing anything quietly on the side, which does make me wonder, incidentally, how come there got to be so many of us. Not surprising Uncle Richard's favourite saying is, 'Where there's a will, there's a way.'

I don't think Ma and Katie would've chosen to live together. Katie thought Ma was a slut who killed her first husband with her excessive desires. (In fact, my father was washed overboard in a weekend fishing expedition.) Ma was overpopulating the world and directly contributing to the slum conditions we were living in; her legs were always open wide either receiving the wherewithal to make babies or spewing out the finished product. Ma thought Katie was an uptight spinster who needed a good you know what, and asked why didn't she get herself a nice man in a wheelchair from the hospital so they could qualify for a state pension and not live with Ma who had never wanted to live with Katie anyway.

Auntie Katie, before she fell asleep, worked at Groote Schuur Hospital in the kitchens. It used to depress her no end. Can you imagine a Cape Coloured woman not being allowed to cook with spices or herbs or flavourings of any kind?

'But it will make them well,' she used to argue to the Matrons, 'if they just have a little *borrie* or a speck of cayenne pepper to stimulate the glands. These spices are medicinal. What about ginger? Didn't your mother give you ginger for your *maagpyn?*' But the Matrons were adamant. No spices. No herbs.

Katie's only ally in that big teaching hospital was young Professor Powell. Katie usually held white people at arm's length. She wanted to respect them, she said, and she couldn't do that once she'd got to know them intimately and realised that there was nothing in them that wasn't also in the most hardened *skollie* or Fancy Boys gang member. But Edward Powell was obviously different, because it was always 'Professor Powell this' and 'Professor Powell that' until one day my mother put her hands on her hips and said,

'Why don't you just let the whitey *naai* you if he's so *bleddy* wonderful?'

Katie tightened her cardigan around her, pinched her lips and wouldn't speak to my mother for a week, which was a great relief as far as the rest of us were concerned.

The truth is that Auntie Katie had a kind of crush on Professor

Powell. More than a crush, really. Katie may have worshipped our Lord every Sunday in Upper Buitenkant Street, but from Monday to Friday Edward Powell of the Neurology Department was her demi-god. He wasn't much older than her himself, but he always called Katie 'Miss Fortuin'. And if we'd heard it once, we'd heard it a million times how one day when it was bucketing down in a typical Cape winter rainburst, Professor Edward Powell of the Neurology Department held his umbrella over the lowly Katie, bottle-washer and cook, for at least five minutes before she dashed to her bus.

Auntie Katie told us with pride how Professor Powell determined who would live and who would die, whose head could be stitched together and whose had to be left like Humpty Dumpty. The ginger-haired Professor presided over the sanity of all who lived on the Peninsula and beyond. Men and women who entered his doors tied up in strait-jackets might leave walking freely once he'd waved his magic scalpel. According to Auntie Katie Fortuin.

As a token of her immense admiration, Katie brought Edward (who was from Natal, and consequently like curry as much as Katie did) home-made rootie rolls and other delicacies, still warm, wrapped in greaseproof paper. I remember Katie getting up at dawn to fold the Professor's samoosas. Stan and Vincent and me would lie in our shared bed, judging from the aromas and the clink of saucepans how far advanced Auntie Katie's culinary preparations were. At the crucial moment we'd fight past each other and the bedclothes and crowd into the tiny kitchen, pleading for just one of these succulent parcels.

It was odd when Katie started to drop off for a *zzz* in the middle of meals or conversations. She was usually such a bustling, tireless woman. Ma said they were working her too hard at the hospital and that white people thought coloured people never needed to rest. But it was more. Katie's personality was changing, because she didn't want to do the things she used to love doing, like walking to Church and greeting everyone along the way, or bargaining with the fruit and vegetable hawkers, or chasing *skollies* who came to pee against our wall. She got into trouble at work, which was also not like her; she was the most law-abiding person. Then one November morning (when she'd already had twelve hours' sleep) Katie stopped folding the Professor's samoosas, climbed into her newly-made bed, and went back to sleep for nearly twenty-five years.

At first Ma thought Katie was suffering from nervous exhaustion, so she moaned a bit about how certain people are allowed to have a breakdown but others have to stay on duty, and then sent me to the hospital to deliver the samoosas. A receptionist my aunt would have described as *kwaai* called Professor Powell to collect the still-steaming package from this snotty urchin.

'Auntie couldn't come. Auntie's sleeping. It's 80c for the samoosas.'

I had memorised these lines and repeated them all the way from Cross Street to the door of the hospital. Professor Powell, for all his deep understanding of the human brain, looked puzzled. He didn't get a chance to question me though, because I was already running back to District Six, hoping I wouldn't get a hiding for coming late to school.

When Auntie Katie had been asleep for three days, Professor Powell visited. The arrival of his smart Cortina in Cross Street created tumult. Children of the neighbourhood crowded round him, laughing and teasing because this was their place, where they held sway, and the tall, thin gingery man was the outlander. He maintained his dignity and was respectfully welcomed by Ma and Uncle Richard who had imbibed some of Auntie Katie's reverence for 'the Professor'.

Ma showed him into Katie's bedroom, which wasn't actually Katie's because it was the room where everybody except Uncle Richard and Ma and the new baby slept. It had a low ceiling and one small, low window with net curtains. There were three beds covered in crocheted spreads, all pushed together, and over the beds hung a plaque of praying hands. Our clothes were in trunks, stacked on top of each other and used as a table. When Ma spotted Edward Powell opening the little picket gate, she had quickly slapped a doily on this stack.

Professor Powell stooped over Katie and shone a light in her eyes.

'Has she been lying in the same position all this time?'

'Oh no, Professor, she tosses and turns sometimes. I think she's having a very nice sleep. I do all the work around here, you know. Now I've got these sheets to worry about too,' she added meaningfully.

'I would like to have her brought in for testing. I'll have an ambulance sent.'

So Auntie Katie was tested. Lights were shone in her eyes. Her pulse was taken and her heartbeat was checked. Her brain was scanned. There was nothing wrong with Katie. She was just a coloured lady sleeping. Eventually, Katie was brought home in nappies, with a special little button on her tummy through which liquidised food could be squirted. A gastrostomy, Professor Powell called it. A catastrophe, Ma said.

'She is doing this on purpose to make my life a misery,' said Ma, tearfully grinding up meat and vegetables. The new baby was crying, Uncle Richard was drinking at a tavern in Horstley Street and we boys were hungry.

'This is my sister's revenge,' said Ma bitterly.

After that, a strange thing happened. It happened gradually, so I can't say when Ma began to change toward the sleeping Katie and became so tender and caring, washing her, feeding her. Always she would put the spices Katie loved in Katie's puree.

'But Ma, we don't have taste buds down there where Auntie Katie gets her food.'

'Don't be cheeky young man. Katie herself said we must give spices to the sick. I'm only doing what she always said.'

Sometimes I wonder if it wasn't the forced removals that made my mother kind. You see, Auntie Katie fell asleep in the middle of it all, in the midst of the weeping, tearing and destruction. Ma sat next to Katie's bedside and told her what was happening. When Katie was 'awake', that is, when her eyes were open and staring, Ma propped her up on the pillows and they'd have a regular chat, except Katie never answered or showed what she thought of it all but only occasionally drooled, which can't be called a reaction.

'Listen, Katie, they are sending us away from here. They say this place is a slum, but actually they just don't like brown people so near their precious city. We have to go to the Flats. There's no shops, no schools, no nothing there. Don't wake up now, Katie, rather just sleep.'

Inevitably neighbours and visitors heard about these strange conversations between Ma and her *non compos mentis* sister. Nobody accused Ma of being *mal* though. Instead, word got round that Katie Fortuin had gone to sleep because of Group Areas, in resistance to it. Then, because people always talk and dream and imagine, it was circulated that Katie wasn't going to wake up till justice returned. Our cottage became something of a shrine to a woman who had turned herself into a barometer of oppression, who refused to be moved.

But of course we had to move Katie, and she came with us first to Elsie's River and then to Mitchell's Plain, where last year I bought Ma a big double-storey house. Now Katie has her own room. All this became possible when I was promoted, in the sense that I stopped being a non-government organiser and became a government organiser. It's the same job but a whole lot better paid. I could've bought Ma a house in Plumstead, but she wanted to stay near the kind of people she's always known, who don't think green plastic curlers is a strange hairdo. In a way, I have Katie to thank for this – the promotion, I mean. If it hadn't been for her I'd probably have died in detention, slipped on a bar of soap you know.

I spent most of 1986 inside Katie's brushed nylon nightie. Sometimes the electricity created beneath the mountain of bedclothes by that skin-warmed garment as my hair rubbed against it, was terrifying. The Security Branch were after me and climbing into bed with Katie was a spur of the moment decision.

'I've got nothing here but an invalid. Search my house, with pleasure,' Ma told the police, and they did.

Their boots on the linoleum made an ominous crunching sound. I lay perfectly still between Katie's thighs, my head on her large cotton bloomers, inside her nightie, under the blankets, under the eiderdown. They said nothing. The linoleum creaked from their weight. It was very hot inside our pink nylon tent, but it smelt good, like fresh laundry. It was only then, when my nose was pressed against Katie's underwear, that I fully understood how well Ma looked after her sister. A stupid thought when you're on the verge of arrest.

When they'd left, I asked Ma what had happened.

'They looked and looked at the bed. The big blond one was reaching his hand out to touch the bedclothes when Katie opened her eyes and stared at him, you know the way she does sometimes. Only this time I think she had a glint of accusation in her eye. Anyway, he drew his hand back.'

For the rest of the year, I was in and out of Katie's nightie, as the occasion demanded. Only the closest family members knew I was home. Eventually the State dropped their case against me and I came out from Katie's nightie.

I worked for various anti-apartheid and non-government organisations and even got a bursary to study further. I met my wife Sandra at a postgraduate seminar. She shares the same ideals as me and was also involved in NGOs and the struggle. We fell in love not over candlelit dinners but at candlelit memorial services and meetings and workshops and late night arguments in Observatory communes. The Mixed Marriages and Immorality Acts have been repealed and there are lots of couples like us so we don't cause much of a stir. It was today, at our wedding celebration that Auntie Katie first showed signs that she'd like to wake up.

Sandra's mother wanted us to get married at her club.

'You coloureds are very welcome these days,' she said.

Sandra was outraged, and said we'd rather get married in Mitchell's Plain. Which we did: today.

Ma has been cooking for days. There's *bredie* for forty guests, stir-fried rice with vegetables (Sandra is a vegetarian), cucumber mousse from the back of a greengage jelly packet, potato salad, rice salad (for people who don't get enough potato salad and stir-fried rice), tomato and onion sambal, little iced cakes, four-tiered trifles, milk tarts galore and I don't know what all besides. Busy as she's been, Ma never forgot Auntie Katie.

Earlier today Ma gave Katie her share of the feast. She propped Katie up on the pillows even though Katie isn't fed through the mouth. Ma feels it's not respectable to eat lying down. As usual, she gave Katie the low-down.

'Now, Katie, today is a great day. What would you say if I told you your nephew was getting married today? To a beautiful girl, and you know what Katie, she's white! How things have changed, Katie, since your day. You should see our guests. They are of every colour. They are all enjoying your spicy recipes, so what I'm giving you today is extra special.'

Then she fed Katie and went back out to our guests. A little while later Sandra and I went in to pay our respects to Auntie.

'Katie,' I said, 'this is Sandra.'

Sandra reached out to take Auntie's limp hand into her own. Imagine her surprise when Katie's hand grasped hers. My aunt, who'd been asleep for over two decades, began to speak.

'Pleased to meet you, ma'am,' said Katie.

'Auntie!' I cried, 'you're awake! It's a miracle! Ma, come look! Katie's awake!'

I clutched Sandra to me. I was so excited and dying to share Katie's awakening with the rest of the family. But the guests outside were making such a racket no one heard my shouts. I looked at my aunt in wonder. She narrowed her eyes, trying to place me.

'It's me, Ricky,' I said. 'Auntie you've been asleep for twenty-four years. So much has happened, so much has changed.'

'You do look like Ricky. And now you've brought your madam to meet me. Are you doing garden work? I always thought they'd apprentice you to learn some trade.'

'No, no,' I laughed. 'It's not like that any more. That's all over now. I've got a good job. Sandra and I are married. You woke up on our wedding day!'

'Married? Then you're in big trouble, my boy. Don't tell anyone. Just don't tell anyone. You could get locked up.'

Then she closed her eyes and went back to sleep. I don't know if it was the shock or the joy of discovering that apartheid was dead. We tried to rouse her again, but to no avail. Ma was very cross to have missed this historic occasion. Immediately she resurrected the old myths about Auntie Katie, who had chosen to be comatose rather than witness the humiliation of her people.

'Why don't you phone that Professor who treats her? I'm sure he should know,' said Sandra, who always makes practical suggestions.

'No, wait a moment. I'm thinking.'

When Ma thinks you can be sure that a scheme is coming soon. I was right.

'Auntie woke up. On which day did she wake up? On the day Sandra and Ricky got married. What was so special about this day apart from wedded bliss? The food is what's different. Spicy food. I gave her nice spicy food in that stoma thing. Katie always said spice was medicinal. Now which spice had this miraculous effect?'

'Don't be ridiculous, Ma,' I said, 'Professor Powell tested her for everything. He's tried everything.'

'He never tried nutmeg,' announced Ma, and went straight to her kitchen cupboard. Sandra helped her heat milk in a saucepan and Ma stirred a whole teaspoonful of nutmeg into it.

'You'll probably kill the old girl,' I said.

'Just watch,' said Ma. Carefully she poured the mixture into Katie's gastric button, speaking soothingly to her sister as she did so. Then we all sat on the bed and waited.

Katie woke up. She looked at me and Sandra and shook her head. She turned around and squinted through the window where all our guests were partying.

'What are all those blacks doing here?' Katie asked. 'Find Desirée and tell her someone left the gate open.'

'I'm here, Katie. Me. Your sister, Desirée.'

Katie looked Ma up and down disbelievingly.

'If you're Desirée then I'm Jesus Christ,' she replied, and went back to sleep.

That's when we gathered the whole family together to witness the official awakening of Katie Fortuin. Ma carefully packed nutmeg into two slow-release capsules she'd emptied. She placed these ceremonially in Katie's tummy opening and stood back to wait for the miracle.

Katie woke up and Katie asked for tea.

As I described to start off with, Ma and Katie have got reacquainted. Katie's met new members of the family as well as old members of the family with new appearances. Professor Powell, who has monitored Katie over the years, has been given the great news. Moments ago he arrived in a state of jubilation, not gingery anymore but peppery, only slightly disappointed to hear how Katie drifted off to sleep again after the tea. We've been sitting in the lounge waiting for Ma's latest dose of nutmeg to take effect.

In between taking these notes, I'm entertaining Professor Powell. Actually, he's so excited he hardly needs entertainment.

'I've been thinking in the car on the way over here, Ricky. Why would nutmeg do the trick? I'll have to take your aunt in for testing, of course, but I hypothesise that she was suffering from a chemical imbalance in the basal nuclei.'

Ma stares at the Professor as if he were speaking Cantonese. Hypothesise? Basal nuclei?

'In the *substantia nigra*. The most uncanny thing, you won't believe.'

'What's so uncanny?' I ask.

'Well, the *substantia nigra* is black. *Nigra*, you know, means black.'

I'm not following, but Ma suddenly nods her head sagely.

'Aah,' she says. 'Katie was so offended by the Group Areas Act that she actually got sick in her negro substance. The part of her brain that contains her blackness, that part got ill.'

'Something like that. Of course we're not talking medicine here. But I think it could make an ironic twist to my article on this amazing case. Coloured woman's anti-apartheid stance has intriguing medical parallel.'

My brother Stan comes in from Katie's bedroom.

'She's awake,' he says.

'Excellent. Now if I can correct that chemical imbalance, she'll stay awake like you or I.'

Since her first reawakening, Katie has gotten used to seeing people aged. She's very pleased to see Professor Powell.

'Come close, Professor,' she says, 'I don't want them to hear this.' Katie looks suspiciously at us over her shoulder. She whispers into his ear, but still I can hear her startling words.

'These people are all mad. They think I'm their relative. They believe that apartheid is no more. You know what, Professor Powell? I think you should get your nice young men in their white jackets and have this lot taken away.'

Thus speaks Katie Fortuin. Her message has been delivered; she has settled back into a sleep Professor Powell promises to cure forever. Ma has summoned the press. There's a gathering expectancy in the house, with neighbours and prominent community members arriving to witness my aunt rise from her bed and greet this new world free of injustice and prejudice.

But I fear the reawakening of Katie Fortuin.

THERE ARE VIRGINS
IN THE TOWNSHIP

Mandla Langa

Much like most human beings, it took me some time to settle comfortably in my trade. My reconciliation with my status as a journalist, that calling which, to many, does not require a lot of soul-searching nor lends itself to a lengthy contemplation of the moral navel, meant an acceptance on my part of a readiness to wound others.

Early in my career I recognised a flaw in my character, a ruthlessness born of my resolve to report and reflect and damn the consequences. In some quarters, this might charitably be interpreted as single-mindedness, a *sine qua non* for effective execution of tasks in hand, a necessary price to pay. In other circles, of course, where my words left a trail of squashed victims much like a snail's viscid emanation, my preoccupations defined themselves as nothing other than recklessness, a trespass against people's privacy and honour, or their notion of these virtues. Whichever way people interpreted my actions, my circle of friends was limited to the few members of the trade.

My eldest brother Jonathan, on the few occasions he visited me in a succession of prison cells that were becoming my second home, would wax lyrical on the merits of friendship in our lives, something that all of us should nurture with every fibre in our bodies. He was fond of pointing out that there were many things happening in our country, with the new society striving to define its role. Many of those we regarded as friends tended to disappear, all using the excuse of being busy. For this reason, then, Jonathan would say, it would be foolish to alienate that small group who stuck by us and remembered us in their nightly prayers. I would listen to all this, my mind wandering, wishing for the appearance of a warder to terminate the harangue. Warders, like cops, are never there when you need one. On looking back, however, I see that he had a point. My discomfort with my brother, the fact that he was a Born Again Christian, did not diminish the gravity of his words. Now that he has disappeared, I miss him terribly. It is as simple as that.

Every person growing up in this country develops a sense of loyalty to friends and family. This is a primal instinct, as essential as breathing. In my case, however, friends and family were a crutch, a convenience which could be discarded at the onset of healing. I am certain that, given the opportunity, I would somehow have found a way of betraying them. In fact, I did betray my parents. They had high hopes for me, seeing me through school and encouraging me to become a lawyer or a doctor, that is, respectable, a credit to the race. I was loth to study, preferring to immerse myself in the picaresque adventures of characters peopling novels by Peter Cheyney or James Hadley Chase, the racy contraband nestling safely behind an exercise book.

My best friend, Arthur Sikhosana, marvelled that I managed to pass at all. It is worth mentioning here that, even with this cavalier attitude to education, I was always at the top of the class. In retrospect, it must be said that it was exactly this disposition which made my education possible. Had I conscientiously swallowed all that Bantu Education bilge which was our daily fare, I would have ended up in a madhouse.

During Standard Four, my English compositions were routinely read to the Standard Six classes, as examples of fine writing, the teachers were wont to say. Even then, I knew – I could sense – that the teachers were somewhat disappointed with my academic performance. They could divine that I had it in me to do better, be a credit to our beleaguered race, and scale loftier heights. I had no intention of being a credit to anybody. As for scaling loftier heights, climbing up a telephone pole and daring others to follow me was enough, thank you. Being good was bad. School was a vehicle for greatness, sure, for success – whatever these meant to an adolescent – but I wasn't going to kill myself or turn myself into a freak in pursuit of excellence.

It is possible that my sense of unease with greatness and a mistrust of success charted the path I would follow later in life. I had seen many great men falter and fall from dizzy heights – and how the people who had thrust them to greatness rejoiced at the inelegance of their collapse.

A case in point was our Principal. Mr Sithole, a strict disciplinarian and lay preacher, was also a closet alcoholic. We knew his secret, having heard him being roasted by a shebeen queen one month-end. His final fall from grace, however, came when one evening he drank himself into such a state that he couldn't tell the toilet from his seventy-year-old father's bedroom, where the hapless old man woke up to a shower of urine. From that day on, Mr Sithole Senior slept swathed in an outsized anorak. 'What do you do', he asked philosophically,' when your son gets so pissed he doesn't know where to direct his pippie?'

At thirteen, my own pippie was stirred by the sight of girls in our school. I was also popular with them, this strange breed being eternally attracted to young men of my ilk who revel in teetering at the edges of precipices. I feared girls and was envious of the freedom in their femininity. The best camouflage, a carapace I wrapped around me, was to make myself as unappealing as possible. Where the other boys vied for Florsheim shoes, grey Barathea slacks and button-down Viyella shirts, I adopted the fashion of slobs: scuffed and loose-laced Bata shoes, baggy trousers and creased shirts. I popped gum loudly, hawked and spat insolently and never hid the fact that I was a smoker. The more I treated the girls with scorn, the more they sought out my company. This perceived ease with which I operated in the world did not endear me to quite a few of my schoolmates; they felt it unfair that this delinquent bested them without seeming to raise a sweat.

Only Arthur Sikhosana, my childhood friend and neighbour, stood by me through these moments of adolescent madness, sometimes earning the wrath of his father in the process. When I was detained in 1976, it was he who campaigned relentlessly for my release; our friendship spans more than two decades, from the heyday of repression when there was an open season on black people, and black flesh was sweet to the palates of police dogs, through the halcyon days of transition where death was as commonplace as mushrooms after a thunderstorm, to this heady new dispensation. It is with this background, then, that what happened between Arthur and me deserves more than a passing comment.

Arthur and I – or, rather, our families – came to KwaMashu around the same time. His mother and father and two elder sisters moved from Mkhumbane, a shantytown which was a precursor of today's squatter camps. His father drove a Durban Corporation truck; his mother worked for some white people in Ridge Road. We had become victims of the Group Areas Act in Mayville. This meant that we had to make way for white people; KwaMashu was the Promised Land. I still remember Jonathan's grim face when we unloaded our belongings from the lorry which had bumped and groaned under the heavy weight. It was when I looked at the clutter of household goods strewn on the ground, within a perimeter that was demarcated by wooden pegs, that I realised that families could certainly accumulate a lot of garbage. While my father was being helped by neighbours to move the furniture into the box-like four-roomed house, my mother sat on a grass mat, looking at the dust swirling behind the disappearing lorry, her face as eloquent as the ages.

It was perhaps in her eyes that I read a message regarding our lives. She tried to make Jonathan and me forget our previous life in Mayville, the rambling house which adjoined our father's church, and our Indian friends, Manilal and Premlal Parboo, with whom we wrestled near the dam, where we played childhood games, all oblivious of what the State had in store for us.

Jonathan was a quiet boy; this caused my parents a lot of anxiety. His dreamy expression meant, for them, that he would become a visionary or a criminal. I was not a problem. As soon as I got to KwaMashu, I reconnoitred the streets, made friends easily and got up to the usual mischief. Arthur was always there, deferring to me in most cases, fighting my battles if the need arose. He was the first boy of eight I knew who owned dogs. He really loved the animals, sometimes purring and addressing them in soft tones as if they were human, threatening us with mayhem if we kicked them. For my part, I didn't see their use. These were just mangy mongrels which made a nuisance of themselves by upsetting dustbins.

Arthur and I ran each weekday to school, the ink bottle and a leather-bound Bible knocking about in each of our suitcases. Although we didn't share a desk, it was known that he was my best friend. He was bigger than I, so I could needle the other boys, comfortable in the knowledge that, if trouble came, he would be there to sort them out.

He was, however, not just a gentle, overgrown kid. Arthur would participate in youthful shenanigans with glee. But he seemed to maintain a certain distance from any messy development. I suspect, now, that he actually initiated some of the capers. During holidays we stole into the churchyard and picked mangoes and guavas, all the time watching for the priest's dogs. If they came upon us, Arthur had a way of pacifying them. I reasoned then that dogs probably took to fat kids. Since I was skinny, I imagined that the dogs were attracted to my barely hidden bones.

Part of growing up included working during school holidays. We were not poor, and my mother worried that I would get into more trouble in 'town', as the downtown area of Durban was known. She didn't trust me alone, or with a group of like-minded boys in the concrete and asphalt jungle which had claimed so many. But, working while a student meant that one got some experience of the real world. It was Arthur's intervention which saved the day. He convinced my mother, I later learnt, that dirtying my hands would make me a more wholesome human being. It was Arthur, also, who benefited more than all of us put together.

We worked in the scullery of a large departmental store. When not wrestling with grime, we were required to serve in the kitchen, spreading a mix of vanilla essence with white Stork margarine on slices of bread. This fare was for the African canteen. In the Indian, White and Coloured canteen, people had their tea or coffee with genuine buttered toast. Young as I was, the country's preoccupation with colour, with putting each national group in a specific pigeon hole, did not escape me. Arthur negotiated for me to be put in his detail, which loaded tripe, pieces of fish, sandwiches and Russian sausages onto aluminium trays. The trays were then installed on a trolley which we wheeled downstairs to the general factory area. Workers came and bought. Since all the food items were entered into a notebook by an Indian chef, Reddy, I took it for granted that there was nothing illegal about the operation. Much later I realised that the figures that Reddy entered didn't tally with the number of items on the trays. What Arthur was doing was to double or treble the amount of goods and then give Reddy a false count. Reddy didn't check, such activity was beneath him. When I caught Arthur out, he agreed to share the spoils. In fact, he organised another trolley. 'These people', he said – meaning Reddy, the white administration, representatives of the whole unjust world – 'are robbing us blind. Just look at the prices on these things, it's daylight robbery.' I couldn't argue with that logic. It vindicated the little robbery of our own. Arthur also rose in my estimation.

After these adventures, we returned to school cockier, more knowledgeable about the ways of the world. We drifted further and further from our parents, or from the methods they used to combat the hostile white world.

The first time Arthur and I started having differences – a time which I should have considered with great care – was over Zodwa, who was without doubt the most beautiful sixteen-year-old at Isibonelo High School.

I was sixteen then, going on seventeen. I had fooled around with members of the opposite sex but, as I have said before, my relationship with girls, dubious and troubled as it was, was strictly on my own terms. Zodwa, however, seemed totally oblivious of my antics; perhaps – and this is twenty-twenty hindsight – they amused her, but she was certainly not fooled. To add to my worries, Arthur began to stay back after school and it was clear that he had designs on her. I then hit on a plan.

'Arthur,' I said one afternoon, 'I think Zodwa is in love with you.'

'What?' he asked. 'G'wan, you. I've seen the way you've been ogling her.'

'No, Arthur. Seriously. I heard her talking to Maisie. She really thinks you're a dish.' This was all bullshit, of course. Zodwa never said anything of the sort. In fact, Maisie had confided in my current girl-friend that *she* rather fancied Arthur. A bit of a laugh, really, since Maisie had a tendency to balloon out as if at will. That she carried a torch for Arthur was a subject that drove some of the more unsympa-thetic students to hysterics; it was tantamount to being fancied by a Goodyear blimp.

I advised Arthur to pursue Zodwa. She was not a common township girl who was mesmerised by flashy cars and meretricious goods. The best route to her heart was via an understanding of her interests. Later, as we hung out on the verandah of Mashiphela's store or under the shade of an umdoni tree, Arthur would tell me about Zodwa. She loved a simple life, going to church, listening to music and reading. While this research was going on, I conducted my own probe. I attached myself to the shift which cleaned the Staff Room, ensuring my access to the cabinets storing student files. I was thrilled at the discovery that her birthday was on 29 May; since it was then the beginning of April, I had about three weeks to perfect my plan.

A certain fever grips Durban during the Easter period. Even though our parents were strong believers – my mother going to church every Sunday in her blue two-piece tunic, the jacket adorned by a white crocheted scarf, and my father looking as grim as an undertaker in his black suit and dog collar – I still couldn't quite grasp the reason for the big to-do over the death of Christ. One of the highlights of the Easter celebrations was the Passion Play. The tickets, as they say here, were as scarce as an Indian policeman in Bloemfontein. For quite a vast section of the black population, attending this performance was out of the question. It was not a racial thing; even the most rabid segregationists could not afford the stigma that would attach to them if they barred black people from the City Hall. Moreover, the company this year had threatened to suspend the one and only appearance in the city if black audiences were prohibited. The show was usually booked out months in advance.

My anxiety about how to get the tickets was solved by the timely intervention of James Firth, a clergyman who was my father's superior. When he visited, I offered to wash his car which was parked in the street. Firth gazed at me from the depths of his blue eyes, possibly thinking that I wanted to hit him for a church bursary. After the obligatory prayers followed by gallons of tea, he made to bid us goodbye. As he moved up the steps to the street, I told him that, as part of an assignment, I was supposed to write about Easter celebrations, and how I had tried to get tickets to the Passion Play but to no avail. Whether he believed this cockamamie story or not I can't tell. But he arranged for me to pick up the tickets from his secretary at the Christian Assemblies Church headquarters on Smith Street.

I remember very little of the play except that it terrified me. This is where I saw the difference between theatre and cinema; here were real people made of flesh and blood, their presence as palpable as Zodwa's clammy palm in my hand. It was easy, then, to understand why some people were weeping in the audience. The journey to Golgotha, for me, anyway, started looking quite real. It represented the hardships, the pain, which people endured every day. Zodwa tightened her grip when they laid down David Horner, the crowned actor who played Christ. She winced at each hammer blow as the nails were driven into Horner – Christ's hands and feet. When I looked at her, she was crying, tears rolling down her face. When the play ended to a rousing chorus, I was myself on the verge of weeping.

The night outside was balmy, rain waiting in the clouds for the famous Durban downpour. The people came out and rushed to their cars. Couples walked, hand in hand, as if the experience inside the theatre had strengthened their commitment to each other. As we walked down the wide street which was being constructed into a one-way, amber lamps shone upon us, on the people, removing whiteness from white faces and investing black people with a regal hue. Here and there policemen stood in twos or threes as if watching out for the beginning of a riot, their eyes shadowed by visored caps. We passed one minion of the law holding an Alsatian that strained against its leash. I looked up at the policeman's eyes. Under the light they were the loneliest, bleakest eyes I had ever seen, cold and grey as cut glass.

As we sat in the Putco bus that was bound for KwaMashu, Zodwa, having composed herself, looked me straight in the eye. 'Do we tell Arthur about this?'

'Why do you ask?'

'Because you know he wants me to be his girl.' She was quiet for a while, looking at the play of light and shadow on the shrubbery outside. She turned her eyes to the scattering of late-night passengers in the bus. 'Isn't that what it is? You're his friend, aren't you, Bobo?'

Instead of answering, I asked her, 'Do you want to be his girl?'

'I don't know.' She swallowed. My princess swallowed. I couldn't take my eyes off her, she was a dream, soft skin the colour of good coffee, eyes as black as night, and lips that seemed to retain their softness even as she nibbled at them with her lower teeth. 'Arthur is ... so proper. The kind of guy a woman would like to get married to one day.'

I felt un unreasoning flash of anger against Arthur. He had no right to intrude, not now.

The bus rolled on. Somewhere up front a radio was playing *mbaqanga*, Mahlathini singing, '*Sengikhala ngiyabaleka*', a group of boys in Wanderers Football Club strip singing along. An old, grey-bearded man in white Zion Christian Church robes got on, followed by a group of women in blue. They sat three or four rows in front. The man stood up and started preaching, railing against the sins of the flesh. I thought of telling Zodwa that some of these men were really fast with women, but thought that would offend her. Zodwa sighed. 'My stop is coming now,' she said. Before I could say anything, she leant forward and gave me a fleeting kiss on the lips. 'Thank you for taking me out. I enjoyed the play.' She stood up. 'I'm not used to scheming, Bobo. But if you don't say anything to Arthur, neither will I.'

I made to stand up to walk her home. She placed a hand on my shoulder. 'Don't worry. I'll be okay. I don't want my folks to see you –

not yet.' Then she walked unsteadily down the aisle. The bus pulled to a stop. I saw her walking towards the path leading to her house in E section. I thought she would turn and wave, but she walked on until she disappeared around a corner. That night, I went to sleep with the memory of Zodwa's kiss on my lips.

My brother Jonathan was concerned. 'You must be careful, Bobo. You've learnt to play this game where you set the rules. But comes a time when you have no power and people come and play your game and you lose. You must never take people for granted. Never underestimate their thirst for revenge.'

'But Arthur is a friend, Jonathan.'

'That's even worse.'

If Arthur knew that I was seeing Zodwa, he never let on. We were still friends, although he was now given to long moments of silence. Schools closed for the winter holidays. Arthur went to his relatives in Mkhuze; I continued seeing Zodwa in what was now a full-blown affair. She took me to meet her father, who hated me on sight. That wasn't surprising. Then she changed schools and was sucked up in the maw of a girls' college in Pietermaritzburg. I wrote her several letters which came back unopened with a RETURN TO SENDER stamp across the envelope. I was wounded by this, I who had never tasted rejection. What was even more hurtful was that I couldn't share my predicament with Arthur. Eighteen months later I was kicked out of the University of Fort Hare after a sit-in. Arthur persevered at the University of Zululand, where he completed his B.Sc.

When I came across him at the Indian Market on Victoria Street, he had changed. I was kicking around at the Banner News Agency, stringing for an assortment of Durban newspapers. The hours were long and the pay scandalous. Arthur was now a serious person, aiming at becoming a geology lecturer. I knew that, even if he showed happiness at meeting me again, something about my condition must have embarrassed him. Seeing him compounded my sense of failure. I knew then that if I was not going to spend the rest of my life wallowing in self-pity, I needed to excel in something. And since journalism was beckoning, I had to make my mark there.

Two months later, Arthur came to my parents' funeral; mother and father had been killed in a car crash in Pinetown. Our heads were shorn of hair, as was the custom, so that death and shaving have become closely associated in my mind. The few uncles and aunts – and a whole battery of cousins – did their best to comfort us. But the pain, the loss, were there, and it was only with their death that I realised how little I knew of my mother and father. What had been their dreams? What had occupied their thoughts, nightly, as they replayed in their minds the events of the day? Because, in those days, every opportunity to go to sleep was an act of defiance, of resistance. I knew that they had loved each other, sometimes to the point where each was interchangeable with the other, my father usually misplacing his spectacles and wearing mother's to read the paper or his Bible, my mother padding into the kitchen, looking smaller in father's terry-cloth bathrobe.

While Jonathan slumped deeper and deeper into depression, Arthur and I were inside the tent, finishing off a bottle of whisky. In a drunken daze I remembered him saying something about Zodwa, and that he was now married and his wife was expecting. I promised to call on him and see his family.

But by that time I was following a lead on corruption in the South African Broadcasting Corporation. In its propaganda against the African National Congress, white radio writers created virulently anti-communist serials which were translated by blacks into African languages. One translator, Themba Nguni, evidently sick and tired of this charade, slipped some liberation movement comment into one play. Knowing that the Special Branch would be knocking at dawn, Nguni went straight to our newspaper and sought me out.

They detained him under Section 6 of the Terrorism Act. But I had a story under my belt. All that was needed was corroboration from other translators. The SABC building was guarded and entry was difficult. I posed as a successful job applicant called in for an interview. I managed to collect a lot of dirt on what some of the Calvinist, churchgoing copy-tasters deemed morally acceptable for black people. In some offices, too, men read pornographic magazines and indulged in bacchanalian raillery. All this was kept under a tight lid. I filed my story and waited for the storm.

It came at 4am in the form of one Warrant Officer Pelser, who, accompanied by two African Security Branch officers as eager as retrievers, took me to the Fisher Street Security Police headquarters. After the obligatory physical and verbal abuse, I was transported to a number of police stations. Jonathan, who was now a minister of religion, gained entry. It was here that he preached to me. Arthur came too. This was strange because a detainee was not supposed to have visitors. I suppose the police thought that my brother or my friend would talk me out of what was called communist nonsense.

But by then I was no mere newsman; I had become news. My colleagues joined in the campaign for the release of detainees. My name made the headlines. I was released nine months later, without being charged.

I was offered a senior editorship, but by then I was being wooed by the *Rand Daily Mail* in Johannesburg. I worked for them until the paper folded under the pressure of greater market imperatives. It was then that Mark Kastner offered me a job with *The Herald*. I couldn't resist the call.

Five years after Mandela's release, I found myself back in Durban. My city of birth also became the arena of my undoing. It is strange how a mundane thing such as the death of someone you might have known as a kid – and possibly not liked – can impact on your life. And how, if you had not gone to a particular event, you might not have met someone who contributed to changing the course of your life. Thomas Manzi's death had this influence on me.

I remember Thomas Manzi as a fierce roughhouse type of schoolboy who talked back to the teachers and harassed us for the few cents of pocket money our parents had given us. I would hear much later that after the June 1976 Soweto Uprising, when young people skipped – the parlance of that dreadful hour for exile – Manzi's parents were so fed up with him that they asked him if he hadn't seriously considered skipping the country. If school was tough, Thomas made it unbearable. If he sat next to you in class, for instance, your fate was sealed. The

teachers, especially Mr Zondi who taught us Geography, had this
terrible habit of posing difficult questions. If no hand shot up, he would
thrash the whole class with a cane. Thomas believed in someone
sacrificing for the collective; when Zondi asked a question, Thomas
would stick the sharp point of his Three Star blade into your elbow,
causing the hand to jerk up involuntarily, resulting in the teacher
pointing at you, the brilliant solver of mysteries, saying, 'Yes, Bobo?
What is an isthmus?' Isthmus? Isn't that what your toothless
grandmammy lisps when she wants to say 'Christmas'? You would
babble some nonsense and of course get caned. It was unfair. Who,
doing Standard Five, under Bantu Education, besides, knew what an
isthmus was?

So here I was, entering the church at Thomas's funeral. I was still
mulling over his death, looking for a place to sit, when a voice said:
'Well, well. If it isn't old Bhongoza himself ...'

Now, I really hate it when someone calls me 'Bhongoza'. My name
is Bobo, no more, no less. However, I controlled myself, ignored the
greeter and concentrated on the throng in the church. It was a motley
crowd, taxi drivers taking a breather in between taxi-wars; church
women in the red and white strip of the Methodist Church, this holy
side for God; some musicians who lugged their instruments waiting for
the moment when they would be required to play; and general
hangers-on. Honoured guests moved silently to the platform, led by a
priest. Family members sat in the front pews. The casket stood on a
bier, wreaths and fresh flowers covering the top, a section of flowers
arranged into a message, WE LOVE YOU DAD.

'Hey, Bobo my bro,' the man behind me persisted, 'how are you?'

This time I turned slowly, composing my face into a smile of feigned
surprise. It was Arthur Sikhosana. Balding profusely and almost visibly
growing fatter, Arthur was still the same boy whose girl I had stolen
some twenty years ago. He wore an expensive-looking dark suit, a
white shirt clasped at the collar by a black bow-tie, and black patent
leather shoes. The bow-tie had an effect of separating his bullet-head
from the rest of the body. It took me a while to realise that Arthur's
companion, a plump, handsome woman who hovered restlessly around

him while clutching a handbag close to her body, was actually Zodwa. She knew that pickpockets were not loth to ply their trade among mourners. Just recently, there had ensued a hue and cry in Munsieville, Klerksdorp, when one of the more nimble-fingered tsotsis made off with a gold wedding ring which some lax mortician had left on the finger of the deceased.

When I saw Zodwa, I felt a pang of guilt, but it was guilt mixed with great relief. Something had changed her from a sharp, self-possessed young woman into a matron of shabby respectability. I knew that what I had done to them was the bottom of the moral totem pole. Both had trusted me at one stage of our lives and I had let them down. Their faces, however, expressed nothing which could have been interpreted as antipathy. Arthur still looked as if he wanted to continue where we had left off, wherever that was, and Zodwa's face was composed, as unreadable as a blank page.

'Arthur,' I cried, spreading my arms wide but still hoping that he wouldn't embrace me, 'what a surprise!'

'Meet my wife, Zodwa.' Arthur shrugged as if introducing his wife was an unpleasant but necessary task. 'This is my old buddy, Bobo. You must remember Bobo?' His smile broadened; Zodwa looked bewildered. From that introduction, I knew that Arthur had known of our little liaison, and that it had hurt him. I wondered whether he would ever forgive me.

I grinned and mumbled a greeting. Arthur steered us to a pew with a sprinkling of mourners. However hard I tried to manoeuvre myself away from the couple, Arthur skirted around and insinuated his bulk beyond the seated people so that I found myself wedged in between the Sikhosanas. I hate funerals as a rule; this one was definitely not going to be a bundle of giggles either. Feeling the warmth of Zodwa's thigh pressing against the fabric of her skirt, I wondered what she was thinking. I remembered those thighs when they were still supple, wrapped around my waist, shit, this was neither the time nor the place to have these thoughts. I had to concentrate on why I was here, my mission.

The service mercifully over, I followed Arthur as we filed out of the church. When we got outside, an easterly wind was rising, ruffling the leaves on treetops, carrying in it a promise of rain. Cushiony clouds scudded across a sky against which swallows flying in formation were framed. Somewhere far, in one of the township houses, a dog barked, to be followed by the plaintive wailing of a child.

Spectators drawn to the hearse stood in ragged groups, some leaning against parked cars. Men took off their hats as eight pallbearers emerged out of the gloom of the church and installed the casket in the hearse. Thomas's girlfriend, Tozi, looking crushed and desirable and infinitely alone, nodded at the attendant who held the limousine door open for her. She entered and sat down. The door clicked shut, a mere whisper of steel against chrome. Then the cortège began its slow movement to the cemetery, the young choristers in black and blue gowns following the procession, stepping in time to the measured tread of the attendant, who wore striped trousers, a swallowtail coat, an Ascot tie and a top hat. The number of German cars confirmed the late Manzi's popularity among the more affluent of the land. Indeed, I couldn't help overhear two urchins standing and gawping with admiration. 'Check that Dolphin,' one said, pointing at a burgundy BMW, 'a gravymobile for amaGents!'

'So, how is Jo'burg treating you?' Arthur asked, not really expecting a reply, pouring me a shot of scotch. We were in his house at D Section. As I tasted the amber liquid, feeling it course down my stomach, I pondered over the day's events. They were fraught with subterranean meanings which portended a darkness that I would have a hard time conquering. It could have been pure exhaustion, or the effect of alcohol, but I experienced a momentary flash, a vision, where I saw a great boulder rolling towards me, my mind screaming, *Move, you fool!* while my limbs defied the command. I fought off an urge to scream, knowing that this was not actually happening. On opening my eyes, I found Zodwa staring at me with a fierce intentness. Shaking myself out of this seizure, I excused myself and went out of the lounge.

'You okay, bro?' Arthur asked, soon standing behind me as I looked at the rain falling on his flower garden. Behind us the small, dark speakers of his expensive CD player issued sweet soul music. When I turned to look at him he was walking back to the kitchen. Zodwa sat paging through a magazine, her legs folded under her body, her shoes on the carpet. Since the door separating the lounge from the kitchen was open, my eyes were drawn to the wood panelling, the pine units and the gleaming aluminium sink. Arthur, having discarded his sombre suit for a loose cardigan, jeans and slippers, was bent in half, his arms working.

I walked back to the sofa and prepared to engage Zodwa in conversation, dreading the prospect, for, really, what was there to talk about? There was just too much to talk about. The music played on amid this profound silence, bringing into the room an ethereal, sorrowful mood; this was deepened by the singing of many voices that were laden with nostalgia and sadness and regret for countless transgressions. These anonymous young singers who raised their voices in praise of an unknown god and who evoked an unseen power, pushed me deeper into the softness of the sofa, a lump in my throat.

A soft, satisfied growl from the kitchen heralded the appearance of a large labrador. It was the dog Arthur must have been stroking when he was bent like that in the kitchen. He continued to caress the animal, his own tone low and soft as he murmured words of endearment. I looked up from the dog and saw Zodwa gazing at the pet with a look of such malevolence it could only have sprung from long pent-up feelings. I understood, as if in a moment of religious revelation, that it was on the dog that Arthur lavished his affection. Zodwa was part of the furniture, an untouched bauble that would be summoned to grace occasions which called for such appearances of respectability. All this communicated to me that she must be an extremely lonely woman indeed. An earlier guilt returned; in not acknowledging what had happened between us, I had effectively put Zodwa at Arthur's mercy, where she was treated like a shop-soiled article, of no account. I felt the weight of what we men do to put women at a disadvantage, where we blaspheme those intimate moments of love and codify them as conquests – we, the eternal swordsmen – while they retreat, maimed, to lick their wounds in that most private, unreachable corner of their hearts.

As Zodwa's eyes softened and misted, Arthur raked us with his own, triumphant that he had finally reached his destination in life: a car, a house, a wife, a dog and freedom. The dog, possibly sensing the tension in the room, gave a cough, then padded to the rug spread near the drinks cabinet. Arthur's movements were now slower and more deliberate, much like a drinker wishing to dispel the impression that he or she is getting sozzled. I have had many experiences with drinking people and I know that when the intake reaches a certain level – especially if there is a little unpleasant issue to be resolved – people can be unpredictable. I knew that it was time to leave. As if seeking to thwart my intention, Arthur picked up the bottle and poured out two measures of whisky into the glasses. 'Top up, bro?'

'Do you see much of Jonathan?' I asked, suddenly feeling a great urge to see my brother.

'Ja, a while back,' Arthur said, 'we collided at one of these Movement dos. He was on the organising committee for Tambo's visit to King's Park.'

'I thought he wanted nothing to do with politics?'

'You'll be surprised how many people have changed.' Arthur regarded his glass, swirling the liquid within. 'There are those we call the six-month wonders, who joined the ANC six months before elections, when it was quite clear which way the cat would jump.' He sipped his drink and twisted his lips. 'It's funny. It's exactly those people who landed cushy government jobs. But Jonathan was in it from the very beginning.'

'Jonathan?' I couldn't visualise my staid, religious brother running errands in the execution of the liberation struggle.

'It's true.' Arthur sounded distracted as if this conversation conflicted with some voice which spoke from inside himself. Then he smiled, urbane and controlled. 'What say we take a drive. Get some air?'

'Have you visited your parents' graves, Bobo?' Zodwa asked. It appeared to me that this was the question she had been waiting to ask the whole afternoon. Arthur turned his eyes to her, favouring his wife with a look which must have been on Balaam's face when the ass challenged him.

I shook my head. The prospect certainly didn't appeal to me. I feared the things such a visit would evoke in me. When Arthur nodded and said that this was a good idea, I felt like someone participating in a game with arbitrary laws, where winning was losing and vice versa. I sat thinking of the dread possibility of being rebuked for neglecting a son's duty. At the same time, I had a feeling of being swept along with schemes which had been hatched long before my arrival in this house. I thought of Jonathan and, without being told, I knew that this couple had actually been supporting him financially, if not spiritually. Which meant that they were paying rent for the house I had left, my father's house. With this sense of shame then, I gathered my briefcase and left the comfort of my seat. While Arthur went to get his car keys, I approached Zodwa and hugged her, taking in the faint whisper of her perfume and hair lotion. She held me tight and I remembered the strength of her clasp, then she pushed me away. I had a feeling that she would later go into the bathroom and wash away the memory of our contact. '*Hamba kahle*, Bobo,' she said, 'and may your gods be with you.' The dog watched us with brown, baleful eyes.

I hesitated at the door. 'Maybe we can talk some time?'

'We'll never talk again, Bobo,' Zodwa said in a fierce whisper. 'Not now, not ever!' In a gesture of dismissal, she bent over the machine. There was a soft hiss as the disk tray slid forward. Zodwa replaced the disk with something upbeat, a tune which both summoned our past and said farewell to whatever had taken place between us. It was a disavowal of any part she had played before, an embrace of whatever the future would offer.

Sunday people, the drunks and the holy believers, brought back the ghosts from the past. We passed them on the streets, my people, moving in a narcotised stupor, their form of dress signifying the crutch of their choice. Women in yesterday's party clothes speaking in harsh, whisky-scarred tones, their partners accompanying them in sullen silence. The men looked dangerous in their suits and hats and shoes that still gleamed in the gathering dusk. Somewhere from inside a house, a snatch of loud music and revellers' voices. Some men, women and children under a bus shelter, the young men's eyes defiant, disconsolate and full of longing.

We hit F Section, where blackened ruins had replaced a shopping centre, speaking of battles that had raged in pre-election days. This was where we danced the latest township jive, smoked the first joint and harassed our first girl. Scrub now abounded in a space formerly occupied by a community centre.

The smell wafting into the car from the street was a smell I remembered from my own youth. Flowers fought exhaust fumes, the eternal struggle of life against death. Although many houses were now electrified, you still came across smoke from wood- or coal-burning stoves billowing out of asbestos chimneys. Hibiscus hedges and bougainvillaea fronted houses, while giant rubber trees kept a silent watch over the street.

On Zulu Road an impi of about forty men dressed in traditional attire danced and beat their shields with knobkerries. This was an exuberant crowd, perhaps from an *imbizo*, a convocation of subjects in a chief's kraal. Instead of people scattering – the healthiest response to armed men – they stood watching, little children pointing at pot-bellied men whose fleshy folds flowed over loin-skins. Some women ululated, urging the prancing warriors on, reliving in their minds the glories of past kingdoms. Since I had covered countless violent incidents involving these warriors' kinsmen, I was surprised at feeling unthreatened as we negotiated our way through this vibrant throng. Looking at the rippling muscles on the bare torsos of some of the younger men, I felt over-dressed and stupid, alien in my Western clothes. I also knew that, second to people involved in struggle, there is nothing more beautiful than people engaged in the celebration of their culture.

We passed my old high school, now bordered by a high barbed-wire fence, the windows burglar-proofed and covered with wire mesh. Weeds and green saplings grew in stubborn abundance around the building, this neglect speaking of a greater inclination on the part of the community to let things go. It was with a mixture of sadness and rage – an emotion which grips one on leaving a hospital after a necessary amputation – that I turned my eyes away from the school which had shaped us and maimed us in equal measure. So many of my classmates were gone, claimed by the streets to become pale imitations of their former selves. Some had found meaning in the struggle, and many more had entered the never-never-land where they nightly pursued the dream of the everlasting rand note.

In the approaching dark, we took the narrow, untarred road to the cemetery. The air smelled of growth, wood-smoke and lumber. Even as we alighted from the car, hearing the call of night birds and frogs croaking in hidden wetlands, I knew that I had been summoned to this terrain by something much bigger than ourselves. Arthur walked beside me in silence. His breath came out in short pants, providing a counterpoint to the raw-edged rising wind. Shadows in the twilight invested the area with strange shapes where the sighing wind carried within itself the unwhispered secrets of the dead.

I followed Arthur to a canopy of wattle where the darkness deepened. It felt as if we had been walking for miles. My skin prickled as I stepped on something soft and squelchy, perhaps a dead rodent, before a feral smell rose and assailed my nostrils. In this dark, which was the most absolute of nights, I was revisited by that epiphanic moment of earlier in the day. What had been straining for expression, something that had been hidden so deeply within the folds of my consciousness, burst forth, unsummoned. I knew, then. Before I could speak, there was a soft snick! of a pistol being cocked. Just then, the clouds above parted and a pale moon gleamed like a polished silver coin. Arthur, his eyes shadowed, stood in the light with the gun hand hanging parallel to his legs.

You must never take people for granted. Jonathan's words echoed from the dead and unburied past. I took a step forward. Arthur lifted the pistol and pointed it at the region of my chest. He was wheezing like an old man. Strange as this may sound, I was not afraid.

'He's dead, isn't he, Arthur?' I asked the question, not really expecting an answer.'You killed him. Jonathan. Didn't you?'

'Your brother seduced my wife, Bobo,' Arthur said quietly. 'Just like you did.'

'You mean you killed him for that?'

'It's not that simple.' Arthur took a step back and sat down on a tree stump. 'When I met Zodwa, she connected me with a past I had forgotten. We got married, but I had a problem.' He swallowed and, as a descending moonbeam highlighted his features, I saw the young Arthur who had been so eager to please, a puppy. 'A sex problem. I couldn't do it with a woman ... how do you say it? I couldn't get it up.' He snickered self-consciously, the way we do when forced to expose our nakedness to strangers. 'I went to medicine men, those rip-off artists, and they cleaned me out. But Zodwa stood by me in all this. She had got some religion, thanks to you and your fucking Passion Play.'

'As I opened my mouth to remonstrate with him, hell, Zodwa had got religious long before I met her, Arthur waved the gun at me, a signal for me to shut up. 'I know what you want to say,' he said. 'But after Zodwa left the girls' college, she went wild. Fucked anything with a penis. When I met her, she was in bad shape. But, because I loved her, I thought I would wean her from her ways. It seemed like a good idea for her to go to your brother and get some spiritual sustenance. Only it wasn't spiritual sustenance he was giving her, your brother. When I found one of those vapid love letters she had written to Jonathan, I confronted her. Then she told me about how you had broken her virginity.' He looked me straight in the eye. 'A virgin is a precious thing in the township, did you know that, Bobo?'

I nodded, thinking maybe non-verbal communication would disarm him. What a mess. Arthur, my friend, carrying all this hate through all these decades, what a bloody mess. The man was certifiable. Obliquely, I thought about a successor who would pick up my spear, or, in this instance, my bulging briefcase, and see my assignment through.

'So I brought him here, just like I brought you,' he went on. 'Funny how people get sentimental over dead parents. Shit, the people are dead, man, resting. Look,' he gestured with the gun hand, embracing the spread of the cemetery,' all those people lying in there, being nutrients and giving real sustenance to the worms. They don't give a flying fuck that you go out there and place fresh flowers and tend to the graves. They're dead. *Finito*, no *manga-manga*.'

Arthur declared that he was a scientist, a geologist. He believed in the immortality of rocks. He knew stones, boulders, pebbles; rock formations, fossils, that was his reality. In the beginning there was rock and in the end there will be rock – rock is the alpha and omega, not human beings. They are transient. In this regard, then, they should stand in awe before greatness, the unchangeable nature of rocks. To this effect, in recognition of their frailty, their insignificance in the face of immutable laws, men mustn't bullshit and fuck other people's wives.

'And you know what happened when I shot him?' Arthur was in full flight now. 'I'll tell you. I got hard. I got hard just imagining it was you I was killing. So,' he asked, brightening up, 'how's that for creative therapy?'

'Arthur ...' I began.

'Shut up!' Arthur screamed. 'Just shut the fuck up!'

He stood up from the stump. 'Lie down, Bobo.' He waved the gun to the ground.

When I got to my knees, he leant forward and pressed me against the wet, mossy ground. I smelled the earth and the grass and the stones. I thought of the briefcase in his car, the BMW, the Dolphin. *Oh God please help me here in this valley of death with this tormented and twisted man who was once my friend help me because I have sinned Hail Mary three times a day I'll even say mea culpa seven times an hour if you deliver me safe how does a bullet feel when it enters your brain do you hear the bang do you smell anything it would be wrong if I voided myself just imagine being dead in such an unflattering position covered in excrement what rots first the guts or the rest of the body is that why when they do an autopsy they take out the innards first do they smell ...Prrrr! Prrrr! I'm already dead and Satan is talking to Saint Peter negotiating over some dubious souls who gatecrashed a celestial party no it's actually ...* Arthur talking on his cellular phone. '... yes, he's here. D'you want to talk to him? Hang on, let me pass him on to you.' He extended his hand holding the dark instrument with a luminous display and numbers. 'Very handy, these little Japanese toys.' When I found it awkward to hold it, Arthur pulled me up into a sitting position. I pressed the gadget against my ear.

'Hello?' I said.

'Bobo?' a voice said through the crackle. 'Where the hell have you been?'

'Jonathan? Is that you?'

'Who did you think it was – the Right Reverend James Firth?' Then he laughed at our little inside joke. 'I'm at Arthur's place. Better hurry up. Will be good to see you.' The line went dead.

I looked at Arthur, who had stood up. He took the phone from my hand, pushed in the aerial and stuck it inside his shirt pocket. He looked up at the moon, his own face resembling the heavenly body. Then he looked down at me, offered his arm. I clasped the proffered crutch and got to my feet. The gun was nowhere in sight. Arthur wrinkled his nose.

'I'll loan you a pair of jeans,' he said. 'They might be a bit wide around the waist, but we'll sort it out.'

'Okay,' I said. I found a packet of cigarettes in my jacket pocket, lit one, blew out the smoke and followed Arthur to his chariot parked in the furze, which would take us to his house where my brother waited with his heart overflowing with love and trembling.

© Mandla Langa 1996

RECOGNITION

David Medalie

When I saw the envelope in which the invitation came, I thought it might be a request for an interview. I still get those occasionally, although fewer and fewer as time goes by. People nowadays don't want to ask me about Kobus and about those years as they did after he died. They think he belongs too much to the past. And I too have become something left over from the past. Let me tell you, that is a sad fate. This has become a young country now, and whether people are pleased about it or fighting against it, that is where their energies lie. Those who do try to recall the past want it to be tough and aggressive. That is certainly not my style. Besides, I am an old lady. I lead a quiet life and would not have it otherwise, but there is still a part of me that does not like to be forgotten; and because I have a responsibility towards Kobus's memory, I would not like him and what he accomplished to be forgotten either. That is understandable. There is a kind of loyalty that must be suspicious of things that are new.

I thought also that it might be an invitation to attend a political rally of the Party. Sometimes I am invited to participate in those sorts of gatherings. I find it hard to refuse, because I know that they want me there to represent Kobus and I suppose they are the last people who still cherish all that he fought for. Yet it is difficult for me to know what to do, for I feel that the Party is no longer the one that he represented so loyally, and that he would not approve of some of the directions it has chosen. Also, I am not a political person in myself, even though I was the wife of the Prime Minister for a number of years. Politics was Kobus's life and, of course, I supported him in every way that I could. But if he had remained a lawyer or I had married a schoolteacher like myself, I would have been quite contented. Politics is a rough business and I am not a rough person. As a child, I did not even like competitive games. Then I found myself having to support Kobus in the most competitive game of all. But I did what was needed and perhaps even more than was needed. I shirked nothing, no matter how unpleasant. I do not say this because I expect praise or gratitude. I say it simply because that is how it was. I must insist on the truth of what was. People are not satisfied with changing the present nowadays, they want to change the past too. I feel I have to protect what I know. I have become strangely jealous of my own life.

Anyway, I tore the envelope open. At first I thought it must be a joke or a trick that someone was playing on me, for I really was never so astonished in my life. I had been so isolated and so removed from what is happening in politics, despite the courtesies extended to me by the Party, that I didn't know that such a gathering was even being planned. And it is the last thing I would ever have imagined likely. The present government could not possibly be favourably disposed towards me – that is, if they ever gave me a thought. Yet, if this was not a hoax, I was being invited to a luncheon at the residence of the President.

I was distrustful. I didn't want to do anything that would make me feel regret afterwards. I didn't want to be used by any group of people for their own political ends, except by the Party, who usually use me very respectfully; and even then I am not entirely happy about it. I am cautious by nature and being married to Kobus for all those years has made me even more so, for he was a careful and scrupulous man, and he taught me a great deal. He taught me more as a father teaches his child than as a man teaches his wife. And I knew so little, even though I had been to the Teachers Training College. But what I learned I have kept with me all my life, for where else does stability lie?

The only way I could establish whether or not it was a joke was to phone up Magdalena. If I received an invitation, then she must have received one too, I thought; and she is more in touch with what is happening politically at the moment than I am. I worked out that there were six widows of former prime ministers or presidents still living. But Magdalena was the only one I could speak to. The husbands of two of them were bitter rivals of Kobus. The third one's husband betrayed him terribly, even though they had studied together at the University of the Orange Free State and were allies for many years after that. Kobus never forgave him and the quarrel went on until the day Kobus died. The fourth widow has Alzheimer's disease – they say she doesn't even recognise her own children.

Magdalena said that it was a genuine invitation. The President wishes to make peace with the past, she said; this is his way of showing that reconciliation can take place. She sounded very excited about it. She was certainly going to attend the luncheon and she urged me to attend it too. I said that I would think about it. Magdalena always loved feeling important; that is one of her little failings. Her husband died in office and so she lost him and the public attention at the same time. I do not condemn her for being that way, but I am different. Even when Kobus was Prime Minister, I did not exploit the powerful position that circumstances had given me, although I worked hard and carried out my duties conscientiously. I like to think that, as a result, I was a dignified and thoughtful presence and a good role model for women generally, not only for those whose husbands were in politics.

Magdalena said that she had already established that the other widows, except for poor Mrs Havenga, were willing to accept the President's invitation. She told me that Mrs Havenga just sits and stares blankly. It is pitiful to see. Her husband had the largest majority in parliament ever achieved in the history of the Party and she remembers nothing of it. All those triumphs are lost to her. She also told me that Mrs Groenewald had not been well, she had a hip replacement last year and other health problems, but she was very excited about the invitation and determined to attend the luncheon. I said politely that I was glad she was feeling up to it; I didn't think it was necessary to remind Magdalena about the great quarrel between Kobus and Jan Groenewald.

Was Magdalena sure that accepting the invitation was the right thing to do, I asked? Was it *politically* the right thing to do? Of course, she said. The President was recognising our importance and the importance of our late husbands. It would be good for the morale of the people who still believed in the old values to see the President extending such recognition and courtesy to us. We owed it to those people. They were in such despair. Their culture was under attack. They struggled to get jobs because of Affirmative Action. They had become outcasts in their own land. Before I put the phone down I said that I would accept the invitation. I still had some reservations, but I kept them from Magdalena. She was thrilled. Every widow would now be coming, she said; except, of course, for poor Mrs Havenga.

You cannot imagine how strange it felt to enter the official residence again after all those years. People feel uncomfortable even when they have cause to enter a house which they once lived in; imagine, then, how disconcerting it was for me to enter the residence where I once, as the Prime Minister's wife, entertained important people from all over the world – Taiwan, Chile, Paraguay. Now I entered as the guest of a man whom my husband fought to keep out of it. It was so difficult for me that I had to think deliberately about my pride before I went in – how much pride I would wear, how I would wear it. It was almost like deciding how to arrange a scarf. The taxi dropped me off and I walked slowly and deliberately, carrying myself without haughtiness but rather as I felt a woman should who is conscious all the time of a solemn duty. I wanted to be worthy of that important thing that had been entrusted to me and that others, despite their own importance, were prepared to recognise in me.

Magdalena was ahead of me and I could already see that she was not behaving in a dignified manner. The President himself was receiving

her at the door and she was gushing over him, not permitting him even
to complete his words of welcome. There was something cringing
about her, I thought; a smallness in her gratitude. I felt ashamed of her
behaviour. I was determined that there would be nothing to be
ashamed of in my behaviour. Someone who was standing near the
President approached me and I told him who I was. He returned to the
President with the information and then the President came towards
me, smiling and greeting me. I shook his hand firmly. I said I was
pleased to be there. I thanked him for the invitation. That was all. I
was ushered into the dining hall.

It looked very different from the room that I had known, the room
that I had redecorated myself a few months after Kobus became Prime
Minister. The colours were bolder. We had painted the walls a light
salmon colour, but now they were reddish brown with a white border.
Not one work of art that we had chosen was still there, not even the
Pierneef or the Van Wouw sculpture. Why was it necessary to remove
those? The Pierneef was a landscape, the Van Wouw was a torso – there
was nothing political about them. In a strange way, the sight of this
redecorated room affected me more than all the other changes I had
seen, such as watching the President being sworn in or the generals
from the army and the air force saluting a black man.

Of course, I showed none of the emotion that I felt. I looked around
to see where I had been seated. Before I could find the card with my
name on it, Magdalena was pointing it out to me and waving at me. It
was not too near to her, thankfully, nor too near to Mrs Groenewald,
who was making a point of ignoring my presence. The seats on either
side of me were still empty. A waiter stepped forward immediately to
offer me a drink. I chose soda water, as I always do.

Gradually the table began to fill up. There were a number of black
women, whom I was surprised to see there. Then I realised that it was
a gathering of political widows of all sorts, including the widows of
people who had fought against the previous government. Black women
and white women were being seated next to one another. The woman
on my left was an Indian woman. She introduced herself, but her name
was not familiar to me. The one on my right greeted me, but did not

introduce herself, so I did not tell her who I was either. I tried to glance at her name card, but it was angled towards her and I could not read it. After that she sat quietly, making no attempt to speak to me or anyone else. She was a young woman, much younger than most of the other women there. She was perhaps less than forty years old.

When the President came into the room, we stood up. He asked us all to sit down. Then he made a short speech. He was honoured to receive us all; he was delighted that we had come. This was a time of reconciliation and dialogue, and we were all participating in that by sitting down to dine together, some of us bitter foes in the past, and showing the country that such things were possible. Then he spoke of those few who were not there, whose health had prevented them from coming. He named them all and said that he would call on them soon. He even mentioned Mrs Havenga, and I wondered whether he knew what condition she was in. He named two women who had managed to come despite recent health problems of a serious nature, and thanked them in particular. One of them was Mrs Groenewald.

Then the President sat down and they began to serve the meal. There was a cold cucumber soup, followed by saddle of venison. Television cameras had been set up and it was strange to think that we were being filmed as we ate. The Indian lady turned to me repeatedly, happy to make small talk, and we spoke about the food and about the President's speech. She pointed out some of the women and told me who they were and I did the same for her, pointing out and identifying each of the widows from the former government. The black woman on the other side remained very uncommunicative. If I spoke to her, she answered briefly, but made no effort to contribute to the conversation of her own accord, so I gave up and spoke to the Indian lady all the time. While the dessert was being served, the President got up and began to move around the table, speaking to each of the women. I could see Magdalena clasping his hand and looking up at him, speaking at length while the television cameras and microphones were focused upon her. I was pleased that I could not hear what she was saying.

When the President got to our part of the table, the Indian lady sprang up and they hugged each other. They clearly knew each other

well. The President enquired after members of her family, they spoke
of mutual friends and acquaintances. Then he moved on to me. He
spoke to me with great courtesy. He knew that I had two daughters and
he enquired after them. He asked me about my health. He wished to
know where I lived. Did I enjoy my retirement from the pressures of
political life? Not particularly, I said; it was a duty that one assumed
without question and gave up when the time was over.

It occurred to me, as we spoke, that he is two years older than I. He
was kindly, polite, yet somehow distant in a way that I could not quite
put my finger on. His eyes are more inscrutable than the photographs
suggest. I was not very pleased with my responses; I felt they were a
little ungracious. I wanted to do more than thank him for inviting me
to the luncheon. I wanted to thank him for the gesture, for the
symbolism. I know the importance of symbolism, for our own culture
is full of symbols. But I didn't know how to do so without gushing like
Magdalena, without yielding something up to him that I was supposed
to keep from him. So I was formal, polite in my turn and controlled.
He passed on.

When he greeted by name the black woman next to me, I felt
startled. I drank some soda water to hide my reaction. Hearing that
name again, the name that had vexed Kobus for so many years and
even after he retired from political life, the name that had been linked
to his throughout the world, was a shock to me. That name had first
begun to inconvenience us before Kobus was Prime Minister – it was
when he was still Minister of Justice. And when he became Prime
Minister, journalists and other people hostile to the government
referred whenever they could to those suicides and accidents that
occurred while people were in police custody; and always they referred,
in particular, to the death of this woman's husband. And perhaps, as
Kobus admitted to me, some of them were caused by police exceeding
their duties, for those were trying times, and in trying times people are
not always at their best. But it didn't mean that Kobus had anything to
do with it. He was a fair man, firm but always fair. And it grieved him
that his name should be linked to such events and I grieved with him,
for I was protective of his reputation as, indeed, I still am.

Yet here was the widow of the most notorious of all those detainees, the one whose death caused an international outcry. I had been sitting next to her throughout the luncheon and I had not known who she was. Now, after the President moved on from us to speak to another group of ladies, we looked at each other and were silent. Her silence made me very uncomfortable. I felt the need to say something, something appropriate to the occasion, but it was difficult to know what to say.

Finally I said, 'I'm sorry, I didn't know who you were.'

'I knew who you were,' she said. We sat silently again. She bent her head to her dessert. It was clear that, if any gestures were to be made, they would have to come from me.

'The President has done a great thing,' I said. 'He has brought us together so that we can make peace with the past and recognise our common humanity. After all, we are all widows. Each of us has suffered a loss.'

She looked up again and seemed to stare at something behind me, something in the far distance.

'Is that what you have come to do – to make peace with the past?' she asked.

I thought for a while before I answered. 'No,' I said. If there was one gesture I could make, it was to tell her the truth. It was a relief to do so. 'I came to make sure that no one is going to take the past away from me.'

When I said that, she blinked and looked directly at me. It was impossible to know what to make of the expression on her face. Only someone who knew her well could have interpreted it, and I didn't know her at all.

'Perhaps we have something in common after all,' she said.

© David Medalie 1996

AUTOPSY

Ivan Vladislavić

Um.

Basically, I was seated at the Potato Kitchen in Hillbrow partaking (excuse me) of a potato. Nothing very exciting had happened to me as yet: I was therefore dissatisfied and alert. Then the King Himself came out of Estoril Books, shrugged His scapular girdle, and turned left. It was the King, no doubt about it, I would know His sinuous gait anywhere. Even in a mob.

It was supper-time, Friday, 15 May 1992. Scored upon my memory like a groove in wax. I lift the stylus, meaning to plunge it precisely into the vein, but the mechanism does not have nerves of steel: the device hums and haws before it begins to speak. (The speakers, the vocal cords, the voice-box, the woofers, the tweeters, the *loud* speakers.) So much for memory, swaddled in the velvety folds of the brain and secured in the cabinet of the skull.

My potato was large and carved into quarters, like a colony or a thief. It had been microwaved and bathed in letcho with sausage and bacon.

Also embrocated with garlic butter (R0.88 extra) and poulticed with grated cheddar as yellow as straw (R1.80 extra). Moreover, encapsulated in white polystyrene.

I was holding a white plastic fork in my left hand. I was stirring, with the white plastic teaspoon in my right hand, the black coffee in a white polystyrene cup.

The slip from the cash register lay on the table folded into a fan. It documented this moment in time, choice of menu item and price including VAT (15.05.92/letch R9.57/chee R1.80/coff R1.90/garl butt R0.88).

Although it was chilly, I had chosen a table on the pavement so that I could be part of the vibrant street life of Johannesburg's most cosmopolitan suburb. A cold front deep-frozen in the south Atlantic was at that very moment crossing the mudbanks of the Vaal. The street-children squatting at the kerb looked preternaturally cold and hungry with their gluey noses and methylated lips.

One of the little beggars was an Indian. Apartheid is dead.

I found myself in the new improved South Africa, seated upon an orange plastic chair, stackable, but not stacked at this juncture. It was one of four chairs – two orange, two umber – drawn up to a round white plastic table with a hole through its middle, specially engineered to admit the shaft of the beach umbrella, which shaft was also white, while the umbrella itself was composed of alternating segments of that colour and Coca-Cola red. My legs were crossed, right over left. The toe of my right shoe was tapping out against a leg of the table the homesickening heartbeat of 'O Mein Papa' throbbing from the gills of a passing Ford Laser.

The King chose that very moment to exit Estoril Books with a rolled magazine under His arm. He paused before the buffet of cut-price paperbacks on two trestle-tables. He examined cracked spines and dog-ears. He scanned the promotional literature.

A saddening scenario presented itself: every book will change your life.

Bundling Himself up in His diet, He turned left, took eight sinuous steps, choreographing heel, toe, knee and hip by turns, all His own work, and turned left again into the polyunsaturated interior of Tropical

Fast Foods. He was a natural. He passed under the neon sign: a green coconut palm inclined against an orange sunset while the sun sank like an embolus into a sea of lymph. Las Vegas Motel – Color TV – 5 mi. from Damascus – Next exit.

Adventure beckoned.

I had consumed no more than 25 per cent of my meal – let's say R3.00's worth – and hadn't so much as sipped the coffee, but I rose as one man, dragged on my trench coat and hurried inside to pay the bill. My white plastic knife remained jutting from the steaming potato like a disposable Excalibur.

'*Danke schön*,' I said, in order to ingratiate myself with the Potato Woman of Düsseldorf.

'*Fünfzig, fünfzehn*,' she replied, dishing change into my palm, and banged the drawer of the cash register with her chest.

Los!

On my way into the night I skirted five children squabbling over my leftovers: three-quarters of a potato (75 per cent), divisible by five only with basic arithmetic.

I sauntered across Pretoria Street, dodged a midnight-blue BMW with one headlight, cursed silently. In the few short minutes that had passed since the sighting, a grain of doubt had jammed in the treads of my logic, and now I paused on the threshold of Tropical Fast Foods, in the shadow of the electric tree, suddenly off balance. Where am I? Or rather: Where was I? Hollywood Boulevard? Dar es Salaam? Dakar? The Botanical Gardens in Durban?

Oh.

The man I had taken for the King was leaning against the counter with His back to me, gulping the fat air down. Blue denim jacket with tattered cuffs; digital watch, water-resistant to 100 metres (333 feet); track-suit pants, black with a white stripe; blue tackies (sneakers), scuffed; white socks stuck with blackjacks.

The Griller assembled a yiro (R9.50). He pinched shavings of mutton from an aluminium scoop with a pair of tongs and heaped them on a halo of unleavened pita-bread. He piled sliced onions and sprinkled the unique combination of tropical seasonings. I turned aside to the poker machine and dropped a rand in the slot.

The machine dealt me a losing hand.

Meanwhile, the spitted mutton turned at 2 r.p.m., like a stack of rare seven-singles in a jukebox. A skewered onion wept on top of the pile. Where the Griller's blade had pared, the meat's pink juices ran, spat against the cauterising elements, which glowed like red neon, and congealed upon the turntable.

I drew the Jack of Diamonds *and* the King of Hearts.

The man I had taken for the King turned to the Manager and spoke inaudibly from the right side of His mouth. There was no mistaking the aerodynamic profile, the airbrushed quiff as sleek as a fender, black with a blue highlight, the wraparound shades like a chrome-plated bumper, the Velcro sideburns, the tender lips.

The Manager amplified the whispered request for more salt.

The Griller obliged.

I kept the Jack *and* the King, against my better judgement.

The Manager cupped a paper bag under a stainless-steel funnel and tipped a basketful of chips (fries) down it. He dashed salt and pepper, shook the bag, and handed it to the King. The King throttled the bag and squirted tomato sauce (ketchup) down its throat like advertising.

The Griller finished assembling a yiro (R9.50). He rolled it expertly in greaseproof paper and serviette (napkin), slipped it into a packet and handed it to the Manager, who passed it to the King. The King took the yiro in His left hand. With His right hand He produced a large green note (bill), which the Manager held up to the light before clamping it in the register.

A flash of snow-white under the frayed cuff when the King reached for His change. Not a card up His sleeve but a clue: sunburst catsuit, doubling as thermal underwear.

The King dropped the coins into a money belt concealed under His belly. He took up the (fries). He swivelled sinuously and tenderly. Anatomical detail: sinews and tendons rotated the ball of the femur in the lubricious socket of the hip. (Nope.) Of the pelvic girdle? (Yep.) He slid onto an orange plastic stool. His buttocks, sheathed in white silk within and black polyester without, chubbed over the edge.

He pushed the shades up onto His forehead. He took out a pair of reading glasses with teardrop rims of silver wire, breathed on the lenses (uhuh), buffed them on His thigh and put them on.

Now I might have hurried over, saying: 'Excuse me. I couldn't help noticing.'

Instead, I looked away.

In the screen of the poker machine His reflection unrolled not one magazine but four: the February issue of *Musclemag International* (*The Body-Building Bible*), the April issue of *Stern*, the Special Collector's issue of *Der Kartoffelbauer* (March) and the November 1991 issue of *Guns & Ammo*. He spread them on the counter, chose the *Stern*, rolled the other three into a baton and stuffed them into a pocket.

He opened the magazine to the feature on Steffi Graf and flattened it with His left forearm. With His right hand He peeled back the greaseproof paper and with His left He raised the yiro. His Kingly lips mumbled the meat as if it were a microphone.

The menu said it was lamb, but it was mutton.

A full-page photograph showed Steffi Graf serving an ace. It captured her racket smashing the page number (22) off the top left-hand corner of the page and the sole of her tennis shoe squashing the date (April) into the clay. It captured the hem of her skirt floating around her hips like a hula hoop. The King gazed at her thighs, especially the deep-etched edge of the biceps femoris, but also at her wrists, with their eight euphonious bones – scaphoid, semilunar, cuneiform, pisiform, trapezium, trapezoid, unciform, os magnum – enclasped by fragrant sweat-bands, and her moisturised elbows scented with wintergreen.

Er.

Then He gazed at the talkative walls. The muscle in His mandible throbbed, the tip of His tongue simonised the curve of His lips with mutton fat. He spoke with a full mouth, He pronounced the lost opportunities under His breath: Hamburger R4.95 – Debrecziner R6.50 – Frankfurter & Chips R6.95 –

He chewed. He swallowed.

Eating made Him sweat. He was fat, He needed to lose some weight. He'd lost (six and a half pounds) in the fifteen years since His last public appearance, but still He was fat. An eight o'clock shadow fell over His jaw, He needed to shave. He needed to floss, there was a caraway seed lodged against the gum between canine and incisor, maxilla, right, there was mutton between molars. He needed to shampoo, His hair bore the tooth-marks of the comb like the grooves of a 78.

He ate, it made Him sweat. A bead of sweat fell like a silver sequin from the end of His nose and vanished into a wet polka dot on His double-jointed knee. He swabbed His brow with the (napkin). He licked His fingers and wiped them on His pants. He got up and walked out.

Wearing His shades on His forehead and His reading-glasses on His nose, He glided over the greasy (sidewalk).

I hurried after Him, pausing momentarily to pluck: the *Stern*, which He had left open on the counter, the corners of the pages impregnated with his seasoned saliva; the (napkin) bearing the impress of His brow; and the sequin. (I have these relics still.)

He took eight sinuous steps and turned left into the Plus Pharmacy Centre and Medicine Depot. He padded down the aisle, between the Supradyn-N and the Lucozade (on the one hand) and Joymag Acusoles: Every Step in Comfort (on the other), to the counter marked Prescriptions/Voorskrifte.

The Pharmacist was a bottle-blonde. She was neither curvaceous nor bubbly, wore a white coat, bore less than a passing resemblance to Jayne Mansfield. The King spoke to her out of the left side of His mouth. He proffered an American Express traveller's cheque and a passport.

Two other customers were browsing: a man in a blue gown, a woman in a tuxedo. She shooed them out and closed the door in my face. There was a poster sellotaped to the glass: Find out about drug abuse inside. Under cover of studying the small print I was able to gaze into the interior.

The King pulled a royal-blue pillowslip embroidered with golden musical notation and silver lightning bolts out of the front of His pants. He swept from the laden shelves into His bag nineteen bottles of Borstol Linctus, sixteen bottles of Milk of Magnesia, twenty-two plastic tubs brimming with multi-vitamin capsules (100s), fifty-seven tubes of grape- flavoured Lip-Ice, three bottles of Oil of Olay, four aerosol cans of hair lacquer, twelve Slimslabs, three boxes of Doctor McKenzie's Veinoids, five bottles of Eno, twenty-five tubes of Deep Heat, a king-size bottle of Bioplus, five hot-water bottles with teddy bear covers, an alarm clock, six tubs of Radium leather and suede dye with handy applicators, a jar of beestings and a box of Grandpa Headache Powders.

The Pharmacist tagged along, jabbing a calculator.

He signed the cheque.

I rootled in a bombproof (trash can).

He took eleven sinuous steps.

The Pharmacist held the door open for Him, and shut it behind Him when He had passed, breathing in His garlicky slipstream.

He found Himself once more upon the (sidewalk) among the hurly-burly of ordinary folk.

I might have made an approach with right hand extended: 'Long time no see.'

Instead, I hid my face.

He breathed. He took off the reading-glasses, He pulled down the shades. He settled His bag of tricks on His left shoulder. He turned right.

The King moved on foot through the Grey Area.

Now He took five hundred and seventy-one sinuous steps and turned right again. Attaboy.

Window-shopping:

He passed Checkers. He passed the hawkers of Hubbard squashes. He passed Fontana: Hot roast chickens. He passed the Hare Krishnas dishing out vegetable curry to the non-racial poor on paper plates. He passed the International Poker Club: Members Only, and the Ambassador Liquor Store: Free Ice. He passed the Lichee Inn: Chinese Take-aways. He gave a poor girl a dime. He passed the hawkers of deodorant and sticking-plaster. He passed the Hillcity Pharmacy, Wimpy: The Home of the Hamburger, and Summit Fruiters. He shifted the bag of tricks to His right shoulder. He passed Hillbrow Pharmacy Extension (a.k.a. Farmácia/Pharmacie). He passed the hawkers of wooden springboks and soapstone elephants. He dropped His Diner's Club card in a hobo's hat. He passed the Café Three Sisters, Norma Jean, Look and Listen, Terry's Deli, The Golden Egg, Le Poulet

Chicken Grill, Gringo's Fast Food, Bella Napoli and Continental Confectioners: Baking by Marco. He passed the hawkers of block-mounted reproductions of James Dean with his eyes smouldering and Marilyn Monroe with her skirt flying. Late, both of them. He passed the Shoe Hospital: Save Our Soles. He passed the hawkers of block-mounted reproductions of Himself with the white fringes of His red cowboy shirt swishing, and the black fringes of His blue hair-style dangling, and the grey shadows of the fringes of His black eyelashes fluttering. Himself as a Young Man. His name was printed on His shirt, over the alveoli of His left lung.

He felt sad to be a reproductive system.

Sniffing, He turned right into the Wurstbude.

'*Guten Abend,*' He said. '*Wie geht's?*'

'*So lala,*' said the Sausage Man of Stuttgart.

The King extracted a pickled cucumber as fat and green as His opposable thumb from the jar on the counter. '*Ich möchte eine Currywurst,*' He said, sucking on the cuke '*mit Senf, bitte.*'

(R4.70.)

He held His breath as the wurst went down the stainless-steel chute. One flick of the lever and the blades fell: the wurst spilled out in cross-sections two-fifths of an inch thick.

'*Fünfundzwanzig … dreissig, sieben, zehn,*' the Sausage Man said.

'*Ich bin ein Johannesburger,*' the King replied. '*Auf Wiedersehen.*'

At the barrel-table outside He ate the lopped sausage expertly with a brace of toothpicks, in the time-honoured manner. He broke the bread and mopped the sauce. He dusted away the crumbs.

Momentarily satiated, shaded, the King moved once more through the Grey Area; once more He moved sinuously; once more He appreciated the cosmopolitan atmosphere. (We both did.)

Now He took two hundred and seventy-five steps (Squash and Fitness Health World, Tommy's 24-Hour Superette, Bunny Chow, Bengal Tiger Coffee Bar and Restaurant, hawkers of baobab-sap and the mortal remains of baboons, Econ-o-Wash, Magnum Supermarket, Jungle Inn Restaurant, Quality Butchery: Hindquarters packed and labelled) and turned right.

He stopped. He parked the bag of tricks. He hitched down the track-suit pants with His left hand and unzipped the cat-suit with His right. He reached into the vent and abstracted a dick.

I was too far away, propped against a fireplug like a gumshoe, to determine whether this organ had charisma. But I was close enough to hear a musical fountain of urine against a prefabricated bollard and to see afterwards on the flagstones a puddle shaped like a blackbird.

He moved. He took one hundred and one steps (Faces Health and Beauty: Body Massage, American Kitchen-City, Hair Extensions International) and turned left into the dim interior of Willy's Bar.

The fascia of Willy's Bar was patched with the gobbledegook of the previous tenant's plastic signage: Julius Caesar's Restaurant and Cocktail Bar, upside down and backwards.

Willy's Bar was licensed to sell wine, malt and spirits, right of admission reserved.

The King and I felt like blacks, because of the way He walked. Everyone else felt like whites. Nevertheless, Apartheid was dead.

I ordered a Black Label and went to the john.

The King sat at the counter. He put on His spectacles and fossicked about in the bag of tricks. He swallowed a handful of pills. He swallowed a Bioplus on the rocks and chased it with a Jim Beam.

He had a fuzzy moustache of curry-powder on His upper lip. It affected me. I hid my face behind *The Star* (City Late) so that I wouldn't feel spare.

We watched the Weather Report together. The cold front was on our doorstep, they said. The King was dissatisfied. I thought He might draw a handgun, but He did not. He just took a powder and pulled a mouth.

I read the Smalls.

Spare is another word for lonesome.

We watched Agenda: The ANC's economic policy.

Ah.

While a party spokesman was explaining the difference between property and theft, the strains of 'Abide with Me' drifted in through the batwing doors.

A far-away look stole over the King's features. He gulped His drink, slapped a greenback on the counter and went out.

I followed after, lugging the depleted bag of tricks and the change (R3.50).

O Thou who changest not, abide with me, the Golden City Gospel Singers beseeched Him. In a moment He had insinuated Himself into their circle, between the blonde with the tambourine and the brunette with the pamphlets.

A chilly wind blew over the ridge from the Civic Theatre. It picked up a tang of Dettol from the City Shelter and Purity from the Florence Nightingale Nursing Home. It swept sour curls of sweat and burnt porridge out of the Fort and wrapped them in dry leaves from the gutters. Tissue-paper and handbills tumbled over the flagstones. The wind coughed into the microphone.

Ills have no weight, and tears no bitterness.

The King opened His mouth. Then He gaped, as if He'd forgotten the words, and shut it again. He would not reveal Himself.

I wept. I wept in His stead. For what right had I to weep on my own behalf? To weep for the insufferable bitterness of being dead for ever and the ineffable sweetness of being born again?

The hymn came to a sticky end. A siren bawled on Hospital Hill. The brunette pressed a pamphlet into my hand: Boozers are Loozers.

I seized His arm and felt a surprisingly firm brachioradialis through the cloth. He shrugged me off – a sequin shot from His cuff and ricocheted into the darkness – but the damage had been done: no sooner had I touched Him, than He began to vanish.

I was moved to call out, 'The King! The King!' The brunette embraced me and cried, 'Amen!' Two hours later I still had the imprint of her hair-clip on my temple.

While I was being mobbed, someone walked off with the bag of tricks.

Laughter: involuntary contractions of the facial muscles, saline secretions of the lachrymal ducts, contortions of the labia.

Vanishing-point: a crooked smile, a folderol of philtrum, nothing.

I hunted high and low for the King, in karaoke bars, escort agencies, drugstores, ice-cream parlors and soda fountains, but found no trace of Him.

I have a feeling in my bones – patellae, to be precise – that He is still out there.

Appendix.

The very next morning I saw Steve Biko coming out of the Juicy Lucy at the Norwood Hypermarket. I followed him to the hardware department, where he gave me the slip.

BIOGRAPHICAL
NOTES

BOSMAN, HERMAN CHARLES (1905 – 1951)
In his writings – both fictional and non-fictional – Bosman strove towards the creation of an indigenous South African literature. His short stories are set for the most part in the Groot Marico area of the North-Western Transvaal. Only one collection of stories, *Mafeking Road* (1947), was published in his lifetime. Posthumous short story collections include *Unto Dust* (1963), *A Bekkersdal Marathon* (1971) and *Jurie Steyn's Post Office* (1971), all edited by Lionel Abrahams. Bosman also wrote two novels – *Jacaranda in the Night* (1947) and *Willemsdorp* (1977) – as well as *Cold Stone Jug* (1949), a chronicle of the years he spent in prison following the shooting of his step-brother. Some of his non-fiction appears in *Uncollected Essays* (1981), edited by Valerie Rosenberg.

CLINE, BRENDAN (1956 –)
Writes short stories, plays and novels. His first volume of stories, *The Six Dead Ballerinas and Other Stories*, was published in 1994. Several stories were also published in *Hippogrif New Writing: 1990*.

DOWLING, FINUALA (1962 –)

A former lecturer at the University of South Africa, she now works as a freelance writer, editor and educational materials developer. Her short stories have won prizes from the Commonwealth Broadcasting Association and *Cosmopolitan magazine*. She has published a study of Fay Weldon.

DHLOMO, H I E (1903 – 1956)

Like his brother R R R Dhlomo (1906 – 1971), he wrote extensively about black history, culture and aesthetics; both are important figures in the pre-Black Consciousness era. A playwright, short story writer, critic and journalist, his works include the play *The Girl Who Killed to Save: Nongqause the Liberator* (1936) and the long poem *Valley of a Thousand Hills* (1941). His *Collected Works* were edited by Nick Visser and Tim Couzens and published in 1985.

ESSOP, AHMED (1931 –)

His collections of short stories include *The Hajji and Other Stories* (1978) – which was awarded the Olive Schreiner Prize in 1979, *Noorjehan and Other Stories* (1990) and *The King of Hearts* (1997). He has also published novels. Among them are *The Visitation* (1980) and *The Emperor* (1984). Has taught at high schools in Lenasia and Johannesburg.

GORDIMER, NADINE (1923 –)

Awarded the Nobel Prize for Literature in 1991 – the first South African writer to be so honoured. Short story writer, novelist and critic. Among her many collections of short stories are *Six Feet of the Country* (1956), *Livingstone's Companions* (1972) and *Jump and Other Stories* (1991), while her novels include *The Conservationist* (1974) and *July's People* (1981). Some of her non-fictional writings have been collected in *The Essential Gesture: Writing, Politics and Places* (1988), edited by Stephen Clingman. A further critical work, *Writing and Being: the Charles Eliot Norton Lectures 1994*, appeared in 1995.

HOPE, CHRISTOPHER (1944 –)

Novelist, poet and short story writer, he has lived in Europe since the 1970s. Novels include *A Separate Development* (1980), *Kruger's Alp* (1984) – which received the Whitbread Literary Award in 1984, and *Serenity House* (1992) – which was shortlisted for the Booker Prize in 1992. A collection of short stories, *Private Parts and Other Tales*, was published in 1981. A non-fictional work, *White Boy Running* (1988), won the CNA award in 1988.

ISAACSON, MAUREEN (1955 –)
Writer and journalist; currently Books Editor for the *Sunday Independent* in Johannesburg. A collection of short stories, *Holding Back Midnight*, was published in 1992. Her short stories have been published both locally and abroad. Worked as a researcher on *The Fifties People of South Africa* and *The Finest Photos from the Old Drum*. Was named National Book Journalist of the Year in 1996.

JACOBSON, DAN (1929 –)
Short story writer, novelist and essayist, he has lived in the United Kingdom since the 1950s. He was formerly Professor of English at University College, London. His work has received many prizes, including the W Somerset Maugham and J R Ackerley Awards. Collections of short stories include *A Long Way from London* (1953) and *Inklings: Selected Stories* (1973). Amongst his longer works are the novellas *The Trap* (1955) and *A Dance in the Sun* (1956). His non-fiction includes the memoir *Time and Time Again* (1985) and *The Electronic Elephant* (1994), an account of a journey through Southern Africa.

LA GUMA, ALEX (1925 – 1985)
Political activism and literary production were closely intertwined in the life and work of La Guma. An accused in the Treason Trial of the 1950s, he left South Africa in 1966. In the latter years of his life he was the ANC representative for the Caribbean and Latin America in Cuba. A novelist and short story writer, La Guma's first work, a novella entitled *A Walk in the Night* (1962), was reissued, with the addition of several short stories, in 1968. His other novels include *The Stone Country* (1967) and *In the Fog of the Season's End* (1972).

LANGA, MANDLA (1950 –)
Writer, screenwriter and columnist; currently Director of Programming for the South African Broadcasting Corporation. Has published one collection of short stories, *The Naked Song and Other Stories* (1996), as well as two novels – *Tenderness of Blood* (1987) and *A Rainbow on the Paper*

Sky (1989). Won an Arts Council of Great Britain Award for Creative Writing in 1991.

MEDALIE, DAVID (1963 –)

Lectures in English at the University of the Witwatersrand. A volume of short stories, *The Shooting of the Christmas Cows*, was published in 1990. Won the 1996 Sanlam Award (in the unpublished category) for 'Recognition', the story included in this anthology.

MZAMANE, MBULELO (1948 –)

Novelist, short story writer, anthologist and critic; currently Rector of the University of Fort Hare. Co-recipient in 1976 of the Mofolo-Plomer Prize. His collections of short stories include *Mzala* (1980) – reissued in 1981 as *My Cousin Comes to Jo'burg and Other Stories* – and *Children of the Diaspora and Other Stories of Exile* (1996). A novel, *The Children of Soweto*, was published in 1982.

NDEBELE, NJABULO (1948 –)

Currently Principal and Vice-Chancellor of the University of the North. He has lectured at universities in South Africa, Lesotho, and abroad. His collection of short stories, *Fools and Other Stories* (1983) won the Noma Award for Publishing in Africa in 1984. In 1991 he published *Rediscovery of the Ordinary: Essays on South African Literature and Culture*. He is also a poet and writes books for children.

SMITH, PAULINE (1882 – 1959)

South African writer of British descent; spent much of her life in England. Her writing centred upon the Little Karoo and its inhabitants. Published a volume of stories, *The Little Karoo* (1925), a novel, *The Beadle* (1926), and *Platkops Children* (1935), a collection of sketches and poems.

THEMBA, CAN (1924 – 1968)

An important figure of the *Drum* generation of the 1950s. Taught English in Johannesburg before working for *Drum* magazine and the *Golden City Post*, becoming associate editor of both in turn. Left for Swaziland in 1963 and died there in exile five years later. His stories and journalism have been collected in *The Will to Die* (1972), edited by Donald Stuart and Roy Holland, and *The World of Can Themba* (1985), edited by Essop Patel.

TLALI, MIRIAM (1933 –)
Has published novels, including *Muriel at the Metropolitan* (1975) – the first novel to be published by a black woman in South Africa – and *Amandla!* (1981), which was banned almost immediately. Has also written a volume of short stories, *Footprints in the Quag* (1989), which was first published as *Soweto Stories*. Wrote a regular column for *Staffrider*. She also works as a researcher and publisher.

VAN WYK, CHRIS (1957 –)
Poet, novelist, short story writer and freelance editor. Co-recipient in 1980 of the Olive Schreiner Award for a volume of poetry, *It is Time to Go Home* (1979). His first novel, *The Year of the Tapeworm*, was published in 1996. Also writes books for children and young adults. Won the 1996 Sanlam Award (in the published category) for 'Relatives', the short story included in this anthology.

VLADISLAVIĆ, IVAN (1957 –)
Works as a freelance editor, with a special interest in fiction and biography; formerly an editor at Ravan Press. Has published a novel, *The Folly* (1993), as well as two volumes of short stories, *Missing Persons* (1989) and *Propaganda by Monuments* (1996). Was co-editor of the commemorative anthology *Ten Years of Staffrider* (1988). His work has won several awards, including the Olive Schreiner Prize and the CNA Award.

WICOMB, ZOE (1948 –)
Writer and academic. Has taught literature, cultural studies and women's studies at universities in South Africa and abroad. Was writer in residence at Strathclyde University in 1990. A volume of short stories, *You Can't Get Lost in Cape Town*, was published in 1987 and has recently been reissued.